LUTHER'S CROSS

TRACY BROEMMER

LUTHER'S CROSS

"Why'd you kiss me at Maeve's?" He breaks the kiss, but he presses his lips to her cheekbone.

"Few reasons," she answers him.

"Like what?"

"Joe. I don't get your deal with Joe." She looks up at him. "I guess I wanted to remind you, I'm your friend. Not his."

"What else?" He fishes for more words that will make his throat and heart burn like he's swallowing whiskey straight from the bottle.

"I wanted to," she admits with a little grin.

The finale is lighting the sky, but he doesn't care that he's not watching it. He wishes this moment with Ellie would last a lifetime. "Do you have a star where even people who don't want to can fall in love?"

"I'm not gonna fall in love with you, Jay." Her words don't mean as much as the fact that she can't look at him when she says them.

Luther's Cross is one of the best books I've read in a very long time. Therese Kinkaide is sure to become a shining star in the women's fiction genre.

—Linda Rettstatt, Contemporary Romance and Women's Fiction Author

Luther's Cross

by

Tracy Broemmer

Originally published under the pen name Therese Kinkaide

Women's Fiction

Published by Tracy Broemmer

Edited by Dawn Peters

Cover Photo: Kim Bush, Bluff View Photography

Cover Artist: Ashley Byland (2018)

All Rights Reserved

Copyright © 2008, 2nd Edition 2018 by Tracy Broemmer
ISBN#: 978-0-9847245-6-7

Dear Readers,

I'm not sure how it's been 10 years since Luther's Cross was published! It seems like just yesterday that I was planning that first book launch party and nervously waiting for guests/readers to arrive and celebrate with me! I had no idea what to expect with Luther's Cross—how readers would receive it and how the satisfaction I got from writing it would drive me to focus so completely on a writing career.

The first book party in 2008 was phenomenal! I'm a writer, but I can't begin to describe to you the feeling I had that first night friends and family gathered with me to celebrate the release of my first published book. I can't tell you how incredibly exciting it was to talk to you—all of you—about the book and how it made you feel and what you thought about it and to hear you say you couldn't wait for the next book.

What I can tell you is that 10 years later, nothing has changed. With every book I write, with every book I publish, I still wait on pins and needles to see how the book is received. I hope I continue to touch your hearts and to make you think. I hope I'm still making you laugh and cry and still bringing you a few hours of entertainment. I hope my books make you happy, and for those books that aren't big happily-ever-after endings, I hope they make you feel less alone in whatever it is you're experiencing in your life.

I have enjoyed every day of the past 10 years on this writing journey. It makes me deliriously happy to know you're still with me on the journey, and it melts my heart and makes me all gooey inside when you reach out to me to share your thoughts. Thank you for choosing my books to read and giving me your time!

This is THE SAME book as the one published in 2008 with a bonus short story added at the end. I hope you enjoy it!

Tracy

CHAPTER 1

ELLIE LIKES TO THINK OF HIM IN ONE OF TWO WAYS, EITHER with the smattering of freckles over his nose and the lopsided smile full of perfect little white teeth as his grubby hands reach to give her the bouquet of dandelions he's picked for her, or resting comfortably in a bed of grass as the afternoon sun warms the tip of his nose. She is sometimes disoriented when she's scrubbing the floor or washing windows, and she stops to check the time only to realize a solid chunk has passed and she's not thought of him. He is in her blood, and it seems wrong somehow to breathe for any length of time without conscious thought of him. But when she thinks of him, it's often in one of these two ways.

She tips her head back and lets it rest against what was once white vinyl siding, but now is the dingy color of regret. It crosses her mind that she has not washed the tiny house down since last summer, and maybe come this weekend, she should do that. Physical labor like this used to be a punishment for the part of her life before him. Now it is simply a means to get by. Her life is divided into two halves, before him and after him. She loves to remember him, but she must

1

always be careful not to wander too far back in her mind. There is a point at which while crossing Bayview Bridge you leave Illinois and cross into Missouri, the state line. You are still on Bayview Bridge, but you've moved from one state to another. She thinks this is like remembering her life; there's a point at which her memories of him cross into memories of who she used to be, even though it's all connected inside her. Crossing into Missouri is one thing; stepping into the person she used to be is quite another, and she simply refuses to do it.

The black velvet sky is alight with stars tonight. She draws her knees up to her chest and loosely hooks her arms around them. Her cement porch is tiny, but now that she sits here alone, it feels as if she could fit an army beside her and still see cement between their government-issued boots. The night air touches her bare legs and lifts a strand of hair from her shoulder, soft as baby's breath. She longs to fill her arms with something but simply pulls her legs tighter against her chest.

She wishes she knew more about the stars. It's not that she doesn't remember or that she wants to replace the stories he used to tell her. But she regrets that she never knew enough to tell him about the constellations. Her stomach sort of drops, the way it did back when she was some other little girl, and her parents took her to the summer carnival, and she spent all her time on the Ferris wheel. The way it does now, each time she thinks of him and wonders if he still sees the stars, and if his voice is bright with excitement and innocence as he whispers to someone else his story about who lives on that star, the one right up there, straight off his fingertip.

Her tears are so much a part of this evening ritual now that she doesn't notice them anymore. They usually come first, and then she feels that knot in her throat where she's unknowingly trapped the sounds of her hurt inside. She wonders if he would somehow know it now if she were to read up on astronomy, as if by wishful thinking she could teach him something across a distance she's pretty sure can't even be measured in miles.

She rubs her face with long, ringless fingers and then wipes her tears on her gray drawstring shorts. It's time to go in. She never stays out past the tears. It's hard to see the stars when her eyes blur with regret. She refuses to let stargazing become a time of grief. Remembering, yes. Grieving, never.

~

Jay?

She pushes herself up through layers of sleep and gauzy images and blinks her crème-colored Martha Stewart curtains into view. Dreams, this time. No nightmares. She knows no Jays, not even in her dreams. Or nightmares, for that matter.

The only Jay she can think of, as her stark little bedroom comes into focus, is Jay Leno. Serious young woman that she is, it never even crosses her mind to snort sarcastically over the possibility of Jay Leno calling her.

"Jay?" she mumbles.

Probably a solicitor. Probably Jay's first day on the job selling new windows by telephone. He's called her by name, and he sounds friendly. Not that she is impressed. She doesn't have a spare dime to buy a can of Coke, let alone new windows for her tiny, five-room house. Or to donate money to the police officers' association—as if Ellie would give the city's finest a penny, if she inherited Las Vegas. Not after all the damned hoops Officer Scott and Detective Farrell had her jumping through a couple of years ago.

"Jay Bryant. From the university. Modern German History."

Oh shit. That Jay. Professor Bryant. Mr. Bryant. She drops her head back to her pillow and squeezes her eyes shut. The words that roar through her mind would singe his ear if she spoke them aloud. She pushes herself up again, on her elbow, and glances at her alarm clock. Nine thirty. Her exam has been over for a half hour already.

"Oh God, Mr. Bryant. I'm so sorry—"

He could flunk her for this. She rubs her eyes just in case they decide to betray her and tear up. A nontraditional student, everything about university life has been hard for her. Everything except the coursework, anyway. For the second time in her life, she has just thrown her perfect grade point average out to the dogs.

"Are you sick?"

Jay Bryant. She's never thought of him as Jay. Just Mr. Bryant. Sick? Yes. She is definitely sick now.

"No. I overslept. I must have slept right through my alarm." It's the dream. She always fights to stay asleep when she dreams about him.

"Can you come in now?"

"Now?" Did he just ask her to come in now? Is he actually going to let her take the exam? She swings her legs over the side of her bed and runs her fingers through her dark blonde hair.

"Yeah. I'm in my office. If you come in now, you can take it."

"Yes." She jumps out of bed immediately and almost drops the phone. "I'll be there as soon as I can."

"Relax." She hears the laughter in his voice. "I'll be here all morning."

Grateful, she hangs up the phone, races through a shower and grabs a quick swallow of orange juice as she runs out the door. Cussing her dysfunctional Tercel yet again, she jumps on her mountain bike and pedals hard and fast across twelve city blocks. She loves to ride, though not always at a break-neck speed. In fact, once upon a time, she would ride so slow it was a wonder the bike stayed upright. Ever mindful of the bright yellow plastic seat that had carried her precious cargo, she had coasted over side streets at a leisurely pace for safety and for fun.

The mountain bike had been a luxury she had allowed herself, even when she hadn't had enough money to buy groceries for a week. Her old purple contraption hadn't been touched since—well, about five years ago. The sporty metallic blue and silver mountain bike had been a garage sale purchase. She had driven the Tercel, probably the last time it had run, to 2900 Sedonia Creek hoping the rich lady of the house had grown tired of some Levi jeans that would just happen to be her size. The bike had been parked on the driveway. She'd never even made it to the garage. Twenty dollars.

The original owner, the teenage son of the rich lady of the house, had been arrested for possession. Ellie knew that song and dance all too well, but she'd answered the woman with only a slight nod. She had to have this bike. The boy, Chandler was his name, had to sell the bike and a few other prized possessions to pay his own fine. She didn't give a damn about seventeen-year-old Chandler and his affinity for expensive scotch or his stiff punishment that came in the form of enforced responsibility.

The woman had thanked Ellie with a friendly smile and accepted the two tens without looking at them. She'd even had the kid help Ellie load the bike in the backseat of the Tercel. The bike had proven good for exercise, as well as for exorcising unwanted thoughts and memories.

Still, at times like this, it would be nice to take her car, never mind that it won't start. She can't afford an estimate, let alone a repair of any kind. As she climbs from the bike and locks it on the metal rack in front of St. Dominic Hall, she says another silent prayer of thanks. She guesses it is a prayer of some sorts. She doesn't really know whom she's addressing. She's just relieved that Mr. Bryant is going to let her make up her missed final exam. It's within his rights, and possibly even his responsibilities, to flunk her.

Her heels might be smoking when she skids to a halt just inside the closet that passes for Mr. Bryant's office. The two flights of stairs she has just climbed to reach the Social Sciences Hall have left her nearly breathless. She apologizes yet again for missing the exam, but he waves her apology aside and hands her the test booklet.

The test, she figures, will be a breeze. Not because Mr. Bryant is a pushover teacher who doesn't challenge his students. But because she finds German history interesting, and because she's always favored essay tests to multiple-choice tests, hands down.

"Define seven of the ten words." He leans over her and skims his index finger over the test sheet. "Short answers. And answer three of the five essay questions."

She nods. It is the same format as the midterm, just a bit longer. A quick glance tells her this test covers old and new material.

"You have two hours. Most people have been finishing within an hour and a half."

She nods and looks again at the test sheet. Blitzkrieg. Easy enough. She signs her name on the front of the pale blue-green test booklet. It is the color of the fluoride rinse she'd had to use when she was in sixth grade and someone had had the bright idea of incorporating dental hygiene into their daily routine. Brushing her teeth with a tiny, generic blue toothbrush had been bad enough. Swishing the awful tasting rinse for a full minute while Mrs. Whalen watched the clock had been enough to make a person want to vomit. If she were the squeamish type, she might feel sick right now just from the memory.

Her long, slender fingers smooth the ugly cover back and grip her pen again to start the test in earnest. She feels half-naked as she writes out four well-worded sentences to define blitzkrieg. Figuring she must have forgotten to put her watch on, she glances absently at her wrist. The silver face informs her that seven minutes have passed since she arrived. Okay, if she didn't forget her watch, it must be something really important. Embarrassing. Like when she dreams that she's left the house without her shirt on. She glances down at herself, seeing the plain gray T-shirt and faded denim shorts. Shoes?

"What?"

Not naked, she realizes, when she sees him out of the corner of her eye. Just exposed. Jay Bryant is watching her from the doorway of the classroom. It doesn't occur to her that he is making certain she isn't cheating. It would never occur to her to cheat in the first place. No, standing in the doorway, right hip and right shoulder propped against the doorframe and arms folded across his chest, he looks decidedly casual and not at all like a college professor.

He smiles, revealing a set of perfect white teeth and a dimple in his left cheek all at the same time. She's never noticed the dimple before. Absently, she wonders why. It's not as if he never smiles during class.

"Do you think you'll need the full two hours?" He drops his arms and moves slowly back into the room.

"No. Why? If you need to be somewhere, Mr. Bryant, it's okay. I blew it. I deserve the F."

"I'm not going to give you an F." He shakes his head and leans his denim-clad butt against the wall to her right. "Actually, Ellie Jordan, I'm just looking at you. And wondering what you were doing last night that kept you up so late that you overslept."

"You are?" She frowns.

"Mm-hmm. Actually, I was wondering too, who you are. I mean, this morning on the phone is the first time I've heard your voice, I think. You've been in this class since January. And you were in my class last fall."

She nods.

"Were you studying?"

She watches warily as he takes two long strides and drops into the seat in front of her. He straddles it backwards and rests his chin on his hands, over the back of the chair.

"You weren't studying. I know that. You don't have to study, do you? I know that much about you."

"How do you know that much about me?" she asks quietly.

"I don't know. Something about you tells me those A's come pretty easy to you."

She sits back in her chair and drops her pen.

"You know the girl who sits in front? Becca. She dates the guy who sits behind her. We've all gone out to lunch together before. And Ryan and Stick? The two guys who always wear their ball caps backwards? They live in my office. I see Krissy at the library every Tuesday afternoon. And I see Mariah at baseball games, because her boyfriend plays right field. But I never see you outside of class."

HE WATCHES HER CHEW NERVOUSLY ON HER PALE LOWER LIP. She wears no makeup. As far as he knows, she never does. As far as he is concerned, she doesn't need it. Her skin is smooth and already glowing with the beginnings of a spring tan. Her pale brown eyes, kind of the color of burnt butterscotch, are fringed with lovely, thick, dark lashes. There's a tiny chip in her front tooth, and he wonders for a moment how it happened. He wonders if he asked her about it, if she would tell him.

"Do you live on campus?"

Now why did he ask her that? Their time this morning is limited. Why ask questions that he's already answered on his own? How many times in the past few months has he glanced through her files in an attempt to learn something new about her? She lives on Lincoln. Her files told him that much. What they don't say, and what he desperately wants to know, is if she lives alone. Is she married? Still living with her parents? She wears no wedding ring, but then again all of her slender fingers are bare. The only jewelry he has seen her wear is the watch.

That's another thing. Who gave her the watch? It's pretty. Understated elegance. White gold that slides over her wrist like a bracelet.

"No. I live on Lincoln."

He wishes he were acrobatic enough to kick himself. She's willing to answer questions, and he asks her the dumbest thing possible.

"I studied for awhile. Then I guess I got caught up watching the stars. It was after one when I went to bed."

"Do you have a telescope?"

"No."

"Astronomy class?" He tries again. He holds the corners of his mouth still, even though he feels a grin just itching to cut loose. She's talking to him. He's been waiting for this moment for a long time.

"No."

"Just kind of a stargazer, huh?"

"You could say that." She nods.

9

He stares at her for a moment, but he almost doesn't see her. She reaches for her pen and starts to fidget. *Don't lose her now, moron*, he thinks.

"See, now, I'm more of a dawn kind of person. There've been times when I've gone to bed at eight just to get up by four. The sky's kinda the color of polished steel then. Ya know?"

She says she does know, then she smiles. It's small and bittersweet, and he senses the smile is more for the person in her memory than for him. "We used to tell stories about the stars," she says quietly. Her words are tinged with sadness; she avoids his intense stare.

He wants to ask her who used to tell stories about the stars. Her parents? Siblings? She and her boyfriend? But he can't. This being the first conversation he has ever had with Ellie Jordan, he doesn't want to seem nosy or rude.

"Mythology? Maybe you should take an astronomy class—"

"No, no." She shakes her head. "Nothing like that. We just made things up. Out of our heads."

He nods. Of course she has a boyfriend. A woman like her has to have a boyfriend. And if not, then she probably has her share of admirers. He'd heard the wistful note in her voice. Whoever made up stories about the stars was someone very important to her.

"Have big plans for the summer?" he asks and hopes he sounds casual. It's not as if he's made up his mind to ask her out. The way his stomach is churning, it's as if he's about to pop the question. He just wants to know more about her. God's honest truth. For over a year now, he has seen Ellie Jordan in his class. Only in his class. Never at parties or dances. Never at sporting events. Never at the library. Always in classes. She has never skipped a class. She never volunteers anything in his class, and he knows some professors might knock her grade down a level for that, but it doesn't matter to him. She is obviously very intelligent and just as obviously very reserved or shy.

Even so, Jay has been divorced for two years. There have been a lot of women since Rylan left him. A lot of dates. A lot of excuses for missed dates, given both by him and to him. A lot of first kisses, as well as first other things. But none of it has ever made him nervous. He's never met a woman yet who could make him jittery the way Rylan had the first time he saw her. Until now.

"No."

He stares at her silently, afraid for just a moment that she'd read his mind. Then he remembers he'd asked her about her summer plans.

"No? No vacation or anything? I mean, besides going home to visit your parents?"

"No trips of any kind. Including going home."

"Hmm." He arches an eyebrow. "Do you work?"

"Why?" she asks suspiciously.

He laughs softly. *Chill, Jay, you're going to scare her away with the third degree.* "Just curious, I guess. Do you?"

"Yeah. I work at the public library."

He raises his eyebrows and nods. She sure as hell doesn't look like any librarian he's ever seen, but he knows instinctively that she is the kind of person who enjoys books.

"And they won't give you a vacation?"

"I don't need one," she says simply. "I wouldn't have anywhere to go anyway."

"What about Memorial Day?"

She shrugs. "What about it?"

"It's two weeks away. Don't you have plans?"

"No." She taps her pen on her test booklet.

He wonders if he's boring her. He sure as hell hopes not, because talking to her has been the most fun he's had since he and his little brother Joe went mudding a few weeks ago, on Maeve and Stash's land. He smiles; comparing four-wheeling with Joe to talking to Ellie is stupid, but somehow it feels right. Talking to her kind of gives him that weird sensation in his stomach, the same way taking a jump and dropping several feet in the air before hitting hard ground does. Like flying. She makes him feel like he's flying.

"My family always has a big picnic at my mom's house."

"That sounds nice."

It dawns on him then. Maybe she doesn't have parents to go home to. Maybe she doesn't have family.

"Would you like to come?" *Whoa! Where the hell had that come from?* He sits calmly, as if he's not holding onto his seat with a white-knuckle grip, waiting for her answer. He's not sure where the hell this idea came from, but now that he's asked her, he can't imagine the picnic this year without her.

She laughs, but she frowns. "To your family picnic? Thank you, but no."

He nods, because even though for a moment there he desperately wanted her to say yes, and for a moment there, it looked like she desperately wanted to say yes, he'd known she'd say no. He takes his cue to leave when she twirls the pen in her fingers like a baton and then sets it to her test booklet, poised and ready to breeze through yet another exam.

"I'll be in my office," he says as he stands. "Just drop it off when you're finished." She glances up at him and nods, but to his disappointment, she turns away from him without saying anything more.

He loves her voice, and he loves the way her eyes had lit with memories when she told him about the stars. His closet-sized office is boring as hell after spending twenty minutes with Ellie Jordan. He drops into his chair, tips it back precariously far, and props his feet on the desk. Nothing to do now but wait for her to finish the exam, unless he wants to start grading the pile of finals on his desk. German history or Ellie? He presses his lips together to hold in the laugh.

Rylan had broken him into such tiny pieces, it had taken his family two brooms and four bottles of glue to sweep him up and put him back together. Half of him wants to pursue Ellie Jordan, ask her out to dinner or a movie. The other half is comfortable watching her from afar.

CHAPTER 2

SHE LIKENS HERSELF TO A TORNADO, THE WAY SHE TORE through her family and left so much destruction in her wake. Tornadoes fascinate her. They always have. Last year, before the Tercel died, she'd driven just north of town to Lima, to see the aftermath of the F3 cyclone that had torn through Canton, Missouri, and then crossed the Mississippi to level the small, rural town of Lima, twenty minutes from Quincy.

Fear had never stood in the way of a thing in her life. She'd watched as the sky turned three shades of gray over yellow over green, until it looked like a bruised Granny Smith apple. The air had tightened around her, until it was still and thick and heavy with the rain and wind that was to come. She hadn't gone inside until big fat raindrops splattered the porch around her. She hadn't taken cover in the dirt cellar until the tree in the neighbor's yard across the street had whipped forward and touched the ground, like a tall, lithe woman doing some ungodly painful yoga stretch.

She'd ridden the storm out in the cellar, armed with a can of RC cola, a flashlight with fresh batteries, and the only Jodi Picoult book she ever truly disliked. She wonders now if she really disliked *Mercy*, or if she just transferred her anger at missing the wild ride outside to the book. She sits back on her haunches and thinks about it for a moment. The characters had not touched her, Jodi's only failure as far as she's concerned. She'd hated Jamie, for no apparent reason; the guy had only done what he thought was best. She'd hated Cameron because he'd been a complete ass and because he reminded her of one of the maintenance guys at the university, and she just couldn't stand that guy.

Nope, not the storm, she decides as she leans forward again to pull the die-hard weed that grows by the sidewalk in her front yard. She envisions herself being seventy years old and still fighting this damned weed. Sweat dampens the wisps of hair that have fallen from her ponytail. She wipes her face on her sleeve and gives one final yank on the weed. As she stands, the offensive greenery hanging from her fingers, she sighs and glances back over her postage-stamp front yard. With an almost imperceptible nod of approval, she heads to the back of her house.

If she ever wrote a book, she'd want to write like Jodi Picoult. She laughs as she rounds the corner of the house and grabs the push bar on the mower. She doesn't know Jodi and she never will, but she figures the woman would be thrilled that some Midwestern chick with a GED rather than a high school diploma thinks she would want to write like her. Not that she has a desire to write. Hell, she really doesn't know what she wants to be when she grows up. She loves history, though, and as she twists the water spigot and picks up the hose, she thinks maybe she should just be a history scholar. One of those insufferable people who walks around with her nose in a book twenty-four seven and spouts off historical facts like sports buffs rattle off baseball statistics. Actually, that's exactly what she'd like to do. Just study history. No, it wouldn't bring her much money, but she's been living just a leg up from hand to mouth for a good ten years. Why should a college education change that?

Even archeology would be interesting. But the university doesn't offer anything of the sort. And she won't leave anyway. She won't leave Quincy for any length of time, so a dig for artifacts in some exotic location might be interesting, but it'd never work for her. The town has been less than welcoming and yet, still less than hostile to her, but it doesn't matter. She can't go anywhere now.

She squeezes the handle on the hose and sprays the loose grass off the top of the mower. She's seen the neighbor to her east watch her clean up ritual. From the look on the old guy's face, she figures washing the mower down after cutting the grass leans a bit toward an obsessive-compulsive disorder. Especially when the mower is a fifteen-buck garage sale gem. She supposes it's kind of funny, the things that her parents taught her back when she wasn't really looking. Things that tend to sneak up on her and bite her in the ass before she realizes what she's even doing. Like spraying the mower off when she's finished mowing. Or rinsing aluminum cans out before she throws them in the recycle bag.

It makes her stomach hurt to think about her parents though, so she doesn't. Now and then she catches them on the outer bounds of her mind, and she rushes at them at a breakneck speed to keep them out. Just the suggestion of their presence makes her feel sick, the same kind of dread that had coiled in her stomach the day she'd stolen Brett Marshall's burnt sienna Crayola crayon in kindergarten. She'd known from the moment she'd picked it up from the floor and put it on her desk instead of his that he would notice. And tell. And she'd be in trouble. He hadn't told on her, but the guilt wore at her until finally, two weeks later, she'd tossed it back on his desk when he wasn't looking.

Guilt is a powerful poison, and she swallows a good

spoonful every morning. She's read some about guilt being a Catholic issue or a woman's issue. She knows better. Guilt is all about how you feel when you do something wrong.

~

MEMORIAL DAY IS FOR REMEMBERING, AND SHE DOES. SHE remembers picnics in the backyard that consisted of raw hotdogs, which she still thinks are disgusting, and grape soda. Oreo cookies, because for him, she didn't mind splurging. A one-on-one baseball game, which always involved more giggling than baseball, and lying on their backs in the grass, finding shapes in the clouds. He was good at that, just like he was with stargazing.

That last Memorial Day, he'd seen an elephant in the clouds, and she'd looked for several long silent minutes without seeing it and finally turned her face to look at him. He'd grinned, and she'd thought he was joking with her, but when she looked again, she'd seen it. An elephant with its trunk raised. And then she'd seen a cloud that looked like a big hand, reaching out to her. She supposes some people would say it was the hand of God, and she supposes that it just might have been the hand of God reaching to take back what was His. The billowy outstretched fingers had climbed her spine and left her chilled. She'd tried to hide her unease by suggesting another inning.

This kind of remembering is dangerous. The good kind has such narrow boundaries she's almost always doomed to fail. She can live with memories, but sometimes the ghosts of the past haunt her and break her down to nothing, and she hates to become that person. She hates to feel, and she hates to lose control, and she hates to break. Each time it happens, it gets just a little bit harder to put herself back together.

Sometimes she runs. She runs to escape, and she runs to

17

search, and she runs to turn the sorrow into a physical hurt. It's always so much easier to deal with physical pain. She's not the squeamish type; she doesn't get all girly and sick at the sight of blood. In fact, when she was twelve, she and Tony Spinelli had bumped noses while they fought over a rebound. The crack of the bones and the jolt of pain had slowed her down, but she'd taken the rebound, put the ball up again for two points, and then turned to see if Tony was okay. They'd ridden to the ER together, had their noses set at the same time in different exam rooms, and then ducked off to the corner of the waiting room to whisper while their parents talked by the triage desk. She'd promised him she wouldn't tell anyone that his nose had bled and hers didn't and therefore she must be tougher than him. He'd kissed her; her first kiss on her mouth, and they were both taped up like hockey players after a night on the ice.

She supposes, as she rides her bike south on Eighth Street, Tony Spinelli was her first love. When her mind starts to click, to remind her of things best left alone, she pulls herself to her feet and pedals like the hounds of hell are following her.

THERE ARE MOMENTS IN TIME WHEN EVERYTHING KIND OF comes to a standstill, and life sort of takes a freeze-frame photo of itself. It's that half a second hang-up when the heart sort of stops, then the blood feels thick and hot when everything sets back into motion, and it's like fire in the veins. Jay's had several of these moments in his life; just yesterday when he'd sped past Forty-Eighth Street on Broadway and saw the cop car tucked neatly behind the bank and had waited for the telltale siren that never came. And the moment when the deathbed vigil over his father had ended, when he'd taken that last breath and only silence had followed. Jay had looked to his older sister in fear, and the dancing, rhythmic line that showed the life left in his father's heart had fallen flat.

And the other day, the moment when Ellie had first realized he was watching her. The moment when she'd turned her head and looked at him, and he'd crossed the classroom to sit with her and talk to her.

He hates that he and Ellie never talked until the final exam. Well, he hates a lot of things, really, but that's his newest and biggest hate. He wishes, since his mouth had invited her to the picnic, that she would have agreed to go. He wishes that he had a reason to call her or go see her. Since she told him she lived on Lincoln, he's ridden his bike past her house a few times. He figures that since she told him where she lived, it's less of a violation to ride past her house than it would be if he'd only known this about her through her school files.

She has never been outside when he's ridden by. He's never really had the inclination to stop and knock on her door. He's decided that she keeps a meticulous yard and wonders if her house is as neat inside. He wonders, too, if he'll ever see the inside of her house. The house itself is tiny, but somehow that seems to fit her. When he rides by, he imagines her sitting on the front porch, watching the stars. Since she'd told him about stargazing, he's found himself up later most nights, sitting out on his patio, looking at the stars and wondering if by chance they are looking at the same one.

Memorial Day is for remembering, and he did spend part of today remembering. He and Maeve always take their mother to mass at the cemetery, and Maddie meets them there. He remembers his father then, of course, and his grandparents. But he spent half the day eating and the other half pounding his little brother into the pavement, playing one on one. Ellie had been on his mind all day, and he'd caught himself wearing a shit-eating grin more often than not. She was sort of like his own little secret, only there wasn't much to the secret because they'd only had one conversation, and the rest of the summer stretched out before him boring and lonely as hell without any hope of seeing her until classes started again next fall.

Apparently his poker face needs some work though, because Maeve had followed him to his truck when he'd made excuses to leave early. It wasn't like it was that early; he'd eaten a second meal there, one he sure as hell didn't need. But in years past, they'd lingered at his mom's house until dark settled in.

Maeve had leaned inside his truck window and simply asked if he was going to go see her. He'd fallen into her trap and said maybe. And that had been the beginning of their game of twenty questions, the one in which Maeve being the pain-in-the-ass older sister asked all twenty and insisted he answer all twenty. He'd failed, though, hadn't even been able to answer half of them, because he still really knows nothing about Ellie Jordan.

HE THINKS IT TAKES A PRETTY SHALLOW PERSON TO FALL FOR another shallow person, and by extension, a damned fool to let said shallow person break his heart. Rylan was shallow, so shallow he could almost see through her. But he'd never stopped to notice that. Instead his eyes had gotten side-tracked by her luxurious brown curls and her big blue eyes. He likes to throw the blame anywhere he can, just so it's not on his shoulders. Yes, it was Rylan who had broken their vows. But he figures the marriage was his fault. He wants to believe he was too young, as if that alone is excuse enough for lusting after a gorgeous woman like Rylan. But he wasn't really that young when they'd gotten married. He was twenty-five years old, old enough to know that beautiful doesn't equal compassionate, and hot, nasty sex doesn't necessarily mean love. He'd taken the chance and asked her to marry him. He doesn't know what the hell she was thinking when she said yes, but he knows it wasn't 'till death do us part.' Six years later, he is a divorced, "Summer Vacation Only Dad," and he hates her for doing this to him. It is one thing for her to leave him; he couldn't have stayed with her after the things she'd done anyway. But taking his son with her had left him with a sadness inside that he can't shake. It has settled into his bones, like a cavity decays a tooth.

Dating is a pointless cat and mouse chase, and he's only participated in that game half-assed since the divorce. Kind of like he's doing the hokey pokey but only with his right side. He's had fun with a few of the women he's dated, but he's never felt that sinking feeling in his heart. The sinking feeling that oddly enough goes up into your heart and your throat as your stomach plummets to your knees and trips you up and makes you act like a jackass in front of that one woman you desperately want to impress. At least not until now. There's something about Ellie Jordan that makes him feel whole enough to want to put himself right back out there on the railroad tracks with an Amtrak train speeding at him faster than he can blink. And that's why he's not surprised when he finds himself on his bike, back in front of her house. Here comes the train. He's going to stop this time.

CHAPTER 3

A FIVE-YEAR-OLD HEARTACHE MAKES NO SOUND AT ALL. EVEN when she cries, and she doesn't very often, her tears fall silently. Since that day, that day when her life had just stopped like the abrupt way a song ends when you drag the needle across a record and the music is gone and you just hear that horrible zzzzzpp and you figure there's a new scratch in the vinyl that's deep enough to be the Grand Canyon, her tears have been silent. She supposes that textured silence is fitting for her to live by. The air she breathes is peppered with regret and guilt and sorrow, and even though she's grown accustomed to it, it still hurts sometimes to swallow a mouthful. She doesn't have that much to say to herself anyway, so most often the silence is welcome.

She is exhausted from the bike ride turned exorcism. Her legs are weak as she puts her toe down gingerly on the side-walk. She swings her leg over the bike and stands beside it for a moment, sucking in huge gulps of the fresh evening air. Her shirt is soaked with the ghosts she managed to sweat out as she rode. The cool breeze chills her as it sweeps up against her and makes the wet T-shirt ride close to her skin, as if the ghosts are trying to crawl back inside her.

The sky is beginning to darken around the edges, the way cookies do when you leave them in the oven too long. She's been gone longer than she thought. Hadn't been a good idea to think about that broken nose and Tony Spinelli. She shakes her head and stands up straight, determined to move before the shadows of those memories can creep in behind her and take her down again.

The old man who lives in the house east of hers is outside having a smoke when she wheels her bike through the yard. He watches her with bald curiosity, as if she's a damned freak from Ripley's Believe It or Not. She's never tried to strike up a conversation with him. He doesn't scare her, but she thinks he's not worth the time if he's going to watch her with that mix of curiosity and suspicion. She considers telling him smoking is bad for his health, but she looks away from his beady green eyes before her voice has the chance to jump out of her mouth.

She keeps her bike locked in the back of her house, inside her very small kitchen. She doesn't trust it out in her makeshift, tumbledown garage. The door locks, but anyone who really wanted to get in could jimmy it a bit and pull it right open. With her bike in the house, all they'd find in the garage is the dead Tercel—good riddance—and the mower. She's learned the hard way to keep her treasures locked up safe inside.

Before she gets in the shower, she grabs a glass of ice water, kicks off her shoes and socks, and pads barefoot to the front door. She wants to get another look at the sky first. It's the sky that keeps her feeling connected to him, because the sky is big enough that somewhere, he's probably seeing the same one. At least that's what she tells herself, because any other possibility is just unthinkable.

Jay Bryant is on the sidewalk in front of her house when she yanks the door open. He's straddling a silver mountain bike, much like the one she's just locked safely away. When he sees her, his face lights up and he offers her a small smile; a million thoughts race through her mind at once. None of them involve how she wished she'd had a chance to take a shower or put on makeup or change her clothes before he showed up. Mostly, she's surprised to see him, and she's half excited about his unexpected visit and half resentful that he's shown up as she was going to look at the sky and remember something good.

"Hi," he says quietly as he walks his bike up her sidewalk. His bike ride has obviously been leisurely, as there is not a drop of sweat on his face or neck. She supposes it's nice that not everyone has demons to run from, but then again, she knows that's an unfair assumption on her part. She knows nothing about Jay Bryant.

"Hi." She gives him a fleeting smile then looks around the quiet street. Of course none of her neighbors are out now to see that she has a visitor. Cosmic plan, she guesses. Nothing good can come of Ellie Jordan, and if there is ever a hint of something positive, no one is looking.

"How was your Memorial Day?" he asks, still straddling his bike.

She drags her eyes back over the neighbors' houses and the grass and the trees and finally up to meet his. Memorial Day sucks, she wants to say, because even the good memories hurt, and like photo albums, once you drag them out and dust them off to look at them, they're a real pain in the ass to put back in the box and put away. It's like after you remember them, the dimensions of each one changes and they don't fit back in your heart the same way.

"Fine." She shivers. The night has grown cooler, and she is still wearing the wet T-shirt. "Yours?"

"Good," he answers with a nod.

She tries to picture her refrigerator in her mind and remember if there is anything to offer him to drink. Possibly a can of Coke, but she's not sure. "Can I get you something to drink?" she offers, hoping to hell she's got a Coke or that he says no.

"No, thanks."

"Can you excuse me for just a minute?" she asks him, because she's got to get this damned shirt off. She's not sure which is worse: the chills she feels coming on or the memory tainted sweat that still touches her skin.

"Sure." He nods.

She carries her water inside, takes a drink and sets the glass on the small, hopelessly chipped Formica table in the kitchen. She yanks her shirt off and grabs a towel from the closet to soak up any sweat still on her skin. Her bra is soaked, so she peels it off too and then grabs an oversized sweatshirt and pulls it on. She doesn't feel sexy; in fact, the only time she did think she was sexy she was too damned young to know what it meant. Finally warm enough to stop the slight tremor, she goes back outside.

Jay watches her sit down and hunch over her bent knees. She folds her arms around her legs and draws them in to her chest.

"You can sit down," she tells him. She thinks it's a wonder her voice isn't rusty, because other than a few words here and there at work, she hasn't used it since the last time she talked to him. He studies her face for a moment, long enough for her to wonder what he's thinking, if he's suddenly remembered her. She lets out a silent breath of relief, one she hadn't been aware she was holding, when he smiles and steps off his bike and props the kickstand. She doesn't want to think he suddenly remembered her. People who remember her act like she might be contagious just from a glance.

"Are you cold?" he asks as he sits down. He's a respectable distance away from her, but she still scoots over, away from him.

"Kind of," she admits.

He nods, and she sees his eyes size her up. Her hair is still damp with sweat; she hadn't looked when she was inside, but she assumes her face is the color of heat from the rigorous exercise. "Were you working out?" he asks. She doesn't hear any ulterior motive in his voice. No ulterior motive, and no censure. He's just asking because he's curious.

She gives him a wry smile and nods toward his bike. "Bike ride."

"Really?" He sounds surprised. "Where did you ride?"

She licks her lips and wonders what to say to him. If she tells him the truth, he'll probably think she's a freak. Most people don't ride from Lincoln Street to Highway Ninety-Six and then double back and follow Thirty-Sixth Street out to Highway Twenty-four and then back again to Lincoln. But she's not most people, and maybe for now, it'd be better if he didn't know that.

"Just around," she hedges.

"So that's how you stay in shape," he mumbles and nods.

She glances at him, but his eyes are so intense she has to look away. "I don't ride to stay in shape."

He nods again and turns his face away from hers. She chances a look at him. His face is expressionless, but it's in that mask of nothingness that she sort of sees that he understands what she's saying.

"I thought you had a picnic today," she says. She stretches her legs out in front of her and flexes her feet. They still have the squiggly little indentations on them from her socks. Her toenails are clean and bare. She curls them under when she sees him looking at them. For the first time in ten years, she wishes she had a bottle of nail polish. "At your mom's," she adds and leans back on her hands. She turns to look at him, hoping to draw his eyes off her legs. She's not one to wear jeans all the time, but she's not into any undue attention drawn to her body either.

"Did." He nods and looks at her with a smile. "I think I gained about five pounds from eating twice. And I smeared my little brother's face all over the driveway."

"What?" She sits up quickly and stares at him with a frown.

"Basketball," he explains.

"Oh," she says and smiles and then adds, "I could take you."

"You could take me?" he repeats with a laugh. "On a court?"

"Court, playground." She shrugs. "I could take you."

"Hot shot basketball player, huh?"

She sees Tony Spinelli and the gusher as she fights the ball away from him and shoots. Tony Spinelli kissing her in the ER. Tony Spinelli with his hands all over her—

"Yeah." She swallows hard and raises her eyebrows then looks away. Why does it have to hurt to remember?

"Take you up on that one day," he warns her.

"Last guy I played against got hurt pretty bad," she tells him. The unspoken words hover in her mouth, but again, she swallows them. She'd hurt Tony Spinelli left and right and every which way and then some. When she'd shredded him down to nothing, she'd taken to hurting herself.

"I'm not scared." He chuckles.

"How old is your brother?" she asks, because she is desperate to get away from basketball and Tony and the rest of it.

"Seventeen."

"Seventeen? And you're, like—" She clears her throat. "Not seventeen. Anybody in between you two?"

He laughs and shakes his head. "Nope. Mom took a thirteen-year break and then had Joe."

Joe. She hates the name Joe, for reasons she doesn't care to remember.

"Just you two?"

"No," he answers. He looks at her again, and she feels like a crime novel, something he's eating up, desperate to find the clues and figure out. "Two sisters. Maeve just turned forty. And Maddie's thirty-seven."

"Wow," she says with a smile.

"What about you?" he asks her. "Do you have brothers and sisters?"

She nods, but she doesn't give him a verbal answer. "What do they do? Are they teachers?"

"Maeve is the assistant district attorney." His voice doesn't drip with pride or arrogance, but his words cut her and slip inside her and make her want to vomit. "And Maddie is a nun."

"A nun?" She forgets the ADA and looks back at him. A nun is almost worse than an ADA. Hell, on any given day of the week, a nun is worse than an ADA. "You're Catholic?"

He gives her a slight nod and an almost bashful grin. "I go to church when I remember it's Sunday."

She laughs softly. She belongs to no religion. Her parents raised her to believe in a higher power, but they were never faithful churchgoers of any denomination. She's not so much afraid of God, because if He's out there, He's already exacted His punishment from her. But she's not really that comfortable thinking about God either.

❧

She's beautiful in a way that Rylan would never be. In fact, Ellie Jordan is every woman Rylan always tried to be. She is natural and comfortable in her skin. He loves that she is sitting with him after a long, hard bike ride and not fretting over needing a shower and makeup and all the shit Rylan couldn't live without. Her skin glows a golden tan, and her hair is falling from what appears to be a hasty ponytail, and her toenails and fingernails are bare. She's beautiful, and she's slipped inside him, and he knows he's a goner.

It makes him a little uncomfortable, the feeling that he could just sit here with her and talk all night. She doesn't say much, but when she does talk, she makes a point. Her laughter is soft and quiet, as if she knows it doesn't have to be loud and harsh to be real. She's a hell of a basketball player, or so she says, and he can't wait to find out for himself. Rylan wouldn't look at a basketball for fear of breaking a nail.

He doesn't want this to be about comparing her to Rylan. He doesn't want Rylan anywhere inside his life anymore, except that she is the mother of his child. Beside him, Ellie folds her body back to the small, compact position she started in, and he wonders if she's cold again. Or if she's suddenly had an attack of self-consciousness and wants to hide herself from him.

Her eyes had gone distant and dark when she'd mentioned basketball, the last guy she'd played against. He wonders who he was and when she'd last played basketball. He wants to learn more about her, but so far, she's stayed on her toes and posed the questions to him. He doesn't mind sharing information about himself, but he wants to give and take here and get to know her too.

"So, how long's it been?" he asks. She cuts her eyes to him, and he has to chuckle when he imagines the many things she might assume he's asking about. "Basketball. How long's it been since you played?"

Her eyes settle back to the familiar burnt butterscotch. She doesn't say it, but she's grateful his question is as simple as basketball. He wonders if she knows her emotions are so easily read on her face. Not her secrets. He can't see to her soul and read her secrets as if they are written there in cramped script. But he can read her emotions well enough to know she does have secrets locked away somewhere.

"Five years since I've shot baskets." Her whisper is thick with emotion she refuses to share. She won't look at him; instead she stares at the front tire of his bike. "Thirteen since I humiliated the last guy on the court."

"And how old were you when you took this guy down?" he asks with a smile.

"Twelve," she answers. "We both broke our noses, but I got possession and scored."

"You broke your nose when you were twelve?" He grins. Before he can stop himself, he reaches out as if he's going to touch the bridge of her nose. He sees the color of panic fly through her eyes when he moves and stops his hand before it ever gets close to her.

"Yeah," she says quietly. "I did. Kinda crooked, right here." She touches the bridge of her nose, but he doesn't see that it's crooked. If it is, it was supposed to be to add just the right touch to an already beautiful face.

"Where are you from?" he asks her. She raises her eyebrows and takes a deep breath.

"Springfield."

"And what about your brothers and sisters?"

She turns her head away from him and takes another deep breath.

"Am I asking too many questions?" he asks when she doesn't answer him.

She nods and tucks a wisp of hair behind her ear then rests her fingertips on her lips. "Nick and Natalie." He sees the effort it takes her to spit the names out. "They're twenty."

"Twins?" He hesitates to ask.

"Yeah." She licks her lips and turns to look at him. In the gathering shadows, he can't see her so well now. He can't see the way her skin glows or the scant freckles on her nose. But he thinks her eyes are suspiciously bright, and he feels guilty. "Don't do that anymore, okay?" she asks.

He knows she wants to look away from him, but she doesn't. She's trying to be tough, and he admires her for that, but he wishes she would see he doesn't expect it. Maybe eventually, if she allows him to come around more often. He nods, and she opens her mouth to speak but changes her mind and presses her lips together and turns her head.

"The stars are out," he says after several long, quiet moments have passed.

She smiles; he sees the way the corner of her lips perk up, even though she's not looking at him. "You know, I was thinking of looking for an astronomy class next semester. Just for fun."

"You should." There's something about the stars that makes her happy. He doesn't know yet what it is, but he hopes maybe someday she'll trust him enough to tell him. He hopes that maybe someday she'll ask him to sit with her and tell stories about the stars. He's not much of a storyteller, but he thinks he could learn anything for her.

For now, he stands because this is her private time, and he doesn't want to steal it away from her. She needs the stars more than she needs him. She looks up at him, and again, he sees a flash of gratefulness and relief before she can get a grip on her emotions.

"Is it safe out here by yourself?" he asks as he throws a leg over his bike.

She laughs, but it's hollow and cold, and he feels it cut through him like a draft in a farmhouse on a winter day. "No." She lifts a shoulder in a lazy shrug. "But I'll be okay."

He nods and stares at her a moment longer, memorizing her upturned face in the pale moonlight. "Goodnight," he says as he turns his bike around. He feels her eyes on his back as he rides away.

CHAPTER 4

Spider-Man is every young boy's hero, Oliver's included, though Jay doubts his son will grow up to be the superhero type. He doesn't think Oliver will ever be an athlete, most definitely not a football player, anyway. There was a time in his life when that would have bothered him, but now there is Oliver, and he is real, and Jay is just proud of him, not of everything he could someday be.

Jay is crazy about every square inch of his son. He has Rylan's hair, the color of melted caramel and milk chocolate, and it's longish and should probably be cut more often, but he loves it just the way it is. It curls over his ears and around his neck, and a big thick shock of it is always falling over his forehead. Really, Jay is surprised Rylan doesn't keep their son in a military buzz. Then again, she's all about keeping up with styles, and the longer, bowl cut is coming back into style.

Oliver is a gorgeous kid and would still be gorgeous, even with a buzz. His big blue eyes, the blue of a midnight sky, are huge and innocent behind his small glasses. Jay loves the way the glasses magnify that innocence. He loves the way his skin is flawless, the perfect mix of cream and peaches and a small smattering of freckles over the bridge of his nose. His voice is a mix of sunshine and music and wonder. His absence is a growth in Jay's lungs and heart that spreads a little more each day. It's a wonder he can still breathe. If Rylan doesn't relent and give him more time with Oliver soon, his lungs will be black, as if he's spent his working years in a mine.

He wonders what Ellie would think of Oliver. One day he hopes to introduce the two of them, but for now, he guards Oliver ferociously to protect him. No woman he has dated since the divorce has ever touched him deeply enough to make him want to share Oliver. He refuses to risk his son's heart until he's tested the waters with his own.

Ellie does have a killer shot. He'd found that out the hard way. A couple of days after their front porch talk, he'd walked to her house since he didn't live all that far away, basketball in hand. He'd found her in the backyard, sitting in a decrepit looking pea green lawn chair, hardback book in her lap. She hadn't jumped or moved quickly, but all the same, he'd seen guilt touch her face when she looked up at him.

He'd asked what she was reading, as she'd asked if he was looking for the Globetrotters. She'd closed the book and handed it to him, John Sandford's newest. He'd nodded in approval and then asked if she wanted to shoot baskets.

Her laughter was a cool breeze against his skin. "Did you bring the backboard? Because I don't have one."

"Park does," he'd answered with a nod toward the alley behind her backyard. She'd taken her book inside and returned a moment later with her keys in hand.

"Don't break my nose," she'd warned him as he carried her lawn chair to the garage. "No insurance."

He'd laughed, stowed the chair in the garage and noted the sorry looking Tercel. "I promise to take it easy on you," he'd said and nodded, then laughed when she'd arched an eyebrow at him.

They hadn't actually played a game, too much physical contact so he hadn't even mentioned it. She'd beat him five of seven games of Horse. He hadn't let her win; there'd been no need for that. Over half of her shots swished the net without ever touching the backboard. She had magic hands; his high school coach would have loved her.

He'd asked if she played in high school. She'd simply mumbled freshman year and dribbled the ball out to three-point distance and sunk yet another shot. He'd asked what position; she'd told him she was a point guard, which surprised him. With her height, he would have assumed she would be a good forward. As he followed her shot with his own and tacked an R on his score, he'd asked her if she'd played other sports. She'd nodded and asked him if he'd played in school. That was the end of his fishing expedition for the evening.

He thinks he wants to see her again, but he knows too much too soon is his quickest ticket to wearing out his welcome. Instead he's been thinking about Oliver, so he picks up the cordless and carries it out to the patio. He can see Rylan in New York; it's right up her alley. But he hates that his son is growing up in a big city. He should be here, where there is room to stretch out and be a boy and grow. Here, where he could catch lightening bugs and dig up worms and play with neighborhood boys.

The answering machine picks up after five rings. He wonders if his message will be heard by other men, if Rylan dates, more specifically if Rylan exposes his son to the men in her life. He hates to think that she probably does.

"Oliver." He doesn't have to fake the smile on his face; the kid puts it there naturally. "It's Daddy. Call me later, buddy, okay? I love you."

The silence that sneaks in around him is absolute. He holds the phone in his lap and stares absently at the neighbor woman's sheets hanging on her clothesline, flapping in the warm breeze. Sometimes when you're alone, life moves too slowly for comfort. He really needs to find something to do with himself before he goes stir crazy.

~

IF SHE HAD THE MONEY AND THE MEANS, SHE WOULD TRY bungee jumping. All her life, really, has been one big jump, and she always seems to land on her feet. She wouldn't say she's ever taken a leap of faith, but she's certainly jumped and felt her stomach hovering around her knees and been half sick with that flying feeling. And still landed on her feet. A leap of faith, by definition, requires faith. She has none. Thinking that there might be a God or some universal conscious doesn't necessarily equal faith. She'd had faith in herself, once upon a time. But about five years ago, it had poured out of her, as if she were a sieve, with millions of tiny holes in her body where anything good would seep out of her.

Quincy used to sponsor a freefall convention and crazy-ass people from all over the world would come to jump out of planes. Ellie is sure that one year bungee jumping was a featured attraction. If she'd had money then, she wouldn't have done it. But now there is nothing to hold her back. Now she wants to add a little danger to her life. Not for excitement, but for added punishment. She's grown too accustomed to this life to feel it as a punishment now. It's time to up the ante. Then again, she figures she'd love skydiving and bungee jumping, and they wouldn't be a punishment.

And maybe that in itself is what she deserves. All the fun things in life and no one to share them with. All the little things in life and no one to share them with. A long life full of missed opportunities and strange faces and no one to talk to her and remind her she is human.

Except Jay. Jay Bryant talks to her. She's not sure why. Actually, she's beginning to think she knows why, and even though she's found she kind of likes his eyes and his voice, and even though he can make her smile, he's dangerous. She needs to push him out and shut and lock the door before it's too late. She will hurt him. By doing nothing but being herself, she will hurt him, and he deserves so much better.

She'd kicked his butt on the court the other evening. And had fun doing it. He was a pretty good shot, but she was better. Her dad had taught her the fundamentals of the sports she played, but she'd been born with her mother's finesse. She has no doubt there are things Jay Bryant could kick her ass at, but she'd won fair and square the other night.

He's not drop-dead gorgeous like George Clooney or Brad Pitt; then again, she's not so crazy about Brad Pitt. He's not drop-dead gorgeous like some of the guys she used to know. But he's cute. He's really cute, and she likes his eyes and his smile. And that dimple. He makes her laugh, and he has a life outside of the confining walls of her house, and so she likes to listen to him talk. But it's got to go nowhere but back to the beginning, because she's not interested in a relationship, and she won't allow one to start. She'll guard her heart and stamp out the festering of anything out of the ordinary, the way she fights that damned weed out in her yard.

If houses were made of clay, Oliver had told him, then people could be too and we could be all different colors. Oliver's favorite color is blue. Not just any blue, but navy blue. Jay imagines houses everywhere made of clay, and the people living inside them made of clay. There would be red people and green and blue people, and he thinks it's cute that his son is delighted with the possibilities. Jay thinks it would be a neat world, because if your house is made of clay and you don't like it, you could just squeeze it in your fist and reshape it into something new and exciting. Likewise, if you don't like the people you live with, you could squeeze them and massage them in the palm of your hand and then sculpt them into someone else, someone you might like better.

The downfall, though, would be the difficulty in changing yourself. Even if we're made of clay, we need someone else to start the process of self-change. We can't just fold in on ourselves and roll into a ball and wiggle around a few times and come out some bigger and better version of ourselves. Besides that, clay gets stiff and hard when it's left out too long, then it cracks and crumbles and sometimes we do that anyway, even without being made of clay.

Oliver had also told him he'd jumped off the diving board at swimming lessons earlier today. Jay is impressed. He'd hated the diving board until he was thirteen. Oliver has ten years on him. Maybe he'll be an Olympic swimmer, Jay thinks, but just as quickly pushes that thought aside. Maybe he'll learn to swim and have fun with his friends at the pool. Above all else, while Oliver is still a child, Jay wants him to have fun.

He checks the chicken and turns it on the grill. His stomach is growling. He wishes it would hurry and get done, though he knows a watched pot never boils. Before he can think twice, he grabs his phone off the redwood picnic table and calls her. He doesn't consider why he knows her number. There is nothing about the way he feels anymore that surprises him. He wants to get to know her better.

"Ellie?" he says when he hears her voice. She stammers for a moment then simply says yes. "It's Jay."

~

TENNIS IS NOT A DATE. SHE DOESN'T CONSIDER IT A DATE. SHE wears old shorts, a plain T-shirt and no makeup. Her hair is loose around her face, and she smells like paint. But she wonders, as she rides her bike to the same park where they'd shot baskets, if his calling her and asking her to meet him at the park to play tennis is a date. She'd tried to beg off, and she really didn't have a racket, but he'd told her he'd bring her one. And no other excuse had come to mind, so here she is, meeting Jay to play tennis.

He's waiting for her when she rides into the park and rolls to a stop at the court. She returns his smile as she drops the kickstand and takes the racket from his hand. It's a nice racket, a shiny red and silver Wilson. She wonders why he has two, but she doesn't ask. She's never been much of a tennis player, but she thinks it would be fun just to hit the ball around. A little bit of fun and a little bit of exercise and time to think of what she's going to say to him when they're finished to tell him they're done.

She's not sure what to say, because technically they aren't in a relationship of any sort. She supposes they are friends now, which only makes it harder. People don't just walk around ending friendships for the hell of it. Or do they? She can't really say, because she's been so disconnected from people for so long, she doesn't really know what they do. Maybe she just needs to clearly define what is developing, or more to the point, make sure he knows what is not developing.

But after they've volleyed the ball back and forth for an hour, she finds herself nodding when he asks her if she likes ice cream. And then they're on their bikes and riding to Dairy Queen, just down the street from the park. He asks her when they climb off their bikes if she wants to sit outside.

She follows his gaze to the picnic table plunked down right on the corner, where pedestrians would have to walk out around it, either in the parking lot or the street, just to get by. When she nods, he says he'll get the ice cream if she wants to watch their bikes and rackets.

He leaves her at the table and goes to get their treats. She watches the light Tuesday evening traffic while she waits. Ice cream used to be a family treat. After ball games or the circus or swimming, her parents took her and her brother and sister for ice cream. Her favorite has always been strawberry. It had come as no surprise to her that he liked strawberry too. Strawberry baseball helmet sundaes. She rubs her eye because it itches, not because the thought of baseball helmet sundaes bothers her, and looks up with a smile when she sees Jay returning with their ice cream.

"Strawberry blizzard," he says as he turns it upside down.

"Jay!" She laughs and reaches for it. "That's ice cream abuse."

He grins and sits down beside her, careful to leave enough room for a third person to sit between them. She appreciates that he understands there is always someone else with them. She wonders how long it will be before he asks who it is.

"What were you painting?" he asks as he spoons a bite of his Butterfinger blizzard to his mouth.

"What?"

"You have paint on your shorts and your shoes." He points to the big splotch of white paint on the toe of her tennis shoe.

"Shit," she mumbles. The shoes are not new, but they have several more miles of wear and tear before she will allow herself to get a new pair. She winces and glances at him, relieved to see that he's amused rather than offended. "Window trim in my kitchen."

"How come?"

She raises her eyebrows and shrugs. "Needed it." She studies him for a moment and notices he's wearing an old Heart concert T-shirt. "Did you see them?"

"Yeah," he answers with a nod. "Couple times."

"What's your favorite song of theirs?"

"Magic Man," he says without hesitation. "What's yours?"

"Alone."

She looks at the splotch of paint on her shoe. It's almost shaped like a fried egg, the uneven, curvy edge. She should say something to him. To make sure they're on the same page. To make sure he knows where she stands.

"Do you like baseball?"

She looks at him with a grin. "I do."

"Cards and Cubs play tomorrow. Game's on TV." She swallows hard and stares at him, waiting for him to go on. "Wanna watch it with me?"

Here's her invitation to walk away. To tell him she's not interested.

"I'm a Braves fan." She hedges.

He clutches at his heart and squeezes his eyes shut. "Don't tell me you like Chipper Jones."

"Of course I do." She chuckles. "My grandpa was a Braves man. Braves and anyone who plays the Cubs."

"Well, we can agree on that, anyway," he says with a small smile. "Do you wanna watch the game with me?"

She remembers other moments in her life like this. When someone has posed a question to her, an invitation of sorts, and she's stood on the precipice of something potentially huge, wondering what will come of it. She blinks and looks at Jay, looks him in the eye and wonders what will come of this. What she knows for certain is it can never be worse than what has already come and gone.

"Yeah." She nods. "I do."

CHAPTER 5

When his sister Maeve was eighteen, and he was nine, he was the bane of her existence. He tortured her when her boyfriends were around and even when she had her usual group of girl friends hanging around. He teased her mercilessly about boys and kissing and making out and zits and everything else nine-year-old boys can think of to use as weapons. Maddie was never as much fun to tease; she was never much into boys, and she never took the bait. He figures now if Maddie had been easier to bother, Maeve wouldn't have gotten the brunt of it.

And if Maeve hadn't gotten the brunt of it way back then, maybe she wouldn't be such a pain in the ass now. She harps on him all the time about finding a woman. A real woman, because she equates Rylan with Barbie. She'd never liked Rylan, and in hindsight, he knows she was just being protective of him. She will love Ellie, and that's why he is desperate to get her out of his house before Ellie arrives.

He'd seen it in Ellie's eyes the night before. She'd wanted to tell him no about tonight. First she'd hesitated to meet him for tennis, and then she'd wanted to say no about the baseball game. It's not really fear he sees in her eyes, but reluctance. She doesn't want a relationship. No romantic involvement, that much is obvious to him. And though he very much wants a relationship with her, he will wait and give her time. He's happy to be her friend, no matter how it all turns out in the end.

But he's afraid Maeve won't be so willing to let things happen naturally. She will scare Ellie, even if sitting alone in the dark on her front porch does not. Maeve wants him to be happy, the way she is happy with her husband of twenty years.

"Why are you rushing me out of here?" she asks him as she pulls the refrigerator door open. "I don't wanna go home. Stash is out of town." She glances at him over her shoulder. "You have steaks marinating in here. One for me?"

"No." His tone leaves no room for doubt.

She closes the door and turns to look at him. He mutters a few choice words that might have made a weaker woman bristle, but his sister is not weak. His sister is tougher than he is. Her rich, hearty laugh fills his little kitchen as she leans her shoulder up against his little white top-freezer Frigidaire.

"You have a date," she says. She has a gorgeous smile. He has to give her that.

"It's not a date, but she'll be here any minute."

"Who is she?"

"Maeve, please?" He hears the desperation in his voice and knows she will pick up on it. "She's very skittish, and if you hit her head-on with that ballsy attitude, you're gonna make her run."

"What's her name?" she asks softly.

"Ellie."

She arches her eyebrows at him. "You're in love with her."

"Going that way, maybe," he admits. "But we're just friends. She's not interested."

"Have you asked her that?" She pushes away from the refrigerator and picks up her purse from his table. "Maybe she is."

"Ellie's different, Maeve." He glances at his watch, takes the steaks from the refrigerator, and sets the dish on the small counter. "She's not into all the games."

Maeve nods. "Okay. I'm outta here."

He follows her to the front door, grateful she is going without a fight. He would like for her to meet Ellie one day, but Ellie is not ready for his family. Of that, he's certain.

"When is Rylan bringing Oliver home?"

They all refer to Quincy as home, when it comes to Oliver, even though he's been living in New York with Rylan for the majority of his life. He loves them all for that. They are as crazy about his son as he is.

"I don't know," he says with a shrug. "You know Rylan."

"Yes," she says as she tugs the door open. "Unfortunately, I do."

JAY'S HOUSE IS NOT MUCH BIGGER THAN HERS. IT'S HER FIRST thought as she stops her bike in front of the small, brown-bricked square. He'd told her just to bring her bike around to the back of the house, and he'd lock it up for her. She steps off it now and walks it around to the back. She stops in her tracks when she sees him at the gas grill. Decked out in faded denim shorts and a short-sleeved, maroon button-up shirt, he looks like the all-American guy. The shirt has a tropical scene on the back, but she doesn't take the time to check it out in detail. She doesn't need a tropical scene. This backyard and the guy and the steak on the grill are working pretty well.

"Hey." He offers her a smile when he realizes she is there.

"Hi."

"Hope you didn't eat." He nods toward the back of the house, where his bike is connected to the wrought iron rail that delineates the outer edge of the patio, with a combination lock.

"Apple," she answers him as she rolls her bike over to stand by his.

"Still hungry?"

She glances at the steaks then looks back at him with a sheepish smile. "Yeah."

"Good." He holds the tongs out to her and opens the combination bike lock when she takes them. She looks at the meat, but it looks fine, and she's never been much of a cook anyway. "What'd you do today?"

"Cleaned out the closets," she answers, gladly handing over the tongs once her bike is locked with his.

"Great fun." He nods. "How do you like your steak? Medium well or ruined?"

"Medium well," she says with a grin.

"My sister likes them ruined," he tells her.

"Which one?"

"Maddie. The nun," he adds. "She and Joe both do."

"Do you have pictures of them?" she asks suddenly. He nods. "Can I see them?"

"Sure." He pulls the steaks from the grill and puts them on a plate. "Do you eat vegetables?"

"Yeah," she answers. "Well, some."

"C'mon," he says. She follows him to the door and then holds it open for him. "Salad's in the fridge."

"You didn't have to go to all this trouble," she tells him. She finds the salad in the fully stocked refrigerator.

"It's no trouble," he answers. "Have to eat anyway."

"Do you cook a lot?"

"I like to," he says with a nod. He grabs two plates from a cabinet above the sink and puts them on the table. "Don't you?"

"No." She watches him with amusement when he puts a steak on a plate and then adds a generous bit of salad to the plate and pushes it toward her.

"What do you eat?" He glances up at her but quickly looks back at his own plate.

"Apples." She grins when he gives her a look. "Hot dogs. TV dinners."

"No wonder you're so thin," he mumbles. "Wanna eat outside? Game's not on for another half hour."

"Sure." She takes the bottle of French dressing from him and pours some on her salad.

"Beer?"

"No, thanks," she says without looking at him.

"Coke okay?"

"Sure."

Outside, she finds it easier to breathe. She knows this time it has nothing to do with the sky. Rather, it's that being alone with Jay inside his house makes her feel completely off balance, like she has one roller skate on and one tennis shoe on. It's been ten years since she's found herself alone with any guy in any small quarters. It's not that she doesn't trust him or herself, simply that it makes her remember things better left alone.

"Why do you have two tennis rackets?" she asks him when they sit down at the picnic table.

He stares at her in surprise, chews the piece of steak he's just stuck in his mouth and then purses his lips, as if he needs to think hard before he can answer her. Just as she decides he's not going to answer, he raises his eyebrows and tugs one corner of his lips up in an imitation of a shrug.

"One was my ex-wife's," he says quietly. "But you're the first person to ever use it."

Ex-wife. It is her turn to stare at him in surprise. She's not sure what to say, so she says the first thing that comes to mind, which is stupid. But once the words fall out, she can't take them back. "She didn't take it with her?"

"No." A storm brews behind his dark blue eyes. "She didn't take that, but she took everything else."

She swallows hard, because she knows what it's like to lose everything that's important. "I'm sorry."

He gives her a small smile and nods. "It's better this way," he tells her. But she wonders if it's better this way why he seems so sad all of a sudden.

SHE EATS LIKE A BIRD, BUT SHE DID FINISH MORE OF THE STEAK than he thought she would. After dinner, she insists on helping him clean up the kitchen. He hates that Rylan has entered the picture, and he hates that he feels Oliver with him, like he's giving him a piggyback ride. He doesn't want to tell her about Oliver. Not yet.

He turns the TV on as she wanders around the living room. His latest picture of his son is in his bedroom; she won't see it. He doesn't mind that she's looking at the pictures in his living room. In fact, he likes that she seems interested.

"This one's Maeve?" she asks, pointing at Maeve's family picture that hangs on the wall above the TV.

"Yeah." He moves to stand behind her. When he breathes, he smells her hair, a mix of something flowery and fruity, like raspberries. He focuses on the picture on the wall and not the woman in front of him. He reaches around her and points to the picture. "Maeve and her husband, Stash."

"Stash?" she asks and glances over her shoulder at him. Her eyes are big and beautiful, and they touch him when he is this close to her. He remembers she is talking to him and grins at her.

"Stephen, but we call him Stash."

"Why?"

"He was pretty tight when he met Maeve. Stashed all his money away, instead of spending it."

"Okay," she says with a quiet laugh. She looks back at the picture and waits for him to continue.

"This is Peyton," he says. "She's nineteen. And this is Luke. He's seventeen."

"Good looking family," she tells him.

"Thank you."

"So this is Maddie?" she asks of the next picture. It looks like a yearbook pose, and he guesses it is, of some sort. Church directory, anyway.

"Yeah, that's Madeline."

"She's beautiful."

Maddie is beautiful, and she does not wear a habit so it is hard to see her as a nun. She has long, wavy black hair and big green eyes. The cowl neck of a red sweater is all that is visible below her chin. He wonders what she will say about Joe. It's not hard to imagine.

"This is my mom and Joe," he tells her when she looks at the last picture, again, from the church directory. Joe looks like the young Elvis Presley, right down to the sideburns. He's a good looking kid, and he's got the girls to show for it.

"Where's your father?" she asks quietly. He is quiet for a moment, not only because she's asked about his dad, but because she didn't make the familiar comments about his little brother.

"He died four years ago," he answers.

"I'm sorry." She turns to him. There is compassion in her eyes, but the two inches that separate them might as well be two yards. She does not touch him, not even to push him out of her space.

He backs up to give her room to move. "He had cancer," he says with a nod.

"Sometimes I think everyone has cancer when they die," she says quietly. She looks at the TV and perches gingerly on the edge of his couch when she sees the game has started. She snorts and raises her gaze to his. "Cubs are up by one already."

"First inning," he answers with a shrug. He sits at the opposite end of the couch. She steals a sidelong glance at him when she thinks he's not looking. "Is your grandpa from Atlanta?"

"No." She laughs and shakes her head. "I don't know where the whole Braves thing came from. But he was a tried and true fan."

"That's un-American," he mumbles.

"Better than the Yankees." She curls her feet up under her and looks at him. He nods. She might be a Braves fan, but she doesn't like the Cubs or the Yankees. If she likes football, he's got a new best friend.

"What was she like?" she asks after two outs have passed, and no runs have scored.

"Selfish," he answers without hesitation.

MUCH TO HER PARENTS' DISMAY, NICK HAD ALWAYS WANTED to be a plumber when he grew up. Well, not always. Until he was six, he'd wanted to be Batman. It was when he was six, when the drain in the kitchen had been clogged and her mom had called a plumber to fix it, that he'd changed his life's career plans. Ellie had always thought he'd just been impressed with the wrench the plumber had used. She'd been repulsed by the old plumber butt joke come true in her own home. Natalie had been too involved in her Barbie dolls to know there was a problem with the kitchen sink or that there was a plumber in the house.

She wonders what they are doing now. Natalie was always a girly girl, and so she envisions her doing something stereotypically female. Like secretarial work. She knows that's unfair to Natalie and to all women and secretaries, but it's the first thing her mind conjures up. Maybe she's a designer, she muses. She used to draw detailed outfits and dresses and tell Ellie she was going to make them one day. Ellie had tuned her out.

Nick had been into science when she left. Lots of avenues to explore with science. She wonders too if Nick played high school sports. He'd been the little league soccer all-star when she'd last seen him.

She's just curious, though. There's no burning desire deep inside to see them, to go home. She will never go home. They have never looked for her; she's not hiding. A simple computer search would tell them exactly where she is. She hopes they never type her name into a Dell and search her out. And visit her. She doesn't want to see them. Ever.

It's getting dark out, but the History channel is showing a special documentary on JFK. She thinks he's interesting. The stars will still be there when the show is over. She lays on the couch, with her eyes on the TV, but she must admit she's not paid much attention to the narrator or the black and white footage. She's thinking about her family and more, really, about Jay's family. Jay's father, who died. And Jay's ex-wife, who left her tennis racket with him.

Selfish. She knows all about selfish. That word had

lodged itself in her gut the other night after Jay had said it. Funny that Jay's ex-wife is selfish. She's afraid now, afraid that she's going to hurt him. The last thing she wants is to hurt someone else.

She gives up on the History channel, rolls off the couch, and turns the TV off. Summer nights have a personality all their own. The air is heavy with cloying heat and humidity, but there is a sparse breeze that slides over her as she steps out on the porch. A million tiny lanterns dot the black velvet sky. She lowers herself to sit down on the step and thinks of him lying in the grass, watching the sky.

She's not surprised when Jay shows up, but his means of transportation tonight is a surprise. He parks his silver Chevy truck in front of her house and climbs out. He's smiling when he rounds the front of the truck and heads up her sidewalk.

"Hey," she says as she scoots over to make room for him on the porch. "What're you doing?"

"Maeve and I went out for dinner," he says as he sits down. "Stash is out of town."

"Where'd ya go?" she asks with a smile.

"Ruby Tuesday. Barbequed ribs."

"Good?" she asks. She's never set foot inside Ruby Tuesday.

"Very. Coupla beers. Good food and my pain-in-the-butt sister." He grins, and she knows he doesn't mean it. "But she bought, so I can't complain."

She smiles and nods. "Yogurt and an apple."

"I thought about calling you to go with us."

"You did?" She is surprised by this.

"Would you have gone?" His eyes are heavy on her as he waits for her answer.

She takes a deep breath and considers his question. She would like to have gone with him. Truth be told, she's not sure she wants to meet Maeve, or Maddie, for that matter, but she thinks she would like to have gone with him. "I don't know," she says honestly.

"If it were just me, would you go?"

She stares at him and suddenly wonders if he's asking her out. She won't go out with him. Instead of answering him, she looks away and stares at the tree across the street. She thinks that she is like that tree that had bent and kissed the ground during that storm. She bends, but she doesn't break. Sometimes she's wished she could just break. Maybe it would be easier if she could break and fall into a million pieces and then blow away in the wind.

"No strings attached," he says quietly. "Two friends grabbing dinner."

She wonders what it would look like; what kind of sound would it make if the tree ever bent so far it snapped? What kind of sound would she make if she ever snapped? She licks her lips and says without looking at him, "Maybe."

When he doesn't answer her, she finally turns back to him. His eyes search her face, but she knows that no matter what he's looking for, he's not going to find it in her. She's empty inside, hollow like everything that made her human has been carved out with a knife. He nods and lets his eyes wander away from hers.

"Would you do me a favor?" he asks. His eyes are drawn to that same tree, and she wonders what he's thinking. Where was he on May tenth last year when that tree had bent and swayed in the tornadic winds that had leveled Canton and Lima? She thinks maybe she will ask him that one day.

"What?" She is hardly in a position to do anyone a favor, but she's curious what he will ask her.

He turns to her again, and she feels a jolt of electricity when their eyes meet. She presses her lips together to keep any unwanted sounds from escaping. "Would you tell me a story? About the stars?"

She stares at him in silence for a moment. It's quite simple, really, to tell him a story about the stars. She has so many folded and tucked away inside her, like blankets stored away in a cedar chest. And yet, he's asking her for the only real piece of herself she has left. He's asking her to share what she has never, in ten years, shared with another living soul.

She swallows hard and looks up at the sky. It's been so long since she's told stories about the stars, she wonders if her voice will remember how to say those words. She puts her hands behind her on the porch and leans back. "See that really big, bright star up there? Right there?" She points with her left hand because he is on her left side, and it will be easier for him to find it when he is close to her.

"Which one?" He leans in so close that she can smell the fresh woodsy aftershave he wears and the beer on his breath. It's almost appealing. She turns her head and looks up at the sky, still pointing. Her breath catches in her throat when he slides his hand up her arm, barely touching her skin and closes his hand around hers. He points at the star she is looking at.

"That one," she says with a nod. She pulls her hand away from his, drops it to her lap and avoids his eyes. Her heart is pounding dangerously hard, and she waits a moment before she tries to speak. "It's called Zanoid."

"Zanoid," he repeats. His deep blue eyes are like the sky when she looks at him. She thinks maybe she could tell stories about his eyes, about the light she sees in them, but those kinds of stories are for other people to tell.

"Everyone there is yellow."

"Yellow?" he asks with a frown.

"Because it's a happy color. Everything and everyone is

yellow. And they build sand castles all day long. And they eat ice cream."

"Strawberry?" He raises his eyebrows.

"No." She shakes her head and smiles. That's a different star, but she doesn't tell him that. "Chocolate. Everybody there likes chocolate."

"Do they have names?"

"Of course they do," she answers matter-of-factly. "Bob and Ned and Fran and Helen."

"And they're all happy?"

She hears those words, but in her head she hears a small voice full of wonder and French fries and ice cream. Her throat aches from holding the sadness trapped inside. She tries to blink her eyes dry, but the more she blinks, the more tears burn her eyes. Finally, she nods and turns to look at him boldly and lets him see her tears. He doesn't flinch or look away or roll his eyes. Instead he looks at her like he sees her, which she cannot fathom because she hasn't seen herself in a good ten years.

"Yeah." Her voice is thick with years of regret and buried memories and yellow people and Zanoid, the star. "They're all happy."

CHAPTER 6

HER AVERSION TO TOUCH HAS EVERYTHING TO DO WITH horrible memories that have nothing to do with abuse or rape. She knows he has to wonder why she does her best to melt away from his touch every time he bumps into her or touches her hand or her arm. It's unnatural, the way she avoids his touch, but she would do it with anyone. She's not been touched in five years. His hand makes her feel like she's a burn victim, and she needs to shed her skin to get away from him. Inside she is deeply blistered and scarred, and so she knows that if he could touch that part of her, he'd be repulsed.

It's a bad sign that they've spent enough time together lately that she misses him now. He'd told her he was going out of town for the weekend, and she'd felt an emptiness inside that threatened to yawn and swallow her whole. She forgot that she was supposed to be independent, that she didn't need him, and she'd asked where he was going. To New York, he'd answered, to visit a friend. He'd teased her then, on his patio as they'd sipped thick strawberry milkshakes that he'd made for them in his blender—he has a blender!—and asked if she was going to miss him. Their eyes had met in the growing darkness, over their straws and rather than lie or pretend that he meant nothing to her, she'd simply nodded.

Within a month, she has grown used to him hanging around her house. She has grown used to watching baseball with him, even if it is the Cardinals. She likes going to the park and shooting baskets or playing tennis with him. The ice cream nights. She likes him. Admitting it makes her feel like she's standing on a rooftop, contemplating suicide. Toes curled over the edge and eyes riveted to the ground twenty floors down. Acceptance and dread woven together inside her and pulling at her with equal force.

OLIVER HAD BEEN THRILLED TO SEE HIM. HE'D LATCHED ONTO him like they were Lego blocks, meant to be stuck together. Rylan hated it, but he didn't care. Nothing about his relationship with his son had anything to do with his ex-wife. With her permission, which he hated having to seek, he'd taken Oliver for lunch. Thank God there are golden arches everywhere, though from the way Oliver had gotten all excited about 'the chicken bicnuggets'—he said it nasally, as if his nose was stuffy—he wondered if Rylan made a habit of feeding him this crap. After lunch, they'd walked around the city for a while, Oliver's tiny little hand inside his own or Oliver on his shoulders, where he could see forever and Jay could safely hold onto him.

After the rest of the afternoon spent at the park, where Oliver showed Jay how he'd learned to pump his swing on his own, they'd gone to Jay's hotel. Sometimes when he'd come to visit Rylan, he ended up staying at her apartment. Sometimes, if Oliver went to sleep early, Jay slept with Rylan.

He'd never been naïve enough to believe that her coming onto him meant anything more than she hadn't had a man in her life for a week or two. She was hot, and if she wanted to hand it over for him to use, he was going to take advantage of her. Use her. He had no respect for her, not after the way things had ended for them.

He couldn't bring himself to look at her on this trip. Before he'd ever left his house, he'd known he wouldn't stay at her place. He didn't want Rylan anymore. He wanted nothing more to do with Rylan and her centerfold body. He had Ellie. In a completely different way, he had all the woman he would ever need again. So he'd booked a hotel, not worrying about the expense. He needed to see his son, and there was no dollar amount that would keep him from spending time with him.

In the gift shop at the hotel, Jay bought Oliver a pair of dark green swim trunks. "Look," he'd said to Oliver as he'd squatted down to look him in the eye. "They have an alligator on them."

"I like the green." Oliver had nodded his approval. "But it's a crocodile, Daddy. See? His snout is much longer than an alligator's."

Jay had simply laughed and nodded and tousled his son's soft hair. "Of course it is. You're right." He supposes, for all practical purposes, his three-year-old son would be classified as a brainy geek. Instead of spouting off the names of baseball players or football teams, he recites scientific facts about animals or the weather. He likes candy bars, but he loves fruit. The kid even eats broccoli and asparagus. He wonders often where it all comes from, but his mother has told him more than once that Oliver is the latent boy inside Jay himself. Maybe, he decides. And he loves his mother for seeing it.

"Why are we getting trunks?"

"I thought we could put them on and go hang out in the hotel pool," Jay says casually. "What do you think?"

Oliver's grin is brighter than all of the stars in Ellie's sky. With their purchase made, they head up to Jay's room and change into their trunks. Oliver watches with interest as Jay undresses and then pulls his navy Adidas trunks on.

"Daddy?" Oliver fits his hand inside Jay's as they head to the elevator in search of the indoor pool.

"What, buddy?"

"Someday, will I be tall, like you?"

"You will," Jay says confidently. He's not all that tall, but to a guy that spends his life looking at people's knees, he probably seems like it.

"Daddy?"

"Yeah?'

"When can I come live with you?"

～

SOMEHOW IT'S DIFFERENT THAT HE'S INVITED HER OVER TO watch a movie. A movie seems to suggest so much more than a baseball game. She'd told him yes when he'd called to tell her he was home from New York and asked her if she wanted to come over and watch a movie. Now she's not sure she should have. A baseball game is a very casual thing that friends do. A movie is something people do for a date.

She steers her bike into his yard and rides on around his house. She couldn't not see him. She's been stir crazy since he's been gone, and that's a sad commentary on her life, because he was only gone for three days. He opens the back door when she steps off her bike. It's hard for her anymore not to notice how good he looks in denim shorts. Good enough that she can forgive him the Cardinal T-shirt.

"Hey," he says as he takes her bike and locks it up next to his. "I missed you."

She nods and presses her lips together, and finally she swallows hard and says very quietly, "Me too."

"Wanna order pizza?" he asks as they go inside.

"Yeah, sure," she agrees.

"What do you like on yours?" He pulls a phone book from a drawer under the kitchen counter.

"Cheese."

"Just cheese?" he asks with a grin. She shrugs and nods and laughs. "Maddie and Luke would love you."

While he orders the pizza, she wanders to the living room and wonders about the friend he visited in New York. He joins her when the pizza is ordered. She turns from the open front door where she is watching the stillness of the summer night and looks at him as he sits down in the corner of the couch.

"How was your trip?" she asks. She doesn't know how to ask who his friend is without sounding too interested or jealous. She doesn't want to be jealous, because it's a worthless emotion to waste your energy on. And because she doesn't want to have the kind of feelings for him that lend themselves to jealousy.

"Good," he answers. "Had a good time."

"Friend from school?" she asks as she walks back to the couch and sits at the opposite end.

He hesitates just long enough to make her wonder again if he was with a woman. She curls into the corner of the couch and studies the copper threads in the throw pillow she folds her arms over.

"Yeah," he finally says. She nods. He wouldn't have a woman in New York and play games with her here, would he? Why wouldn't he? First of all, cheating and sleeping around are commonplace; she knows that by experience. But most importantly, they are not involved. They aren't dating. Jay's never held her hand. She doesn't want him to hold her hand. So why should it bother her if he went to New York to get laid?

It does bother her. The thought is like a popcorn hull stuck between her teeth, stubborn as hell as she tries to pick at it and make it go away.

"What movie are we watching?" she asks, looking for surer ground to stand on.

"I rented *Seabiscuit*," he answers. "Is that okay?"

"Yeah."

"Ellie?" he says softly. She looks up with sharp eyes, but she holds down the shiver that his voice traces along her spine. "I really did miss you."

She stares at him for a long, silent moment and pictures herself on that rooftop, teetering on the edge of something huge and unknown. "I know," she whispers. "Me too."

He turns the TV on, and she pretends to watch the sitcom reruns, and finally the pizza comes. She has to smile when she sees he's ordered half cheese and half pepperoni. Nick and Natalie loved pepperoni pizza. They eat in the living room, and when they are finished and the movie is on, she finds herself stretched out on his couch. He is spread out on the floor. The movie interests her, but she decides she doesn't care much for Tobey McGuire and decides she doesn't necessarily need to see *Spider-Man* anytime soon. She finds herself watching Jay more than the movie, wondering what he's thinking and what he did in New York and what he does when she's not around and how it came to be that she wonders these things about him. When the movie is over, she's sure to have her eyes on the TV so he doesn't catch her watching him.

They are both tired so instead of riding his bike alongside her when she rides home, he puts her bike in the back of his truck and drives her home. She feels different tonight, but she's not sure if it's because they watched a movie together or if it's because she's still wondering about New York.

"Ellie," he says as he wheels her bike into her kitchen through the back door.

"Yeah?"

"I need to ask you something."

She holds her breath, waiting for the other shoe to drop. Waiting for him to ask her out. Waiting for him to tell her about New York. She resists the urge to cover her ears and shake her head. She doesn't want to hear anything he's about to say.

"Maeve is having a family cookout this weekend," he tells her. "Do you wanna go?"

She swallows her surprise and her immediate fear, but it creeps back up like acid reflux. This is almost worse than anything she worried he might say. He wants her to meet his family, including the assistant district attorney and the Catholic nun.

She wants to go. She is scared sick at the thought of meeting them, but she wants to go. Because if she doesn't go, he'll be there and she'll be here. Alone. Since Jay's been hanging around, she finds it harder being alone.

"Yeah," she whispers. "Yeah, I wanna go."

CHAPTER 7

ADRENALINE. NERVES. HE REFUSES TO THINK OF THAT FEELING as butterflies, because guys don't get butterflies. The rush of nervous energy he always felt on game day was much too powerful to be butterflies anyway. Had to be adrenaline that stepped up to the plate with him and carried him through each baseball season with a three hundred batting average. Nerves had dogged him the first few weeks he'd stood in front of a classroom and repeatedly told himself he was the teacher. Nerves had messed with his head when he'd gotten involved with Rylan. He's finally beginning to feel more comfortable around Ellie; the nerves have calmed, and he just enjoys being with her.

Ellie is nervous about Maeve's cookout. She hasn't said much about it, but there's this pinched expression she gets on her face now and then, and he thinks he knows her well enough to know she's thinking about meeting his family. She's been quiet this week, more so than usual. They had played tennis Monday and watched a Cardinal game Tuesday afternoon and, just last night, they'd gone for a run together. He's seen her every night this week. It's dangerous, what he's doing. He knows that. He's playing with fire, and even though he knows she doesn't want to do it, he's going to get burned. He's won her over as a friend; of that, he has no doubt. But he sees her looking at him sometimes, like she's wondering about him and where he's wanting to lead her. She is a tangle of need and want and innocence and guilt, and Jay wants to take that tangle and free her and study every strand of emotion that defines her so he can understand her.

She is looking at him now, sitting beside him on her front porch. She'd skipped the ice cream tonight, but now she is watching him eat his. She sips her soda and looks away from him and looks up to study the stars. She doesn't wear perfume, but he has come to recognize her scent. It's a mix of soap and lotion, not a flowery lotion, but something that smells good and clean, and he supposes keeps her skin soft. He doesn't know. He rarely touches her. When he does touch her, in a completely appropriate way, she freezes, though she recovers herself quickly as if she doesn't want him to notice that it bothers her. He wonders what is in her past that makes her shrink away from him. He worries that someone hurt her, violated her, but he can't ask. Not yet.

"Ellie?" he says quietly. She turns her head to look at him. He's eating a hot fudge sundae. He holds the spoon out to her, lots of fudge pooled on top of the ice cream. "Want a bite?"

He's not sure if he's testing her or pushing her or just offering her a bite. But he holds his breath as her eyes sweep his face for a long moment of silence before she leans forward and reaches out to cover his hand with hers. He watches as she slips his spoon between her lips and then draws it out again, the ice cream gone. She licks her lips and swallows and thanks him. He simply nods, because right about now he feels like a lovesick teenager. She'd put his spoon between her pale lips and sucked the ice cream off and just right now, all he can think of is how badly he wants to kiss her. Instead he clears his throat and looks up at the stars.

"Can I tell you a story about the stars?" he asks her.

"You have a story about the stars?" She smiles, and he almost forgets the stars.

"Well—" He shrugs. "—it's not mine, exactly. But someone told it to me."

"I wanna hear it," she says with a nod.

He and Oliver had sat out on the balcony of their hotel room after swimming and ordering in a pizza. He'd told Oliver Ellie's story about Zanoid and then asked him to tell him one. He had known his son would love the star game and that he would have a good star story inside him.

"Okay." He sticks his spoon back in his plastic dish and points upward. "See that star up there?"

"Which one?" she asks and leans closer to him to find his star. Oliver's star.

"Right there." He drops his hand and reaches for hers. Her eyes are wide and innocent when she looks up at him. He lifts her hand in his and points again at Oliver's star. "It's the little one. Kind of faded, next to that big cluster right there."

She licks her lips and glances at him and then looks back at the sky. "I see it."

"That's Maladorny," he begins. He loves the way her eyes are bright with excitement when she turns her head and smiles at him. "On Maladorny, they don't talk. They sing. They eat marshmallows for breakfast. They play kickball, and they read books about jungle animals."

She stares at him in wonder and nods and smiles. "Do they have names there?" she asks him softly.

"They do," he answers. "Bobby and Freddie and Johnnie and Mikey."

"I love it," she whispers. "I wish I could go there."

He smiles and finds his eyes drawn to her lips again. He wishes they could both go there, to Maladorny or Zanoid. What if he and Ellie and Oliver could go to a happy star and live there forever? She clears her throat and looks away again, but this time she doesn't look at the stars. She stares at her yard, as if she is simply desperate not to look at him.

"Ellie—"

"Don't," she says quietly. "Please. Don't."

He wonders if there is a star up there where she could be happy. He wishes he could find it and bring it to her.

She'd dreamt that night of Maladorny. She and Jay were there, and they were holding hands. She'd liked the feel of his big hand curled around her fingers. His rough skin against her softer skin. He'd slipped his arm around her waist when she wasn't looking, but when she'd finally realized he had let go of her hand and then felt his hand on her hip, it felt good enough that she hadn't moved away from him.

She hates today. She hates the nerves that plagued her at work, not that she'd slipped up and put any books on the wrong shelves. She could do her job blindfolded, she thinks. She loves books, the feel of the covers in her hands and the words on the pages that paint these incredible stories that take her away from her life. She could be happy working at the library forever. But she hadn't eaten a thing at lunch. She was so hungry when she'd gotten home, she'd given in and eaten some crackers. She'd been tempted to eat more, but she didn't want to make herself sick before going to Maeve's house.

He'd thought about kissing her last night. She knows that, just from the way he had looked at her. She'd stared at him boldly, almost daring him to do it, but when he'd left, and he hadn't kissed her, and she hadn't given him a chance to say what was on his mind, she'd been relieved it hadn't happened. Relieved because she's afraid of what she feels for him. And she thinks kissing him would be a big mistake. She doesn't know what the hell she's feeling, the lightheadedness when she thinks of him. The butterflies in her stomach when she woke up this morning and thought of her dream, of being with him on Maladorny. The way she misses him when he's not with her. She doesn't know what this is, because she's never felt this way before.

She'd stressed all day over what to wear, and she hates that. She's not a shallow person; at least, she isn't anymore. And she hates that she's letting this get to her and make her be someone she's not. Then again, it's not like she has a huge wardrobe anyway. She finally settles on a pair of faded Levi shorts and a lavender knit shirt and then goes outside to sit on the porch and feel sick and wait for Jay.

He comes for her within a half hour, and the butterflies in her stomach flap their wings and remind her that she really kind of wants to stay home. She avoids his eyes as he rounds the truck and hurries up the sidewalk to sit down by her.

"Hey," he says quietly. She glances at him, relieved that he is wearing denim shorts and a pale green button-up shirt. She is surprised to see brown leather sandals on his feet. It seems almost wrong to see his bare feet after all this time.

"Hi." She smiles and lifts her eyes to meet his, then looks away.

"Still wanna go?"

She jerks her eyes back up to his. Does he not want her to go now? Is this his way of saying he's changed his mind?

"I want you to go," he says softly, as if he can read her mind. "But I know this makes you nervous."

She presses her lips together and nods. "I wanna go," she tells him.

"Okay." He stands and reaches for her hand. When he pulls her to her feet, she slips back inside to grab her keys, lock her door, and grab her own sandals. He walks behind her down the sidewalk and opens her truck door for her. "You painted your toenails," he says with a small smile when he looks down and notices the pale pink on her toenails. She feels the blush climb her neck and the butterflies in her stomach threaten to morph into birds. She had indeed bought a bottle of nail polish and painted her toenails. Now it seems like it was a stupid idea, and she wishes she wouldn't have done it.

"Jay," she groans. "Don't do this."

"Don't do what?" he asks, ducking down in front of her, when she lowers her chin. "Don't notice that you look beautiful? C'mon, Ellie, don't get freaked out on me because I noticed you painted your toenails."

"This isn't a date," she whispers and finally looks up at him. "We're not dating, Jay."

"I know." He nods. He reaches for her hands and holds them in his.

"It's just—" She licks her lips and stares at him and wonders how to say what she wants to say. She doesn't even know what she wants to say. She just wants him to know they aren't dating. She wants to be sure his family knows they aren't dating. "I don't want your family to think—"

"My family," he says softly as his thumbs rub small circles over the backs of her hands, "is anxious to meet you. Simply because we're friends."

"Friends?" she whispers.

"Ellie." He lets go of her left hand and slides his fingers over her jaw and around the back of her neck. She shivers at his touch and tries to pull away from him, but he steps closer. It's daylight, and she's standing beside his truck, inside the open door, and his fingers are on her neck. His eyes are deep blue, and they're safe, and she inches closer to him.

"I have nothing to give you." Her voice is thick with need. He draws her closer until her forehead rests against his lips.

"I won't take anything," he says against her skin.

She closes her eyes and feels him beside her. Feels his warm fingers curled around her neck and his lips against her forehead and the heat of his body just inches from hers. Afraid that if she doesn't move, she will melt into him and cease to exist as Ellie Jordan, she steps back from him. She tucks her hair behind her ear and avoids his eyes.

"You okay?"

"Yeah," she says with a nod.

"Still wanna go?" he asks as he lets his hand fall away from her. She nods. "We'll leave whenever you're ready."

She nods and climbs up into his truck. She's not sure what just happened. She doesn't want to date him, and he isn't pushing her, and now she's hung up in what it felt like to have him so close to her. His touch makes her hurt so deep inside she'll never be able to reach it and soothe the hurt away. Instead of feeling comforted, she's cold now. He's a streak of warm, bright color in her black and white life, and since she's used to seeing so much gray, it hurts to look at him.

He watches her as he introduces her to Maeve. She seems okay, but he knows she is scared, and he hates that. He watches, but he doesn't hover protectively beside her. He doesn't want to smother her. He just watches her eyes, because he knows that if she decides she needs him, he'll see it in her eyes first.

Because he's watching, he sees the moment the

tension slides from her shoulders. Maeve is talking to her; he's not close enough to hear their conversation, but he can see the way Maeve has already accepted her in the easy way she talks to her. She'd never been able to talk to Rylan. Five minutes after meeting Ellie, she's yakking the poor kid's ear off. Ellie seems fascinated by Maeve. Her eyes are like her stars at night, all bright and happy; the smile on her lips reaches right into her heart and makes her almost glow.

She turns to him when he approaches them and hands Ellie a Coke. "Thanks," she says with a smile that is all for him. It hits him like a damned dart right in his heart, and the burn tingles all the way down through his stomach and into his toes.

"Jay, get her a beer," Maeve says as Ellie pops the top on the Coke can.

"I don't drink," Ellie says with a shake of her head. She seems comfortable telling Maeve this, and though Jay has figured this out for himself, he wonders why she feels okay saying the words to Maeve but never to him. Maeve simply nods and shrugs and asks Ellie if she's hungry. They wander off to the kitchen together, and Jay is left holding his beer, staring at the piano in the sitting room. He shrugs and makes his way to the backyard, trusting that Ellie is in good hands.

He finds Maddie on a lounge by the pool. It strikes him yet again how beautiful she is. Her black hair dusts her shoulders. She wears khaki capris; her feet are bare. The leather sandals she's kicked off are halfway under the chair. The green sleeveless blouse she wears is the same green as her eyes. She smiles when she sees him.

"Hey," she calls and sits up straighter.

"Hi, Maddie." He grins and sits down on the end of her chair. "Long time, no see."

"Not my fault," she reminds him. "You can visit me."

"Been busy." He knows as he says it that it's an excuse. He

doesn't visit Maddie at her little house by St. Romuald's church because really he doesn't know what he'd say to her. He loves her, just because she's his sister, but he is always on edge around her, worried that he will say the wrong thing. Not because she's a nun, but because there is a deep fault line in her relationship with Maeve. One he can't begin to understand, and he's always felt closer to Maeve. Somehow that makes him feel like he's standing on that fault line and if he makes any sudden moves, the ground will open up and swallow him, and he's afraid he'll suffocate.

She gives him a look that tells him she knows he's lying, but she lets it slide. He's always telling her little white lies like this, and she's always just letting it slide. He thinks someday it would be nice to get to know her, but he really doubts it will ever happen.

"I thought you were bringing your friend," she says as she glances around the patio. Stash, Luke, and Joe are goofing off by the grill, but she's obviously looking for Ellie.

"I did," he answers. "She's in the kitchen with Maeve."

"Figures," Maddie mumbles with an eye roll. He notes that the big eye roll must just be a female thing, not a female on the prowl thing. "I wanna meet her."

"Okay," he says.

"No, I mean, take me in there and introduce me to her." She thumps him on the back. He almost loses his grip on his beer, so he shoots her a look of warning. She laughs and climbs off the lounge chair. "C'mon, cowboy."

"Maddie," he says as he stands and reaches for her. His fingers brush her arm, and he pulls his hand away quickly. She rolls her eyes again, clearly frustrated with him, though he's not completely certain why this time. "Take it easy on her. We're just friends—"

"Friends." She arches her eyebrow and nods at him. "Sure, Jay."

"No." He tries again. "I mean it. Be nice to her."

"What do you think I'm gonna do?" she asks quietly. "Eat her heart for dinner? I just wanna meet her."

He stares at her for a moment, again wondering who she really is. He has never been close to her the way he's close to Maeve. Not even when he was younger. Finally he nods. He follows Maddie inside, through the screened in breakfast nook and to the kitchen. He finds Ellie and Maeve slicing vegetables for a salad tray, and his mother is crushing strawberries. The three of them are talking and laughing, and he feels like an intruder when they realize he and Maddie have joined them and stop the conversation.

"Ellie." He steps closer to her and touches her arm. "I take it you've met my mom."

"I have," she says quietly. "Maeve introduced us."

He smiles at her and glances at his mother. She smiles, but it is a simple smile that implies absolutely nothing.

"This is my sister, Madeline," he continues, and he looks at Maddie. "Maddie, this is my friend, Ellie."

"I'm happy to meet you," Maddie says graciously as she steps forward to shake Ellie's hand. Jay sees the curiosity in his sister's eyes, the nerves that come back for seconds in Ellie's eyes, and something vicious and hateful in his sister Maeve's eyes. He thinks maybe he should ask Maeve what happened between her and Maddie that makes them act like strangers. He decides he really doesn't want to know.

"Hi, Maddie," Ellie says. Her eyes are still shaded a bit with nerves, and that bugs Jay because Maddie can't see the true color of them, how beautiful they are, when she's nervous. "It's nice to meet you."

Maddie plucks a piece of celery off the salad tray and ignores the look Maeve gives her. She sits on a stool at the island where the other three are working. "Jay says you're a Braves fan," she says with a smile. He remembers that he had told them that, one of very few things he's really said about her.

Ellie grins and shrugs. "Yeah. Die-hard."

"Dare to be different." Maddie raises an eyebrow. "I hate baseball. I'm a hockey fan."

Maeve stares hard at Maddie for a moment and then looks away. She finishes slicing the cucumber she's been working on, washes her hands and waits for Ellie to finish with her last piece of celery. She picks up the tray and carries it outside. Jay glances at his mother, wondering if she understands the tension between Maeve and Maddie, if she knows the root of the problem.

"Ellie," Jolene Bryant says. "Quit working so hard. Go sit out by the pool and relax."

Ellie offers his mother a big smile. "I'm fine, Mrs. Bryant, but thank you."

"Call me Jolene," she says in a tone that tells Jay she's told Ellie this once already. She sets the big bowl of strawberries in the stainless steel Sub-Zero refrigerator and wanders on outside.

"Why do you like hockey?" Jay asks Maddie when it is just the three of them left in Maeve's huge, open kitchen. He looks around the big room and decides he could fit half his house here. Maeve and Stash have money to burn, but they are the salt of the earth.

"I like the contact," Maddie says with a shrug. "More excitement than baseball."

He nods, but he's thinking that's just one more thing he's never known about this sister. She stands and reaches for Ellie's hand and pulls her toward the door.

"C'mon," she says with a smile. "Mom's right. You should be out by the pool."

Jay follows them out, but he stands with Stash by the grill. Joe and Luke are in the pool now. Jay glances at Maddie and

Ellie, wondering what Ellie is thinking, wondering if she likes his family or if she's feeling trapped. He watches Ellie as she relaxes by the pool, wondering if she's looked at Joe. He wonders again about Maeve and Maddie and turns to ask Stash about them but again decides he doesn't want to get involved.

When dinner is ready, Ellie searches him out, and he makes certain they sit together. As much as he'd wanted to introduce her to his family, he finds this isn't as much fun as the nights they have spent alone together. He misses the quiet of her front porch or the tennis court or his patio where they sit together and breathe and talk when there is something so important it has to be said. He wonders what she would say if he leaned toward her and whispered in her ear that he misses her.

They are squeezed in at the picnic table, between Maddie and his mother. Ellie's leg is flush against his. Her skin is warm and soft, and he wonders how in God's name he can walk away from this and not want to touch her again. Joe and Luke get caught up in a conversation about a party they'd gone to the weekend before. It quickly turns off color, and Stash tells Luke to mind his manners. Jay's mother gives Joe a look, and Ellie squirms a bit beside him. Knowing she doesn't want to draw attention to herself, he simply lays a hand on her leg, closer to her knee than her hip. To his surprise she covers his hand with hers and links her fingers through his when he turns his hand palm up.

Years ago, she was just getting started at ten o'clock. Now it's just after ten, and she's exhausted. She'd enjoyed herself at Maeve's house, but it has been so long since she's had to be on for a social event that it doesn't come naturally.

The concentration involved in being on her toes and being normal has worn her out. She'd watched Jay play a few hands of Euchre with Stash, Maeve, and Joe. She'd talked some with Jolene, though there really wasn't much to say. The night air that had stolen in around them outside on the patio had been soft and warm, like a light throw over her bare legs. The pool water lapping behind her had all but put her to sleep. The one time she'd begun to feel overwhelmed, she'd looked up and seen the stars and remembered him and thought of Zanoid. And then she was okay.

Jay is quiet on the drive back to her house. She wonders if that means she hadn't performed well enough. She'd felt him watching her all evening, and it had made her feel a touch uneasy and a little bit protected. An odd combination, and she supposes this is yet another reason why she feels so drained.

He walks her to her door, and even though she's tired, she doesn't want to go in. She doesn't want him to leave, but she doesn't want to ask him to stay either. She'd held his hand tonight, and that scares her. It scares her that she'd done it, and it worries her that he will make something out of it, something bigger than what it was. She'd just needed something to ground her in the present, because she'd been dangerously close to fading ten years into the past.

She glances at him when they're standing on the porch, but she looks away quickly.

"Do you want me to go?" he finally asks her.

She swallows hard and looks up at him. "No."

He nods. She sits down in her spot on the porch and waits in silence while he sits down in his spot.

"Thank you for going," he says quietly. "I know you were uncomfortable."

"I enjoyed it," she tells him. "I liked them."

"Really?" he asks quickly. She turns her head to look at him, surprised to see the look of fear on his face.

"Really." She nods. "You have a nice family."

"Maeve didn't come on too strong?" he asks. "She means well, but she tends to meddle."

Ellie shakes her head. "I liked her."

"Good," he says, and he nods and looks away. "I saw you watching the stars."

"Just felt a little overwhelmed," she admits. "The stars make me feel free."

"You know what?" he whispers. She raises her eyebrows in question, waiting for him to continue. "I'm glad you went with me. But I missed this."

"What?"

"Just you and me," he tells her. His words drag over her back like nails on a chalkboard. She tries to take a deep breath, but it feels like she's breathing in quicksand, and she's smothering. "Ellie, just this. I just missed talking to you and listening to your voice."

She licks her lips and stares at him. Her eyes burn with tears that she cannot hide from him, so she doesn't even try. Instead she nods. "I know. Me too."

CHAPTER 8

It's almost lethal, that moment in your life when you realize something you've always known to be true is nothing more than a myth or a cruel joke. That disappointment, the disillusionment just swells up inside your stomach and then your chest, and it expands like a balloon and pushes at your guts and makes it hurt to breathe and move and talk. And then you can't say the words that make it real. You can't verbally acknowledge that you were dead wrong about something, because saying it out loud makes it true.

Ellie was seven the year she'd snuck out of bed on Christmas Eve. She hadn't snuck down the stairs to catch her parents in the act of playing Santa. She'd believed with all her heart she was going to sit on the steps and catch Santa himself sliding down the chimney. She'd watched them for a long time, as they set out presents under the tall, skinny tree she had helped them decorate. Her father had always lifted her on his shoulders to put the star at the top of the tree. She was getting too big for that he'd said this year, too tall and lanky for him to lift her that way. That alone had been too much disappointment for her to deal with. But when she'd watched her parents as they set out presents, both of them laughing and smiling and obviously enjoying their parental Santa duties, and finally realized what they were doing, her stomach had hurt so bad she could hardly crawl back up the stairs to her bedroom.

She'd cried herself to sleep, one arm curled tight around her bedraggled teddy bear that she'd called simply H, and one hand resting on her belly where she'd rubbed the ache away. In the morning, she'd pretended it hadn't happened, because she knew that her life would change once she admitted she knew the truth.

There are other things that make her hurt like that, things that make her gasp for air as if she has been buried in mud, and she's clawing and clawing to get free. When she gets to the surface and breathes, she doesn't speak of what suffocates her. She is afraid that once she says something, she will set something unwanted in motion.

She worries that Jay will read more into the night at Maeve's than she wrote there. She'd needed a friend; hell, she'll admit she needed him. But she thinks she needs him on a very different level than the way he might need her. She's afraid to say this to him, because once it's out, it might snowball until any sort of bad thing could happen. Mostly, she doesn't want to lose him.

Jay's sisters had fascinated her. There is a dangerous undercurrent with them, and Ellie wonders if Jay has ever noticed it. She figures most likely not, because he's a guy, and most guys probably wouldn't notice it or wonder much about it if they did. Then again Jay isn't like most guys.

It amazes her that Maddie is a nun. She is serene and beautiful. Her skin is porcelain, pale and smooth and perfect. Her green eyes are emeralds, but they are inquisitive and cool. She'd been welcoming to Ellie, though in a very different way than Maeve had been. Ellie hopes to see them again sometime, but she worries that if she does, they will assume there is more to her and Jay.

When he calls her now, she never tries to think of an excuse to not see him. She likes him. She wants to spend time with him. But it is still important that he stay on the same page with her. Since she held his hand at Maeve's, she has been more accepting of his touch; she doesn't panic when their hands brush in the popcorn bowl or when he touches her hand to get her attention. But she is still on guard for the first time he might touch her with more than friendship on his mind. She can't let that happen.

He thinks Oliver might like a puppy. He's spent several days now considering the idea, having a puppy here for his son when he gets to bring him home for a visit. If he had to admit it to anyone, he wouldn't, but he kind of wants a puppy too. A dog, for companionship. Well, actually, he wants more of Ellie, but he figures sublimating that desire with a dog might be a good idea.

They have solidified their friendship, almost like they dumped their common ground into a cement mixer, and then stood together as the cement was poured into a sidewalk form over the rebar and then hardened overnight. He loves that they have reached this point, that she knows he cares about her. That he knows she cares about him. If this is all she will ever give him, he'll accept that. But he sees more in her eyes sometimes, and as long as there is the potential for more, he will pursue it.

Maeve had loved her. She'd shown up at his house the day after the cook out to tell him that.

"She's special," she'd said with a nod. "Take care of her."

"I will, as long as she'll let me," he'd answered.

It means a lot to him that Maeve likes her. He is so close to Maeve he likes to share a lot of his life with her. He wants to draw Ellie into his family and share her with them. He also thinks Maeve is a good judge of character; she'd been right about Rylan. And now she sees something special inside Ellie.

He wonders what Maddie thinks of her. Hell, he wonders what Maddie thinks of anything. Hockey? He'd never known she was a hockey fan. Really, he knows nothing about her. She plays the piano, at least she did when she was younger. She has a scar on her knee from a bike crash when she was fifteen. She renounced Satan and men and physical pleasure and that's about all he's sure about when it comes to Maddie.

Ellie doesn't answer her phone when he calls, and he wonders where she is and what she's doing. He just saw her last night, but he was hoping to see her again. Not many days go by now that they don't see each other and do something together. It bothers him that she might be doing something without him. But she is not his, so she has every right to some private time and life and secrets. He just wishes he knew the way inside her heart, invited. He doesn't want to slip inside her and peek without her knowledge. He wants her to ask him in.

His house is small, but it's too damned big and empty when she's not there. He locks up behind him and jumps on his bike. Instead of making a left in front of his house, he heads to the right. He knows where he's going, even if he isn't completely comfortable visiting her. But maybe he's old enough to get to know his other sister.

〜

HE FINDS HER ON HER KNEES IN A SMALL GARDEN BEHIND HER small house, next door to the rectory. He knows the population of nuns in Quincy has dwindled down to almost none. In fact, the convents have been torn down or are no longer in use. He supposes that's a sad commentary on today's youth and religious vocations, but the thought makes him squirm so he pushes it aside.

She looks up when she hears him coming. Her face is shadowed and hidden under the large brim of a straw hat. A smudge of dirt outlines her cheekbone. She smiles, but it's not really a big smile, and it doesn't reach out and grab him and say, *Hey, Jay, glad you're here.* She looks away and pats the dirt down around whatever the hell she's been working on and then stands up. Her knees are dirty. He looks away, because that's not a good thought to have about your sister, especially your sister who is a nun.

"So," she says as she heads to the back door of her house. "You don't visit me. Ever. Until I meet your girlfriend. And now you show up. Why does my opinion matter?"

"What?" Her offensive comment and cool voice catch him off guard. Aren't nuns supposed to be charitable? Happy? Her voice literally dripped cynicism.

"I'm not stupid, Jay," she tells him as he follows her inside. His eyes sweep the bright yellow kitchen, looking for clues about who this woman is. There is a big round clock on one wall, above the tiny two-person table. A plaque on the far wall that he figures says something sunshiny and happy and probably about Jesus. And a crucifix on the wall by the doorway to what he thinks is a hallway.

"I never said you were stupid, Maddie," he answers.

Without asking she fills two glasses with ice and then pours tea in each one. He takes the one she offers him, figuring he's got till the tea's gone before she kicks his ass out the door.

"Did Maeve like her?" she asks as she leans against the counter behind her.

He frowns, suddenly disgusted at the way Ellie is being batted about like a tennis ball. "Ya know what? I'm not here about Ellie." He sets his glass on the table. "I like Ellie. I don't care if you do or if Maeve does or if Mom does."

Maddie raises her eyebrows slightly. "Kudos to you, if you mean that," she says quietly.

"What's going on with you and Maeve?" he asks suddenly, as if he's made of courage hard as nails.

She laughs and shakes her head. "Trust me. You don't wanna go there."

"Why don't you like her?"

She stares at him for a moment and licks her lips and then looks away. "Ever ask her that about me?"

"No."

"Well, don't." She takes a drink of her tea and then sets the glass on the counter. "Some things are better left alone."

"You're my sister, Maddie. I feel like we're strangers."

"Maeve is your sister, Jay," she corrects him. "I'm just here. Let it go."

What the hell does that mean? She gives him her back, busies herself with rinsing out what looks like a clean sink. He sighs, glances at the tea he'd really kind of like to drink and reaches for the door handle.

"Jay," she says as he pushes the door open.

"What?"

"I liked her."

He turns back to look at her, but the kitchen is empty behind him. Unnerved, he wanders outside and around to the front of the house where he'd left his bike. He wants his family to like Ellie, but really, he likes her and that's enough. Right now he is more intrigued by the act Maddie just put on.

~

NATALIE BROKE HER PINKY TOE WHEN SHE WAS FIVE. SHE didn't clear the wall in the living room as she hurried to her bedroom, and she'd caught her toe on the corner of the wall. Ellie, who had been sitting on the couch reading a book, heard the big, nasty crack, and then Natalie had gone white as a sheet. Ellie had climbed to her knees on the couch and peeked over the top to look at the broken toe. It stuck out at a ninety-degree angle to the rest of her foot.

Ellie feels like that toe in comparison to her family. She sticks out at a ninety-degree angle to the rest of them. She hadn't let them tape her up and stick her next to Nick and Natalie. Instead she'd split, a choice she doesn't regret all that often.

She wonders why Jay didn't call her last night. A million old insecurities weigh her down, and she hates that. Feeling human makes her feel weak and worthless. She doesn't want to need anyone, and she sure as hell doesn't want the fear of needing someone who may not need her back. She'd walked to the grocery store, because her refrigerator was completely bare, but she'd only been gone an hour at the most. It shames her to think she'd lain down on the couch, waiting for him to call, and finally given up and gone outside to the stars after it was ten thirty and obvious he wasn't going to call.

Even as she'd watched the stars, she'd half expected him to come by. He hadn't. She'd wrapped her arms around her knees and watched the stars and felt lonely for more reasons than one. The tears had come pretty early so she'd gone to bed before midnight, with no call or visit from Jay.

She hops on her bike after work and rides four blocks to the north and three blocks west and finds herself in front of his house. It is the first time she's dropped by his place, uninvited. She imagines all sorts of greetings, including one where he's entertaining someone else and doesn't want company. She forces herself to remember the way he looks at her and talks to her, and then she rides her bike to the back of his house.

She finds him on the patio, with the cordless phone pressed to his ear. He smiles when he sees her, a warm, welcoming smile that puts her wildly thumping heart at ease. She parks her bike by his and then joins him at the picnic table when he pats the table beside him.

She sits by him, but she doesn't watch him while he's on the phone. It feels odd listening to his end of the conversation. Finally he thanks the person on the other end of the line and hangs up.

"Hi," he says and puts the phone down.

"I didn't mean to interrupt."

"It's okay." He shrugs. "Trying to find a dog."

"A dog?" she repeats.

"Mm-hmm." He offers her a smile. "I missed you last night."

"Me too," she answers. She looks away from his dark eyes. Where was he? If he missed her, why didn't he call her?

"That guy had terrier puppies," he tells her. "But he sold the last one earlier today."

She smiles and shakes her head. "Why do you want a dog?"

"You don't like dogs?" he asks her.

"Sure." She shrugs. "I guess I just wonder why you want one all of a sudden."

"Not much all of a sudden," he says defensively. "Did you have a dog when you were little?"

"Yep." She avoids his eyes.

"What was its name?"

"Simon."

"You had a dog named Simon?" he asks with a laugh.

"What's wrong with Simon?"

"Makes me think of that old, electronic game, with all the

colors," he answers and ducks away from her hand as she reaches to slug his shoulder.

"Jay?" she asks when the quiet comes to sit with them.

"What?"

"Why didn't you call me last night?" She doesn't look at him when she says this. She can't. Instead she looks at the toes of her shoes. The paint stain is still there.

"I did," he answers softly. "You weren't home."

She swallows hard, relief flooding her veins like a drug. "I went to the grocery store," she whispers. "I was only gone about an hour."

"I'm sorry." He sighs and reaches out and touches her hand. "I thought maybe you just needed a night to yourself."

"I had five years of nights to myself before I met you." The words fall out of her mouth before she can stop them. She looks at him, horrified, and shakes her head. "I'm sorry. I don't expect you to babysit me. I just—"

"Five years," he says softly. She watches when he reaches for her hand and links their fingers. "Why?"

Of all the things he could have said to her, this is not what she expected. She stares at their hands and wishes for just a moment that she could tell him everything. That he would understand instead of judging. That he would put his arms around her and forgive her instead of blaming her.

A tear falls from her face to his arm, and she reaches with her free hand to wipe it away. She presses her lips together and turns her face away from his eyes.

"Okay," he says gently. "Tough question. Will you answer a different one for me instead?"

She nods, but she still avoids his eyes.

"Why does it bother you when I touch you?"

"It doesn't." Her voice breaks, and she clears her throat, hoping to put the pieces back together.

"It did," he reminds her. "Up till that night at Maeve's, you were afraid to touch me."

She takes a deep breath and lowers her head, until her chin touches her chest.

"Don't." He lifts her chin with his free hand. "Don't hide from me. If you can't answer me, it's okay. Just say so."

She looks at him out of the corner of her eye, but even that is too much. So she lets her gaze drop to their hands again.

"Ellie," he whispers. "Did someone—"

"No," she interrupts him, but her word is quietly spoken. "No, it's nothing like that."

"Okay," he says simply. "I don't know what it is, but you can't know how relieved I am that it's not that."

She licks her lips and nods her thanks.

"I've been alone for five years, Jay," she finally tells him. "Alone. Except for people I see at work and people I see at school. And they don't count," she adds. "Because I see them. They never see me."

"I do."

She nods. Her hand shakes a bit when she reaches up to pull her hair behind her ear. "It's just hard to go from being invisible to being someone's friend and everything that involves."

He squeezes her hand but says nothing. The silent comfort slips into her fingers and slides down deep inside her.

"Wanna go for a walk?" he asks her after a few moments of silence have passed.

"Yeah." She sniffles and takes a deep breath and tries to get a grip on her emotions.

"Let me lock up your bike," he says and squeezes her hand again. She watches him as he chains her bike next to his, and she feels her stomach settle back into place. She was so afraid that his absence last night meant something bad, that he was tired of her. Or that he did have a woman somewhere.

"So," he says as he takes her hand again and they start walking. "Who named your dog Simon?"

"I did," she answers with a laugh.

"What kind of a dog was Simon?"

"A mutt." She shrugs.

"Best kind."

"Did you have a pet when you were a kid?"

"Dog." He nods. "Rocky."

"Like the fighter," she says with a laugh. His fingers tighten around her hand, and she feels a tight squeeze up in her chest, somewhere around her heart.

"How'd you get to the store?" he asks.

"Huh?"

"Bike?"

"No." She almost laughs. "I had a few too many bags to carry to manage them on a bike."

"Car?"

She does laugh at that. "Won't start. Hasn't started in a couple years."

"Let me look at it for you," he offers.

"You don't have to do that."

"Then call me next time, and I'll drive you to the store," he tells her firmly. "And I will take a look at the car."

"No." She rolls her eyes. "It's dead. Leave it alone."

"Where'd you find it anyway?" he asks with a grin. "Side of the road, dead?"

She gives him a small smile. "Stole it."

"Yeah, right."

"I did," she says quietly. "It was my dad's. He drove it to work everyday."

"Where did he work?"

"Brady, Longlett, Jordan, and Shear." She recites the names as if they are long-lost school facts. "Accounting firm."

"And your mom?"

"Had her own business." She avoids his eyes. She doesn't want to talk about her family.

"Which was?"

"Pottery. She was an artist, and she had a small studio in the back of our house."

"Really?" He sounds genuinely interested so she knows it's time to cut him off.

"Where were you on May tenth last year?"

"May tenth?" he repeats and frowns. "Should I remember May tenth?"

"Tornado," she reminds him.

"Oh." He nods. "I was at my mom's. I'd just cleaned her gutters out. We ended up playing Aggravation in her basement for an hour or so."

"Aggravation." She nods. "Wow. Haven't played that in a long time."

"Where were you?"

"What?"

"When the tornado blew through?"

"I watched as much as I could from my front porch. When it started raining, I went inside. Eventually went to the cellar."

"And what did you do in the cellar?"

"Took a book and a flashlight with me. Jodi Picoult book."

"Really?" Jay asks with a smile. "Maeve reads her books."

The talk stops momentarily as a trio of young boys on skateboards flies by them on the street. Ellie flexes her fingers; she loves the feel of his skin against hers. He lets go of her hand and glances at her.

"Don't," she says and reaches for his hand. "I didn't want you to let go. Just—"

"Just what?" He watches her as they walk.

Embarrassed and backed against a wall, she doesn't know how to answer him. She turns her head and studies the yards they pass by. Some are small and neat, and some are small and the grass is overgrown and toys cover more area than the grass. She thinks someone should go up and knock on the doors and tell these people how quickly things can disappear.

"I just like this," she says quietly. She squeezes his hand again and then lets her thumb slide back and forth over his.

"Ellie?"

She turns to look at him. "What?"

"Maeve always has a big Fourth of July party," he begins. "It's fun. There'd be more people there. Friends and stuff. Do you wanna go with me?"

Fourth of July. She hasn't celebrated the Fourth in years. It's just become another night to sit on her front porch and watch the stars.

"If you don't want to," he goes on when she doesn't answer, "we could hang out at my house, if ya want. Or your house." He stops walking and draws her up short. "Really, I don't care about Maeve's party. I just want to spend that time with you."

She's not crazy about the idea of a party. "She'll expect you there," she says softly. "I'll go."

"We could go for awhile. Go back to your house." He rubs his thumb over her knuckles.

She nods. They start walking again, and she remembers the dream she had, the dream when she and Jay were walking hand in hand on Maladorny. This is even better.

CHAPTER 9

SHINY, GLITTERY THINGS USED TO CATCH ELLIE'S EYE. SHE'D always loved her mom's rings; the diamonds in her wedding ring had been her favorite; her birthstone, a sapphire, a close second. She'd bought the watch several years ago, shelling out a bit too much money for something that simply told time. She'd needed the watch, because back then she had more in her life than her job, but she hadn't really needed to drop so much money on something just a little bit fancy.

She's worn the silver chain around her neck every day for the last six years. At first, it had felt foreign to her. Heavy, although it was a very fine, dainty chain. After awhile, she forgot it was there. It became a part of her body, and she'd sooner lose a finger than take it off. She never pulled it out to lie over her collar, never played with it or turned it to put the clasp in the back and make a wish, never showed it to anyone. She simply wore it every day, as one more desperate way to keep him with her.

The Fourth of July looms ahead of her, three more calendar days, and she sort of dreads it and looks forward to it. If she's honest with herself, she has to admit she would like to get to know Jay's family better. But she knows they, in turn, will want to get to know her better, and she's not willing to share much of herself with them. It also makes her nervous to think of a big party, with more friends than family. She's not a people person. But she wants to be with Jay, and she wouldn't think of asking him to miss his sister's party.

She locks her bike up with his; he'd given her the combination the other night, after their walk. She taps at the back door and hears him call for her to come in.

"In the living room," he calls. He looks up at her when she enters the room. She laughs when she sees there is a big ball of fur in his lap.

"Jay," she says cautiously. "That's not a dog. That's a caterpillar on steroids."

"Hey." He chuckles and pats the floor beside him. "Come help me name this dog."

She crosses the floor to sit by him, an amused grin on her face. "How about Kitten?" she asks sarcastically.

"Kitten?" he asks. His big hand nearly covers the fluff in his lap. "Jeez, you wanna give my dog an identity crisis?"

"Seriously." She reaches to touch the furry head. "Is there a dog under there?"

"Yep. Wanna hold him?"

"Sure," she answers as she takes the dog from his hands. The warm little body snuggles up against her chest. She closes her hands around him and holds on. "He's scared," she says quietly. "Shaking a little."

"He likes you," Jay tells her.

"When did you get him?"

"This morning," he answers. "I called you, but you must have been at work."

"Yeah, I was." She nods. The puppy climbs down from her chest and over her lap and puts his nose to the floor to explore his new home. She watches him with a half smile on her face. "So what's his name?"

"I don't know yet," Jay answers. "I told you I need help naming him."

"How about Simon?" she offers with a giggle.

"No way." He gives her shoulder a playful shove.

"George."

"I like that," he says and purses his lips in thought.

"Oh, get real." She laughs. "You can't name that fur ball George."

"I kind of like it." He shrugs.

"Jay, you don't want me to name your dog," she says quietly.

"Why don't I want you to name my dog?" he asks. She's not sure how it happened, but suddenly they are facing each other, his right shoulder to her left shoulder. She meets his eyes for a moment, realizing she's not really sure how any of this has happened, how she's found herself surrounded by Jay and always feeling like she needs more of him to feel whole inside.

Her stomach falls a bit, but her heart pushes to her throat. She watches him as if time has stopped, and his house and the dog and yesterday and tomorrow have all faded away. The pain in her chest, where her heart was before it crowded her throat, is almost unbearable. It suddenly feels hot in the small room, as if they are sitting cross-legged on a star, engulfed in the heat, but her hands are cold. His blue eyes swallow every inch of her face as he leans toward her, and she wants to cover herself, hide from him, from what he's about to do.

His lips are soft and warm against hers. Her breath

catches in her throat and huddles there with her heart as he gently rubs his lips over hers. She parts her lips so she can breathe. When he moves just an inch and rests his forehead against hers, her lips are cold. The room pitches forward, and she feels like she's falling. Into Jay. It's a little like being drunk and knowing you've had too much as you reach for the next bottle. The room spins around her, and she lifts her hand to reach out and grab onto something solid.

She lets her eyelids fall, to block out the rest of the world so she can feel his hand as it strokes her face and then her neck—or to pretend this isn't happening; she's not sure. He moves again; his breath hovers over her lips. She breathes cautiously with him until she feels the tip of his tongue trace her lip, and her heart stops, and she can't breathe.

This time when she lifts her hand, she reaches for him until she gets a handful of his shirt. She lets her fingers climb up over his shoulder until she splays them wide around the back of his neck.

"Ellie." He whispers her name over her lips. She can't answer him. She has no voice, and talking right now would ruin this, make it different somehow. Remind her that she can't do this. Instead she pushes the bad stuff, the memories, from her mind and rushes to close it so they can't come back for awhile. She wants to kiss him back, but she can't. She hasn't done this in so long; she was someone completely different the last time she kissed anyone.

And this is different. Kissing Jay is different from the rest. He's gentle, and they're friends, and this means something to her and it has to be special because this is as far as it can ever go. She sighs with relief when he senses that she is stuck and slides his tongue inside her lips to touch hers. He tastes like mint and sugar; his tongue is warm and soft against hers. Her hand slides over his face, and she delights in the feel of his six o'clock shadow against the palm of her hand. The kiss is long and soft, and it ends and starts over again and again, until Ellie feels little paws climb up over her lap and against her chest, soft fur against her neck.

"I think someone's jealous," Jay whispers as he pulls away from her. She doesn't trust herself to open her eyes, because she's afraid this is a dream and when she opens them, she'll be alone in her bed and this kiss with Jay will not exist in the real world. Jay nuzzles her neck, kisses her just below her ear and adds in a thick voice, "I don't blame him."

She breathes heavily, as she tries to bank the fires inside and pull all the pieces of herself that have slid out of reach back together. Her eyes flutter open, and she half expects to find parts of her heart and soul strewn about Jay's living room floor.

She touches the puppy, more to get a grip on herself and her thoughts than to comfort him. Jay covers her hand with his. She glances up at him, but she can't hold his gaze. Her eyes lower over his lips, and then she looks at the puppy. What now? What do you do to yourself when you break your own rules?

"Wanna take George for a walk?" he asks quietly.

"You can't name him George," she says and laughs softly. She sinks her teeth into her lip when he cups her chin in his hand and forces her to look at him. This kiss is there and gone, and the way she wants more tells her it's time to move. A walk sounds like a good idea.

"His name's George," Jay tells her. "My best friend named him that."

She lets him pull her up from the floor and links her fingers through his. Her stomach pitches and heaves a bit, as if she's just stepped off a roller coaster. Her heart still beats so loudly she thinks they could dance to its rhythm. She doesn't ever want to let go of his hand, but she hates herself for what just happened. No matter what she does now, she'll hurt him. She'd promised herself she wouldn't hurt anyone again, and with one touch, Jay has reduced her to who she used to be. She hates the person she used to be.

Careful not to look at him, she waits while he puts a long red leash on George and then follows him outside.

FRENCH KISSING COULD BE A FORM OF TORTURE; IT'S HELL when the guy who is kissing you has no finesse and thinks it's sexy just to jam his tongue down your throat. She remembers some of those kisses and some of those guys, even though she tries not to. It had taken Tony Spinelli a few kisses to get the nerve to kiss her with his tongue. He hadn't really been that bad, not as good as Jay, but still not so bad. It's all the guys and kisses in between Tony and Jay that Ellie wishes she could forget. Then again, she needs to forget Jay's kiss too, because it can't happen again. She remembers the way he tasted and the gentle way he'd touched his lips to hers, giving her time to say no. Waiting for her to kiss him back or push him away. She still feels his hand on her neck and the kiss he'd placed just below her ear before they'd gone outside to walk George.

And he's calling the damned dog George. It feels like something pretty heavy happened in his living room the night before, between him asking her to name his dog and that kiss. She's not ready for things to spin out of control and dovetail and fall straight to hell. She's not ready to jump in blind and burn herself up in some crazy fling that will break the place in her chest where she used to have a full heart. She's not ready to show her true self to him and then watch him haul ass out of her life.

He nudges her arm with his elbow.

"What?" she says softly, but she doesn't look at him. She's

looking at the tree across the street and thinking of him playing Aggravation with his mother in her basement while a severe storm blew through the area. She thinks it was probably kind of fun, maybe cozy. Her eyes burn just a bit when she thinks of his cozy game of Aggravation and her flashlight and Jodi Picoult book. She blinks hard and gets the wetness out of her eyes. God, she hates to cry.

"You okay with Maeve's party?" he asks quietly. She turns to him, a tiny little voice inside her wondering, again, if he regrets asking her.

"When you do that," she tells him, "you make me feel like you want out."

He takes her hand and lays it palm to palm over his. "If I told you how far in I want to be with you, I'd scare the hell out of you." His dark eyes rage with emotion that does indeed frighten her. "So I'm trying really hard to play by your rules. I'm trying to do this right."

"We're not doing this, Jay," she whispers. "I told you—"

"We are doing this, Ellie," he says gently, but his tone allows no room for argument. "You can pretend we're just friends if that makes you feel better, but this is real, and it's big, and it's both of us."

She takes a deep breath and looks away. She can't stand the hope in his eyes, the hope and the love and the way he's just laid it all out in front of her. He's wide open for her to slash his throat with a knife and watch him bleed out and walk away.

George perks up for a moment, moseys over to her feet and plops on them.

"Even my dog loves you," Jay says. Without looking she knows there is a small twist of a smile on his lips.

"Don't." She shakes her head. "Don't use that word."

"Why?"

She thinks maybe she should get a dog. A dog would love

her unconditionally, even after she introduced him to the girl she used to be. The dormant woman who has lived inside her, the one Jay brought to life just last night.

"Because I don't like it," she answers. She sighs and pulls her hand away from his and then leans back on the porch to look at the stars.

"Got another story for me?"

"Yeah," she says with a nod. "Yeah, I do."

He scoots closer to her. "Which star?"

She takes his hand and points to a small star, just a bit west of the tip of the tree across the street. "Bangwazzle," she says quietly. "They don't remember things there. No matter what happens, when they go to bed at night, they're all happy. And they all sleep well. And they wake up the next day and start fresh. They don't even know there was a yesterday."

She feels him staring at her; her face is burning where his eyes are touching her. She wets her lips with the tip of her tongue and then turns her face toward his.

"Was it that bad?" he asks her.

"What?"

"Kissing me. Was it so bad you wanna forget it?"

She feels the kiss again in the tingle of her fingers. "It was so good I wanna forget it," she whispers.

He sighs and turns his head away from her for a moment. She watches him curiously. He lowers his head and rubs the back of his neck and finally looks back at her. "Maybe I can help." He avoids her eyes, like he's uncomfortable saying this. "Maybe talking about whatever you don't talk about would help."

She chews on her lip, wishing she could lay it all at his feet. Wishing that talking about it would be enough to make it all go away. What would it be like to lose this leaden anchor around her neck and live without the sorrow and guilt?

"On Bangwazzle, they don't have to forgive, because they don't remember the bad things." She swallows hard. "People here remember." Her voice is so thick it almost gets stuck in her throat. "And they don't forgive."

CHAPTER 10

IT HAD TAKEN JAY ALL OF THREE DAYS TO LOSE HIS VIRGINITY, once he'd decided he was ready. At sixteen, he'd done Allie Karrigan in the backseat of his pile of junk Chevy Impala. In retrospect, he supposes it wasn't his finest moment, groping and panting all over her. Then again, she hadn't really seemed to mind. She was a senior, and rumor had it that she was a good time. He'd never really added to the rumor, but he sure hadn't squelched it either. When he was eighteen, he'd taken a few weeks to coax a sixteen-year-old virgin into his bed. In his two years of sexual experience, he'd improved both his performance and his endurance, but in retrospect he thinks it was a horrible experience for Tara Rafferty. He'd been in Rylan's pants two days after he met her. None of it means anything to him now.

He wants to make love to Ellie. He wants to hold her and love her and make her see what he sees when he looks at her. She's wounded inside, and he is desperate to get to her hurt and make her better. He's in love with her, and he figures she has to know that, even though he hasn't come right out and said it. He can't say it, not yet. She would panic and run, and he can't lose her. Hell yes, he wants to kiss her and take his time undressing her and run his fingers over her skin. Feel her body pressed up against his. Sleep with her curled in his arms. But he'll wait and do this right, because the day after they make love is as important to him as a night in her bed.

He wonders if she splurged for the party. She's wearing dark Hilfiger jean shorts and a sleeveless red blouse. The red is gorgeous on her; he wishes she would wear it more often. As he follows her through Maeve's house, he can't help but let his eyes wander over her shorts and down over her legs. Her skin is dark with a summer tan, but he knows it's from working in her yard. She doesn't lie out just to worship the sun; she considers it a waste of time. Her toenails are a different color tonight, a dark, frosty raspberry color. He loves the color, but he doesn't comment on them because it bothers her when he notices her looks.

He loses her near the kitchen, figures Maeve grabbed her as they walked by, and he wasn't looking. He steps outside through the breakfast nook and flashes Joe a grin when he slaps a cold beer in his hand.

"Wha's up, Jay?" Joe asks with a smile.

"Not much, man," Jay answers. He twists the top off the Michelob and takes a long drink. It's hot enough to melt skin, so the cold beer goes down smooth and welcome.

"Bring your girlfriend?"

"I brought Ellie," he says quietly.

Joe shrugs. "Whatever."

"Mom here?" Jay asks him. He surveys the backyard; there is already a huge mix of people milling about. Ellie won't like this. He has to take a deep breath and remind himself that she's an adult, and she's okay with his sister. They can eat dinner, visit for awhile, and then make a break for it.

"Yeah," Joe answers. "She's inside talking to Maddie."

Jay nods. Maddie. He hasn't seen her since the day he'd

ridden his bike over to her house. No sense in visiting her again, when that talk hadn't gone all that well. He takes another swig of his beer, grabs a handful of chips from the bag on the picnic table, and heads back inside. He just wants to look at her. He wants to see a smile on her face as she talks with his sisters and his mom.

~

SHE SEES HIM WHEN HE STEPS INTO THE KITCHEN, BUT SHE'S listening to Maeve talking about Stash throwing her in the pool the weekend before.

"Fully clothed," Maeve groans. Ellie laughs, her eyes darting back and forth from Maeve to Jay and back to Maeve again. In their flight, she catches a frown on Maddie's face. Ellie glances back at her as she slips off the barstool and makes her way out to the backyard. Ellie watches her go and then looks back at Maeve, not surprised that Maeve doesn't seem to notice Maddie has left the room. She offers Jay a smile as he approaches her.

"Need anything?" he asks quietly. She melts into his touch when he rests his hand on the small of her back.

"No, thanks," she answers.

"Worried I'm telling stories about you, little brother?" Maeve asks with a smirk.

"The only stories you could tell about me would be good stories." He pops his last chip in his mouth and reaches around Ellie to grab a brownie.

"Would you quit?" Ellie smacks at his hand. He offers her a bite of the brownie, which she takes with a smile. As she chews, she feels Maeve's eyes on her.

"You guys bring your suits?" Maeve asks them.

"Nope," Jay answers.

"Ellie?"

"I don't have a suit," Ellie tells her.

"You don't have a suit? You don't have a swimsuit?" Maeve asks in disbelief. Ellie shakes her head and takes another bite of Jay's brownie.

"A brownie and a beer?" Maeve shoots Jay a frown. "Yuck. You're not right."

"Your dad used to do that all the time," Jolene reminds Maeve.

"True," Maeve says with a nod. "But he wasn't right either."

Jay laughs and traces his hand up over Ellie's back. "I'm gonna go see if Stash needs help with the grill. Can't leave him out there too long with Joe."

Jolene follows him out, and Ellie finds herself alone with Maeve. She takes a long drink of her bottled water, mostly to avoid Maeve's eyes and comments.

"Have you slept with him yet?" Maeve asks her.

She chokes on her water and sets her bottle down hard on the counter. "No."

Maeve grins. "I'm sorry. That slipped out. Jay made me promise to behave, but I couldn't help it after watching you two share the brownie."

A laugh bubbles up inside Ellie, but it sounds foreign when she hears it slip out. It's been so long since she's talked to a girl friend. Since she's said stupid things like this to a girl friend. She misses Blair. It's almost a physical ache inside her, the sudden way she feels Blair's absence in her life. She is horrified to realize there are tears in her eyes. Damn Jay Bryant for making her remember how to feel.

"Hey, I'm sorry," Maeve says quietly when Ellie sniffles and covers her eyes. "I was just teasing. I won't—"

"No." Ellie rubs her eyes and paints on a threadbare smile. "It's not that."

Maeve stares at her expectantly. She is not like Jay, who is afraid to push her too hard and send her running scared. Maeve wants an explanation. Ellie presses her lips together and raises her eyebrows.

"You made me think of Blair." Her voice is almost cool and distant. She hears it float far away from her, as if the words came from someone else.

"Who's Blair?" Maeve asks gently, but with the same bold certainty that Ellie will answer her.

"My high school best friend," Ellie answers. "She was killed in a car accident when we were sixteen."

"I'm sorry." Maeve touches her hand, but she is quick to move away. Ellie wonders if Jay has told her she does not like physical contact.

"Blair and I spent most of our freshman and sophomore year of high school drunk," Ellie confesses, even as she wonders where the words are coming from. Why is she telling Maeve this? She's never been tempted to tell Jay. "Ironically, she was killed by a drunk driver."

"Is that why you quit drinking?" Maeve asks quietly. Ellie looks away when she sees how Maeve's eyes shine.

"No," Ellie answers honestly. "I think that made me drink more."

Maeve blows out a big breath and busies herself with rinsing dishes to put in the dishwasher. "And I reminded you of her?" She keeps her back to Ellie.

"Girl talk," Ellie says wistfully. "I miss that."

Maeve turns to look at her again. "Door's always open," she says quietly. Ellie nods, grateful for the standing invitation but afraid to ever take Maeve up on it.

"Need another Coke?" Jay asks her. She looks up from her perch on the end of a lounge chair. She's been thinking about Blair, and thinking about Blair leads her to thinking about other things she doesn't want to think about. She is still holding her empty Coke can.

"No, I'm fine," she finally answers him.

"Can I sit down?" he asks her. She nods, assuming he'll sit on the cement in front of her. Instead he swings a leg over the lounge chair and drops to sit directly behind her. No one notices the bold move except Ellie. She sucks in a sharp breath when she feels the hard wall of his chest behind her. "You okay?" His breath tickles her ear.

"Yeah," she says with a nod.

"Are you lost in thought? Or are you watching these hot shots play volleyball?"

"Lost in thought," she answers quietly. She hadn't even realized the bunch of teenage boys were playing volleyball in the pool.

"Yeah?" He cocks his head to study her face. "Because it looked like you were checking out the hot shots. Especially Joe."

She glances at Joe. The kid is gorgeous; there's no doubt about it. But something about him turns her off. It's not him; he really seems like a nice kid. It's every emotion that he yanks to life inside her. He's every guy she remembers, and he's her when she was in school, and for that alone, she doesn't like him.

She leans forward a bit and turns to face Jay. His eyes are wide and uncertain when she reaches for him and cups the back of his head in her hand and leans forward to kiss him. Surely one more kiss won't change things that much between them. She brushes her lips over his and comes back to do it again when she feels his lips part under hers.

"I came here with you," she reminds him as she turns around again.

He slides his arms around her waist, slowly, to give her

time to tell him no. She appreciates that he's sensitive to what she wants and needs, but she sinks back into him and lets him fold his hands over her stomach.

"Can we get out of here yet?" he whispers. "Go down by the river and watch the fireworks?"

Before she can answer him, Maddie approaches them and sits on the end of the lounge chair next to them. "You guys look pretty cozy," she says with a smile.

"We were just talking about heading out," Jay answers in a cool tone. "Let George out for awhile."

"Who's George?" Maddie asks with a frown. She takes a sip of her tea.

"My dog."

"When did you get a dog?"

"Last week."

"Guess I didn't know that." She frowns again.

"Yeah, well, you might know more about me if you visited now and then," he says quietly. Ellie covers his hands with hers. His hands are cold. He sounds angry; Ellie has never seen him angry. Maddie takes the words like a left hook in the jaw, but she rights herself quickly and even smiles at him.

"You're right, Jay," she says simply. "Maybe I'll do that."

"What was that all about?" Ellie asks when Maddie leaves them alone.

Jay sighs. "You ready?"

"Sure. Whenever you are."

GEORGE WANDERS THE BACK OF HIS TRUCK, NOSE DOWN, AS IF he's going to find some good snacking. Jay watches him for a moment, but he can't concentrate, sitting leg to leg with Ellie on the tailgate of his truck.

"Jay?" she says quietly.

They are parked up on Third Street, where they are alone, but far enough up on the bluff to see the fireworks when they start. He turns his attention back to her, leaving George to sniff out the rest of the truck bed alone.

"Hmm?"

"What's with you and Maddie? And Maeve?"

He raises his eyebrows and shrugs. "I don't know what the deal is with Maddie and Maeve. They rarely speak to each other, and when they do, they're cool and bitchy. I don't know," he repeats.

"What about you? You and Maddie earlier. What was that about?"

He sighs. "That night you went to the store? I rode my bike to Maddie's house—"

"She has a house?"

"Yeah," he says with a smile. "I know. It's hard to think of her that way. There aren't enough nuns around to keep the convents open anymore. She lives in a house by the rectory."

"So what happened?"

"Nothing. Really. She made a comment at Maeve's last cook out that I never visit her. So when you weren't home, I decided to visit her. Maddie and I have never been close. Not even when we were younger. I feel different with her because she's a nun, but really, that's just an excuse, I think. I've never been close to her, and I think it's because I'm close to Maeve."

"They don't seem to like each other much," Ellie mumbles.

"They used to. When I was a kid, they were close." He remembers the way they were always together, riding their bikes or watching TV or studying. "Anyway, I asked her the other day what the deal was with her and Maeve. She pretty much said it was none of my business."

Ellie raises her eyebrows. "That's sad. I like them both,"

she tells him. "Two very different people, but I do like them both."

"What were you talking to Maeve about? In the kitchen when you were alone with her?"

She stares at him for a moment and then looks away.

"She said something. Kind of funny. Made me think of this girl I used to be friends with."

"What'd she say?" he asks softly. He's not certain because it's getting dark, but he thinks a dark blush climbs her neck and floods her face.

"She asked if I'd slept with you yet," she says with a grin.

"Dammit, I'm sorry, Ellie—"

"No, it's okay," Ellie says quickly. She touches his leg that is still pressed against hers but moves her hand quickly. "She was teasing."

He nods and looks up, out over the riverfront below them. It's nearing eight thirty; the fireworks will start soon. "What about this girl you were friends with?" He holds his breath. Why can she tell Maeve things that she seems hesitant to share with him?

"She was my best friend," she whispers. "We were inseparable." He waits silently for her to go on. "She was driving home from basketball practice one night. Drunk driver hit her. Killed her instantly."

"Oh God," Jay says as he looks away from her. "I'm sorry."

"Blair and I…" She licks her lips and looks out toward the river. "We were the party crowd. Drank a lot." She swallows hard. "I can't tell you how many nights we drove home after drinking. Maybe it was karma. Just got her at the wrong time, because I wasn't with her."

"You didn't hurt anyone," he tells her.

"Not with a car," she clarifies. "But we could have." She rubs her eyes. "I hate myself for saying this, but sometimes I think she got off easy."

He lets those words sink in through his skin and slip into his bloodstream. Within seconds, they make his stomach churn and his head hurt. "Dying?" he asks her. Her friend got off easy dying?

She nods. "Dying at sixteen would have been easier for me than dying and still living at twenty."

What the hell does that mean? Dying and still living? What the hell could hurt her so badly? "Ellie—"

He looks up to the sky when he hears the first boom of the fireworks.

"Wow," she says softly. She wipes at her face again, never taking her eyes off the mix of red and green sparks in the night sky. He watches the next several colorful blasts in silence, happy to have her beside him and all to himself.

"You know, I wanted to tell you," he finally says. She looks at him, waiting for him to go on. "On Bangwazzle they don't remember so they don't have to forgive. But then they can't love."

George sticks his cold nose on Jay's arm and then hikes his paws up to climb through them and settle himself on Ellie's lap.

"You don't wanna love me, Jay," she whispers.

"Little too late," he answers. He leans toward her and touches his lips to hers. She tastes like summer and rain and the chocolate brownie they'd shared as they'd snuck out of Maeve's, by the side gate in the yard. She kisses him back, still uncertain, but with more confidence than she'd had that first night. He slides his fingers around her neck and up into her silky hair. A soft groan escapes his lips and melts in her mouth when she touches him. Her small hand climbs his shirt again, until her fingers scrape up the front of his neck and then cup his chin and splay wide over his cheek.

"Why'd you kiss me at Maeve's?" He breaks the kiss, but he presses his lips to her cheekbone.

"Few reasons," she answers him.

"Like what?"

"Joe. I don't get your deal with Joe." She looks up at him. "I guess I wanted to remind you, I'm your friend. Not his."

"What else?" He fishes for more words that will make his throat and heart burn like he's swallowing whiskey straight from the bottle.

"I wanted to," she admits with a little grin.

The finale is lighting the sky, but he doesn't care that he's not watching it. He wishes this moment with Ellie would last a lifetime. "Do you have a star where even people who don't want to can fall in love?"

"I'm not gonna fall in love with you, Jay." Her words don't mean as much as the fact that she can't look at him when she says them.

CHAPTER 11

HER DREAMS ARE NEVER GRAY; THEY ARE EITHER GOOD DREAMS or nightmares. The nightmares far outnumber the good dreams. On the Fourth of July, she has a nightmare. It's one that she has often. She is wandering through her backyard, and her yard rambles over hills and down other hills, and she keeps walking and searching, but she cannot find what she is looking for. Birds perch on power lines and watch her, but they are birds of prey, not the pigeons and red birds she sees every day. They watch with beady eyes as she searches and wait for her to give in and admit defeat. She thinks they know what she looks for and where she should look, but they offer no help. Instead they wait for her to give up, so they can swoop in and suck the rest of her life from her.

To anyone else, it wouldn't be a nightmare. It is not only her nightmare; it is her life.

Jay calls her after work and asks her to come over. She thinks she would have anyway. She has gotten comfortable just showing up at his place. She has gotten used to hanging out with him, watching TV, playing basketball, lying with him on the couch while they both read. She's gotten used to needing his presence in her life. After a quick change of clothes, she heads to his house, anxious to see him and George. She finds them in the backyard; Jay is tossing a tennis ball. George can barely get his mouth around it to carry it back to him. He drops the ball and trots to Ellie when she wheels her bike around to lock it up with Jay's.

"Well, there goes my doggy loving," Jay mutters. He sits down on the picnic table and watches her when she squats down to pet George.

"You're cute when you're jealous," she tells him as she scoops George up and carries him over to the table.

"Careful." He warns with a sly smile. "I might think you're flirting with me."

"I think we're a little beyond worrying about that," she mumbles.

"Wanna play pitch and catch?" he asks her. She laughs. He'd bought a second ball glove that he now keeps at his house so she can't give him hell for buying it for her. They've played pitch and catch often, but it always deteriorates into burn out. Both of them end up so sore they can hardly move the next day.

"Sure." She glances at him and arches an eyebrow. "If you think you can handle it."

"Bring it on," he says with a wicked grin. She stands, and he tosses her the glove. It's a nice glove, a soft, light-colored leather Nike glove, and she loves it. She loves the feel of it on her hand and the smell of it and even the memories it brings to life inside her. Hot summer games and the sun beating down on her and sweat wetting the visor she always wore over her ponytail when she played left field. The snap and pop of the ball in the glove or the funny, metallic clink of the ball hitting the aluminum bats. She sort of misses it. Not so much the people on the field or the people in the bleachers, but the game.

They start out slow as usual, but they quickly zip the ball back and forth hard enough to sting each other's hands. She loves to cut loose and throw like this.

"Hey, you wanna go get something to eat?" he calls after awhile.

"Now?" she answers. "Am I hurting you?"

"You wish," he yells with a laugh. "I'm hungry. I waited for you to eat."

She catches his next throw but holds it in her glove for a moment. "Really? You waited for me?"

"Yeah."

She thinks about that for a moment and then throws the ball to him.

"So this is how you two spend your time."

Ellie catches the ball again and turns to see Maddie leaning a shoulder against the corner of the house watching them. She swallows hard, her stomach kicking in with the guilt and the nerves. It's a gut reaction; intellectually she knows this, but she can't help it. Guilt is her most familiar feeling. It shadows her so closely it is like her second skin.

"Hey, Maddie," Jay says. He walks up to the house and offers her a smile. George stirs and lifts his head to study her from his spot under the table. Ellie watches him trot over to sniff Maddie's canvas Keds.

"This is George?" Maddie asks with a glance down at George and then back at Jay.

"The one and only," Jay answers with a nod. "Ellie and I were just gonna go get something to eat. Wanna go with us?"

"No, thanks," she answers. "I was just out walking and thought I'd stop by."

"How about pizza?" he suggests. "We could have one delivered."

"No, really," Maddie shakes her head, "I've already had dinner. You guys go ahead."

"Be right back," Jay says as he hurries inside the house. Ellie glances at Maddie. She doesn't feel as comfortable with Maddie as she does with Maeve, and she hates that, because she figures it's probably obvious.

"You've got a good arm," Maddie says quietly.

Ellie laughs. "So does Jay. We can't play pitch and catch without playing burn out."

"Did you play in high school?"

"Um." Ellie swallows hard and nods. "I did. Freshman and sophomore year."

"What position did you play?"

"Left field."

Maddie flashes a smile at her. "I played center."

"You played softball?" Ellie can't get her mouth closed before the words slip out.

"Why is that so hard to believe?" Maddie grins. "I do a lot of things normal people do."

"What else do you do?" Ellie asks with a small smile.

"I teach kindergarten," Maddie answers. "I play the piano. I sing, if I feel like it."

"You teach kindergarten?" Ellie reaches and almost touches Maddie's arm, but she lets her hand fall before her fingers make contact. "I'm not shocked. I just think that's cool."

"I've taught kindergarten for about five years," Maddie says simply.

"Do you like it?"

"Most days." Maddie looks up when Jay comes back outside.

"Do you work tomorrow?" he asks Ellie. She notices he's changed his shirt. He holds his keys and his wallet in his hand. She nods. "Maeve called while I was inside. She said to tell you to come over and check out the pool."

"Yeah," Ellie mumbles and shakes her head. "I don't have a suit."

"So get one," Maddie tells her. "I'm gonna head home. I'll talk to you guys later."

Ellie watches her walk toward the front of the house and then disappear down the sidewalk. She looks back at Jay, still trying to picture Maddie playing centerfield.

"You didn't tell me she's a teacher."

"Oh." He frowns. "Guess I didn't think about it."

"Because you don't see past her vocation."

"She say that?" he asks quietly.

"No, I did." Ellie looks around for George.

"Already put him in the house," Jay says. "You wanna get something to eat?"

"Sure." She nods. "But I don't have any money on me."

"I'll buy," he tells her as they head to the back, where Jay's truck is in his small garage.

"You don't have to keep buying—"

"I don't have to," he says with a nod. "But I want to."

ELLIE ORDERS A CHICKEN STRIP BASKET AND A COKE. HE orders a peppercorn sirloin and a baked potato and a bottle of Michelob. She says she likes chicken, but he's planning to make her eat some of his steak. He watches her look around the dining floor of Ruby Tuesday.

"I've never been here before," she admits after the waitress brings their drinks.

"I kind of thought that," he says quietly. She watches him pour his beer into a glass. "Can I ask you something?"

"Yeah." She nods and takes a drink of her soda.

"Does my drinking bother you?"

She stares at him silently for a moment. He watches the

emotions play her face, from surprise to guilt. Guilt? Why does she always have that look on her face, like she's waiting for the other shoe to fall? Like she's been a bad girl, and she's ready for a punishment to be handed down. She'd had that look when Maddie had found them playing pitch and catch in the backyard earlier.

"No," she finally answers. "I trust that you're responsible. You aren't gonna drink too much and then get in your truck and drive home."

He has to fight to hold the smile down. She cares. God, it feels so good to hear the way she cares, the way she loves him, when she refuses to admit it. "No, I won't. Got too much going on to do that." He takes a drink and sets his glass down. "I meant, does it bother you? If I drink like this. And then I kiss you goodnight."

"You mean am I an alcoholic?" she says with a nod. "No, I'm not. It doesn't bother me. It doesn't offend me. It doesn't make me wanna run out and buy a six pack."

He reaches across the table to hold her hand. She watches him link his fingers through hers, but she says nothing. What he really wants to do is sit with her on her side of the booth. Put his arm around her. Pull her in close.

"What made you quit drinking?" he asks softly.

She licks her lips and looks away from him. She's not going to give him a straight answer on this one.

"I was sixteen," she whispers. "Something just came up."

He nods, takes another drink and squeezes her hand. "Hey, I have a proposition for you."

She giggles. "I think my answer is no," she says with a smile. "Unless we're talking joint custody of George."

He smiles, but her words touch him on the heart. He has to tell her about Oliver, soon. She needs to know, and he wants her to meet him and love him, and he wants Oliver to be crazy about her. He will be. Oliver is very trusting and loving, and that's why he protects him from the dating games in his life.

"I'd let George stay over now and then, if you'd let me come too." He takes a gamble. He thinks she probably knows he wants her this way, and yet, he's been on such good behavior, maybe he's not made his intentions clear.

She raises her eyebrows and laughs quietly.

"What's your proposition?" she asks as the waitress returns with their food.

"You like history. Right?"

"I love it," she answers.

"I'm thinking I want to write a book. I've always been fascinated by ancient Egypt."

"And?" she asks with a shrug.

"And?" he repeats with a smile. "I want you to write it with me."

She raises her eyebrows in surprise. "You want me to write with you? You don't even know if I can write."

"Your research papers are very well written and very interesting."

"Jay, I don't know what to say," she says quietly. "Writing a book like that implies a long-term relationship."

"You going somewhere?" he arches an eyebrow.

She stares at him for a long, silent moment. "You scare me when you say things like that."

"No, I don't." He shakes his head. "I scared you before, but I don't now."

"You don't," she agrees. "But what you want does."

He cuts his steak and offers her a bite. She takes the bite in her mouth, and he watches her as she chews it. His breath catches in his throat, and his stomach sinks down into his lap. He doesn't remember feeling like this for a woman. Ever.

They both have so much to share. But he knows they can get past the secrets. He hates whatever she hides, because it hurts her. But it doesn't matter to him; whatever she hides can't change the way he feels about her.

～

ELLIE FINDS HERSELF WONDERING ABOUT MADDIE. SHE KNOWS nothing about the Catholic religion. She doesn't know what separates a Catholic's beliefs from a Lutheran's beliefs. She doesn't know what a nun does, other than consider herself married to God and not have sexual relationships with men. It surprises her to realize that she is curious about Maddie and curious about Catholicism. It scares her, more than it surprises her. Maddie's green eyes are sometimes like sea glass, and sometimes the way Ellie catches her looking at her makes her feel transparent. Like Maddie sees right through her. She doesn't want Jay's sisters to read her. She doesn't want someone with a direct line to God to see too far inside her and unearth who she really is and have a talk with God or Jay.

When she leaves work the next day, she finds herself carrying a book about religion in her canvas tote bag. Just some interesting reading material, she promises herself as she unlocks her bike and sets off for home. As she rides, she thinks about Maeve's swimming pool. It would feel really good, right about now, to peel off the clothes and jump in. It's got to be ninety-five in the shade, and the only air that moves is the wind her bike makes as it cuts a trail home.

She and Blair used to live at the pool. When they were younger, they were at the community pool almost every summer day. They had taken swim lessons together from the time they'd been four. Blair loved the high dive, but Ellie had always loved simply swimming under water. She wonders now if that's because she likes to stay hidden.

Doesn't matter now. She can't imagine putting a suit on.

She hasn't owned one since she left home. Back in the days when she played in the water with him, she simply wore cut off shorts and old T-shirts. She wouldn't know how to relax at a poolside now if she tried.

She barely gets her bike pulled inside the house and her bag tossed down in the spare bedroom, the one she hates to venture into, when she hears the knock at her door. Mostly, she knows it's Jay, but her mind races with the possibilities. Then again, why would anyone come looking for her now? It's been too long for anyone to care.

He gives her that trademark grin when she pulls the front door open. She swallows hard over the lump in her throat and waits for the air to break up the knot in her lungs and her heart before she tries to speak. "Hey," she finally says. "What's up?"

"Just get home?" he asks, leaning a shoulder against the doorframe.

"Yeah."

"Wanna go to Maeve's? Stick your feet in the water?"

She laughs and steps back to let him inside. He's been inside her home before, but only in one half of her house, the half with the kitchen and living room. He waits expectantly for her answer. Hell yes, sticking her feet in the pool sounds like a better evening than snuggling up to her book on Catholicism.

"Sure," she finally answers. "Let me change clothes really quick." She hates that she has to dress in business attire and ride a bike to work. Stepping out of her khakis and pulling on cut-off denim shorts feels incredible. So good that she thinks she doesn't need to go to Maeve's house. But if Jay's going to Maeve's house, she wants to go to Maeve's house.

"Hungry?" he asks when she joins him in the kitchen again.

"Yeah, but you're not buying anything tonight," she tells him.

"I haven't eaten." He shrugs. "Let's grab some tacos on the way to Maeve's."

She laughs. "Yeah, that's on the way." She gets her first really good look at him for the day and sees he's wearing dark green swim trunks with a white Hard Rock shirt. Chicago. "You been there?" she asks, pointing to the word Chicago on the shirt.

"Couple times," he says with a nod. "Have you?"

"Not Chicago," she answers quietly. "Few other ones though."

"Maybe we can go someday."

She rolls her eyes and slips her sandals on. "Yeah, we can just drive to Chicago for a night out."

"We could take the train and spend a weekend," he suggests.

"Jay." She gives him a warning glance. He heads for the door when she grabs her keys. "Hey, I like the green trunks."

"Thanks," he mumbles. She wonders what he's thinking as they head out to his truck together. "Did you know a crocodile's snout is longer than an alligator's snout?"

A long moment of silence creeps by as she stares at him over the bed of his truck. Finally she laughs and shakes her head and says that she thinks she may have known that at one time. He hits Taco Bell, orders enough food for an army and hands her a Mountain Dew as he pulls out of the drive thru lane.

"What do you do through the day? When I'm working. What're you doing?" She turns sideways in her seat to look at him.

"Sometimes I work in the yard. Help Mom with some stuff at the house. Work on lesson plans for next semester." He glances at her. "And think about you."

She doesn't blush, but she feels a flash of intense heat zap her from head to toe.

"Ellie?" he asks quietly.

"What?" She finds an interesting spot on the floor of his truck and glues her eyes to it.

"Do you ever think of me?" From the corner of her eye, she sees him reach his hand over across the seat to lay palm up at her side.

She lays her hand over his and thinks about how quickly this man has become her life. "Yeah. I do."

Maeve laughs at him as he chows down on his huge Taco Bell order. Ellie eats two tacos and sips at her Mountain Dew while she's waiting for him. When Joe and Luke join them at the table, Maeve asks Ellie if she wants to go on out to the pool. She feels Jay's eyes on her as she follows Maeve outside.

"You really don't have a suit?" Maeve asks her as she pulls her shirt off over her head. She's wearing a two-piece, black with tiny bits of red splattered over it, like someone shook a paintbrush at her. She's tan everywhere Ellie isn't, and she's got the body of a twenty-year-old model.

"No, I don't," Ellie answers. Maeve steps out of her khaki shorts. Her hips look as good as the rest of her body. Ellie hopes she looks as good in another fifteen years, but then she wonders why it matters.

"Do you work Saturday?" Maeve asks as she lowers herself to sit on the edge of the pool.

"No. Why?" Ellie kicks off her sandals and sits down beside Maeve.

"Wanna go shopping? Bet you could find a cute suit on clearance now."

The water is cold on her feet and legs, but it feels so good, she simply sits for a moment and wiggles her toes. She never took him to a pool. For a second she can't breathe. Her eyes fill, and when she feels Maeve's eyes on her, she has to look away. Why hadn't she ever taken him to the pool? Something so simple, but she'd never done it, and now thinking about it makes her ache all over, like she has the flu.

"Sure." Her whisper is thick with regret and tears.

"You okay?" Maeve asks quietly. Ellie stares at Maeve's hand on her leg; the burgundy nails are sexy and the emerald cut diamond catches the evening sun. She nods, but she cannot find her voice. "Everyone has something to run from." Maeve pats her leg and then moves her hand away. "You're safe with us."

Ellie looks up quickly and meets Maeve's eyes. A laugh slips out, but her eyes fill again. She wipes at them and laughs again, thinking how far off the mark Maeve is. Ellie Jordan, safe in a family with an assistant district attorney and a Catholic nun.

"I haven't felt safe in a very long time." She works the words out over the sandpaper in her throat.

"Do you feel safe with Jay?" Maeve's voice is gentle, as if she senses that she must tread lightly over Ellie's feelings.

"Sort of." Ellie shrugs. She avoids Maeve's eyes and watches the sun bounce off the blue water. "I feel safe from everything else when I'm with him." She swallows hard and glances back at Maeve. "But he scares me."

"What do you mean?"

"Sometimes when I think about him, I feel like he's with me. Like he's got his arms around me. But sometimes thinking about him makes me feel like I'm about to jump out of a plane."

Maeve raises her eyebrows. "Have you ever been in love?"

"No."

"Because that's what it feels like." Maeve presses her lips together. "To me anyway. Like I can face the world when I'm with Stash. He makes me stronger. And then there are times when he just looks at me, and I feel like I'm breathing through smoke and fire, and I burn inside and get all dizzy."

"I'm not in love with Jay," Ellie says simply.

Maeve nods. She looks up when the guys step outside and make their way to the pool. Ellie clears her throat and blinks away any tears left and smiles up at Jay.

She spends the evening on the side of the pool, legs in the water, watching the rest of them play volleyball. She is drawn to Maeve, who is sexy and relaxed and having a good time. It amazes her, the difference between Maeve and Maddie. Joe and Luke are good-looking guys, and they're kind of cute, the way they goof off while they play. They remind her of herself and all the guys she knew in school. It makes her feel funny, the way you feel when you're tempted to do something even when you know it's wrong. The way she'd felt at the first big party she and Blair had gone to, when some guy she'd never even seen before had put a plastic beer glass in her hand. She hates it that they make her think this way, because they are part of Jay's family too.

Jay looks so good in his trunks and nothing else that she has to keep reminding herself not to stare. He looks solid through the chest and shoulders; she's hugged him enough to figure he's solid through and through. His skin is an even shade of golden brown, which tells her he spends a good bit of time in the sun, most likely right here in Maeve's pool. He looks like a beach bum tonight, and that thought scares her, so she pushes it out of her mind.

Darkness falls, but they linger in the pool. Maeve offers her a glass of wine, which she turns down. They sit side by side in lounge chairs once the night is full and watch the guys in the pool. Maeve doesn't talk much, but Ellie senses she is lost in thought about a case she's working. She knows Maeve can't discuss it, but she'd heard her refer to the Wittmer case on the Fourth of July. Ellie knows from reading the paper that Alec Wittmer is being tried for murdering his son.

It's nearing ten o'clock when Jay takes her home. His trunks have dried, and he's got his shirt on, but she keeps thinking of the way he looked in the pool. He follows her into her house and watches her kick off her sandals.

"Can you stay for awhile?" she asks quietly.

"I want to," he answers with a nod.

"Want something to drink?"

"No, thanks." He reaches for her hand. "Wanna go look at the stars?"

She nods but neither of them moves. Her lungs swell up inside as he rubs his thumb over her hand. She reminds herself to breathe, and he steps closer to her.

"Ellie." His whisper dances on her stomach and pushes it down to her knees. She licks her lips when his fingers trace her jaw and then cup her chin. This kiss is different. No less gentle, but more urgent. Sort of demanding. She breathes over his lips when he breaks the kiss and then trails his mouth over her jaw to her ear. She slides one hand over his shoulder and rests the other on his hip.

"Jay," she says softly as he nips at her neck. "I don't wanna do this."

"Are you telling me no?" he asks as he slides his arms around her. "Tell me no, Ellie."

She can't say no. There is so much fear and need and desire in her stomach and throat and mouth that she can't get the word *no* to come out. Her eyes close as his lips come back to hers. She moans softly as he slips his fingers under the hem of her shirt. "Jay," she whispers.

"I love the way you taste." His voice surrounds her, like she's kissed him so deeply she's slipped inside him. Her fingers climb the back of his neck and play with the fine hair over the collar of his shirt.

"Don't stop." The words are out of her mouth before she knows she is thinking them. She covers his hand with her free hand and pushes her shirt up, asking him for more.

"Are you sure?" he asks her. He pulls away from her to look at her. To hear her.

Ellie is not a virgin, but she's never made love. Tomorrow looms ahead of them like a storm cloud. He won't love her when he sees inside her, but right now, she wants to feel this. She wants to know what it would be like to make love to Jay. To feel his arms around her, to sleep next to him.

"I'm sure." She nods. She's not sure. She's not sure because she's used to bike rides with Jay and shooting baskets, and she loves George, and she loves looking at the stars with Jay. She's not sure she can go back to being alone once he's gone.

She wonders, when he kisses her again, if he can feel her trembling. His hands skim over her skin again, and his teeth nip at her lips and her chin.

"I love you," he whispers as he presses kisses to her chest, above her T-shirt.

"Don't say that," she tells him as she covers his hands again with hers.

"Are you sure?" he asks again. She pushes his hand up again and nods when he inches her shirt up further. Her stomach jumps as he pushes her shirt up and then she helps him pull it off over her head. She watches his eyes as he looks at her, suddenly scared and sick and sure this is a bad idea. His eyes stray over her face and down over her white lace bra and her bare stomach.

"Jay?" She licks her lips. *Why isn't he moving?* A blush creeps up her neck and floods her face. Her shirt is on the floor, but it seems a million miles away as she stands there, embarrassed.

"Ellie, you're beautiful." His voice is low and tight, as if it's painful for him to speak.

She reaches for his hand, because she needs him. "Kiss me," she says softly.

His fingers skim lightly over her breasts and down over the lace bra. She closes her eyes.

"What's this?" he asks. His fingers climb higher on her chest and touch the silver chain around her neck. She opens her eyes. He's holding the cross in his hands. It's a small, silver, Celtic cross.

"It's Luther's Cross," she whispers. "Jay. Please?"

He steps closer to her, but his lips barely touch hers before he moves back again. "Who's Luther?"

"Jay. I thought—"

"I know." He nods. "I want this. But I need to know who Luther is. I can't make love to you if you're in love with someone else."

"I'm not in love with Luther," she says softly.

"But you love him, or you wouldn't be wearing his cross."

"I love him." She nods and takes his hand again. "I wear his cross everyday. Please make love to me." She links her fingers through his and steps close enough to kiss him.

"Ellie." He pulls away from her again. "Who's Luther?"

"He's my son."

CHAPTER 12

JAY DROPS THE CROSS TO HER CHEST AND TAKES A STEP BACK. *Her son? Luther is her son?* He regrets his move, the step away from her, the second he sees the look of defeat cross her face. She presses her lips together and reaches to pick up her shirt. He watches, his stomach still pushing hard against his heart and shoving it up into this throat. *Her son? Ellie Jordan has a child? Where is he? How old is he? What happened with Luther to make Ellie this beautiful, tortured woman?*

He catches her arm as she stares at her inside-out shirt, as if it is a puzzle she's forgotten how to work. She glances at him, and he sees so much emotion in her eyes, he tightens his grip on her to hold himself steady. To hold her steady. She squints, and her eyes shine, and she looks away.

"Ellie." Jay slides sideways, trying to maintain eye contact with her. She closes her eyes tight. He watches the tears slip and trickle over her face. He wants to pick her up and hold her. He wants to soothe her, to make the sadness, the pain go away. He wants to see her smile. He wants to know about Luther. She is still struggling with her shirt, so with gentle hands, he takes it from her and turns it right side out and then puts it back in her hands. He knows, as she pulls it back on, that she's about to show him the door, so he sets himself directly in front of her and digs in. He's not going anywhere.

She turns her back to him and drops her head to her hands. Her shoulders shake, and she ducks away from him when he lays a light hand on her back. "I need you to go."

"No," he says quietly.

"Please?" Her voice comes out sideways, and he thinks from the soft cry he hears that it must have hurt.

"Don't push me away," he whispers. He touches her again, a gentle hand on her back, and he moves again to stand in front of her. "Ellie?"

She steps forward into his arms and lays her head on his shoulder. Rylan had never cried on him. Rylan hadn't often found a reason to curl into his arms and lay her head on his shoulder, no reason other than sex anyway. He'd held Amie Sanders when her boyfriend had dumped her their junior year of high school. But nothing had felt quite like holding Ellie tight against his body, coaxing the tears and the sadness from her, asking her to share it with him.

Her heartache is silent but strong. She buries her face against his neck and slides her hands up over his back and shakes against him, but she cries quietly. Jay cups the back of her head in one hand and smoothes his hand over her back in long, slow circles, wishing maybe to ease the sorrow up from her lower back and into her throat and finally from her lips. He wants to take it away.

He thinks she's never cried about this before. Whatever she carries inside, she's carried alone and she's never given herself time to grieve. He hates that she's been so alone, and he tightens his hold on her. He won't let her go. Her fingers dig into his shoulder, and he thinks she's afraid he is going to disappear.

"Ellie?" he whispers as he tucks her hair behind her ear. "Will you talk to me?"

She shakes her head and pulls away just enough to rest her forehead against his collarbone.

"Please?" He traces his fingers over the length of her jaw and cups her chin in his hand. "C'mon," he says softly. He walks her backwards to the couch and then slides around so he sits down first and draws her into his lap. He wonders if she will bolt if he loosens his arms around her, if she'll realize what she's doing, what she has already said to him. He takes a chance and slackens the circle of his arms around her and breathes a sigh of relief when she melts against him and lays her head in the crook of his neck.

He knows better than to think she will say much. He knows it will take a hammer and chisel to get inside her and read her secrets. But he needs something. He needs her to give him just a little. He wants to know everything about her, but right now, he needs just a little piece of her past. He needs to know about Luther.

"How old is he?" he finally asks; his voice is gruff with need and love and a little bit of sadness.

She sighs, and he hears the ragged edges and knows she's not finished crying. Her breath is warm on his neck. "Nine," she whispers.

Nine. She has a nine-year-old son. Where is he? What happened? He lays his head back on the couch and counts to five. He wants to ask, but he knows once he opens his mouth to ask these questions, a million more will gush out, and she's not ready for that. She's like a timid animal, backed into a corner, and his questions will either make her run for cover or charge and attack him.

"You can go," she mumbles against his neck.

"What?" He lifts his head and looks down at her. She is

pale and ghostlike against his shoulder; her lashes rest against her cheek.

"Are you sitting here wondering how to walk away?" She opens her eyes and stares at his neck as if she is afraid to look him in the eye. "It's okay, Jay."

He ducks his head and presses his lips to her head. "I don't want to go, Ellie. I'm trying to figure out how to ask you about your son. What to ask you about him. Without scaring you away."

She closes her eyes again. He knows she is searching for a dark, quiet place inside where she can be alone again and hide from him. She doesn't want to talk about her nine-year-old son, named Luther. Where is he? Jay leans over her again and touches his lips to her cheek. To his surprise, she lifts her head and turns just enough to touch her lips to his.

"Jay," she says softly. She kisses him, strong and greedy, and she tastes like sugar and spice and need.

"Ellie, no," he mumbles as she rises and shifts around on his lap. He knows what she is doing when she straddles him and drags her hands up to rest on his shoulders. She kisses him with a bold desire he has not seen in her since he's met her. On any other day, he'd be undressing her right about now, moving swiftly toward making love to her. Right now, he can't. She's using her body to put him off. She's willing to give him her body but not her heart. He wants all of her; he'd be kidding himself to think one or the other would satisfy him.

"No?" she whispers as she nips at his lips. Her fingers tease the back of his neck. He can't hide the way his heart is thundering in his chest. If she leans any closer, she'll feel his heartbeat against her. If she slides any lower in his lap, she'll feel the proof of his desire. He turns his head to hold her off. She leans her forehead against his face. She's crying again. "I thought you wanted this."

"Not like this." The words are too big for his throat and his mouth, and they hurt as they come out.

She touches his chin and turns his face back to hers. Her eyes are bright with tears. She licks her lips and strokes her thumb over his lower lip. "Please?"

His sigh is heavy with frustration. He wants her, and he hates this look of desperation on her face. He hates that she's willing to give him sex, after the way she hated his innocent touches, in exchange for not talking about what's in her heart. "Can't we talk first?" He tries again.

She laughs softly, but it's a sad sound. He slides his hands up over her back when she drops her head to his shoulder. "I've never made love, Jay," she whispers. "No one's ever made love to me." She sits up straight again and looks him in the eye. "Show me what it's like?"

His blood rushes south. She's tragic and beautiful at the moment, and he's tasting her again before he can remind himself that this should wait. His hands are in her hair; her body is pressed hard against his.

"Not here, Ellie." He breaks off a kiss and fights to come up for air.

"What?" Her face twists with confusion and what looks like pain.

He pushes her a bit and stands, still with his arms around her. She realizes what he wants and takes him by the hand and leads him to her bedroom. He sees the tremble in her hand when she reaches to pull back the quilt on the bed. She turns back to him.

"Are you sure?" he asks quietly. His hands slide under her shirt and find warm, soft skin. She nods and rests her cheek against his. Her hands settle on his hips. Gentle kisses and hands slide and roam and touch. When they are naked, they slip between the sheets. Hot skin and cool sheets. She is a tangle of long legs and soft, silken skin and hair that smells like raspberries. His hands greet every inch of her body as his lips follow and get to know her more intimately. Her soft sighs of pleasure and her hands that finger-comb his hair and splay wide over his shoulders push thoughts of Luther and Oliver and Rylan out of his mind.

He holds her the first time, when he simply touches her, and she falls over the edge of the earth. He holds her and kisses her, and before she comes down to touch the earth, he whispers again and asks if she's sure. She simply closes her hands around his neck and rearranges her body under his. He eases into her slowly and then raises himself to his elbows so he can look at her. His eyes touch the silver chain, the silver cross that lies now on the curve of her breast.

He makes love to her, and he thinks he loves her and Luther and all that she's been through and all that she is afraid of. She stares back at him, and he sees something in her eyes that he never saw when he made love to Rylan. He sees that she loves him, but he knows it's likely she will never say it. He looks hard to see through her fear and guilt and sorrow, to see deep inside her where she still loves Luther, where she loves him. He watches her teeth dig into her lip and her eyelids slide shut and then he lowers himself over her and presses her into her mattress and brushes her lips with his.

She doesn't call his name. She cries softly and breathes heavily and hangs onto him, both arms wrapped around his shoulders.

"Ellie?" he whispers. He lowers his head further and tugs her earlobe with his teeth.

"Mm?"

"Where is he?" he asks, because even though he's still inside her, he wants more. He wants to be in her heart.

"He's gone, Jay," she says softly. He doesn't know what that means, but he knows this is all she will give him tonight.

She is vaguely aware that she is cold now. She'd slept plastered to him, his arms around her and his breath hot on her neck. But now she is cold. Eyes still closed, she rolls to her back and reaches blindly across her bed. There's no one there. Hope has gossamer wings like a butterfly, and she feels it flying away from her as she opens her eyes. He left while she was sleeping. She expected exactly this to happen, so she's not surprised when she sits up and sees all traces of Jay Bryant are gone from her bedroom.

It is nearing seven o'clock; her alarm will go off in a few moments to remind her she has to get up and go to work. She stretches and turns the alarm off and climbs out of bed. She is still nude; she'd slept clothed only by Jay. Cold again, though it's a cold from inside and she knows this, she slips on the nightshirt she usually sleeps in and wanders through the house. The cold slice of the knife draws no blood when she passes through each room and finds that Jay is gone, and he's left nothing behind. Not even a note. She hadn't realized how much she'd been hoping to find a note until she didn't find one, and now she stands in her bedroom and swallows hard because she wants to cry because Jay left her after she'd told him about Luther. She wants to cry because Jay had drug all the old heartache about Luther back to the surface.

She'd been afraid to tell him. She hadn't even told him the details. She'd given him the first sentence of a novel, and he'd already bolted. It hurt to realize she'd trusted him. He'd seemed so sincere; she had almost believed he wouldn't run from her when he learned the truth about her. Almost.

Why had he said he loved her? She showers quickly, drinks a glass of juice and dresses for work. She'd rather he'd never say the words than to say them and not mean them. It doesn't matter anyway. He might have said he loved her, but

Jay Bryant had just taken her back ten years and changed the woman she'd become back to the girl she'd run so hard to get away from. She strips her sheets off her bed and carries them to the kitchen so she can wash them when she gets home after work. She wheels her bike out of the kitchen and then shuts and locks the door on the memories Jay brought back to life inside her.

Today she remembers that alone and lonely are two entirely different things.

CHAPTER 13

ALEC WITTMER KILLED HIS SON. MAEVE HAS NO DOUBT IN HER mind that the son-of-a-bitch beat his son to death. Alcohol, though consumed, is not to blame. There are no mitigating circumstances. The bastard had landed a blow upside seven-year-old Gentry Wittmer's head that killed the boy. And the lovely wife and mother had watched him do it. It is her job to convince the jury that Wittmer did indeed have a history of abusing his children and that this time the attack had ended in murder, rather than simply bruises or broken bones. Maeve's good at her job. She'll get Wittmer convicted. But working this case still drains her. She hates violence, and she really hates violence toward children.

She sits back in her chair when her brother whirls through the office door. A glance at the gold watch on her left wrist tells her it is just after eight o'clock. Jay looks disheveled and actually, all-out pissed off, for this early in the morning. He paces the floor of her less than opulent office, bites off a string of expletives that would have earned him an arched eyebrow from their mother, and then moves to close her office door.

"What?" she finally says. It's not that she doesn't care. But she doesn't have all day. When Jay decides to be pissed off, it can stick to him forever, the way gum sticks to the bottom of your shoe when you step in it. She will try the Wittmer case in front of Judge Allensworth in a few days. She needs every spare moment to make sure she's prepared.

He sighs and lets loose with a long groan of frustration. She watches him quietly as he drops to a chair in front of her desk. He rubs his face; he's done it since he was a small boy, rubbed his face when he's tired. His gaze locks on hers as he drags his fingers back through his thin blond hair.

"Jay?" she prompts. "I go to trial in a few days. What's wrong?"

"I just left Ellie's," he mumbles. She stares at him in shocked silence. She'd expected this to be about Rylan. Maeve is convinced that Rylan is the devil in disguise. She hates the woman; the only good thing she can think of involving Rylan is Oliver. And now that Rylan has actually given birth to Oliver, she hates her all over again.

Ellie? What had Ellie done to Jay to hurt him? She'd sensed a lot of turmoil inside Ellie, but she never thought she would hurt her brother. In fact, she worries that Jay will somehow hurt Ellie, unintentionally. It seems like a possibility, given that Ellie appears to want to love Jay but doesn't trust herself to do so.

"What happened?" she asks quietly. She drops her pen on the open file on the desk in front of her.

"Shit," he groans. "I left her. Goddammit, I walked out in such a hurry I didn't even write a note."

"Jay?" Maeve asks and cocks her head in question.

"I gotta go back." He stands to leave but stops at the door

and looks back at her with a frown. "What time is it? She's already up. She had to work today. Dammit."

Maeve stands and rounds the corner of her desk. She takes Jay's hand and leads him back to the chair. He doesn't sit. Instead he stares at her for a long, silent moment.

"Rylan called me this morning."

So it is Rylan. Maeve raises her eyebrows, but she waits quietly for him to go on.

"Six o'clock. She called to tell me she and this guy she met are going to Jamaica."

Maeve holds her breath. No wonder Jay is so upset. This has something do with Oliver and Ellie.

"She's gonna pack Oliver off to this daycare place. It's like a boarding school, Maeve. What kind of mother goes on a trip with a man she just met and leaves her son with absolute strangers for a week?"

Your ex-wife. Maeve holds the words back, because she doesn't want to hurt Jay. She lays her hand on his upper arm and gives it a gentle squeeze.

"Get yourself on a plane and get your son, Jay," she says firmly.

He nods. "I know. I have a flight out at six. Earliest I could get." He takes a deep breath and then looks her in the eye again. "I was at Ellie's when she called."

"At six this morning?" She rests her hip on the edge of her desk. He nods. "You were at Ellie's at six in the morning? What were you doing at Ellie's so early?"

He raises his eyebrows and gives her a pointed look. "I spent the night with her," he finally mumbles.

"You spent the night with her. Like sitting outside with her? Or watching movies and you fell asleep?"

"No." He shakes his head and turns away from her. "Not like that."

"Oh, Jay." She sighs and ducks her head.

"Maeve, I'm in love with her."

She looks up and watches him rub the back of his neck. "She doesn't know, does she? She doesn't know about Oliver. You spent the night making love to her, and she doesn't know about Oliver. And you got that phone call and flew out the door and left her to wake up alone."

He turns to look at her with sad, tired eyes. "Gets worse than that."

"What?" she asks quietly. She presses her lips together, wondering what the hell could be worse than what he's already told her.

"She"—he swallows hard and shrugs—"she told me something last night. She finally let me in, just a little bit."

Maeve stands and paces. She was right. Jay has just hurt Ellie unintentionally. And she's afraid it's the kind of hurt that will leave a mark on Ellie's pale heart. "Why didn't you at least leave her a note?"

"I don't know," he snaps. "I was so damned mad at Rylan I wanted to scream. I just had to get out. I had to get the flight. I have to get Oliver, Maeve. I can't let her do this to my son."

"Jay," Maeve says sharply as she turns to him. "I know you have to get Oliver. I understand that. But you owed Ellie some sort of explanation for leaving. Was it the first time you slept with her?" He doesn't answer, but she figures it was from the sullen look on his face. "Fix it. You've got a few hours before you have to leave for St. Louis."

"I can't." He shakes his head. "She's at work, Maeve. I can't just barge in there and make a scene—"

"She works in a public place. You don't have to barge in. You can walk in. And find her. And walk right up to her and talk to her."

He stares at her for a moment, obviously lost in thought. Finally he nods and takes a step toward the door. Maeve goes back to her desk and sits again. She picks up her pen and watches her brother open the door.

"Jay?" He turns to look at her again. "Did it matter?"

"What?"

"What she told you last night. Did it matter?"

"It matters," he answers firmly. "But not like you think."

SHE WATCHES THE WASP TRY TO RIGHT ITSELF ON THE windshield of Jay's truck. It had landed when Maeve had pulled into the drive thru lane at McDonald's. As she'd watched, it had managed to crawl over the windshield wiper and flip upside down, and now it's struggling to get back on its feet so it can get a solid take off. She feels like that wasp, struggling to get back on her feet so she can put some distance between herself and Jay. Why had she agreed to this? She can't, for the life of herself, remember why she'd given in and agreed to ride to the airport with Jay and Maeve.

When she'd looked up, while on her knees reshelving cookbooks that dated back to the 1950s—why anyone would want to look at them she didn't know—and seen Jay approaching her, she'd felt a rush of heat touch her face and make her fingertips tingle and make the woman inside her burn. And then she'd remembered that she'd told him about Luther, and she'd spent the night with him but woke up alone, and the heat was gone and only ice was left in its wake.

"Ellie." He'd waited for a long time for her to say something, to acknowledge that he was standing there in the cookbook aisle with her, but she hadn't. She wasn't really sure what to say; she simply knew she didn't trust herself or her voice. "Ellie." He'd tried again and squatted down beside her. "Will you look at me? Please?"

She'd sighed and given in and looked up at him. She wonders now what he saw on her face, in her eyes, because even now she's not sure what she feels beyond the need to fly away and be alone.

"Can I explain?" he'd asked her.

"I'd rather you didn't," she'd mumbled, her gaze still locked on his. "Let's just let it go at this. Okay?"

"I don't wanna let anything go," he'd said softly. He'd touched the back of her hand, curved around a fat book with a worn blue cover. She'd jumped like he'd laid an iron on her skin.

"It's better this way," she'd said simply.

"Nothing's better this way." He'd scooted in closer to her and stroked his fingers over her chin. "Something came up—"

"Don't lie to me," she'd said boldly and turned her face away from his touch. "You owe me the truth. If it bothered you about Luther, at least have the decency to say that to me. Don't make this about something else."

He'd dropped his knees the rest of the way to the floor and taken her hand in his. "The only thing that bothers me about Luther is that he's not with you, and that makes you sad."

She'd stared at their hands, rather than look him in the eye.

"Ellie, do you remember my cell phone ringing this morning?" He was so close to her now, she could feel his breath on her lips. She shook her head. "It was on the table by your bed. It rang, and you picked it up and handed it to me."

"I was dreaming," she'd answered softly. Of Luther. She would have done her damnedest to ignore any interruptions when she was dreaming of Luther. Maybe his phone did ring, and she just didn't remember it.

"It was my friend in New York," he'd pressed. "He needs some help."

She'd swallowed hard and wondered why he couldn't have taken five minutes to wake her up and tell her that. Or at the very least written her a note. Her eyes had burned with tears she didn't want him to see.

"I'm sorry," he'd whispered. "I should have left you a note. I was so upset I just left without thinking. I had planned to come back and tell you what had happened."

She'd looked back at him. His lips had touched hers gingerly, and he'd said those words again and this time, she'd shaken her head and flattened a hand on his chest and pushed him away. "Don't tell me you love me."

"I do love you, Ellie," he'd said the words over her lips and into her mouth.

She'd pushed him back again. "I lose the people who love me," she'd said simply. He'd backed off, but he'd practically begged her to ride along with him and Maeve to Lambert Airport in St. Louis. He was flying out at six, and he had to hit the road soon, and he really wanted her to be with them. She'd actually had to ask for the afternoon off and now, as she sits between Jay and Maeve in the front of his truck, she wonders just what the hell she's doing here.

Maeve, who is driving and has told her with a wink she's always wanted to drive Jay's truck, hands her a Coke, which she passes to Jay. She sips the next one Maeve hands her and then passes Jay the bag with the sandwich and fries. She's not hungry. Not at all. She is a basket case, really, sick about what she'd done with Jay and what it says about her. Sick that she'd told Jay about Luther. Smothering in memories of childish laughter and memories of Jay's laughter and his touch and his kiss.

"C'mon," Maeve says, nudging her with her elbow. "I got a two cheeseburger meal. You eat one, and I'll eat one."

She glances at Maeve and when their eyes meet, she sees a flicker of understanding. Jay has told her more than that he needs a ride to the airport. That thought spikes a million nerves inside her. Surely, if her memory is jogged, Maeve will remember her. But all she sees so far is that bit of under-standing and some compassion.

Because she doesn't want him to know how badly he hurt her, she eats Maeve's other burger and makes small talk with her. Jay is quiet on the passenger side of the truck, so quiet he's almost sullen. She wonders again what kind of friend he's running to rescue and if his friend is who's on his mind right now. She swallows the need to be the heartache on his mind with a mouthful of Coke. His fingers brush over the back of her hand, and she thinks it was accidentally on purpose that he touched her. She remembers the wasp then and looks at the windshield, hoping to find it on its feet. It's gone. She wonders when it flew away.

"I'LL BE BACK IN TWO DAYS." HE TURNS TO HER WHEN THE three of them are standing in front of the security check at the airport. She and Maeve can go no further. This is good-bye. She stares into his eyes and feels this goodbye in more ways than one. If he left her bed without talking to her this morning so he can rush off to help another woman, she has nothing left to say to him. She glances around and realizes they are virtually alone in the middle of a sea of people at the security checkpoint. Maeve has stepped away to give them some privacy.

She licks her lips and swallows hard. "You don't have to bother coming back for me," she whispers. She hates the way her voice quivers, because she hates to hurt this way after so many years of not caring or needing anyone in her life.

"Ellie." He runs his hands up her arms and sinks his fingers into her shoulders. "Why do you say that? I promise I'll be back—"

"It doesn't matter," she says with a shrug. "Not after last night. This morning—"

"I'm sorry about this morning," he says again. "I know I was a jerk to leave you like that. And I'm sorry. It had nothing to do with you. With Luther. This is just something I need to do."

She stares at him in silence and then finally breaks the heavy gaze.

"Will you come with Maeve? When she comes back to pick me up?"

"Who's in New York, Jay? Who in New York was more important than me this morning?"

He closes his eyes and sighs. "I didn't want to tell you this way, Ellie."

"Another woman?" she asks quietly. She looks up at him and raises her eyebrows.

"God, no." He cups her chin in his hand and rubs his thumb over her lips. "I promise you there's no other woman."

She waits silently for him to answer her. When he doesn't, she turns her head and pushes his hand away from her face.

"My son," he blurts out and reaches for her hands. "I'm just going to get my son. And I'll be back in a couple days."

Betrayal hurts like nothing else. The stick of a needle, a hard hit to the back of the head, seventeen hours of hard labor. None of it hurts the way it hurts to find out someone you care about has deliberately kept something from you. She stares at him in stunned silence. Her heart catches and then starts again, and the force of the blood pounding out through her body makes her ache everywhere. She can feel the rush of heat in her face.

"Your son?" Her voice is deceptively strong and cool. She hadn't told Jay about Luther, but Luther is different. She can't just go get her son and introduce him to Jay. Jay's son is obviously very much a part of his life, and yet, he kept him from her.

"Ellie," he sighs. He glances at his watch. She backs away from him.

"Go," she says with a shrug.

"Please come back with Maeve when she comes? I want you to meet him. I want you to understand this."

She thinks of Luther and laughs. It is a hollow laugh bent around the edges, like an empty two-liter bottle. "I think I understand this better than you do," she whispers. "You were right to keep him from me."

"I love you," he tells her again.

She shakes her head. "Either way you lose." She watches him turn and walk away, head through security and down the ramp that will lead him to the plane that will take him to his son. She feels someone's arm brush up against hers, and she knows without looking that it's Maeve. She wants to resent that she is here. That she knows things about Jay and his son that she doesn't. She wants to hate her because she is Jay's sister, and Jay hurt her. She wants to be alone.

She can't though. None of the above. She can't be alone and get back home. She can't hate Maeve, because she likes her. She doesn't resent her, because even though she is standing by her side, she's not saying anything, and she's not pushing Ellie to talk.

"You ready?" Maeve finally asks. Ellie turns away as Jay looks back over his shoulder and waves to them.

"Yeah," she says quietly, her gaze on the floor. "I wanna go home."

CHAPTER 14

SOMETIMES SILENCE IS SO THICK YOU CAN SLICE IT AND DICE IT or split it with an ax, like it is fresh firewood. The silence that rides home between Maeve and Ellie is palpable. It breathes, and it schemes, and Maeve knows she cannot push Ellie. She cannot push her to talk or to listen. As much as she wants to stand in her brother's corner and cheer him on, she can't. She can defend his need to bring Oliver home, but she cannot defend the way he walked out of Ellie's house this morning. She wants to stick her hand in the pile of puzzle pieces beside her on the truck seat, the pieces that put together would resemble the Ellie Jordan she'd met earlier this summer. But she can't. This is not her battle. As much as she loves Jay and as much as she likes Ellie and wants to see them together, she cannot grandstand and show off her wonderful brother. She hurts for Jay, because she cannot imagine her children having a parent like Rylan. And she hurts for Ellie, because she is a woman, and a night spent making love with someone special—and she knows just from watching the two of them together that it was making love with someone

143

special—should never be followed by a morning of waking up alone.

Ellie's silence lasts until the Citgo station in Troy before she turns to her and asks very simply, "What's his name?"

"Oliver." Maeve wants to say more, but she doesn't. It's not the right time. She doesn't know when the right time will be, or if there will even be a right time. But she drives in silence, hoping Ellie will say more. When Ellie remains quiet, Maeve reaches over and turns the radio on. "This okay?" she asks quietly.

"Sure," Ellie says with a nod.

Maeve sighs and taps her fingers on the steering wheel. "Still wanna go shopping Saturday? For a suit?" She watches Ellie out of the corner of her eye, sees the way Ellie opens her mouth to answer her and then thinks better of it and closes it again. She sees Ellie close her eyes and sigh silently.

"Not really," she finally answers.

"Just because you're angry with Jay doesn't mean you have to take it out on me."

"I'm not angry, Maeve." Ellie sounds resigned, almost bored, as if she expected something like this to happen.

"You should be," Maeve tells her. "You have every right to be pissed off at Jay."

Ellie gives her a sharp look. "He told you, didn't he?"

Maeve raises her eyebrows. "He told me he spent the night with you, yes, but only because he had to explain the circumstances, and because he was really upset. Mad at himself."

Ellie licks her lips and looks away from Maeve. "It was a mistake."

"Leaving you this morning was a mistake," Maeve agrees.

"Last night was the mistake," Ellie corrects her in that same, resigned tone.

Maeve bites her lip to distract herself from saying all the

things in her mind. *Why was last night a mistake? Why are you so sad and quiet, Ellie Jordan, at an age when you should be on top of the world?* She sighs and runs her fingers through her short, dark hair. Ellie glances at her.

"Why?" Maeve asks. She winces when the word falls out of her mouth. So much for minding her own business.

"What?"

"Why was last night a mistake?"

Ellie stares at Maeve for a long moment before she looks away. Maeve sighs and turns her attention back to the road. Traffic is light. She watches a rusted-out beige Chevette muscle its way into her lane several cars ahead of her.

"I was fine before Jay came along." Ellie's voice is a bit harsh and rusty, and Maeve wonders if she's crying.

"Fine," Maeve repeats.

"I didn't need anyone," Ellie whispers.

"You didn't?"

"I don't," Ellie says firmly.

THE TEARS COME EARLY TONIGHT. ELLIE IGNORES THEM AND watches the stars. She needs to feel connected to him tonight, because she feels disconnected from everything else. She carries this hurt with her everywhere, everyday and after so many years, it had dulled to the vague throb of an old injury. Since Jay poked at it last night, it has consumed her thoughts and her heart. She misses Luther.

She feels her stomach jump when Jay's truck pulls up in front of her house. Then she reminds herself that Jay is in New York with his son. She passes a hand over her eyes to dry her face and watches Maeve round the truck. In one hand, she holds George's leash. In the other, she carries a six-pack of Michelob.

George ambles up the sidewalk, nose to the ground. Ellie watches in amusement as he sniffs at the weed she's been fighting since she moved into the house. He lifts his hind leg and waters it. She chuckles and shakes her head. When he hears her laugh, he tugs at the leash and hurries to climb over her feet. Maeve walks by her, into her house, and Ellie says nothing. She scratches behind George's ears and then lifts the dog into her lap. Holding George is familiar and comfortable, but she misses Jay.

When Maeve returns, she hands Ellie a cold brown bottle. "Thought you might like a beer."

Ellie looks up at Maeve and raises her eyebrows. "I don't need a babysitter."

"How about a friend?" Maeve asks quietly. She sits down beside Ellie and takes a long drink of her beer. "A girl friend who isn't sitting here thinking about getting you into bed."

"Ouch," Ellie says with a crooked grin. "Am I not your type?"

"Married," Maeve answers with a smile. Ellie snorts and takes a drink of her beer. It is good and cold and smooth and goes down easy. Too easy. She licks her lips and closes her eyes and refuses to remember. She is walking that bridge from her new life into the old life, and she'd sooner jump off and drown in nothingness than go back to what used to be.

"I can't do this," she says softly. She sits the beer down and looks away.

"Are you an alcoholic?"

"No," she answers. "I'm a lot of things, but that's not one of them."

"Then relax," Maeve tells her. She touches Ellie's arm, but she's quick to move her hand away. "Look, I know you're upset. And I understand that. If I were you, I'd have torn into Jay with both hands. But I've come to think of you as a friend."

"It's not Jay's fault," Ellie whispers.

"It is, and it isn't." Maeve shrugs. "Will you go with me when I pick him up?"

"Maeve," Ellie says quietly. She studies the toes of her shoes and sees the splotch of paint and remembers the night she and Jay had first had ice cream together. She tucks her hair behind her ear. "I don't wanna see him again."

"Ellie," Maeve says quickly. This time when she touches her arm, she is slow to move away. "C'mon. You can't mean that. You guys are best friends. You have something real. Don't let one mistake take that away."

"It's not even that he left," Ellie continues as if she hasn't heard Maeve. "It's what I told him before we were together. It's all the things he made me remember about myself. He and Oliver are better off without me."

Ellie studies the stars again, part of her wishing Jay were here with her telling her a story. Part of her wishes she'd never met Jay Bryant, the man. Her life would have been much simpler if he'd stayed Jay Bryant, the professor. Now she's made a mess of that simple relationship, and really, why in the hell should that surprise her? She's good at screwing things up. She's been doing it far too long to lose her knack.

"What the hell?"

Ellie turns her head quickly to see what Maeve is muttering about. Maddie is walking up the sidewalk. She flashes Ellie a smile before she turns to Maeve with a look of annoyance. Practiced annoyance, Ellie thinks.

"What are you doing?" Maeve asks, the second Maddie is close enough to hear her.

"Mom told me Jay went to New York again," Maddie answers in a tight, clipped voice. "I thought I'd check on Ellie."

"Do you have a car?" Maeve asks her. Her voice is heavy

with frustration. "God, Maddie, you can't just walk around town like this at all hours—"

"It's just after nine o'clock," Maddie reminds her. "And I live on this end of town. Maybe you aren't aware of that."

"It's dark," Maeve answers. "Think God's gonna save you from some jackass kid who decides he wants to attack you?"

Ellie rubs her hand over George's back and reaches for her beer.

"Beer's in the fridge," Maeve mumbles. Maddie disappears inside the house.

Ellie glances at Maeve. "Why do you hate her?"

Maeve stares at her silently. Ellie feels the night close in around them. The sky behind Maeve is a darker, deeper blue, and it suddenly feels like it rests just beyond Maeve's shoulders. It's as if she could reach over Maeve's shoulder and pull the midnight blue and the glittering stars down around the woman, like a blanket. A million crickets give soundtrack to this otherwise silent movie. They are so loud suddenly that Ellie wants to shout at them and shut them up. Her shoulders are tight, and her head hurts and still, she misses Jay.

"Because I do," Maeve answers simply, as if this alone should answer every question Ellie might have about the two of them. As if this alone explains why it's okay for her to hate her sister, the catholic nun.

"Is the feeling mutual?" Ellie asks quietly.

Maeve snorts. "What do you think?"

Ellie turns away when Maddie comes back outside with a beer in hand. She sits down beside Maeve. They are crowded together on the porch now. It seems like it's been a million years since Ellie could sit and watch the stars by herself. She thinks she misses the solitude. But she sort of likes the two women who now share her porch, both of them, even though it is like sitting with night and day.

She doesn't think Maddie hates Maeve. She wonders if

Maeve believes she does or if Maeve wants to believe she does.

"Maeve, do you remember Cal Nichols? Graduated with me."

"Mm-hmm." Maeve presses her bottle to her lips but doesn't take a drink. "Who wouldn't remember him?"

"Remember when he and Jeff Evans got arrested for drunk driving?"

Ellie watches Maeve turn and look at Maddie, as if she's wondering what prompted this stroll down memory lane.

"Hard to slide under radar when you're doing ninety dragging down Main," Maeve mumbles.

Maddie laughs quietly and takes a long drink of beer. "You're a fine one to talk," she says quietly. Ellie sees the grin on her face; kicked up another notch, it might be considered a leer.

"Never got picked up for drunk driving," Maeve tells her with a shrug.

"Doesn't mean it's okay to do it," Ellie mumbles. She looks up quickly, when she realizes she's spoken aloud. "I don't know how many times Blair and I got in the car, past the legal limit."

"Bygones," Maeve says softly. Maddie chokes as she swallows another mouthful of beer.

"Didn't know that word was in your vocabulary." She licks her lips and glances at Maeve.

Ellie stares at the two of them and wonders what their story is. She wonders if she and Natalie would treat each other this way if they knew each other now. This is the sort of relationship they had had the last time she'd seen her sister. Then again, she'd been sixteen, and Natalie had been eleven. Kids are supposed to argue and bicker over stupid, inconsequential things. Adults aren't. Adults are only supposed to bicker and hate each other over serious things.

That thought gets stuck in her head, and Ellie wonders if they looked hard enough if they could see it in her eyes.

She looks back at the street again and wonders what Jay and his son Oliver are doing. She would wonder what Luther is doing, but she fears she knows the answer to that, and it's not one she's comfortable thinking.

"You're a DA," Maddie continues. "What do you know about letting bygones be bygones?"

"So just because you work for God, you've got the forgiveness market cornered, huh?"

"I think I understand the concept a little better than you do," Maddie says quietly. She takes a long drink of her beer and then looks up at the sky. "Do you remember looking at the stars with Dad?"

"With the telescope," Maeve adds wistfully. She, too, looks up at the stars.

"You guys had a telescope?" Ellie asks them. Jay has never mentioned a telescope.

"Dad did," Maddie tells her. "It was ancient, though. Half the time you couldn't be sure if you were looking at a star or the neighbor's kitchen lights."

"You looked at the stars with him?" Ellie's throat is so thick with emotion she can hardly speak. One more night. She'd trade anything, including Jay Bryant, for one more night of sitting on the porch, looking at the stars with Luther.

"I did," Maddie answers with a nod. "Maeve spent more time trying to scope out the hot guys in the neighborhood. She used to watch Eric Morgan work out. Watched Eric Morgan make out with Susan Crain once."

"Oh, bullshit." Maeve rolls her eyes.

"You watched the whole thing," Maddie says.

"All ten minutes of it." Maeve almost laughs. "You were

jealous. If you'd been the one to see it, it would have been fine." Maeve turns to Ellie. "She told on me."

"How old were you?" Ellie asks.

"Thirteen," Maeve answers. "Eric was seventeen. Hot guy."

"Was that the end of the telescope?"

"Yep," Maeve says. "Thanks to St. Maddie."

Maddie lifts a shoulder. "Rather be a saint than a sinner."

"Oh, that's real," Maeve mumbles as she takes another sip of her beer.

Ellie snorts softly. She's most definitely not choosing sides. She couldn't if they asked her to. If Jay hadn't told her they were cut from the same cloth, she'd never believe these two are sisters. Maybe one of them was adopted. She takes another drink of her beer and stands up. George lets out an excited bark as she wraps the end of his leash around her hand.

"What're you doing?" Maeve asks her, surprised by Ellie's sudden movement.

"Taking George for a walk," she answers simply.

"In the dark?" Maeve mumbles.

"I dare someone to hurt me, Maeve." She licks her lips. "Don't wait on me."

"Ellie!" Maeve calls after her as she and George take off down the sidewalk. She ignores her. She's not afraid of the dark. Luther is gone. What more could she possibly lose?

CHAPTER 15

SHE'S ALWAYS HEARD THAT THE SINS OF THE FATHER ARE
visited upon the son. But in her case, it's the sins of the
mother that are visited upon the son. At sixteen, most girls
aren't cut out for motherhood. As she recalls, at sixteen, she
wasn't cut out for human involvement of any sort, let alone
motherhood. Luther had paid dearly for the life she'd led,
and there is not a day that goes by that she does not come
face to face with that regret.

Regret is now what makes her unfit for human involvement. Regret over Luther and regret over getting involved
with Jay consumes her. When Maeve asks her again to ride
with her to pick Jay and Oliver up from the airport, she says
no. Maeve, clearly upset and yet determined not to say
anything, had simply nodded and then reminded her that
they had a shopping date for tomorrow. Ellie shook her
head, but Maeve told her she'd be over to get her around
noon for lunch and shopping. She'd left her no room to
argue, simply turned and walked back to her forest green
Sebring convertible. She was intimidating in her gray power

suit and matching gray heels. Ellie had watched her slide into the driver's side of the convertible and drive away without a glance in her direction. She hoped she didn't call her before she left her office to head down to Lambert Airport to get Jay. Ellie didn't want to cave; she couldn't afford to anyway. Rather than think about it any longer, she'd eaten her banana and headed off to work herself.

Reshelving books is a mindless job, and for the first time she resents the amount of time her job gives her to think. Luther is so heavy on her mind since she'd told Jay about him that she feels as if he is riding on her back, his skinny little arms wrapped around her neck and his bony knees pressing into her sides. She's dreamt of him each night now since talking to Jay, and she awakes in a fog, not sure if the dream is reality. If she could walk into his room and find him there, sprawled out, St. Louis Cardinal sheet kicked to the foot of his bed.

She misses Jay so much she's caught herself near tears just thinking about him. She hates herself for letting him get so close. This is her fault. She'd known the first night she'd sat on the porch with him and looked at the stars that she was playing with fire. The two of them are going to burn before this is over, and now there is Oliver. Hell yes, she wants to meet Oliver. She envisions a miniature Jay with curly blonde hair, bright blue eyes, and a killer smile. She wants to meet Oliver, but she knows she will love him with just one look, and loving him will hurt him and her and Jay.

She dreads the moment he will be back in town. He'll come to her. He'll come and he'll want to know why she didn't ride with Maeve, and he'll ask her to understand why he left her that morning. Yes, the timing was horrible, but if it was something to do with his son she understands. And she understands why he kept Oliver from her, even if he won't say it. She is not good for him and Oliver, and they are far better off ending everything there is or was between them. She understands this because she thinks she loves him. And if she loves him, she knows she has to want what is best for him. She is not what is best for anyone. She never has been, never will be.

Making love to Jay had been special. Not to be dramatic, but really, it is the thing in her life, except having Luther, which means the most. Luther's birth is a bittersweet memory, and anyone who knew her in her old life would say she is lying when she claims it meant something to her. Anyone in her old life would say she is lying when she says she loved her son. Anyone in her old life was just like her, and therefore, she wants nothing to do with the bunch of them.

Jay was right to keep Oliver from her. But she can't help but feel the sting of his omission. What if he knew her and that's why he'd kept Oliver a secret? What if he remembered her, and he'd believed the things he'd heard about her or read about her? What if he had kept Oliver from her because he doubted her? She steps into an aisle of ancient travel journals, where she is certain she will be alone and takes a deep, calming breath. Her throat aches, but she breathes slowly. She hates Jay Bryant for making her cry, and with one last steadying breath, vows to herself that he won't do it again.

Maddie likes to imagine what people would say if they knew she liked to drive with hard, crashing music like that of Evanescence blaring. She is a far cry from a good Catholic, really, let alone an obedient nun. The truth is like someone putting a cigarette out on her skin, so she seldom lets it surface. This evening though, as she drives to Ellie's house, she can't help but consider her own issues, her own guilt. She recognizes it in Ellie, as one junkie recognizes another, and she would like to help Ellie take the guilt by the horns and rush at it headlong and beat it. But she still avoids her own story; there is little hope that she can lead Ellie to any personal peace.

She thinks it is funny, in a sweet way, that Ellie was stunned to learn she'd played softball. That she plays the piano and teaches kindergarten. She figures the shock would have been even greater if she wore a habit. Perhaps that is part of what she wants Ellie to learn. Physical appearance, clothing included, don't make a person. It is what is inside that matters. Don't judge a book by its cover. Dig a little deeper. Investigate. Find out what makes a person tick.

Ellie is not outside when she parks her Buick by the curb. She is careful to turn the CD down, but she doesn't turn it off. She locks her doors when she slips out of the driver's seat, mindful of the way Maeve had given her hell the other night for walking by herself after dark. Maeve. Maeve has always known what is best for everyone. And it has always irritated her to no end.

She taps on the screen door, but she sees Ellie sitting on the floor in front of the couch. Ellie looks over her shoulder and sees her. The shadow across the screen hides the look in Ellie's eyes, so Maddie can't be sure of what she's thinking.

"C'min," Ellie calls. Maddie steps inside. Ellie's face is red from exertion; tendrils of her hair are matted to the sides of her head, the rest pulled back in a ponytail. She wears athletic shorts, a sweaty T-shirt with the sleeves cut out, and running shoes. She climbs to her feet and offers Maddie a smile. Her breathing is slow and deep, as if she's finally caught up with herself. "Just got home."

"Bike ride?" Maddie asks, because she knows Ellie and Jay often ride together.

"No." Ellie swipes the back of her hand over her forehead. "Went for a run."

"Ah," Maddie says and nods. "Have you eaten?"

"No." Ellie bends at the waist and stretches her legs. "I was gonna have an apple," she says as she stands up straight again.

"Well, I was gonna see if you wanted to go grab something to eat," Maddie tells her.

"Sure." Ellie looks so surprised by her answer that Maddie almost laughs. *Sometimes our mouths betray us*, she thinks. "Mind if I take a quick shower?"

"Not at all."

Maddie sits at the end of the couch while Ellie showers. She stares mindlessly at the TV. Ellie had been watching the Discovery channel. The show about eye surgery does not interest her, but she has no desire to change the channel. TV has never been her thing. She was a dreamer when she was a kid, and now that she is older, she reads. She reads anything and everything she lays her hands on.

Ellie is ready within fifteen minutes, which Maddie thinks is wonderful, and she wishes Ellie could teach Maeve this trick. On the rare occasions she and Maeve do anything together, and they are very few and far between, it takes Maeve a good hour to get ready, and that doesn't include the shower. Ellie's wet hair is pulled back again, in a sleek ponytail. She wears denim shorts and a navy ribbed T-shirt and sandals. Maddie is glad she is wearing capris. It seems to make people ill at ease when she dresses in slacks and proper blouses, as if that clothing thing makes her unapproachable. She guesses though, really, she is a bit unapproachable, just because she spends so much time alone. Growing up in Maeve's shadow has taught her to live as quietly and unobtrusively as she can. She hates that this makes her seem aloof, when really she is just a bit weary and very independent.

They decide to walk to the barbeque joint on Twelfth and

Filmore. Ellie glances at the Buick as they walk past it. She raises an eyebrow at Maddie.

"Yeah, I know," Maddie says with a soft laugh. "But I have to drive a sensible car."

"Better than the dead Tercel in my garage," Ellie mumbles. She looks away, leaving Maddie to wonder what she is thinking.

"What's wrong with it?" Maddie asks.

"Won't start."

"Jay could fix that," Maddie tells her. When Ellie doesn't answer her, she realizes Jay is off limits. "I'm sorry."

Ellie shrugs but still says nothing.

"Look, I don't know how close you and Jay are, but can I just say one thing and then I promise I'll drop it?"

"What?" Ellie sighs. She glances at Maddie, but she won't hold her gaze.

"Jay and I aren't very close, but even I can see the difference. You've made him come alive."

"Jay and I might have been good as friends," Ellie says softly. "But we crossed that line, and that was a mistake."

"Why was it a mistake?"

"Because it can't go anywhere," Ellie answers her. "Including backwards."

"Why can't it go anywhere?" Maddie asks her, but Ellie does not answer. "I'm a good listener."

Maddie senses that she's making Ellie more uncomfortable. The tense silence finally eases a bit; the charge in the air fades away as they round the corner of Twelfth and Filmore and walk past Dairy Queen. She wonders if Ellie's reluctance to talk to her is because she's a nun or because she's Maeve's sister.

~

SOMETIMES MEMORIES ARE SO VIVID THEY ARE LIKE OIL paintings, hanging there before your eyes. Each brush stroke is visible, tangible, as if you could reach out and touch it and feel the texture of the paint on canvas. As she sips her Coke, Ellie sees herself and Jay sitting on the picnic table at the corner, where they'd eaten their ice cream that first night. She is surprised to see herself as happy, skittish, maybe, but happy.

Maddie joins her at the picnic table, so she pulls her eyes away from the table on the corner in front of Dairy Queen. She studies Maddie when the woman watches an old black Cadillac creep down Filmore. Her skin is so smooth and pale, even this late in the summer, she still looks like a porcelain sculpture. How does a woman this beautiful give up her right to make love and sleep in the right man's arms?

"Why did you do it?" Ellie asks before she realizes she is going to speak. She winces and wishes she could catch the words before they hit the air and make sound, and Maddie hears them. But she can't. Maddie turns to her, her face a mosaic of guilt and fear. Not fear. Terror. Ellie swallows hard, wishing double now that she could have stopped those words.

"Do what?" Maddie's voice is just a whisper. Her eyes are wide, but Ellie doesn't think they are wide with doe-eyed innocence. Maddie has the look of a woman who has done something desperately wrong and knows she can no longer hide it.

Ellie stares at her for a long, quiet moment. She wants to search inside Maddie and find the root of that horrible terror. No one should have to feel this way, and Ellie has grown very fond of Maddie. She wonders if this is how they see her. A woman broken and stitched back together. A woman whose face is always hidden in shadows of guilt.

A flash of heat and nerves uncurls in her stomach, like a

firecracker has exploded inside her, and the silent, but deadly heat has burned her. The root of Maddie's terror and guilt is the root of the bizarre tension between her and Maeve. Whatever Maddie is guilty of is the reason Maeve hates her. She is more certain of this than anything else in her life.

Ellie takes another sip of her soda and tears her eyes away from Maddie. She wants to know, and that's dangerous. It's dangerous to set herself up between Maddie and Maeve, when she is drawn to both of them. She can't walk the fine line between them if she knows what crossroad separated them.

She looks back at Maddie, to find the look of panic gone. She wears the mask of cool indifference that Ellie has seen many times before. "What made you decide to become a nun?"

Maddie's eyes go so distant, Ellie thinks she can almost see a new world in them. Not hungry anymore, she picks at her sandwich as she waits for an answer. Ellie finds herself curious about God and nuns and being Catholic and faith and forgiveness. And yet, she can't imagine a world where every breath and every blink of her eye belongs to God.

"Not what you'd think," Maddie finally answers. Ellie frowns but says nothing. Instead she takes a bite of her sandwich and wishes she were hungry, because the barbequed pork chop is delicious, and it's not often she splurges like this.

"And what would I think?" she asks after a long stretch of silence.

"Devotion to God," Maddie answers simply.

"You're not devoted to God?"

Maddie takes her time answering, taking a bite of her own sandwich and watching a steady stream of cars pass by them on Filmore. Ellie often wonders about the conversations and the lives lived in cars and houses that pass by her world, and she wonders now if Maddie does the same. For Ellie it's wistful, because she always wonders if those other people are happy when she's not.

"I am now," Maddie says with a small shrug. She pins Ellie with serious eyes and then shakes her head. "Ya know what? That's a lie. I'm no more devoted now than when I first became a nun."

Ellie takes a moment to mull that over. "Then why did you choose this life for yourself?"

"First of all," Maddie tells her. "I'm not unhappy. I may not be living the life I thought I would be when I was younger. But I'm content."

"You shouldn't have to settle for content," Ellie says quietly.

"Okay, maybe not." Maddie nods. "But you shouldn't have to settle for alone."

"This is where my life led me, Maddie," Ellie answers uncomfortably. "Actually, life's been too easy on me after the things I've done."

"Like your son?" Maddie asks her boldly. Ellie feels the blood drain from her face, and in the part of her brain that has not frozen in a panic, she wonders if she now wears the look Maddie has just discarded.

"How do you know about Luther?" she whispers, praying that Jay told her. She'd prefer to think Jay told her secret, as much as that would hurt, than any other alternative.

"I read the paper," Maddie answers quietly. "Every day."

Ellie shoves her sandwich away and covers her face with her hands.

"How long have you known?" she asks from behind her small barrier of protection.

"Since the first night I met you at Maeve's." Maddie reaches for her hand. "Ellie."

Ellie jumps away from her and drags her fingers back through her hair. "Why didn't you say something?"

"Because my brother is in love with you and has been since he's known you. Because I liked you, and I wanted to get to know you."

Ellie stares at Maddie silently. Her heart races. She takes a deep breath and swallows it hard and tries to steady herself. "Do Maeve and Jay know?" Her voice is tiny, and she hates that she's giving away how scared, how vulnerable she is.

"No," Maddie answers. Ellie wipes her hands on her shorts, but they are damp with sweat, and she can't wipe the nerves away. "I haven't said anything."

"How can she not know?" Ellie hears the life fall out of her voice. "How can she be who she is and not know?"

"It didn't go to trial," Maddie reminds her.

"Oh God." Ellie sighs and covers her face again. She grinds the heels of her hands into her eyes. In the kaleidoscope of colors there, she finds the green of Maddie's eyes and the brown of Maeve's eyes and the blue of Jay's eyes. She is naked there, on the picnic table, and the people she has fallen in love with are staring at her and seeing inside her to that black heart she has tried so hard to keep hidden. "I have to go." She drops her hands to the table and pushes herself up. Her knees are weak, and she wonders if she has the strength to walk the five blocks back to her house. She wishes she had the strength to take a left at the corner and walk to the highway several miles south and walk out of her life and disappear. Maybe she should just die trying.

"What happened to Luther?" Maddie ignores her. Ellie drops back to her seat and stares at Maddie again. She opens her mouth to answer her, to tell her what happened to Luther. To tell her how her life is nothing now, without Luther. She can't make the words come out. She chews on her lower lip and then looks away. If it is this hard to tell Maddie who she is, how could she ever hope to tell Jay?

She looks back at Maddie and raises her eyebrows. What she planned to say doesn't matter now. Those words are stuck somewhere under her heart, but they're not important. There's only one thing she can say to Maddie right now. "I didn't kill my son."

CHAPTER 16

OLIVER IS HOME NOW, AND JAY IS WHOLE IN A WAY THAT ISN'T possible when his son is gone. And yet, Ellie did not ride with Maeve to pick them up at the airport. Ellie doesn't want to see him. Ellie chose not to come and meet Oliver. He doesn't blame her, not at all. He just hates that the pieces have fallen this way. He hates that he hurt her, because he loves her. What he had with Rylan is a shadow of what he feels for Ellie, and he wants her in his life. In his and Oliver's life. He needs her.

Oliver loves George, and the first night his son is home, he finds himself in bed with his son and his dog and still missing Ellie. He craves the closeness he had with her that last night. The way she'd held him. She'd clung to him, but not in a desperate way. It had been like they were made to be together, skin to skin, and once they'd discovered each other that way, neither of them had wanted to let go. She'd slept in his arms, and he'd lain with her, with his arm around her, wondering about Luther. Now, with the ball of fur between him and his son, he wants Ellie there to complete his family.

He thinks that Ellie would be wonderful with Oliver. He

knows the kid can turn any woman into a sucker for his big blue eyes and brown curls. He hopes Oliver will melt Ellie's heart. He won't use his son to get back in her good graces, but he wants her to be as crazy about him as he is. It was after eleven when Maeve dropped them off, so he didn't call her. He figures she was on her porch watching the stars. Probably thinking about Luther, and that makes him wonder again what happened to her son.

He hopes Maeve can get Ellie out of her house tomorrow. For an afternoon of lunch and shopping. It would be good for Ellie, and he thinks Maeve would enjoy it too. Maeve had been unusually quiet tonight, even with Oliver, and that bothers him. He supposes she is concerned about the Wittmer case she will be trying. Maeve has never settled for mediocrity in anything, and her job is no exception. He has no doubt she'll put Wittmer away, but he worries that it will take a toll on her.

When he closes his eyes, he sees Ellie again. In her bed, in his arms. He doesn't want to push her, but he wishes she would have said she loved him. Somehow he needs to see her tomorrow. He needs to tell her about Rylan and Oliver, and he wants to know about Luther.

SOMETIMES THE WHITE FLAG OF SURRENDER TEMPTS HER. IT'S A lonely world she lives in, at times, and the fact that no one would ever guess that makes it even lonelier. She has it all; therefore she's not really entitled to go to pieces or feel this way. When she does she hides it. Often Stash sees through her. They talk a lot; he is the constant in her life when all else is shimmery and distant, as if she is looking at life through a veil of tears. But Stash travels often, and she finds herself alone more often than not lately. She used to get the most bang for her buck as she could when she was alone—bubble baths, fluff romance books, Lifetime TV, and shopping. Now it gives her too much time to think.

Ellie is gorgeous and so completely oblivious to it that it makes her heart hurt. She is simple and genuine and beautiful, and Maeve wants her for her brother more than she wants anything in her life right now. Ellie will be wonderful with Oliver; she's sure of this. What she isn't sure of now is how to corral Ellie back into Jay's arms without being too obvious.

Lunch had been a quiet affair. Ellie had been much too quiet. Maeve guesses there is something more on her mind now than there was the other night. But she doesn't have a clue what it might be. Ellie had eaten a Caesar salad and answered questions Maeve asked of her, provided they were not personal questions. Maeve had learned that she slept with a nightlight until she was five. She used to play Kick the Can daily with neighborhood kids, and her favorite color is blue. She'd gone silent when Maeve asked her about seeing Jay.

The bikini that Maeve insists Ellie try on is perfect. It is black with a flash of silver, outlines her curves—and she does have curves though she hides them under her clothes—and accentuates the breasts she hides as well. Ellie flat out refuses to buy it. Next Maeve brings her a tankini, in a size six, grumbling all the way that someone she knows, besides her daughter, can wear a size six. The tankini is red, and it's gorgeous on Ellie as well. But Ellie vetoes it, and Maeve knows it is the color she's objecting to. It is too loud for someone as reserved as Ellie.

The black one piece that Maeve brings her is perfect. It is low-cut in the back, low enough to be sexy, but it covers enough in front that it doesn't bother Ellie. It is textured and elegant, and though Maeve is careful not to say so, it cuts a perfect fit to Ellie's lithe body. Jay will love it. Then again, Maeve thinks Jay would love Ellie in burlap.

Maeve doesn't even offer to drive her home. Instead they go straight to Maeve's house, where Maeve suggests they relax by the pool. She sees the fleeting anger cross Ellie's face, but it passes quickly. The girl simply nods and excuses herself to use the restroom and put the new bathing suit on. Maeve changes quickly, pours herself a glass of wine, and waits in the kitchen for Ellie to return.

When she'd come home last night after dropping Jay and Oliver off, she'd caught Luke with a girl. It has happened before, and in her opinion, it is getting out of hand. Stash laughs it off. Were it Petyon with a boy, he'd be on the warpath. Maeve thinks there is something fundamentally wrong with seeing a young girl's hands wrapped around your son's bare ass as he hammers said young girl against your living room wall. She'd simply slammed the door to get his attention and waited, eyes averted, for them to get themselves put back together and the girl to disappear. She'd grounded him, of course, and he'd apologized. But they both knew Stash would lift the punishment when he returned from San Antonio.

"What're you thinking about?"

She turns when she hears Ellie's voice. It startles her to realize she misses this. She misses talking to someone other than Stash. No, she'd never think of cheating. She's as in love with Stash today as she was the day she'd married him. But once, in another lifetime, she'd been close to her sister. It's unnerving to realize twenty years later that she misses her. She needs Ellie, maybe as much as Ellie needs someone to talk to. Her stomach sours just a bit; she's fifteen years older than Ellie Jordan. It doesn't feel right to need her so much, so soon.

"Luke," she answers quietly. "Want a glass of wine?"

"Are you going to consider me standoffish if I say no?"

"No." Maeve feels Ellie's words torpedo her heart. "God, Ellie, I don't wanna make you think I'm forcing you to drink. I just thought—" She stops herself and shrugs and shakes her head. "I just thought the other night that you could use a beer. I know you were hurt."

She watches Ellie lick her lips and nod slowly. "I know you're not forcing me to do anything, Maeve," she says softly. "It's just that it's early. And I'm not used to drinking anymore. And one glass of wine is enough to knock me out."

Maeve nods. "Okay. How about a Coke?"

"That'd be great," Ellie says, but she avoids Maeve's eyes. "Maeve."

"What?"

"I did." Ellie clears her throat and blows out a big breath and then looks back at her. "I needed a beer. And I needed a friend."

Maeve opens her mouth, because she really wants to know if the friend she needed was Maddie or herself. She can't say it though, so she simply shakes her head and reaches into the refrigerator to grab Ellie a Coke.

The sun is bright, and true to late July in Illinois, the air is so thick and heavy, it feels as if they need diving masks and oxygen tanks to breathe. Maeve throws two rafts in, jumps into the water and gracefully climbs up to sit on one of them. She watches with amusement as Ellie dives head first into the deep end. She has to keep Ellie around to keep her close to Jay.

"God, this is great." Ellie sighs as she climbs up on the other raft. "I haven't done this since I was sixteen."

"What did you do when you were sixteen that ended that life?" Maeve asks her. She maneuvers so she is now lying on the raft, on her back, eyes closed. But she puts a hand up to shield the sun from her eyes and studies Ellie through slitted eyes.

Ellie, still sitting on her raft, stares silently at the water. Finally she lifts her head and looks at Maeve. "Some mistakes you just can't take back." Her whisper is thick, but her eyes are dry.

"I know all about those mistakes, Ellie," Maeve says quietly. She lives with one of those mistakes, and she suffers the consequences of that mistake every day of her life. It weighs heavily on her now; the older she gets, the more it haunts her.

She hears Ellie clear her throat. "What about Luke? You said you were thinking about him earlier. You looked upset."

Maeve laughs sarcastically and looks away from Ellie's serious eyes. "Last night when I got home, I found him banging some girl against my living room wall."

Ellie groans, but she says nothing. Maeve is glad for that, because really, what could Ellie say to that that would mean anything? He's an all-American kid? He's good looking so he should be out with girls? As long as he's using protection, there's nothing to worry about? Maeve has heard it all before from Stash, and it gets old. It doesn't matter that he's being careful, if he's being careful. He's her baby, and it bothers her that he's grown up enough to be playing with sex.

"It's not the first time," Maeve mumbles. "I grounded him, but we both know it means nothing. Stash'll let him go out when he gets back home."

"You guys don't agree on parenting?" Ellie asks her.

"Usually we do, but Stash doesn't seem bothered by the girls. He thinks as long as he's being careful, it's okay. And I guess I want to know he's being careful." Maeve splashes water up over her tan, trim stomach. "It's just a little bother-some to walk in on them. In my house."

"I'm sure it is," Ellie answers.

"They never seem to make it to the bedroom," Maeve says with a sigh. "God knows I've been there, but maybe not so much when I was his age."

"You weren't having sex when you were Luke's age?" Ellie asks curiously. Maeve glances at her again and finds that she is lying on her stomach, chin propped on her folded arms.

"I was, but I don't think it was ever so good I couldn't wait to get to a private place to do it," she answers with a chuckle.

Ellie arches an eyebrow and nods. "Good point."

"I got pregnant when I was seventeen," Maeve says quietly. The words gush out of her mouth, and they reverberate around the pool area, suddenly very loud in the stunned silence that follows. Maybe Ellie is stunned she got pregnant. She is stunned that she just told Ellie her secret.

"Peyton?" Ellie frowns.

"No." Maeve wipes at her eyes, wishing she'd have washed her face before coming out. Her eyeliner will smear with tears, and it'll smear with pool water, so it will do no good to dive in and get wet.

"What, then?" Ellie asks. Her voice is quiet, almost reverent, as if she knows Maeve is handing her heart over to her.

"I had an abortion," Maeve whispers. "No one knows but me and Maddie."

Ellie stares at her in silence for several long moments. She is dying to know what Ellie is thinking, but she will not ask. It is enough to know Ellie will not judge her; she's sure of this or her subconscious wouldn't have thrown those words out when she wasn't paying any attention.

"Stash doesn't know?" Ellie finally asks. It's not what Maeve expected her to say. Not really what Maeve wanted her to say, but it could have been worse, she guesses.

"No."

"Why tell me?" Ellie asks her.

Maeve flips off the raft and goes under. Maybe she shouldn't have said it. Maybe she is wrong about Ellie. When she surfaces and pushes her hair back off her face, Ellie is watching her.

"I don't know," Maeve finally answers. "I guess maybe I want you to know that we all make mistakes. And a lot of us make the kinds of mistakes you can't take back."

Ellie nods. "I made that kind of mistake with Jay the other night," she says quietly. "We were good friends. That should have been enough."

"Sometimes it is enough," Maeve agrees. "But why should it have been enough for you?"

"It's more than I thought I'd have." Ellie shrugs. "Jay deserves better than me."

"Jay doesn't think there is anyone better than you," Maeve tells her.

"Maeve," Ellie whispers. "You know what I mean. I can't give him anything. I have nothing."

"You love him," Maeve says simply.

Ellie shrugs and raises her eyebrows. "Doesn't mean I can make him happy."

"You do make him happy, Ellie," Maeve answers. "And you know that. He deserves a chance to love you. He deserves to know all of you and to love all of you."

Ellie takes a deep breath and looks away. Maeve takes this as her cue that this conversation is over. "So. What'd you do last night? I missed you on the drive to the airport."

"Maddie came by," Ellie tells her. "We went to that barbeque place by Dairy Queen."

"Maddie." Maeve narrows her eyes at Ellie, wondering who else she knows by the name Maddie. "Maddie? My sister Maddie?"

"Yeah."

"Wow." Maeve nods. "Didn't realize you guys were close."

"We're not close," Ellie says and sounds put out by Maeve's jealousy. "First time I've ever really talked to her, outside of the family get-togethers."

Maeve climbs out of the pool and reaches for her towel. Ellie is lying on her back with her eyes closed when she sits down on the end of a lounge chair and takes a sip of her wine.

"Is it because of the abortion?" Ellie asks. She doesn't move a muscle. Her eyes are closed; she is soaking up the sun as if she's done this every day of her life.

"What?"

"Is that why you hate Maddie? Does it have something to do with the abortion?"

Maeve stares into the glass of white wine. She's not sure why she brought this up, because thinking about that day always makes her heart beat so hard she thinks she's going to have a heart attack. Thoughts of that day will hover over her now for a day or two, and she'll swear there's something inside her, scraping away every bit of her insides and her dreams and the flesh and blood that makes her who she is. She's up enough on psychology to know that this is her biggest inner conflict, and that heart in her throat, can't breathe feeling is her anxiety and shame over what she did. Someday she supposes she's going to have to work through those feelings.

She doesn't look at Ellie, but she knows she hasn't moved. She feels her eyes on her now though, and she feels like maybe she shouldn't have told Ellie because maybe now Ellie will only see her as a woman who killed her own child instead of a friend.

Eyes wet, throat aching with the loss of her child and her sister, she simply shrugs. "Sort of." She manages to breathe the words out over the loss in her throat. They are spoken so softly she wonders if Ellie will hear them.

~

THE ONLY TEST SHE'S EVER FAILED IN HER LIFE IS THE LIE detector test Detective Farrell had suggested she take to clear herself. Twice she'd taken it, and twice she'd failed it. Farrell had been pleased; she could see it in the wicked gleam in his eyes. He'd wanted to send her up the river. From the start he'd pinned his suspicions on her, and he'd been like a damned pit bull, with her ankle between his teeth, trying to drag her down into the guilt. She hates him as much as she hates the people she used to call friends.

She has a super-size headache and a nice tan line in the shape of a deep V on her back from her afternoon in the pool. The headache, she thinks, may be more from Maddie and Maeve and Luther in her head vying for attention than from the sun. She's in too deep with them not to care. But she's not naïve enough to think she can be a bridge between Jay's sisters.

He shows up after seven. She is surprised, really, that it took him this long. Then again if he knows what Maddie knows, she's surprised he bothered to come back. She closes her book, *Daughters of God*, which is actually a bit disappointing and climbs off the couch to answer the door. All day she's reminded herself that she's not good enough for him, at least not in the new boundaries of their relationship. They might have made it as friends, but she can't let him waste his time with her looking for any kind of love relationship.

When she sees him, though, when their eyes meet, she remembers. She remembers the way his lips had brushed over her skin, almost reverently. The way his hands had touched her, possessively, the way she felt safe in his arms. She remembers that he'd said he loved her.

"Hi," he says quietly.

"Hi." She doesn't trust her voice. He can't know how she's

trembling inside, wishing he would touch her. Slide his arms around her and draw her against him and say those words again.

"Came to look at your car," he tells her.

"What?" She almost sniffles so she coughs to hide it. She tucks her hair behind her ear with an unsteady hand.

"We came to look at your car," he repeats. "Oliver's the brains behind the operation, but I do the manual labor."

"Oh my God," she whispers. She'd been so busy absorbing the details of Jay's face, the way the skin around his eyes crinkles when he smiles, that she hadn't even noticed his son standing beside him. Testament to who she was, who she still is. "Oh my God."

She lets her eyes slide slowly down, until she sees a riot of unruly brown curls and big blue eyes behind big round glasses. A smattering of freckles dust a tiny, pert nose, and a dimple sits close to a killer smile. He's perfect. Oliver Bryant is perfect, and she's in love, and she's in pain, and she desperately wants to pull him close to her and smell the little boy smell that she sometimes misses so desperately that she sits in Luther's closet just to try and find it again.

"You must be Oliver." Her voice is a little bit rough and a little bit soft, and her eyes are wet with tears. She blinks them away and squats down in front of Jay's son. One more day. Just one more day with her son. One more day of picking up Legos and Hot Wheels from the floor. One more day of Peter Pan pajamas and Superman underwear. She'd give the rest of her life for one more day.

"Yeah, I'm Oliver." He grins at her, and she sees Jay in his smile and his eyes. Dammit, but she's sunk now. She longs to reach out to him and touch him, trace the line of his nose or feel the silky touch of his hair against her fingertips. Instead of touching him, because she will taint him, and she would sooner die than mark Jay's son, she curls her hands into fists and rests them in her lap.

"Hi, Oliver," she whispers. She tries to laugh, and maybe to the boy, it sounds like a laugh. But she knows Jay has to know she's about to fall apart. "I'm Ellie."

"My dad told me about you," he says, still with that contagious grin on his face. "He likes you."

She ducks her head and bites her lips to keep the sob inside.

"What do you say we go check out Ellie's car, Ol?" Jay asks. "I bet we can fix it."

"Sure, Daddy."

Jay's fingers trail lightly over her shoulder as he and Oliver step inside and head through her house. She stands and steps out onto the porch. It's too early for stars, but there is not enough air to breathe inside. Luther's presence is so heavy on her shoulders, she simply sinks to the porch and covers her face with her hands.

Some days it's the life he'd lived that hurts her. Some days it's that she misses fixing peanut butter and apple jelly sandwiches and trimming the crust off and cutting them in perfect triangles. Some days it's that she misses reading to him. Some days it's that she misses his arms around her and the way he'd pucker his lips up for a kiss. Some days it's that she hates that people could think she would harm him.

Today it is everything.

CHAPTER 17

RYLAN HAD COMPLAINED FROM THE MOMENT SHE'D FOUND out she was pregnant about losing her perfect figure, stretch marks, and backaches. She'd been beautiful while she carried Oliver, but she'd never been happy about it. She'd tried to nurse Oliver, but Jay thinks she did it to be fashionable. She had never been abusive toward him, but she'd never gone out of her way to be overly maternal either.

Jay wonders what sort of mother Ellie had been. He figures she probably hadn't been too happy to find out at sixteen that she was pregnant. But he wonders if she'd cared for her son more than Rylan had cared for theirs. Ellie'd loved Luther; he'd seen that within the first five seconds when she'd seen his son. It had taken every ounce of self-control she had to keep her hands to herself. She'd wanted to touch Oliver; he'd seen it in her eyes. Maybe she wanted to give him five and remember the way Luther's small hands had felt against hers. Or maybe she'd wanted to hug him and remember what it was like at night when she tucked Luther in. It bothers him that she'd held herself back. He wants to share his son with her. He wants to make a life with her, and she's fighting him so hard every step of the way. They need to sit down and talk, and he needs to know what she thinks she's done to deserve this desolate life she's created for herself. He needs to know why she stole her dad's beat-up Tercel and why she doesn't look back and why Luther no longer lives with her. It doesn't matter to him. Losing Luther to his father or giving her son up for adoption, whatever choice she had to make, only matters in as much as it hurts her. But he needs to hear it, because she needs to say it so she can move on.

Right now is not the time; he knows this. They can't sit down tonight and talk, because Oliver is here. But they need to talk soon because he hates every minute of his life without her in his arms.

The Tercel needs a starter, so it will be an easy fix. He tells Oliver this as they leave the garage and head back to her house. Tomorrow he will go to Western Auto and get a starter and fix her car. Oliver fits his small hand inside his as they enter Ellie's kitchen. The front door is open, but she is not there.

Jay wonders if she went for a walk. He calls for her, and still holding Oliver's hand, makes a pass through the rooms situated in the small square that boxes her inside this sad life. He finds her in what he had thought to be a spare bedroom, what he now assumes was Luther's room. She is stretched out across a twin bed; dried tear tracks mark her face. There is something shiny and smooth and colorful under her cheek.

"You okay?" he asks quietly as he perches on the edge of the bed.

"I read this to him," she whispers. "Every night."

He sees that it is a book under her cheek. She lifts her head and pulls the book out from under her face and hands it to him. *I Promise I'll Find You* is the title of the book. Jay flips through it. The illustrations catch Oliver's eye, but Jay skims over the words. A mom promising to find her son or daughter, no matter where he or she might disappear to.

"I lied, Jay." She turns her deep rum colored eyes to his and licks her lips. "I lied to him. I can't find him."

～

WHEN MADDIE WAS THIRTEEN, SHE PLAYED "FÜR ELISE" FOR A piano recital. She still loves the song. She loves the classics, and honestly she loves some of the old gospel hymns as well as the new Christian rock music. But she loves the other stuff too. She means no disrespect to God; in fact, she thinks it's just another way to praise Him. If someone has a talent, shouldn't he or she use it?

Her fingers slide over the piano keys with ease. She longs to sing, but she can't. Not here. Not now. The church doors are open, and anyone can wander in as they please. If she's playing music, odds are they will not recognize the song. If she's singing, they might recognize lyrics or at the very least ask about what she is playing.

She'd almost come undone the other night with Ellie. It scares her, the way the truth had surfaced immediately and threatened to spill from her mouth. She'd buried this secret years ago. Too many lives are at stake to let it slip now. It's not a matter of trusting Ellie or not trusting Ellie. It is simply that no one can know. It is that once a hidden truth is spoken or whispered, it has a way of inching into the light of day and taking control over everyone and everything, and she can't let that happen.

Suddenly she feels someone watching her. Assuming it is Robert, she stops abruptly and lifts her head. It is disconcerting to find that she is still seated at the grand piano in the front of St. Romuald's church. Robert, Father Robert Harte is not standing by the piano, the way she usually finds him when she's playing. In fact, he's nowhere to be seen. It is Ellie she feels watching her. The girl is sitting in a pew several rows back from the front. From the distance, she can't see the expression on her face.

"Ellie," she says softly. Her voice carries, so she knows Ellie hears her. She stands and makes her way to the pew and sits a careful distance from her. Of course she is surprised to find Ellie here, but she is careful not to let Ellie see this. She thinks it would make Ellie uncomfortable to make a big deal out of a visit.

"What were you playing?" Ellie asks, a look of concentration on her face.

"'Breathe No More,'" Maddie answers. "Evanescence."

Ellie looks shocked. "That's what I thought, but." She shakes her head.

"All music is a gift from God." Maddie shrugs. "Except maybe Marilyn Manson's noise."

Ellie chuckles. "You're good."

Maddie shrugs and smiles. "Stress relief."

The thick silence of the church settles around them. Maddie has always loved the hush inside a church. It is so pervasive, it's a noise all its own. She studies Ellie's face and notices the way Ellie cannot look her in the eye.

"I met Oliver last night," Ellie finally says. Her words are small and quiet, but they are powerful.

"Can't help but fall in love with Oliver," Maddie says with a smile. She loves Jay's son. No matter that she and Jay have never been close, and that maybe Oliver will not grow up knowing much about her, she loves him.

Ellie nods but says nothing. Maddie watches her rub the palm of her hand over her shorts. Finally she glances at Maddie. "What's it like to be Catholic?"

Maddie stares at her for a long time, wondering how to

answer her. She recognizes this question as Ellie reaching for something solid to hold onto. What she says here could make the difference in how things end up for her brother. "It's a place to belong," she answers simply. "It's sanctuary."

"It's a crutch," Ellie mumbles.

"It's what you make it," Maddie concedes.

"Do you think I did it?" Ellie asks. She leans forward and grips the pew she is sitting on. Her knuckles are white as she holds on, waiting, Maddie supposes, to be condemned yet again. "Do you think I killed Luther?"

"No, I don't," Maddie answers sincerely. "But Ellie?" Ellie raises her eyebrows but says nothing. "You feel guilty of something. You wear it like a shield. Like armor."

Ellie simply nods.

"You can be safe from that here."

HIS TRUCK IS IN FRONT OF HER HOUSE WHEN SHE COASTS DOWN the sidewalk and stops the bike to hop off. She wonders what he's doing here. Her front door is closed; she's never given him a key. She wheels her bike around the side of the house and wonders as she passes the window to the room that used to be Luther's if Oliver is with him. She imagines a cartoon version of herself split right down the middle; half of her wants to see Jay's little boy again and half of her hopes she never has to see him again.

Jay is coming out of the garage as she reaches the back-yard. He smiles when he sees her, and she feels it curl around her heart and warm her from the inside out. She stands and waits for him, watches him walk toward her. He wears the usual denim shorts, but he sports an old T-shirt with the sleeves cut out. His forearms are wiry and sinewy; his biceps are well defined and hard. She looks away when she realizes she is admiring the golden tan of his skin and the way the sun lights his blonde hair. That perfect body had moved with hers several nights ago and brought her pleasure she'd never really experienced before. She wants to experience all of it again, and the fact that she wants him makes her angry.

"Hi," he says around his smile when he catches up with her.

"What're you doing here?" she asks, because she doesn't want to get caught up in his smile. She unlocks her back door and walks her bike inside. Jay follows her.

"Fixed your car," he answers.

"What?"

"Yeah, I know you doubt me because I don't have the brains with me today." He grins. "But I took care of it. Starter was bad."

"You put a new starter on it?" she asks with a frown.

"Yeah." He shrugs. "Pretty simple."

"Jay, I don't have the money for that right now—"

"Don't worry about it," he says quietly.

"I'm not gonna let you pay for this—"

"Then pay me back," he answers. "Whenever."

She stares at him, angry that he'd done the repair without telling her. Angry that she still wants him. Angry that he'd broken her defenses and she'd made love to him and thrown the best friendship she's ever had out the window. She sighs and looks away. "Where is Oliver?"

"He's with my mom," Jay answers with a small smile. "Probably gonna end up pulling the 'can I spend the night?' thing."

Ellie swallows hard. If Oliver spends the night at Jolene's, Jay is free from now until tomorrow. She doesn't want to be alone with him. Not anymore.

"Where were you?" he asks as he leans against her

counter. He'd left his tool kit by the door. Her eyes are drawn to his arms, folded across his chest.

"I went to see Maddie," she answers absently.

"My sister Maddie?"

"Yeah." She nods and lifts her gaze to meet his.

"Why?"

She frowns at him and finally shrugs. "Why not?" She is leaning on the refrigerator, but she pushes herself away and walks past him to the living room. When she turns to see if he's following her, he runs into her. She sucks in a deep breath when their bodies touch, but he doesn't step away. Instead he slides his arms around her waist.

"Ellie," he whispers.

"Don't." She shakes her head, but when he lowers his head toward hers, she closes her eyes and waits for his kiss. It is a cautious kiss; he rubs his lips over hers and then turns his head a bit and presses them to the corner of her mouth.

"Can I talk to you?" he asks. "Can we just sit down and talk?"

"It doesn't matter." She shakes her head. "It doesn't change anything."

"What's to change, Ellie? We made love the other night." He dips his head lower and touches his lips to her neck. "I know I shouldn't have left you that way. I know I hurt you at the airport when I told you about Oliver."

"You were right to keep him from me," she says quietly.

"Why?" He lifts his head to look her in the eye. "Why was I right to keep him from you? Ellie, I want you to love him. I want you to love me. I want—"

She shoves him back with a hand flat against his chest. "I can't give you what you want."

"What about the other night?"

"We had sex, Jay. People do it all the time." She turns her

back to him and ducks her head. No amount of pressure she squeezes into her neck touches her headache.

"I made love with you, Ellie," he corrects her. "You were there. You know the difference."

"It doesn't matter," she snaps and turns back to look at him. "It doesn't matter what you call it, Jay. It can't happen again."

"Why can't it happen again?" His words are loud and tinged with anger. "Because you enjoyed it? You don't let yourself enjoy much in life. Is that the problem? Making love with me cramped the self-punishment you live?"

Stunned by his anger, she stares at him in silence. She backs away from him and gives him a small nod. "Yeah, that's exactly it, Jay," she finally says calmly. "That's it."

"Don't do this." He steps backwards and leans on the wall.

"Why can't we just go back to the way it was?" Ellie lowers herself to the couch.

"Because I love you," he answers as he pushes himself away from the wall. She looks up at him when he stands in front of her. "And I can't pretend that I don't." He squats down in front of her and rests his hands on her bare knees. "Ellie, I saw more love for my son on your face last night than I ever did with Rylan."

"Maybe I was thinking of Luther." She licks her lips and shrugs and tries to tear her eyes from his.

"I know you were." He nods. "How could you not think of your son? But that doesn't mean you didn't feel something for Oliver."

"Jay." She cups his chin in her hand. "He's beautiful. Your son is beautiful. I'd have to be blind not to see that." Jay takes her hand in his and kisses it. "He even told you how to fix my car," she says with a tiny smile. "But you're both better off without me."

"Can you let me decide that?" he asks her. "I've protected

my son from everything. I've never told any woman I've dated that I even have a son. I wanted to tell you. I've been thinking about how to tell you. I never wanted Oliver involved in this part of my life. Not until I knew for sure. I trust you, Ellie. I trust you not to break my son's heart."

"There's something you need to know, Jay," she says quietly.

"Wait." He touches his finger to her lips. "When I left that morning, I didn't want to go. I didn't want to leave you." He brushes her hair back and leans forward to kiss her cheek. "I wanted to wake up and watch you sleep in my arms. I wanted to make love to you again, in the morning. In daylight, where I could see you. Watch your eyes as I touched you. I didn't want to leave you."

She nods. "I believe you." She rests her forehead against his chin. "But it still doesn't matter."

"Rylan called," he goes on, as if she hasn't spoken. "She was going to put Oliver in a day camp. Like a boarding school thing while she went to Jamaica with her latest boyfriend. I had to leave to get everything together to go after him."

She smacks her lips together and nods again. "I understand, Jay," she tells him. "I wish you would have left me a note, but I understand that your son comes first."

"I meant to get back to you before you had to leave for work."

"How old is he?" She wipes at her eyes.

"Three."

"He has your eyes," she says as she traces his lips with her fingertip. "Your smile." She smiles, though her eyes are still wet with tears she hasn't cried. "Even has your dimple."

He brushes her hand aside and then touches his lips to hers again. Ellie slides her hands up his chest as he nibbles on her lower lip. But she pushes gently until he backs off.

"Jay." She presses her lips together and shakes her head. "What happened was a mistake. I can't let it happen again."

He sighs and leans forward a bit to drop his knees to the floor. "Why is it a mistake? What's wrong with two adults who love each other being together?"

"I never said I love you."

He looks away and leans back against her coffee table. "Dammit," he groans. "I know how you feel about me, Ellie."

"No," she corrects him. "You don't." She stands up and wanders a few steps away from him. "You don't really know anything about me."

"Not for lack of trying," he mumbles.

She takes a deep breath and turns to look at him. She's never hated herself as much as she does right at this moment, but she has to shove him back to protect him and more importantly, Oliver. "Jay, five years ago I was arrested for killing Luther."

CHAPTER 18

SHE DOESN'T LOVE HIM. SHE'S NEVER LOVED ANYONE AFTER the first time she fell. But she supposes in some strange, detached way, she cares about him. Detached. That's it in a nutshell. Since she'd turned nineteen, she's been separate from everyone. She blames herself for the way she sometimes feels isolated, but then again, this is mostly how she likes it.

He'd left her bed before five this morning. He'd slid in beside her only a couple of hours before that. Sometimes she wonders what it would be like to have him for a night, to have any man in her bed for a night. To sleep in his arms, not just offer him her body for the taking. And then again, she's lived this way for so long, she's not sure she could have it any other way.

She wonders what Maeve would think if she knew the truth. Well, not that truth, but the truth about what kind of life she leads now. How devoted she is to her calling. With that thought, she climbs out of bed, glances at her alarm clock and heads to the shower. It is just before seven. She has just enough time for a shower and a quick cup of coffee before she heads over to mass.

She thinks about Ellie often, so it's no surprise to her that she's thinking about her while she's in the shower. In the beginning when Jay had first brought her around, and she'd kind of heard faint warning bells go off and finally made the connection from Ellie Jordan to Elaina Nicole Jordan, she'd sort of wondered about this girl who had been arrested for the murder of her own son. She hadn't looked like a murderer, sitting there in Maeve's kitchen. But then again, most people don't. And no one had ever accused Ellie of premeditated murder. Maybe she'd had a bad day and snapped and hit him and killed him. Sort of like the Wittmer case. Except that the police claimed there had been previous abuse, and Alec Wittmer was a drunk. Wealthy drunk with a four-car garage and an MD after his name, but a drunk just the same.

Maddie had gone back to the archives at the library and dug out the old reports about Elaina Nicole Jordan to refresh her memory. She'd even seen Ellie there a couple times, but Ellie hadn't seen her, and Maddie hadn't gone out of her way to be noticed. Words printed in black on white can be very damning. Maddie's thankful that she had the opportunity to meet Ellie and that she's now getting to know her. She likes her. And though she is in the business of forgiveness, she doesn't believe for a minute that Ellie killed Luther Jordan. Ellie has some serious guilt that she chews like bubble gum, but Maddie would stake her life on her innocence.

Jay had been wrapped up in his life with Rylan. In the way his life with Rylan was unraveling when Ellie had been arrested. It's no wonder he doesn't remember it. Maeve was working in the prosecutor's office, but she had been a little lower on the assistant district attorney totem pole at the time. Not to mention that the case hadn't ever gone to trial.

Maddie thinks if she were to drop the name Elaina Nicole anywhere around Maeve, she'd remember it all in a heartbeat. She won't do it though. It is Ellie's business to tell Jay and Maeve, if she wants them to know. It is Maddie's business now to wait for Ellie, to see if she will come back to her for spiritual guidance, for lack of a better term. The sooner Ellie can work through the guilt she insists on dragging around with her, the sooner she will be free to give herself to Jay and Oliver.

∽

"I GOT PREGNANT," ELLIE SAYS SOFTLY. SHE IS STARING AT Maeve's TV, but she's not paying much attention to the movie. Once upon a time, she'd liked movies with the Brat Pack, but after all that she's done *The Breakfast Club* doesn't have all that much appeal. She feels Maeve's eyes on her, but she is reluctant to meet her friend's gaze. She has just opened the proverbial can of worms, and she almost shivers because she can feel them oozing and slithering over her skin.

A loud crash of thunder draws her eyes to the window. She loves rain. A flash of lightening gives Maeve's late afternoon darkened house a surreal shimmer. She turns on the couch, curls her bare feet up under her and watches the rain. "Where were you last year? The day of the tornadoes?"

"Here," Maeve finally answers. "I'd just finished mowing. Stash was trimming. We waited it out in the basement. The kids were with friends, but they both called to let us know they were okay."

"The worrying never stops, does it?" Ellie whispers.

"When did you get pregnant?" Maeve asks her.

Ellie looks up when she sees movement out of the corner of her eye. Maeve moves from the loveseat to sit at the opposite end of the couch. She turns and mimics Ellie, legs drawn up under her and eyes on the storm outside the window. Ellie takes a deep breath. Behind her Molly Ringwald is demonstrating her amazing talent of applying lipstick while she wedges the tube deep in her cleavage. Ellie shakes her head, because she finds herself thinking ten years ago, she could've done that too. Ten years ago, she was that ignorant.

Ten years ago she was worse.

She sees Maeve reach for the remote, but she reaches for her hand and shakes her head. "Don't. Please. I need the background noise."

"Okay," Maeve nods.

"You asked me the other day," Ellie says and glances at Maeve, "what I had done when I was sixteen to end that life. I got pregnant." She waits for Maeve to shrug and point out that it happens to the best of them. She expects Maeve to frown and tell her that getting pregnant at that age is not the end of the world, not anymore.

"And what happened?" Maeve tilts her head a bit and waits for her to go on. Unnerved by her gentle voice, Ellie lowers her head and closes her eyes.

"I didn't want him," she admits. "I didn't wanna be pregnant."

"Not many sixteen-year-olds do." Maeve nods.

"I didn't work," Ellie says so softly that she wonders if Maeve can even hear her. "Didn't have money for an abortion. So I took it out on him."

"On the baby? Or the father?"

Ellie barks a bitter, empty laugh and looks up boldly. "I didn't know who the father was."

"Were you raped?"

Ellie doesn't know whether to roll her eyes at Maeve's apparent naiveté or hug her for trying to believe the best about her. "No."

Maeve nods silently, watching and waiting for her to go on.

"I found out I was pregnant not long before Blair was killed." Ellie raises her eyebrows and blows out a deep breath. Her voice shakes, but she keeps a tenuous hold on her emotions. "I hated. Life. I hated my life. I hated the guy who'd hit Blair and killed her. I hated Blair for leaving me. Alone with this kid I didn't want." Ellie still feels the worms crawling all over her skin, and now she feels warm, sticky tears slide over her face. She has not ventured down this road in so long, she's forgotten how much it hurts. "I hated myself. I hated the baby I was carrying."

Maeve nods. "I've been there, Ellie," she whispers.

"I hated the name Luther," Ellie continues. "I wanted a boy, so I could name him Luther and just hate him. Forever. So I could blame him for how screwed up my life was."

Maeve wipes at her eyes but waits quietly for Ellie to go on. Ellie watches the storm again and catches bits and pieces of the movie.

"When did that change?" Maeve finally asks her.

Ellie turns her head a bit and looks at Maeve from the corner of her eye. "The second he was born." Her whispered words are punctuated by a loud boom of thunder. She wishes she were at home, because this storm is getting more vicious by the minute, and she wonders what her neighbor's tree is doing. She wonders if it is bowed over to sweep the ground or if this will be the storm that finally breaks it.

ICE CREAM IS ALWAYS BETTER WHEN SHARED. JAY KNOWS THIS. His son knows this. He watches Oliver offer Ellie a bite of his dripping vanilla cone and prays that Ellie will not turn him down. It is huge in his heart that Oliver wants to share with Ellie, and he hopes Ellie will see it this way too.

"It's dis beanilla," Oliver tells her with a shrug. "You wanna taste?"

Ellie, who is holding her own sundae, a baseball helmet sundae, looks down at Oliver, and a huge, sloppy grin lights up her face. Jay's chest swells in relief. She is pushing him away like a defensive tackle on the line of scrimmage in a football game, but he sees it in the smallest things she does; she loves him. No woman who can look at his son with those big moony eyes and a grin that says 'I wanna kiss your freckles off your nose' can be guilty of murder. Whatever happened to Luther, and he still doesn't know any details—damn Ellie for being so damned stubborn—he knows in his head and his heart that she didn't hurt him.

"I'd love a taste," she tells Oliver. Jay watches her sit down on the picnic table, the one where they'd sat together that first time to eat ice cream. Oliver climbs up beside her, practically in her lap, ice cream dripping over her bare legs and lifts his cone to her mouth. She slides her tongue out to touch the ice cream and raises her eyebrows in appreciation. "I love it."

Oliver smiles at her, a soft, precious smile that stomps the hell out of Jay's heart. *Dammit, Ellie, how can you not see how much we love you?* She nods toward the Royals baseball helmet in her hands. "You wanna try mine?"

Oliver eyes the sundae with a mix of excitement and trepidation. "What kind is it?"

"It's vanilla ice cream with butterscotch on it," she tells him. She glances up when Jay sits down on the other side of Oliver.

"What's butterscotch?" Oliver asks with a frown.

"What's butterscotch?" she asks and leans back to study

Oliver with narrowed eyes. "You've never tasted butter-scotch? It's the best."

"For real?" Oliver asks. She laughs softly and glances at Jay again.

"Yes, for real," she answers. She dips her spoon into her sundae and then holds it out for Oliver to taste. He stares at her thoughtfully as he savors it and then swallows it. "Well?"

"Tastes kinda buttery." He nods and shrugs.

She laughs and looks at Jay again. The laughter fades away, and there is nothing left between them but a small smile and a small boy.

"When are we gonna start working on that book?" Jay asks her. He takes a long pull from his chocolate milkshake.

She's confused by his question; he can tell from the way she's frowning at him as if he's speaking Russian. "I'm not gonna write that book with you," she finally answers. "I can't."

"Well." He shrugs and nods and looks away. "Then I guess I'm not writing a book."

"What? Why not?" She shakes her head. "Jay, you don't need my help on that—"

"I don't need your help," he says quietly. "But I need you."

She swallows hard and stares at the ice cream in the cup. It is melting fast.

"Can you keep that?" Oliver points at the cup.

"Yeah," she answers and offers him that soft, genuine smile. "I used to get them all the time." She still smiles, but Jay sees the sadness in her eyes that Oliver is too young to notice. "I would get them for this other little boy."

"Who?" Oliver asks eagerly, the prospect of a playmate enticing.

"His name was Luther," she answers.

"Is he your little boy?"

"He was," she says and clears her throat. "But he doesn't live with me anymore."

Oliver considers this for a moment as Ellie picks up a napkin and tries to wipe away the melting ice cream from his little hands.

"You want this helmet when I'm done with my ice cream?" she asks him as if this thought has just occurred to her.

"Could I really?" His eyes are huge with excitement and disbelief.

"Of course you can," she answers. She glances over Oliver's head and sees him looking at her. He stares at her boldly, daring her to look away. She holds his gaze for a long time, as if she knows he's issued a challenge. But finally, she lowers her eyes and looks at his lips and finally looks away. As long as she says it like this, he can hang on and wait forever to hear her say the words.

WHEN YOU TAKE A PICTURE THROUGH GLASS, REFLECTIONS always taint the subject you're trying to freeze. Doesn't matter how good you think the shot is going to be; when you get your film developed, it is always a disappointment to see those shots. You never end up with what you think you've captured. Ellie knows this; her mother had taken countless snapshots of her and her brother and sister when they were younger, standing in front of the glass wall at the gorilla habitat at the zoo and pictures of the dolphins swimming under water at the aquariums in Chicago and Orlando and pictures of the mountains or the sunset, shot through the windshield of the car. It's always a letdown, comparing those pictures to what you remember of real life.

She wonders what sort of glass Jay is looking through to

see her, to think that he can capture her and not be disappointed when he compares her to the ideal woman in his mind. She will come up short to any comparison, and he will be disappointed. It's as simple as that. It's hard for her to push him away, because she enjoys every moment she spends with him, and right now, she's head over heels with Oliver, and she's desperate to see him as much as she can. Which isn't fair to Oliver.

Maddie is playing something that sounds churchy today, but Ellie still enjoys listening. She knows Maddie senses her presence; she can see it in the way Maddie'd tensed up as she had slid silently into the pew several rows back from the front. Ellie figures it is bad enough that she could slink inside a church after all these years and all these things that she's done, but she thinks somehow that sitting in the front pew would be like thumbing her nose at God. She would have done it gladly back in her old life. But since God or someone had taken revenge on her, she is a different person, and she avoids confrontation.

When the piano music stops and the heavy hush fills the air, Ellie looks up to find Maddie slowly walking toward her.

"Hey." Maddie offers her a small smile.

"Didn't mean to bother you," Ellie says quietly.

"You're not bothering me." Maddie leans a hip against the dark walnut pew and folds her arms over her chest. "I wondered if you would come back."

Ellie sighs and looks away. "I don't know what to do with myself anymore."

"What do you mean?" Maddie cocks her head sideways and frowns.

"He's become my life," Ellie admits in a whisper. "I feel the most complete when I'm with him. When I'm at work, I'm thinking about him. I'm researching the Catholic Church and the history of the Catholic religion in Quincy. I'm looking up stuff about ancient Egypt. I'm thinking about sharing ice cream with Oliver." Ellie stops and looks up at Maddie. Half of her wishes she could hit rewind and take back everything she just said. She's just admitted to Jay's sister that she's in love with him. The other half of her wants to keep talking.

"What's wrong with that?" Maddie asks with a shrug.

"When I'm not with him and I'm not at work, I'm looking for you. Or hanging out with Maeve. This isn't me, Maddie." Ellie stands up. "He made me remember there's a huge hole inside me, and he makes me want to fill it."

"Maybe this is you," Maddie corrects her. "Maybe you've been lying to yourself."

"Believing that this can work is lying to myself," Ellie tells her. She swallows hard and looks away from Maddie's sharp green eyes.

"C'mon." Maddie touches Ellie's arm. Ellie follows her out the side door of the church and across a small patch of dried, burnt grass. Maddie slows to study a garden and then turns to look back at Ellie. "What's your favorite flower?"

Ellie raises her eyebrows and shrugs and grins a bit sheepishly. "I don't know. I guess I never really thought about it."

"These are daisies," Maddie says as she fingers a bright red flower. "I love daisies."

"Is this your garden?" Ellie asks her as she looks around. They are behind a small house with yellow siding and neat white trim.

"Yeah." Maddie nods. "This is my house."

"I didn't—"

"You didn't know nuns could garden? Or you didn't know we could live in houses?" Maddie arches one eyebrow up and grins at Ellie.

"Maybe both." Ellie laughs softly. "I just. I don't—why would a woman like you dedicate your life to God?"

"Define a woman like me," Maddie says before Ellie can regret the offensive question.

"You're beautiful, Maddie." Ellie shrugs. "You have to know that."

"So what you're really asking is why did I give up sex?"

"You don't mince words, do you?" Ellie grins.

"I don't," Maddie answers with a shake of her head. "I don't see the point." She reaches for Ellie and takes her hand and leads her to the back door. When she unlocks it, Ellie follows her inside a small but bright and cheerful kitchen. "Tea?"

"Thanks." Ellie nods.

"I fell in love when I was nineteen," Maddie tells her as she busies herself getting out glasses and ice. "I'd had a few boyfriends in school, but I'd never been serious about anyone. It wasn't that I wanted a celibate life. Not at that age. I just never felt strongly enough about any boys to get that involved."

She sets a glass on the table by Ellie and then sits down across from her. Ellie lowers herself into the chair as Maddie takes a sip of her tea. "That all changed when I was nineteen. I fell head over heels for this guy."

"So where is he now?" Ellie asks quietly. Her heart is sort of tapping a bit harder, as if it is a hammer gently tapping away at a thumbtack. Maddie is talking to her. She's getting in deeper and deeper with Jay's sisters, and the thought kind of makes her stomach jumpy, the way it sometimes used to feel when she'd get caught up in a catfight with her girl-friends back in school. The monkey in the middle is not particularly a good place to be. Ellie wishes she could put the brakes on here and walk away.

Maddie simply shakes her head. "He was off limits," she answers evasively. "Maybe that's why I fell so hard. Maybe that added to the excitement."

"But what happened?" Ellie pushes.

"I got pregnant and left town. Mom sent me away to this home for wayward girls. I carried the baby and delivered her out of town, signed the adoption papers and found myself so lost, I didn't know what to do."

Ellie nods. This is a feeling she is familiar with. Lost. Empty. She knows exactly what that big, empty hole inside Maddie had felt like. The one that threatens to yawn and devour her and make her live in the dark forever. She didn't officially dedicate her life to God, but she sure as hell alienated herself from anyone who might have cared. "So you turned to the church." Ellie's voice is a bit hoarse with emotion.

"It was a good place to hide," Maddie says softly. "To forget."

"Do you regret it?"

"Joining the church?" Maddie clarifies. "No," she says when Ellie nods. "I told you the other night, I'm content."

Ellie wonders about the baby Maddie gave away. She wonders if that kind of loss hurts the same way the sudden, unexpected loss of Luther hurts her. She wonders how Maeve and Maddie, who both experienced the loss of a child, can waste their years hating each other.

"She doesn't know," Maddie finally mumbles.

Ellie doesn't pretend that she's not following her. Instead she sighs and shakes her head and says softly, "She should know."

"And Jay should know that you're in love with him," Maddie answers quietly.

CHAPTER 19

Luther loved ketchup. She had often teased him, asking if he wanted a little hotdog with his ketchup or if he wanted ketchup on his ice cream. He would always screw his little face up into a frown and shake his head at her as if she was crazy. Oliver does not like ketchup. He'd asked her to get him a hotdog, while all the adults were busy either playing volleyball in the pool or manning the grill. Ellie had felt a surge of powerful, protective love when she'd felt his cold, wet little hands touch her neck, and she'd left the pool volleyball game without a second thought to get him what he'd asked her for. Thank heavens he'd caught her just before she'd squeezed ketchup on his hotdog.

"Do you want anything on it?" she asks him. She is holding his Zoo Pals paper plate in her hand, water dripping from her wet suit. She feels Jay's eyes on her as she waits for Oliver to answer her. Oliver nods. "Mustard?"

"Don't like mustard," Oliver says as he shakes his head.

"You don't like mustard or ketchup?" Ellie asks in disbelief. "What do you want on this hotdog, Oliver Bryant?"

Oliver giggles and points to the jar of relish on the picnic table next to Stash's beer bottle.

"You want relish on your hotdog?" she asks doubtfully.

Stash, who is watching over the pork chops on the grill, chuckles and nods at Ellie. "He loves pickled relish," he tells her. Ellie shakes her head and imagines trying to get Luther to eat pickled relish on his hotdog.

"Ol, I woulda gotcha a hotdog," Jay says as he approaches them. His trunks are dripping water all over the patio. Oliver squeals in delight when Jay picks him up and tosses him over his shoulder. "I'll do that, Ellie."

"It's fine," Ellie answers. "I got it." She knows that when she leans over, Jay has a straight shot view down the front of her suit. Oddly enough, the thought kind of warms her and she finds herself wishing he could slide the straps off her shoulders and pull the offending material out of the way so she could press her naked skin against his. "Want anything else, Oliver?" she asks when she is done spreading a small spoonful of relish over his hotdog.

"Chips," Oliver says. He is still hanging upside down behind Jay's shoulder.

"Would you put him down?" she mumbles as she puts a handful of chips on Oliver's plate.

"Man, you sound like a mom," Jay groans and pulls his son back over his shoulder and then leans over to set him on his feet. She looks up silently, her eyes meeting Jay's. For a moment she wonders what it would be like if Oliver were her son. Her son with Jay Bryant. Playing with them in the pool, reading Oliver bedtime stories and fighting over the sheets at night while she slept with Jay. Guilty, she looks back at Oliver's plate. Her stomach curls in on itself and knots in a familiar way; the food on the table makes her feel a little green. Wondering about having a baby with Jay makes her feel as if she is discounting the wonderful son she lost, as if she is sweeping Luther under the rug.

"Thank you, Ellie." Oliver beams at her when she leans over and puts the baby koala bear plate in his hand.

"You're welcome," she says softly.

"Would you sit by me?" he asks hopefully.

"Ol, Ellie might wanna go back and play again," Jay tells his son. Ellie can't help herself. She touches Oliver's wet ringlet curls that drip water down the back of his neck. He has spent the better part of the day floating in a Mickey Mouse ring while the adults play volleyball. "I'll sit with ya, buddy."

"I don't mind." She looks up at Jay.

Jay watches her sit down with Oliver. She wonders if it bothers him that Oliver has gotten so comfortable with her. In a way it bothers her. She loves this little boy already, and it's going to kill her when he has to go back to New York. She's also realized that when he and Jay are around, she's a bit ill at ease wondering if Jay thinks she's horning in on his time with his son. Like right now.

"Want some juice, Oliver?" Jay asks.

Oliver takes a big bite of his hotdog, and relish drips over the end of the bun on his hand. He looks up at Jay and grins and nods. Ellie laughs just because his grin makes her happy, and he wears his green pickled relish all over his hand just the same as Luther wore his bright red ketchup on his.

"Hey," she says and taps the ear of the koala bear plate. "What kind of animal is this?"

"Koala bear," Oliver says around a mouthful of hotdog.

"Very good," she answers with a smile.

"They live in Australia," he goes on. She raises her eyebrows.

"How old are you?" She lowers an eyebrow and studies him.

"I'm free," he says seriously.

"Are you sure? Because you're so smart, and you're so strong, there, dude, I'd think you'd at least have to be five."

Jay hears her and grins as he sets a Juicy Juice box beside Oliver's plate.

"Dad, am I free?" Oliver asks him, taking another big bite of his hotdog.

"Slow down." Jay chuckles and shakes his head. "You're gonna get a tummy ache." Ellie watches him wipe Oliver's hand clean with a napkin. "You are, indeed, three."

Oliver looks back at Ellie and giggles. "Yep, I'm free."

Ellie lifts her gaze to look at Jay over the top of Oliver's head. He's smiling, but his blue eyes probe hers for something deeper than the moment warrants. Slowly, she closes her eyes and turns her head away. He is looking for things that don't exist inside her.

"Aren't you gonna eat too, Ellie?" Oliver asks her. He holds a chip in his hand. His blue eyes watch her curiously, and with a smile, he offers her the chip.

"Ellie's gonna eat a pork chop. Like Daddy," Jay tells his son. Ellie winks at Oliver as she takes the chip from him and pops it in her mouth.

"You like porch cops?" Oliver asks with a frown.

"I do," she says with a straight face. "You like pickled relish?" She glances at Jay again. He gives her a lopsided grin and a lazy shrug.

When the pork chops are ready, Oliver stays nearly pressed up against Ellie's side as she eats. She loves the feel of his little body up against hers, but she finds herself overwhelmed with thoughts of Luther. While she picks at her pork chop and sips her Coke, she remembers an afternoon of playing in the water with him. She remembers his baby soft skin turning a lovely bronze under the summer sun, his squeals of delight as she sprayed him with the hose or tossed water balloons at him, the ornery giggle when he'd soak her with the hose.

Oliver is talking to Maeve, and Jay is talking to Stash. Maddie is not here—Ellie does not know if she was invited—and Luke and Joe are yakking at the end of the picnic table. She needs a moment, because suddenly she feels as if someone is standing over her with heavy hands on her shoulders to hold her down under the water. Memories of Luther smother her. She stands slowly, finds her towel on a lounge chair and wraps it around her waist. She glances at Maeve, who arches an eyebrow in question. Ellie shakes her head and slips inside the house.

She uses the restroom, but even when she washes her hands and finds herself with no excuse to stay inside, she can't go back out. She can't go back and sit with Oliver and not call him Luther and pull him into her arms and hold him and never let him go.

The soft tap on the closed door does not surprise her. She wonders if it is Jay or Maeve who has come to get her.

"El? You okay?"

Maeve. Ellie takes a deep breath and opens the door. She doesn't trust her voice, so she looks at Maeve, meets her eyes, and looks away quickly.

"What? What is it?" Maeve asks gently.

Ellie shakes her head. "Just needed a minute."

"Is it Jay?" Maeve tilts her head and watches Ellie closely.

"No," Ellie whispers.

"Oliver?"

Ellie turns her head, but she doesn't answer Maeve.

"What? Ellie, is he bothering you? If you don't want him hanging on you, you just—"

"Maeve." Ellie's voice is tight. "He's not bothering me."

"Then what's wrong?"

Ellie presses her lips together and raises her eyebrows.

She wants to talk. She wants to break down and cry on Maeve. She trusts that Maeve would hold her and let her cry as long as she needs to without even knowing what hurts her. Even if Ellie couldn't say a word, she thinks Maeve would patiently let her cry until she could get herself back under control.

"Luther?" Maeve finally breaks the silence. Ellie nods. "You never told me. I don't know where he is."

Ellie swallows hard and meets Maeve's gaze. "Neither do I," she whispers. She sees a shadow on the wall behind Maeve and turns her head as Jay comes up behind her.

"What's going on?" he asks, obviously concerned.

"Nothing," Maeve answers without looking at him. "Ellie just needed a breather."

Ellie doesn't look at him, but she feels his heavy stare.

"You sure you're okay?" he asks her. She nods and waits for him to leave before she looks at Maeve again.

"I would like to know," Maeve says as if they have not just been interrupted. "I would like to know what happened, and I want to help you, even if all I can do is listen."

Ellie nods and rubs her eyes. "I can't right now." Her voice melts in emotion.

"Yeah." Maeve nods. "I know. I understand." She touches Ellie's hand. "But whenever you're ready."

"Thank you." Ellie licks her lips.

"Can I just ask you something?" Maeve is uneasy, which trips Ellie's nerves. She nods, but she holds onto the counter with a white-knuckle grip. "Does Maddie know?"

Ellie can't lie to Maeve. She can't begin to tell her the truth, not tonight. But she can't lie to her.

"I didn't tell her," she says honestly.

"Ellie." Maeve raises her eyebrows and looks down at the floor.

"Don't." Ellie slides her arm around Maeve's shoulder and gives her a tight squeeze. "I love you both."

WHEN DARKNESS FALLS, ELLIE IS EXHAUSTED FROM THE LONG day in the sun and the pool play and the rush of loss she'd felt earlier. She flops on a lounge chair and retreats into herself. For comfort. For protection. Stash asks her if she wants to play cards with them, but she begs off. Truthfully, what she wants to do is go home and remember what it was like to be alone and not lonely.

Jay and Maeve are partners against Stash and Joe. Luke has just left to pick up his current girlfriend. Oliver whines to Jay that he wants to go home, and Ellie doesn't blame him. She's tired too, and what fun is a game of euchre for a three-year-old? She is just about to call to him when he remembers she is camped out on a lounge chair and turns to her with a shy smile. She gives him an answering smile and a small nod of encouragement. He grins and breaks into a run.

"Be careful!" she calls just as he catches his toe on the leg of a lounge chair and sprawls out across the cement. "Oh God!" She flies out of her chair and rushes to help him up. Big crocodile tears slide off his cheeks, but he cries very quietly. Ellie lifts him up as Jay hurries over to them. The blood from his knees smears over the shorts Ellie has changed into.

"Ol," Jay says as he reaches for his son. "You okay, buddy?"

Oliver cries louder and clutches at Ellie's neck. "I want Ellie," he says and buries his face in the crook of her neck.

"Oliver, you're getting blood on Ellie's shorts. Let Daddy look at it." Jay lays his hand on Oliver's back.

"Jay, it's okay." Ellie smoothes a hand over Oliver's back. "I'm not worried about my shorts."

"Maeve," Jay says and looks back over his shoulder. Maeve is standing behind him. "Got some peroxide?"

"No!" Oliver yelps. "No, Daddy, it's gonna burn."

"No, sweetie," Ellie says softly. "It won't burn. I promise. It won't hurt."

Ellie follows Maeve inside, with Jay close at her heels. Oliver is still crying, with his head buried in the crook of her neck. Maeve leads them to the same bathroom Ellie had sought sanctuary in earlier and takes the peroxide and Band-Aids from the medicine cabinet. Ellie sits Oliver on the edge of the sink, but he clings to her.

"Sweetie, I promise it's not gonna hurt," she whispers as she kisses his forehead.

"Want Daddy to do it, Ol?" Maeve asks gently. Oliver nods, and Maeve hands Jay the peroxide and steps out of the way.

As Jay dabs a cotton swab with peroxide over Oliver's bloody, scraped-up knees, Ellie examines the palms of his hands. Both are covered with angry red scrape marks from trying to catch himself as he fell. She kisses both and blows gently on them, and she's finally rewarded with a small, teary-eyed smile.

Before Oliver can blink, Jay has both knees bandaged. Oliver gives them a quick, sad look and then looks back at Ellie.

"What's wrong, Bud?" Jay asks.

"Mommy has SpongeBob Band-Aids," he says quietly. Ellie sees the look of surprise cross Jay's face. Maeve tousles Oliver's hair.

"I'm sorry, baby." She kisses the mass of curls on top of his head. "Peyton and Luke just don't like those kinds of Band-Aids anymore."

Ellie has to laugh at the thought of macho Luke with a SpongeBob Band-Aid.

"Daddy'll get some, okay?" Jay asks his son.

Oliver nods, but he still looks sad.

"Oliver," Ellie says as she finger-combs his hair away from his face. "I don't have SpongeBob, but I have Scooby Doo. I can get them for you later when Daddy takes me home. Would that be okay?"

She feels Jay's and Maeve's eyes on her, but she watches Oliver, relieved when he flashes her a grin and wipes at his eyes.

"Were they your little boy's?" he asks her. She lets the tears slide unchecked and answers him with a small nod. "Will he care?"

"No, sweetie." She licks her lips and laughs sadly. "I don't think he will."

"Are you ready to go home, Oliver?" Jay asks him.

"No," he answers.

"No?" Jay frowns, but he is smiling.

"I wanna sit on Ellie's lap while you play cards," Oliver tells him. Jay glances at her, and she imagines she can see the caution in his eyes. Is it because he doesn't want her close to his son? Or because he is worried that she doesn't want to be close to him?

She feels Maeve watching her as she reaches for Oliver and picks him up when he raises his arms to her.

"You have blood on your shorts," Jay reminds her.

"It's okay," she answers with a shrug.

"Ellie," Maeve says as they all file out of the bathroom and back out to the patio. "Need anything to drink? Want a brownie or anything?"

"No thanks," Ellie answers. "I'm fine."

She lowers herself into the lounge chair with ease, still holding Oliver in her arms. She knows Jay still watches her, and she still wonders what is going through his head. Oliver still whimpers just a little, but he is calmer now. He snuggles in close to her as Jay and Maeve sit down again at the picnic table.

Ellie lays her head back against the chair and closes her eyes. The laughter and chatter from the table surround her and comfort her. The little boy in her lap brings back happy memories that make her want to cry.

"Oliver," she says softly and opens her eyes.

"What?" His reply is small and sleepy.

"Want me to tell you a story?"

"Yeah." He tips his head back and gives her a big grin.

"Okay," she answers with a smile. "Look at the star up there."

"Which one?" His eyes are dry, but now they shine with excitement.

"That little one over there." She points with her finger to a bright little star next to a huge cluster of stars that look like they hang from the corner of Maeve's house.

"I see it, Ellie." He nods. "It's Neverland."

Ellie looks at him curiously. "Really? What do you know about Neverland?"

"That's where little boys go who don't know where their mommies are."

Ellie winces and bites her lip. "Oh, Oliver."

"It's okay, Ellie." Oliver touches his fingertips to Ellie's cheek. She takes his hand in hers and kisses his tear-wet fingers. "If Luther is there, Peter Pan will take care of him."

She nods, because she wishes Luther were there in Neverland, living the adventuresome, exciting life the lost boys live, with Peter Pan and Wendy taking care of him.

CHAPTER 20

"What happened to Luther?" Jay feels like he's at a blackjack table, and he's just told the dealer to hit him. He watches Ellie's face, catching each of the signs as they happen. She is shutting down now. Her warm smile slips bit by bit until her mouth is small and tight, and the sparkle in her eyes dims until they are the same haunted golden brown he remembers from the first day he sat down to talk to her over her final exam.

They are sprawled on the living room floor; somehow they have become intertwined as they lay here talking and playing games with Oliver. It has been a fun, relaxed evening, and he wants to know what the hell happened to Ellie's son, so he's gambled and asked the million-dollar question.

Oliver is asleep on the couch, thumb in his mouth, George curled in a ball at his feet. It is just after ten, and Jay knows Ellie's going to tell him it's late, and she needs to get home. He doesn't want to argue, but he wants to know what she's thinking. And he intends to find out what happened to Luther.

"Kid disappears, the parents are the first suspects," she mumbles as she sits up to pull away from him.

"I don't believe for one minute that you did anything to your son," he says and grabs her arm. She fights him as he pulls her back into his arms, but she won't fight too hard, because she doesn't want to wake Oliver. "You can't treat my son the way you do, and then think I'm going to believe you hurt your son."

She licks her lips and looks at him from the corner of her eye. "Am I getting too close to your son?" she asks him quietly.

He doesn't want her to change the subject, but this is a worthy question, and he decides to answer her. "Ellie, I want you here in my house, tucking my son in every night before you come to my bed. I want you waking up in my arms, and I want—"

She pushes him away and shakes her head. "No."

"You'd walk out on him?" he asks her quietly.

"That's not fair." She presses her lips together and glances at Jay over her shoulder. "He's your son, not mine. And he lives in New York. And you and I are nothing to each other—"

"We're lovers, Ellie, whether you wanna remember that or not."

"We were," she corrects him.

"Can you sit there and tell me you don't want me again? You don't think about what it was like? You don't remember the way we fit together—"

"Stop it," she hisses. It's not so much a blush, as heat, that floods her face. She wants him. He feels the blood rush to his groin when he realizes she does still want him.

"I can still taste you, Ellie," he whispers. He reaches again and trails his fingertips over the back of her neck. "I still feel your skin against my lips—"

"Jay." She catches his hand and pulls it away from her neck.

Instead of pulling her back to him, he scoots closer to her, links his fingers with hers and presses his open mouth to the back of her neck. Her ponytail brushes his face.

The fresh raspberry scent of her shampoo slips inside him and makes his heart pound and his fingertips tingle.

"Please stop," she says, but she turns her head to look at him. He slides in even closer and tips his head to catch her lips with his. If she says no again, he'll stop. If she puts her hand on him and pushes him away, he'll stop. But she doesn't. She parts her lips under his and raises her hand to touch his face. Her fingers draw a chill from his body as she rakes them gently into his hair and then cups the back of his head in her hand.

He eases her to the floor and kisses a trail from her lips to her neck.

"No," she whispers as he cups her breast.

"Ellie," he groans. He traces a small circle over her breast and feels her nipple bead under her shirt and her bra.

"Not with Oliver here, Jay," she says softly.

He lifts his head and checks to see if Oliver is still sleeping. The boy hasn't moved. "Okay." He nods, and even though he's desperate to get her naked and slide over her body and bury himself inside her, he's grateful that she's got the presence of mind to remember this is wrong with his son here. "But tell me."

"What?"

He props his head on his hand and rests on his elbow to look at her.

"What happened to Luther?" he asks her again. Her eyes fill, but she's determined not to cry. "Don't tell me what anyone else said. Tell me what happened."

"He wanted to go outside." Her voice is hoarse with the emotion that fills her eyes. "He loved to be outside."

"Typical boy," Jay says with a nod.

"No." She swallows hard and turns her eyes away from his. "He wasn't a typical boy. I had a lot of problems delivering him."

Jay touches her chin and turns her to face him. "It's okay," he urges her gently.

"We used to play in the rain, because he hated being cooped up inside." She sighs and closes her eyes. "He liked to dig in the dirt. He loved worms. Frogs. Baseball."

He watches her as she raises her hand and finds the silver cross around her neck. Her long, elegant fingers close around it.

"He found this cross one day when he was digging in the backyard. I was washing the windows outside, and he started yelling, all excited about it. You'd have thought he found gold. He brought it to me, hopping from one foot to the other while I looked at it. I was just glad it wasn't a worm. He liked to bring me worms, and we'd have to name them and then go through this big process of letting them go free and wishing them well." She shivers and opens her eyes.

A moment of silence passes between them.

"He told me he wanted me to have the cross. Said it was Luther's Cross." She wipes at her eyes, but he catches her hand and shakes his head. Tears slide over her face and down into her hair. "I bought the chain, and I put it on and I've never taken it off since that day."

"I think any little boy would be lucky to have a mom like you," Jay says softly. She sobs and turns her back to him. Again, instead of pulling her back to him, he scoots close to her and puts his arm around her. "What happened, Ellie?"

"I was cleaning the house. I had the bathroom left to do and he begged me to go outside." Her words are broken with emotion. She shakes against him, so he gathers her as close as he can. "I let him go out. I went out about ten minutes later."

Jay knows what is coming. He knows now what she is going to say. He wants to say it for her, so she doesn't have to feel the words form in her throat and come out of her mouth again. But he knows she needs to say it. Maybe if she says these words to someone who loves her, she can get past the way it hurts, the way the guilt eats her up inside.

"He was gone."

"I'm so sorry." He is surprised to hear the tight tremor in his own voice. "God, I'm sorry."

"He just vanished, Jay. I looked everywhere for him. I walked our block. I walked all over, looking for him. I was afraid to go too far, afraid he'd come back and I wouldn't be there. I looked everywhere. I couldn't find him."

"And they blamed you."

"They arrested me," she answers. Her voice is dead calm. "They pretended to look for him, like they were humoring me. And then they arrested me."

Jay kisses her head and gently pulls her ponytail holder out. He strokes his fingers through her loose hair. "You still don't know?"

"No."

MAEVE CAN COUNT THE NUMBER OF TIMES SHE'S BEEN TO HER sister's house on one hand. She is uncomfortable here, completely out of her league, and she knows it shows. She wonders if Maddie feels the same way at her house. If so, she handles herself much better than Maeve does. Maddie always looks cool as a cucumber, and that's just one thing about her that drives Maeve to distraction. The only time in their adult lives that Maeve has seen Maddie passionate about anything was the night after a pool party several years back, when she'd awakened after two in the morning and heard voices by the pool. When she'd tiptoed downstairs, she'd been shocked to find her sister wrapped only in a man's arms, lying under him on a chaise lounge, a look of ecstasy on her face. It is a picture that stays front and center in her mind anytime she sees Maddie, and it's very hard to look through it or around it and see the flesh and blood woman.

She has never seen Maddie passionately angry, not since she became a nun. Actually, she's just never seen her sister deeply invested in anything. It always seems as if Maddie just glides through life and nothing affects her, nothing hurts her, nothing angers her and nothing makes her happy. Maeve feels a twinge of regret for Maddie as she climbs out of her car and stares at the little yellow house where Sister Madeline lives. She wonders if there is anything left of the young girl who loved grape popsicles and playing Ghosts in the Graveyard and rode her bike with her feet up on her handlebars when their mother wasn't looking.

Maddie answers the door several long, excruciating moments after Maeve knocks. Maeve hates standing on the small front porch, waiting to be invited in. There is a tiny part of herself that knows the truth as she stands and waits for the door to open. She's heard it said that the truth will set you free, but she doesn't believe it. The truth, at least in her case, makes her stomach queasy, the way she used to feel when she was pregnant with Luke and Peyton, and she'd get up in the morning and smell Stash's coffee. She hates standing here, waiting to see Maddie, because she thinks honestly if their roles were reversed, she might not let herself in. She thinks she might not like herself too much, and that irritates her because technically she's done nothing to Maddie.

"What's up?" Maddie asks as she steps back to let her in.

She is wearing a short pink robe; her hair is loose around her shoulders.

Maeve catches herself before the vicious words tumble out of her mouth. Maddie is stunning and sexy in her robe, and she looks satisfied, and Maeve almost asks her if she is alone. Maeve, though deeply shaken after seeing Maddie with Stash's friend Greg Marshall, had never mentioned it to her sister. Rather, like everything else, she'd let it fester deep inside.

"Mom's sick," she says instead. This is, after all, what she's come to tell Maddie.

"You couldn't just call?" Maddie wears a puzzled look.

"What?" Maeve knows the words are coming now, and she can't stop them. "Am I interrupting something?"

Maddie raises her eyebrows in surprise at Maeve's direct attack. "No. I was reading the paper and drinking a cup of coffee. That okay with you?"

"Didn't you go to mass today?"

"No, I didn't," Maddie answers boldly. "Don't you have to work today?"

The words chip at Maeve's armor and leave a definite dent. She has been in court for two weeks, arguing the Wittmer case. She is drained, and she is disheartened, and she knows that even if she gets Alec Wittmer put away, there will be another drunk or sober son-of-a-bitch who will hurt his children and keep her hard at work.

"Jury's deliberating," she says quietly. "I needed a break."

Maddie nods. She does not smile, but the hard look on her face softens a bit. "Want some coffee?"

"Please," Maeve answers with a small nod. She follows her sister to the tiny kitchen at the back of the house. The paper is indeed spread out over the table. Maeve remembers the way Maddie used to study when they were in high school, spread out all over the dining room table, taking up every inch of space available. She wonders for a brief moment what Maddie might have been if she hadn't gone insane and become a nun. Would she still have been a teacher? Maeve knows Maddie is smarter than she is; her grade point average in high school had always been two or three tenths of a point higher.

"What's the matter with Mom?" Maddie asks as she pours Maeve a cup of coffee. Maeve sits down and watches her sister take the powdered creamer from the cabinet above her microwave. She remembers without asking how Maeve takes her coffee.

"Jay took her to the doctor yesterday," Maeve says. She curls her hand around the cup as Maddie sits down across the table from her. "She has pneumonia."

"Oh boy," Maddie groans. "Did he admit her?"

"No." Maeve looks up at Maddie. "But he probably should have. She's got a horrible cough."

"Doctor Einhaus?"

Maeve nods.

"He's good," Maddie says softly. "He'll watch her."

"I know," Maeve agrees. "Just makes me think of Dad."

Maddie nods and looks away.

"Rylan called Jay," Maeve finally says to break the heavy silence that now hangs over them.

"Time for Oliver to go home?" Maddie asks.

"She's coming here to get him," Maeve answers with a nod. "I hate to see him go."

"Me too." Maddie smiles. She's beautiful when she smiles. Maeve can't deny that. Well, she's a beautiful woman, but the smile softens her features and makes her seem approachable.

"He's really gotten attached to Ellie," Maeve mumbles. She sips at her coffee and stares at Maddie's refrigerator.

"We've all gotten pretty attached to Ellie," Maddie corrects her.

"She's a good girl."

Maddie arches an eyebrow, but she doesn't say anything.

"What?" Maeve asks.

"You know, she's almost the same age your first baby would be now."

Maeve wants to thank her for bringing the abortion up, but truth be told, she's already had this thought. She's already worried that she's gotten so close to Ellie in some godforsaken attempt at getting to know a child she aborted years ago. She meets Maddie's eyes, but she is quick to look away. Guilty. Yes, she fears she might be guilty of seeking some sort of close relationship with Ellie because she reminds her of the child she willingly got rid of.

"Are you using Ellie to assuage your guilt over what you did?"

"Maybe," Maeve says and swallows hard. "I like Ellie, and I want to see Jay happy."

"Maybe." Maddie raises her eyebrows, but Maeve knows she is not convinced.

"I told her."

Maddie takes a drink of her coffee and folds the paper up. "Told her what?"

"I told Ellie about the abortion."

Maddie stares at her in shock. "Why? Why would you do that? My God, Maeve, your own husband doesn't even know."

"She was talking about Jay one day," Maeve says with a shrug. "About how she wasn't right for Jay. And I just wanted her to know that people make mistakes and still live full, happy lives."

Maddie nods. "So you think the abortion was a mistake?"

"Of course I think it was a mistake," Maeve answers. "It's something I regret every day of my life."

"What if you'd have had that baby and kept it, and it would've changed things for you and Stash?"

Maeve presses her lips together. "I love him, Maddie," she says quietly. "He's my life."

"So if you had to choose, you'd choose him over that child?"

"I didn't even know Stash when I was seventeen." Maeve sighs in frustration. "Why are you doing this?"

Maddie shrugs and shakes her head. "I don't know. Maybe I'm just curious."

Maeve pushes her cup away and clears her throat. "Mom wanted to have a get-together at her house. For Oliver. But since she's not feeling well, I'm gonna do it."

"Of course you are," Maddie says calmly. "The Taylors have a pool party at least once a week."

"It's for Oliver," Maeve says again. "Will you be there?"

"I wouldn't miss it," Maddie answers her.

RYLAN IS COVER GIRL BEAUTIFUL. ELLIE HADN'T EXPECTED this. She doesn't know why, exactly, because Jay is good looking, and he's charismatic and charming, and why couldn't he get any woman he set his heart on? There is a small sliver of Ellie that feels plain and even ugly by comparison to Rylan. But mostly, she doesn't care. Rylan is the epitome of all that she left behind when she gave birth to Luther.

She has long, rich, chestnut brown hair that falls around her shoulders and over her back in loose curls. Big blue eyes are framed with thick, lush lashes, and her smile is beautiful. Empty, Ellie decides, but beautiful. Her body belongs on the cover of Cosmopolitan, Ellie thinks, so she is not surprised later in the evening when she learns that

Rylan posed for Playboy just before she and Jay were divorced.

The thought makes her cringe for several reasons, the first, of course, being how much that must have hurt Jay. The second was the fact that Rylan had a centerfold body, so Ellie figures she did a lot more for Jay in bed than she ever could. And of course, everything about Rylan brings back memories of Ellie's former life.

She manages to stay low on the radar all evening at Maeve's house. Oliver gives her a big hug when he sees her, but he is quick to grab Jay by the hand and drag him to the pool. Oliver is milking every second with Jay, and it's painfully obvious he doesn't want to leave his dad. The fact that Rylan intends to take this little boy and make him live in New York City again where he can't play ball with his dad or dig up worms in the backyard makes Ellie hate her. And yet, she knows that's not fair. Things may not have worked out between Rylan and Jay, but that alone does not give her cause to judge what sort of mother Rylan is. After all, most people, if asked, would question what sort of mother she had been.

"You didn't eat much," Maeve says as she and Ellie clean off the picnic table.

"I'm not hungry," Ellie answers. She has sensed a strange coolness from Maeve today, and it leaves her feeling uneasy. She doesn't know what she's done to offend Maeve, other than be herself. She glances back at Maddie as she follows Maeve inside. Would Maddie have told Maeve what she knows?

"You're not letting Rylan get to you, are you?" Maeve asks once they are alone in the kitchen.

Ellie stares at her for a long, silent moment. She finally moves, picking up a plate and scraping the remainders of dinner into the garbage can. "What's to get to?" she asks without looking at Maeve. "She's nothing to me."

"She's Jay's ex-wife," Maeve answers as she takes the plate from Ellie and puts it in the dishwasher.

"And Jay's a friend," Ellie tells her with a shrug.

Maeve nods slowly and shrugs. "Fine. Have it your way," she says quietly. "But you're twice the woman Rylan is."

Ellie frowns. She's wondering what other things Rylan has done to warrant such hatred from Jay's family. It only drives home the fact that if they'd known her all those years ago, she'd have been hated too. Sure, she didn't like Rylan, on principal alone. She's Jay's ex-wife. She has a child with Jay. She's Oliver's mother. In Ellie's book, those things alone are enough to dislike her. But none of that should matter to Jay's family the way it matters to her.

"Good grief, it's hot out there," Maddie groans as she joins them in the kitchen.

"Get in the pool," Maeve suggests. She grabs another plate and scrapes it off to put in the dishwasher.

"Yeah, I'll just jump in with clothes on," Maddie mumbles. "I wish Barbie would leave. But I wish she'd leave Oliver with us."

"Well, we agree on something." Maeve leaves the last of the plates to Ellie and begins putting leftovers away.

"What's wrong with Rylan?" Ellie finally asks.

Maddie snorts. "Did you look at her?"

"What? She's gorgeous? You hate her for that?"

"She's plastic," Maeve corrects her, still busy with the leftovers. "You're gorgeous."

"So she had a boob job and graced the pages of Playboy," Ellie says with a shrug. "I know that must have hurt Jay, but is that it? I mean is that reason to hate her?"

"She doesn't spend time with Oliver," Maddie says as she refills her glass with ice and water. "He goes to daycare every day. And Rylan is a model. She doesn't have steady hours. She just never wants to be bothered with him—"

"But she has SpongeBob Band-Aids," Ellie says softly. "I mean—" She swallows hard and looks from Maeve to Maddie. Both of them are staring daggers at her. "You don't live with them. How can you judge what kind of mother she is, if you aren't there living with them?"

Maeve turns her back to Ellie to run water in the sink.

"What, Maeve? I'm just asking a simple question." Ellie glances at Maddie again. "Most people I know would say I was a bad mother, and I wasn't. Not after I had Luther. He was my life. Maybe—"

"I walked in on Rylan in bed with Joe."

Ellie and Maddie stare at Maeve, both stunned at her outburst.

"What?" Maddie finds her voice first.

"I went to Mom's one night. I'd been working out of Dad's office, because Luke was having a party here. I left a file over there, and I went to get it. Mom was out. I think it was her bowling night. I heard Joe with someone, so I hurried to grab the folder and get out. I recognized her voice—"

"But are you sure it was her?" Maddie asks doubtfully.

"Damn straight I am." Maeve turns around to stare at Ellie and Maddie. "I went straight to Joe's room to confront her."

"And they were having sex?" Maddie asks.

"They were busy," Maeve answers. "Seems I caught them before they could seal the deal, but yeah. She was putting the moves on him."

Ellie stares at the counter, finally understanding Jay's jealousy toward Joe any time she happened to look his way. How must it feel knowing your brother was messing around with your wife?

"Joe was just a kid," Maddie says quietly.

"Yeah," Maeve agrees. "A good looking kid. And Rylan took advantage of that. Score one for her."

"He could've said no," Ellie says quietly. She could've said no. All those times she'd found herself alone with different guys, in bedrooms and closets and backseats, she could've said no. She could have said no and saved Luther the horrible, short life he'd had.

"I didn't say he was without blame." Maeve's voice is flat. "He knew what he was doing, and yes, he damned well should've said no."

"Did you tell Jay?" Maddie asks her.

"I didn't want to, but he was moping around about Rylan one night. He said he thought she was messing around with someone else." Maeve turns to look at Ellie. "And she was. Someone else besides Joe." She looks back at Maddie. "I just got so upset that night. I blurted it all out. I didn't mean to hurt Jay. I just wanted her out of his life."

"Jay and Joe still talk," Maddie says thoughtfully.

"Yeah." Maeve raises her eyebrows. "Jay took the high road. Go figure." She starts putting pots and pans in the sink to wash. "I'm not sure I could do that."

Ellie sighs and backs away from the counter. She turns to go outside, but Maeve calls to her. "Where ya going?"

Ellie stops and turns back to Jay's sisters. "I'm Rylan." She swallows hard, faces the firing brigade, and takes a deep breath. "I'm everything you just said. I was Rylan and Joe and thoughtless and selfish and I could've said no."

CHAPTER 21

It's like a preheated oven outside. Ellie feels as if someone draped a wet wool blanket over her head, the air is so wet and heavy with humidity. She spots Jay talking to Rylan, while Oliver splashes in the pool. Her skin burns, as if everywhere accusing eyes stare at her. And yet, she knows she's being ridiculous. She has just given Maeve and Maddie both a big shove in order to back them away and close her heart to them. She guesses they are as stunned by what she's just said as she was to learn that Joe messed around with Rylan.

Stash offers her a beer, and she is prickly and pissy, and she wants to snap at him to go to hell. She wants to go home and sulk in private. She wants to erase this summer from her life and start it over and be alone. Instead she simply smiles at him and shakes her head.

"Oliver was just looking for you," he tells her.

"He was?" She grins, because how could she not be happy knowing Oliver was looking for her?

"He wants you to get in the pool again," Stash says with a chuckle. "Wants Ellie to fly him like an airplane."

Ellie laughs. Earlier she'd pulled him along in the pool and pretended he was an airplane. He'd actually started kicking his feet, but he'd warned her in a very serious three-year-old voice not to let go of him. Ellie doesn't want to get in the pool again. Not even to play with Oliver. She doesn't want to be near Jay and Rylan. There is something about the way Jay looks at Rylan that bothers Ellie. Without thinking too far into it, Ellie knows it's jade green jealousy eating her up inside. He may not love Rylan anymore, but any man with a pulse would be attracted to her.

Jay will never love her when he sees inside her. He would never saddle himself with another Rylan, and Ellie will not let him drape another selfish woman around his son's neck. She looks around, but she finds nothing to do with herself. Jay and Rylan occupy one end of the pool. Luke and two of his friends are at the other end of the pool. Stash is flopped in a lounge chair, quietly drinking a beer. Ellie does not feel she knows him well enough to sit and talk to him. And tonight is not the night to get to know him. Jolene is napping on Maeve's couch, and Maeve and Maddie have yet to come back outside.

It crosses her mind that she should simply say goodnight and go home. When Jay had offered to pick her up earlier, she'd begged off. She wants Jay and Oliver to have as much quality time together as possible before Oliver leaves tomorrow, so she wants to stay out of the way. She'd driven her car over, secretly thrilled that Jay had fixed the heap of junky metal for her. Not that she would give up the bike. She loved the freedom the bicycle gave her.

"Ellie!" Oliver squeals when he sees her sitting on the edge of the picnic table.

She offers him a smile and wanders slowly toward the small, broken family. Rylan greets her with a smile. Although Jay introduced them earlier, they have not said much to each other. She's not sure how she feels about Jay introducing her as his friend. She does know that if he'd have said she was his girlfriend, she would have been angry. And she also knows that Rylan saw right through the word friend, and she knows they've slept together at least once, if not many times.

"Are you gonna get in again?" Oliver asks hopefully.

"No," she answers, but she sits on the side of the pool and puts her legs in. Jay, who is in the pool, heaves himself out and excuses himself. Ellie glances at Rylan and wishes she'd have gone with her first impulse and headed for home.

"I forget how humid it is here," Rylan says. There is no other immediate noise, just the soft splashes Oliver makes and the quiet chatter of Luke and his friends at the other end of the pool. Ellie finds herself remembering nights like this, ten years ago, when she and her friends had been the rowdy teens at the other end of the pool. Nights when she'd have so much to drink she couldn't remember the following morning how she'd made it home. Nights when instead of splashing in the pool she was locked in an upstairs bedroom with the star quarterback or class president or biology teacher, sliding skin to skin between the sheets.

Unexpectedly her thoughts turn to Tony Spinelli. She wonders what he's doing now.

"How long have you and Jay been seeing each other?" Rylan asks her.

Ellie looks at her and finds herself wondering about the Playboy pictures and how Jay must have felt about it. She doesn't bother to correct Rylan, to tell her they aren't seeing each other. "Just since May," she finally answers.

"He loves you, ya know," Rylan announces. Ellie fights the urge to get up and walk away. She has no desire to sit here and play nice with Jay's ex-wife. She really doesn't want to listen to Rylan tell her that Jay loves her. What's she supposed to say to that? That she knows? That she loves him too? "I never wanted to hurt him, Ellie," Rylan continues. "But I didn't really love him."

Again Ellie wonders what she's supposed to say. Is she supposed to defend Jay? Hook her claws into Rylan and take her down? Engage in a long philosophical conversation with her? She's never had a boyfriend, other than the couple of months that she and Tony were dating, never mind the fact that they never actually went out on dates. She's never had a boyfriend's ex-girlfriend or ex-wife to deal with. Sure, she had plenty of girls that hated her, that looked at her with the same sort of contempt that Maeve and Maddie held for Rylan, but that sort of hatred never got personal.

"Why did you marry him?" She surprises herself with her question. "If you didn't love him?" She stares at Rylan, waiting for an answer.

"I don't know," Rylan answers. Ellie wonders if she's being honest or just taking the easy way out. "I liked him. We had fun together. The sex was great." Rylan shrugs. "Maybe I thought I would learn to love him."

Ellie would not have to learn to love Jay Bryant. She loves him so much right now, she hurts inside. But she has nothing to offer him, just a sordid, regretful past that she cannot change or outrun. She's certain she could send him running, just a word about the life she led would send him packing. She really needs to say that word and save them both from any further heartache.

"Jay deserves so much more than that," she says quietly as she stands up. She doesn't know if she's talking about the way Rylan treated him or the fact that she is nothing more than a child whore who got caught and had to straighten up and be responsible. She finds her towel and dries her legs off, slips her sandals on and looks around the patio. This time she's going home.

"Ellie?" Oliver calls. "Are you leaving?"

"Yeah," she says and offers him a sad smile. "I'm gonna go home, Oliver."

Oliver paddles over to the side of the pool. Ellie kneels down and lifts him from the water. "I don't wanna go home, Ellie." His lower lip trembles.

"You'll be fine, Ol." Her voice is tight with a mix of emotion, not the least of which is missing Luther. What would she have said to Luther if she'd known it was the last time she would talk to him? The last time she'd kiss his baby-soft cheek and tousle his dark blonde hair? Goodbye somehow seems inadequate after the way she'd loved him so completely for five years. "Your mom misses you. You need to be with her."

"But I miss Daddy when I'm with her," he whispers.

"I know, baby," Ellie says with a nod. Her eyes burn. Behind her, she hears muted conversation. Maeve and Maddie have come back outside. She was hoping to escape before they realized she was still here. "And Daddy misses you too. But your mommy loves you."

"Will you miss me?" he asks. His big blue eyes mirror the sadness in hers.

"Every day," she answers sincerely. "Can I have a hug?"

He comes willingly into her arms, swim trunks dripping wet against her shorts. She wraps her arms around him and pulls him close. He links his arms around her neck and squeezes her so tight he traps the air inside her lungs.

"I love you, Ellie," he tells her.

She pulls away from him to look him in the eye. "I love you too, Oliver."

She kisses his cheek and then stands and turns away from Rylan. She doesn't care to cry over Jay and Oliver and Luther in front of Rylan. Or Maeve or Maddie. Not tonight. She folds her towel and finds her keys and runs square into Maeve on her way to the door.

"Don't go like this," Maeve says quietly.

"I need to," Ellie answers.

"El, come on. Let's talk—"

"I can't tonight." Ellie licks her lips. "I can't. I just need to be alone."

Maeve nods. "Okay."

"Thanks for inviting me," Ellie mumbles.

"You know, whether you like it or not, you're part of this family now." Maeve's fingers close around her wrist.

"I walked out on my last family, lock, stock, and barrel," Ellie reminds her. "Don't trust me, Maeve."

"Ellie," Maeve calls, but Ellie keeps walking. She says a quiet goodnight to Maddie and Stash, who sit at the picnic table, drinking beer. Maddie is shuffling a deck of cards.

The cold hush of Maeve's house chills her. She is wet now from her goodbye hug from Oliver. And she is alone. Funny how she feels more alone at this moment than she did the morning Jay called her about her final exam. The more she is around Jay and his family and the more she loves them, the more she remembers of herself and hates what she used to be and wonders if a person can truly change.

"Are you leaving?" Jay asks. He's in the living room, apparently checking on Jolene. She's asleep on the sofa; the TV is on the game show channel.

"Yeah."

"I'll walk you out," he says quietly. She doesn't argue with him, because she doesn't want to wake Jolene. He slips his fingers through hers as they step outside. She wishes for just a moment that she could rewind time and go back to those first nights on her front porch, back when it was just her and Jay.

When they stand in front of her car, she turns to him and finds herself near tears again. "This is hard for you," she says softly. He gives her a curt nod. "I'm sorry, Jay. I know what he means to you."

"Yeah," he mumbles. "I just don't get why she had to drag him all the way to New York."

"I know." She nods. He looks so sad. Alone. He looks like he feels as alone as she does at the moment. She slides her hands up over his shoulders and steps close to him. He sighs against her lips when she touches them to his. "I love you, Jay." She does in every way possible, but it's cruel for her to say the words. He doesn't understand that because she loves him, she will do anything for him. Including saving him from herself.

IN THAT SOFT, COMFORTABLE SPACE WHERE YOU HOVER between dreams and the real world, she remembers making love to Jay. The way his hands had touched her with tenderness and something akin to reverence. The way he'd kissed her, as if she tasted like caramelized sugar glazed over ice cream. He'd filled her completely, and he'd been both gentle and demanding at the same time. She wants to be filled with him again. She wants to feel his weight on top of her and feel his body pulse inside hers and feel his breath against her ear as he tenses over her. She's fought the need for him since she woke up to find him gone the first time he'd made love to her. The only time he'd made love to her. Part of her is desperate to wrap her legs around his hips again and run her hands over his bare back, and part of her is disgusted by the feelings he's created within her. It's a constant war inside her that pounds inside her head and makes her stomach ache.

When she was younger she'd had fun playing with sex. She'd lived for the thrill that she could make the guys want her. The popular guys. The older guys. Whoever she wanted to mess with. She knew at the time she was making a name for herself, a bad name, but she didn't care. She was doing the sports gods and a few academic geeks who happened to be blessed with good looks and a few teachers. It was a rare thing for her to actually enjoy the act, but the power was a trip. She and Blair would go out on Fridays and score and then come back and share details.

She'd never told Blair that her first time had been with Tony Spinelli. Out of all the guys she'd been with, and it made her cringe now to think about all of them, Tony was the closest to Jay in the way he'd touched her and kissed her. No, he hadn't taken her to the big O, but he'd wanted to. They had been so young. She had been his first too, and he was so nervous, so afraid that he would hurt her or embarrass himself. It had hurt but not horribly, and he'd been so good to her when it was over it didn't really matter. He'd kissed her all over, trying to make up for the pain he'd caused her. They'd been together a few times after the first. It got a little better, but it wasn't until Ellie did her biology teacher that she knew what the big O was. He'd stoked her with one hand, clamped the other over her mouth and then slid inside her, all inside the small supply closet in the back of the biology classroom.

None of them really compared to Jay. Not the whole package. Not the way he talked to her and listened to her and touched her and kissed her and fit her body like he was made for her. She hates herself for that first time she'd cheated on Tony, for the hurt in his eyes when he realized she was screwing around with a senior basketball player. She hates herself for falling in love with Jay. She hates herself for all of the guys in between.

She wonders if Tony and Luther and all the guys in between are what led her here to Jay. And if so, she wonders what the hell she's supposed to do about it.

Forgiveness is not doled out like a special treat, at least not by God. Maddie's pen hovers above her lesson plan book, but her mind couldn't be further away from planning for a new year of kindergarteners. Today has been a day when she has thought of little else besides the daughter she gave up. Truth be told, she's been thinking of the baby since last night, when Maeve blurted out to her and Ellie that she'd found Rylan and Joe in bed together. No, her daughter is never far from her mind or heart, but she has become very adept at folding that little piece of the past up and tucking it away.

If she's going to be honest, she has to admit she'd never much cared for Rylan either. Even before the proverbial shit had hit the fan, and it had gotten out that Rylan was having an affair. But how can she explain that instant dislike to Ellie? How can she condemn Rylan for the life she led, when Ellie claims she was the same kind of person Rylan is? It's not so much that she holds Rylan in contempt for what she did. She just never felt a connection with her, and she never believed she was what was best for Jay.

She's fascinated that Jay knows about Joe and Rylan and still speaks to him. They don't hang out together every spare minute they get, and yet, Maddie believes they are as close as brothers with their age difference can be. Then again, what does she know? She spends the majority of her family life on the outside looking in. Correction. She spends the majority of her life on the outside looking in; she belongs nowhere.

She is worried about Ellie, and she knows Maeve is worried about Ellie. And Maeve fears they've scared her away for good. Maeve, who had taken to heart Maddie's worries over her abortion, is now afraid that Ellie walked out for good last night. But there is so much more to Ellie. She is a complicated person with layers and layers of guilt and love and fear and regret. She loves Jay too much to walk away now. Where she will go from here, Maddie would never claim to know. But she doubts that Ellie will simply walk away.

Ellie's past does not matter to Maddie, except that it matters so much to Ellie. Maddie hopes that Ellie will continue to delve into this personal soul-searching mission she has started but hates to admit to. It has been hard for her to not pick up the phone today and call Ellie. That is Maeve's style. Push. Except, of course, when it comes to their relationship. Maeve walks around the heart of who they are and who they were as if they are a fire burning, and she fears getting too close to the hot coals will leave her with burn scars.

Maddie knows it is best not to waste time thinking about Maeve. What they had is long gone, and what Maddie finds saddest of all is that Maeve doesn't even know why they now live like distant strangers.

～

"DID YOU SLEEP WITH HER LAST NIGHT?" ELLIE ASKS QUIETLY. Jay is sitting on the floor in front of his couch. Ellie is curled in the corner of the couch, eyes glued to the TV. She is looking at Martin Sheen, but she hasn't paid a bit of attention so she has no idea what's on.

"What?" Jay lays his head on the couch and closes his eyes.

"Did you sleep with Rylan?"

"No. She and Oliver slept in my bed. I took the couch."

Ellie tries to turn her mind off. She has tortured herself all day with images of Jay and Rylan together. She reaches for him and combs her fingers through his curly hair.

"But you've slept with her since the divorce." She's not

sure why she's pushing this. It's not like hearing him admit that he has slept with his ex-wife after the divorce is going to make her feel any better.

"I did," he admits. "But I haven't since I met you."

"She's a lot more woman than I am," she says softly.

"No." He opens his eyes. "She's not. She's very pretty, yes, but she's not you."

"She's gorgeous, Jay."

"Are you jealous?" he asks with a tiny grin. He turns so that he can look up at her.

"I don't know," she answers honestly. She holds his gaze for a long moment, but she gives in before he does. She looks away from his intense blue eyes and watches George chew on a tennis ball that is almost bigger than he is. Jay's house is quiet now; the quiet is so loud it almost screams Oliver. It's quiet the way her house was after Luther disappeared. Ellie imagines it is like a cartoon house, tall but sucked so thin that the outer walls almost touch.

"You know what I wanna know?" Jay's fingers trace over her leg.

"What?" She is breathless from his touch.

"How you can stand it. How you live from day to day not knowing where he is. How you don't lose your mind wondering—"

"I do," she whispers. "I lose my mind every day wondering where he is."

He reaches for her, and she slides off the couch to sit by him. He pulls her into his lap and puts his arms around her.

"At least I know I'll see Oliver again," Jay says softly. Ellie rests her forehead on his shoulder. Tears wet her face, but she lets them fall. "I'm sorry about Oliver. I know he came on like a freight train with you—"

"Sssh." She turns her face to his neck and presses her lips to his skin. "Don't. I love your son, Jay. He's beautiful." She lifts her head and touches her lips against his chin, his jaw, his lips. He opens his mouth, but he waits for her to make the next move. She strokes her tongue inside his lips, relieved when she feels him kiss her back.

She's not sure about what she's doing. She's uncertain on so many levels. She wants to make love to him, to lie in his arms and sleep through the night and wake up with him. But she knows tomorrow she will feel regret come crashing in on her like the roof caving in on some dilapidated building. She will forget the woman she is right now, the woman who loves Jay and wants to show him that. She will become the selfish, whoring brat she used to be.

It has been years since she felt the power she used to have over guys. And now she's seen Jay's ex-wife. She wants to strip her clothes off and offer her body to Jay, but she can't help but remember the perfect curves of Rylan's body.

"Stay?" he whispers against her lips.

She swallows her doubts and nods reluctantly. Tonight she wants to love him, because she keeps thinking about the way Rylan hurt him. But she knows that tomorrow she will hurt him. She has to tell him that she is just another Rylan.

CHAPTER 22

SHE'D GIVEN HIM EVERYTHING. THEY'D MADE LOVE WITH AN abandon that had both shocked him and thrilled him. But she is still holding back. She is still guarding her heart from him, and even though he holds her now as close as he physically can, he hates the distance between them. He knows that when she leaves his bed in the morning they will go back to the less than warm friendship they have slipped into since the first time they made love. He wants to change it, to keep her here and keep her from walking away, but he doesn't know how. Ellie carries so many secrets inside, he's afraid he'll never get deep enough inside her to really know her.

He watches her for several long minutes and then glances at the clock. It's after three, and he's been watching her lay awake for nearly an hour.

"What are you thinking?" he whispers as he scoots closer to her. His leg is draped over hers; his arm lies possessively over her waist. He presses his lips to her bare shoulder as he waits and wonders if she will answer him.

She is so long in answering that he decides she simply

isn't going to say anything. He sighs and kisses her shoulder again and closes his eyes.

"This is the first night." Her voice is soft and heavy with emotion.

"First night?" he repeats, eyes still closed.

"The first night I've been away from home," she whispers, "since he's been gone."

She's afraid. She's lived the past five years glued to the little square box she'd raised her son in, just in case he ever came back. Jay feels the way her heart is squeezed tight in her chest, because the pressure slips through them, and his heart squeezes, and it feels for a moment like he can't breathe.

"You're afraid he'll come back," Jay says gently. "And you'll be gone."

"Mostly," she says, rolling over and looking at him with dry eyes, "I'm afraid he's dead. Most kids that are abducted are found dead."

He nods. "Ellie?"

"What?"

"Let me help you look for him." He traces the curve of her jaw with his fingertips. Her face glows a surreal blue in the bright light from his alarm clock.

She shakes her head. "It's been five years, Jay," she says quietly. "I wouldn't even know where to start."

"Maeve." Jay finger combs her hair off her face. "She's got connections."

"No." She looks away, and again, he wonders what is going on with Ellie and Maeve. When they'd made it to his bed earlier and started all over again, the phone had interrupted them. It was Maeve. Ellie had gone rigid when she'd heard Maeve's voice. Maeve had asked if he'd heard from Ellie all day. She'd wanted to press him for details when he'd said he was busy, but she'd finally let him go. "I can't open myself up to that again, Jay. I can't let myself hope that I'm gonna find him."

"But you can't let him go either," Jay says and raises his eyebrows.

"I just try to hope that even if I never see him again, there's someone out there who has him. Who's taking care of him for me."

"It's hard to keep that hope."

She nods. "When all you hear on TV is that another child's body was found dumped in a ravine or a lake, it's really hard to hold onto hope."

"Do you have pictures of him?"

She nods again and glances at him, but she won't hold his gaze.

"Can I see one sometime?"

She pushes gently at his chest until he moves. He watches her slide out of bed and reach for her clothes. She steps into her panties and shorts and reaches for her bra before he sits up and grabs her wrist.

"What are you doing?" he asks.

"I was gonna wait until morning to do this, but I can't." Her voice is thick with regret. "I gotta go."

"Why?" He climbs out of bed and holds her hands in his. "I just asked to see a picture of your son. I want to be close to you, Ellie Jordan, but so help me God, you make it damned near impossible."

"Luther was born with FAS—"

"FAS?" he repeats with a frown. "What? And what does that have to do with you leaving—"

"Fetal alcohol syndrome," she says sharply as she plows her fingers back through her hair. "He looked different. Had all the features of an FAS baby. I drank myself sick with him, because I was desperate to miscarry him. I didn't want a kid."

He nods. "Okay. You were sixteen. You didn't want a baby. I get that—"

"I didn't just not want a baby, Jay!" she yells. "I couldn't afford an abortion, so I tried to drink him away. I made him sick! I hated him so much that I made him sick!"

"You were a kid." Jay's voice is tight and controlled, but he knows she feels the anger seething just behind his words.

"I was a kid." She laughs sarcastically. "I was a selfish little slut, and I took it out on a baby, and I messed him up for life."

Jay watches her finish dressing. When she leaves his bedroom, he grabs the cargo shorts he'd worn earlier and scrambles into them, careful as he tugs the zipper up.

"What are you doing?" he snaps as her fingers close around her keys that lay on the kitchen table.

"Going home," she says simply.

"At three in the morning? You're gonna walk home at three in the morning?" he roars. "My ass, you're gonna walk home at three in the morning. Stay here and face this, Ellie. Face this Goddamned ridiculous fear and get it out in the open—"

"Fear?" she whispers. "What fear? This is my life. This is what I did, and this is what I do now."

"You made a mistake," he says quietly. "And you're determined to punish yourself for the rest of your life to pay for it. Nobody cares what you did when you were younger—"

"Thanks." Her voice thick with anger and hurt, her eyes bright with unshed tears, she pulls his back door open.

"Stop." He slaps a hand against the door and shoves it closed. "Please, just stop." His heart beats so wildly that he wonders if he's going to have a heart attack, so he forces himself to relax. "Sit down with me and talk to me."

"It doesn't matter, Jay. I'm no better than your ex-wife, and I won't let you make that mistake again—"

"Sit down and talk to me," he says again. "You owe me that much before you fuck me and walk out for good."

"I just told you," she sobs. "Everything that you and Maeve and Maddie hate about Rylan is all inside me. It's all who I am."

"What do Maeve and Maddie hate about Rylan?" He tilts his head a bit and stares at her curiously. Whatever they said has left a deep bruise in Ellie. She was skittish before, but she's running scared now.

She folds in on herself, shrinks right before his eyes. Her shoulders slouch, and she ducks her head and covers her face with her hands. Jay steps toward her and puts his arms around her waist and tries to pull her close. She fights him, but she eventually drops her head to his chest.

"Just let me go? Please?"

"I love you," he says as he presses his lips against the top of her head. "I don't wanna let you go. I don't ever wanna let you go. I want you to trust me. And I want you to be happy."

"I was good before we started this," she mumbles.

"You were numb before we started this," he corrects her. "Jesus, Ellie. Trust me enough to know I see you. This isn't about Rylan. This isn't about how I feel about your past. This is how you feel and what you think you deserve."

She sighs and rolls her head against his chest. "I can't, Jay. I can't put this on you. I can't ask you to love me."

"You don't have to ask me to love you." He rubs his hand over her back in a slow, steady circular motion. "I love you so much that every time I think you're about to walk out on me for good, I feel like I'm gonna have a heart attack."

"I never wanted this to happen between us."

Her breath is hot on his bare skin.

"But it did," he says gently. "And it could work, if you would let it."

She takes a deep breath and lifts her head to look at him. "I have to work in a few hours, Jay."

"Then come back to bed, Ellie." He cups her face in his hands. "Sleep with me."

"Jay—"

"I will give you whatever time you need to get through this. To trust me enough to tell me. Just stop trying to walk away from me. Stop pushing me away."

"The longer I love you, the more you're gonna hurt me when this is over." She looks up at him with sad eyes.

"I'm not going anywhere. If this is ever over, it's because you walked away."

She touches his lips with her fingertips. "And what if I walk away for you?"

"Then you don't love me. You can't love me and make those kinds of decisions for me. I'm a big boy, Ellie. I know what I want. And I know what I see in you."

SHE CAN'T HELP IT. SHE'S NEVER LIKED RYLAN, AND HELL YES, finding Rylan putting the moves on Joe and finding out that she slept around on Jay pissed her off and pushed her dislike into flat-out hatred. She can't apologize to Ellie for the way she feels. But she hates that Ellie sees herself in Rylan and has finished that syllogism with Maeve and Maddie hating her. Nothing could be further from the truth. Maddie has never said so, but Maeve knows she thinks as much of Ellie as she does.

Her muscles are in knots, and the delicious backrub Stash had given her last night just before he'd made love to her didn't put a dent in the stiffness she feels. She has a headache, and it has Luke and Peyton and the Wittmers and Ellie and the abortion written all over it. No amount of Advil is going to knock it. She's not really sure anything could knock it at this point. Maybe two weeks alone with Stash at some posh resort would be a good start, but really, she's not even sure that would do it.

She groans and lays her head on her desk when the doorbell rings. As far as she knows, she is home alone. Luke may have come home while she's been tucked away in her office, but she's not certain. Stash is at a business meeting, and she knows not to expect him home for another hour or two. Before she can make herself move, she hears her front door open and close and then a sharp knock on her closed office door.

Today she hates her job. And she wishes she was single and childless and stranded on a deserted island, and no human beings existed except those who are there to wait on her hand and foot.

"What?" she says so quietly she doubts whoever is knocking on her door can even hear her. She manages to lift her head as the door opens, and Jay steps inside.

"Hey."

She sighs and sits back in her chair. "What?"

"What? You called me last night to talk," he reminds her. She knows. Even after the backrub and the long, languid lovemaking with Stash, she'd still been on needles and pins thinking about Ellie. She'd slid out of bed and tiptoed downstairs and called Jay close to midnight. Jay had been cold and direct and told her he was busy.

"Yeah, I know," she mumbles. She rubs her face with her fingertips and then drops her head back against her chair. "I'm sorry I bothered you."

"You look tired," he says quietly as he sits down on the chocolate brown loveseat just inside her office.

"Ya think?" she asks sarcastically.

"What's up?"

She stares at him for a moment, arches an eyebrow and finally shakes her head. "You don't wanna know."

"I do wanna know," he corrects her. "If I didn't want to know, I wouldn't have asked."

She sighs again and lowers her arm to her desk. She picks up her pen and twirls it in her long, red-tipped fingers. "Okay, for starters? Wittmer got off on murder one. The son-of-a-bitch beat his kid to death, and he gets five years for manslaughter."

The look of shock on Jay's face says a thousand words. He is disappointed in her. No more than she is, but it still hurts to see it in her little brother's eyes.

"Money talks, Maeve," Jay says quietly. "Happens all the time."

"Sure." She shrugs and nods. "Fuck the law, if you've got enough money to bend it, right?"

Jay nods. "You did your best."

"Then I'm losing my best," she answers. "Five years ago, I'd have had the bastard convicted of murder."

"What else?" he asks.

"Luke," she says as she pushes her chair back and stands up. "Luke got busted for marijuana a couple days ago."

"Why didn't you tell me?"

"I'm telling you now." She paces to the far wall of her office and studies the oil painting that hangs there. It is a landscape done by some obscure hand that touched Maeve's heart seven years ago when she and Stash had vacationed in Maine. She loves the ocean. Just the lifeless rendering here on her wall reaches out to her and calms her.

"Possession?"

"Yeah," she answers with a nod.

"He's a kid." Jay shrugs.

"Tell me that when Oliver gets busted for pot or alcohol,

Jay." She turns to look at him. "Peyton is shacking up with her psychology professor."

"And I'm involved with a student." He shrugs again.

"He's twenty years older than she is," Maeve says quietly.

"Wow."

"Yeah, wow." She nods. She leans a hip against the front of her desk and folds her arms over her chest. They stare at each other for a long, quiet moment. "Have you talked to her?"

"Oh, I've talked to her," he answers. "I talked to her. At three o'clock this morning, I talked to her. We both did a little yelling, blew off a little steam. I did a little begging. She was gonna walk out."

"She was with you?"

"Yes."

"When I called you? She was with you?"

"Yes, she was with me. In my bed, when you called."

This time Maeve breathes a sigh of relief. "Good."

"No." Jay stands up. "Don't give me good. I wanna know what the hell you and Maddie said to her the other day. I wanna know what's got her running for cover."

Maeve licks her lips and averts her eyes. "She's got a lot—"

"What did you say to her?" Jay snaps. His anger is palpable in the small office space. Maeve stares at him in surprise. He's never shown her this kind of anger. Not even when she let it slip about Rylan and Joe.

"I didn't say anything to her." Her voice rises a bit. "She wanted to know why we hate Rylan."

"And what did you tell her?"

"Because she's fake. Inside and out. Because she took Oliver from you. Because she's selfish." Maeve stands up straight. "Because she hurt you."

"You told her everything?"

"Yeah, I did," Maeve answers with an indignant shrug. "She has the right to know what split you two up. You should have told her that a long time ago—"

"You should back off and mind your own damned business." Jay's voice is dead calm.

"Look." Maeve takes a deep breath. "You brought her into this family. I can't speak for anyone else, but I'm crazy about her. I like her. Even if you two don't work out, I care about Ellie. She asked me a question. I told her the truth."

"Does she talk to you?"

"About?"

"Luther."

"She's told me she has a son," Maeve answers quietly. "She told me how she hated being pregnant. That she didn't want him."

"That's it?"

"Yeah." Maeve gives him a slight nod. "That's it."

"She's fragile, Maeve. She's like a piece of crystal, and you went raging through the china shop the other night and all but shattered her."

Maeve turns her head when she feels her eyes burn. "I didn't mean to hurt her. I just answered her question. I can't change the way I feel about Rylan. Not even for Ellie. But that doesn't mean I would condemn everyone in Rylan's shoes."

"Why didn't you tell her that?"

"She wouldn't listen. Jay, I tried." Maeve moves again to the back of her desk and drops into her chair. "I tried."

"You didn't try hard enough." His words slice through her like a fisherman's blade, filleting the daily catch.

"I know she has secrets, and I know whatever she's hiding consumes her." She looks up at Jay as tears slide from her eyes. "Jay, I told her something about myself that no one but Maddie knew. I told her my deepest secret, because I wanted her to see that even when you make mistakes, you can go on. I wanted her to see that I'm not perfect. That I would never judge her for whatever she hides."

Jay stares at her curiously, but he doesn't ask her to share her secret. She wouldn't anyway. She could never tell Jay about the abortion. About the way the fear had bloomed inside her and sucked up her whole body until she felt like she was possessed by some demonic force. She could never tell him about dragging Maddie with her, holding Maddie's hand so tight she cut her with her fingernails. She'd cut her and drawn blood.

"What more can I do?" she whispers.

CHAPTER 23

IF SHE WAS DROWNING AT SEA, AND THERE WERE PEOPLE nearby, she would call for help. She would scream bloody murder until someone threw her a life preserver. She would clutch at any hand that reached toward her to pull her from the water and save her. She is drowning now, but it is not water that fills her lungs and threatens to tow her under and suffocate her. It is the past and the guilt and Luther and Maeve and Maddie and Jay that are drowning her. And they are the same people who stand nearby and watch her struggle and reach for her to help her ashore.

She is not surprised to find herself at Maddie's house. Though her heart is heavy, her mind is blank. She doesn't know what she will say, only that she needs to say something. She jams her hands deep inside her pockets as she waits. Beads of sweat trickle down the middle of her back. She sucks in thick, heavy air like an emphysema patient taking a drag from a cigarette.

She looks up quickly when she hears the door open. Maddie offers her a smile and pushes the screen door open. "Hey."

Ellie takes a shaky breath and steps inside. Suddenly instead of reaching for a hand to help her ashore, it feels as if she is jumping overboard. "Hi."

"Ride your bike over?" Maddie asks as she shuts the door.

The cool air moves over Ellie, and she breathes easier. "No. I walked. Just needed to get out. Stretch my legs."

"Sit down." Maddie nods to the pale blue sofa behind Ellie. "I'll be right back."

Ellie wanders to the sofa and perches nervously on the edge. Why is she here? She can't get her head on straight enough to know what's really bothering her. How the hell can she expect anyone else to understand her?

Maddie comes back a few minutes later, carrying two Coke cans. She hands one to Ellie and then drops at the other end of the couch.

"Thanks," Ellie says quietly. She pops the can open and takes a long drink.

"I thought you might not come back."

Ellie slides a careful glance toward Maddie, but she doesn't answer her right away.

"I have so much going on in my head right now, I can't think straight."

From the corner of her eye, she sees Maddie nod. "I know."

"I failed two lie detector tests," Ellie says as she stands and walks to the bay window where the late afternoon sun throws a burnt orange light into Maddie's living room.

"Proof of nothing," Maddie says quietly.

"Proof of something," Ellie argues. She watches an elderly couple across the street; the man helps the woman up the porch steps of a red-bricked bungalow. "Luther had Fetal Alcohol Syndrome."

Maddie is silent behind her, but Ellie refuses to look back at her to read her expression. Instead she lets her eyes wander the length of the now empty block where Maddie lives.

"Could've been much worse, but I had to quit the drugs when I was pregnant."

"Why?"

"Couldn't afford them," Ellie says quietly. "I traded the sex for drugs, a lot of times. No one wanted me when they found out I was pregnant." She is calm. The picture of collected. She glances at Maddie. "So I drank as much as I could. Drank my dad's stuff. Friends' stuff. Went to as many parties as I could get invited to. Probably smoked a pack a day. Again, I bummed from friends when I could. Used money I'd saved from babysitting jobs. Whatever it took."

"So you wanted to lose your baby." Maddie's voice is flat.

"Yeah, I did." Ellie turns to Maddie and leans on the wall behind her. She watches Maddie consider her words carefully.

"I hate that you wanted to lose your baby," she finally says. "That you sold yourself out for what you did. And mostly, that for whatever reason, you felt so alone you couldn't go to your parents or a teacher or some trusted adult for help." Ellie opens her mouth, but Maddie shakes her head. "But that doesn't change how I feel about you."

"Shouldn't it, though?" Ellie asks quietly.

"You're more than your actions. There's so much more to a person than the things he or she does. The mistakes we make." Maddie scoots forward a bit on the couch. "Don't you think, Ellie?"

Ellie takes a deep gulp of air and closes her eyes. "I don't know what I think, Maddie. How can you look at me and say that this stuff doesn't matter, doesn't change how you feel? After what you and Maeve said about Rylan the other night?"

"Okay." Maddie nods. "Here's the deal. I can't speak for Maeve. Well, I can, but I won't. First of all, Jay's our brother.

Hell yes, we're gonna bend over backward to protect him. Second, I don't think I really hate Rylan. I just don't care for her. I never did. I don't think she and I exchanged a total of five words when she and Jay were married."

Ellie presses her lips together. She stares defiantly at Maddie.

"I do think she was vain. She was too uptight about her manicure to dig in a garden. To play basketball with Jay or to play with Oliver. She was a married woman, and she had a boob job done so she could pose for Playboy. She messed around on Jay twice, outside of what Maeve said about Joe. When they divorced, she took Jay's son and moved across the country. And my guess is she's not any better at mothering him now than she was when he was a newborn."

Ellie shakes her head and holds up her hand. "I understand everything up to that. You can't possibly judge her as a mother, if you aren't around to see her with Oliver. Look at what I did to my son."

"You were sixteen. She's a grown woman—"

"I love my son with everything I have. But I tried to kill him. I tried to get rid of him—"

"Ellie, you have to let that go. You were a good mother. You did right by him after—"

"How do you know that?" Ellie's voice is tight and rough with emotion. "How do you know I was a good mother?"

"Because I trust you," Maddie answers simply. "I look at you, and I see your grief and your guilt, and I see the way you fit into my brother's heart and my family, and I trust you."

"You can't judge Rylan without being there—"

"Okay," Maddie concedes. "You're right. Maybe she is a good mom. But—"

"But what? Why does there have to be a but? Why can't you just say she might be a good mom?"

Maddie stands and takes two long strides to stand in

front of Ellie. "She's not you. I watched you with Oliver, Ellie, and you touched me. You loved that little boy, just the same as if he'd been your son." Ellie ducks her head to hide the tears in her eyes. "That's how I know you were a good mother to Luther. You made a few mistakes when you were younger, but you are a good person. You are tender and compassionate and giving. And my brother is in love with you, and my nephew is in love with you, and you would do well to wake up and realize that people can make mistakes and go on and be happy."

"But none of that means she's—"

"No, none of it means she's a horrible person," Maddie agrees. "And I'm sorry. But as I said in the beginning, he's our brother, and we're a little over protective."

Ellie turns away from Maddie. She rubs her face with her hands and paces back and forth over the hardwood floor. "It's just…"

"It's just what?" Maddie coaxes her. "Just say it."

"I wasn't good to him when I was pregnant. And I'm not proud of what I did—"

"I know that," Maddie says. Her voice is close behind Ellie.

"And because of those things I did, when Luther went missing, people accused me of hurting him. The police accused me. Arrested me. And people. People who didn't even know me came out of the woodwork to point their fingers at me. I was a good mom, Maddie," Ellie says as she turns around to look Maddie in the eye. "Nothing meant more to me than my son."

"I know," Maddie whispers.

"And maybe standing out here on the sidelines, Rylan doesn't look like such a good mother. But maybe she is. Maybe everything she did to Jay makes her a horrible person. But maybe she's good to Oliver."

"Okay." Maddie nods. "You're right. Maybe Rylan is good to Oliver. I guess Maeve and I just got caught up in the illusion with you and Jay together with Oliver. And we connected the dots where maybe they shouldn't have been connected."

"Maddie, I love Jay more than I ever thought I could love someone. But I'm not good enough for him. I have nothing to offer him, and I'm not good for Oliver."

"I disagree."

Ellie stares at her defiantly. Finally, Maddie backs up a step and nods toward the couch and the coffee table. "Drink your Coke."

"Can I ask you something?" Ellie asks her as they return to the couch.

"Sure." Maddie takes a big drink of her Coke.

"Do you ever wonder about the child you gave away?"

"No."

Ellie is surprised by Maddie's firm, immediate answer. She holds the Coke can en route to her mouth, finally remembers to move. She takes a sip and then lowers her hand to her lap. She turns the can in small circles on her bare leg.

"No? Just no? You don't wonder at all?"

Maddie sighs and raises her eyebrows. "Yeah, I wonder, Ellie. But I don't really want to know. I can't know. If she came looking for me now, she'd destroy too many lives in the process. I only hope that she's with a good family who's taking care of her."

Ellie wonders for a moment about the lives that would be destroyed. Certainly Maddie's life as a nun would take a hit, but what other lives would be affected? The people who have been behind her and supported her religious life? The priest? Parishioners maybe?

"Maddie?"

"Hmm?"

"I wanna go to church," Ellie says almost timidly. "Can I? Can I come to church and sit in the back and see what it's like?"

Maddie's look of surprise slides easily into a welcoming smile. "Of course you can, Ellie. Weekday masses are at six thirty and eight."

"I work at eight." Ellie shakes her head. "I could do six thirty."

"You're more than welcome," Maddie says softly. "But can I ask you something?"

"What?"

"Are you doing this for Jay?"

"No," Ellie says honestly. "I'm doing it for me."

MADDIE KNOWS SHE WILL REGRET IT, BUT SHE PARKS HER CAR in Maeve's driveway and steels herself with a deep breath. She needs to talk to Maeve for a moment, and with school starting the day after tomorrow, this might be her only time to grab a few minutes with her.

The brick house is gorgeous, but Maddie sort of hates it, because it is Maeve's fortress. Maeve is very down to earth with everyone but Maddie; she tends to use the house and the pool and every other rich girl toy as a weapon against Maddie, to hold her at a distance. Maddie has grown so tired of it that she seldom feels it anymore. But today is a day when she feels the loss of her sister keenly. Actually, she's been reminded of the relationship she used to have with Maeve and missed it often in the days since Ellie has become a part of their family.

"Maddie." Maeve is surprised to see her. Maddie thinks she should feel a boost of one-upmanship right about now, since she's taken Maeve by surprise. But she doesn't. She is just weary of being here, and she's wondering what kind of hateful thing Maeve will pull out of her pocket to say to her today. Surely, there will be something. Maeve is a kick-ass prosecutor, and therefore, she has an entire arsenal of words that sting and tones that burn.

"Can I come in for a minute?" Maddie asks quietly. Maeve is dressed in navy walking shorts and a plain white knit shirt. She is holding a glass of wine, and from the dull look in her eyes, Maddie assumes it is not her first glass of the day. She slides a cautious glance at her watch and wonders why Maeve is at home, drinking at three thirty in the afternoon.

"I finished up some paperwork here at home," Maeve explains. Her eagle eye had caught Maddie checking her watch, of course. "It's kind of been a rough week, so I thought I'd have a glass of wine."

Maddie shrugs.

"Can I get you a glass?"

"No thanks," Maddie answers quietly. "I was at Mom's last night. She seems to be feeling better." She follows Maeve back to the kitchen.

Maeve stares at her over her wine glass. Maddie slides onto a barstool and watches Maeve take a sip. "And you couldn't call me to tell me that?"

Maddie sighs, but she counts to three before she answers her. "I had some errands to run, so I thought I'd come by for a minute."

"Errands." Maeve repeats the word. "What kind of errands does a nun have to do?"

"Jesus, Maeve," Maddie hisses. "How much have you had to drink today?"

"Hey," Maeve says with an innocent shrug. "I'm curious. I know nothing about your life."

"I had to get toothpaste," Maddie answers. "Because I do

brush my teeth. And I got some dishwashing liquid. And I went by Forresters' School Supply to get a few things for my classroom. That okay?"

"Sure," Maeve mumbles with a nod. Maddie watches her retrieve two bottles of water from the refrigerator. She takes one with a quiet thank you when Maeve hands it to her. "I'm glad Mom's feeling better."

"She was outside for awhile, but the humidity was kind of hard on her. She couldn't breathe too well, so I talked her into going back inside. She was working on a puzzle when I left."

Maeve laughs softly. "Remember that winter scene puzzle she did? Thousand pieces of a million shades of gray and white."

"And she had it half way done, and Jay and his friend Mike Walch upended the card table. I thought Mom was gonna skin him alive."

Maeve chuckles. "She probably should have. Wouldn't have hurt him. Mike too, for that matter."

"Mike was hell on wheels." Maddie raises her eyebrows and remembers her brother's friend's antics. The kid had been tall and lanky and fun and because of his fun-loving personality, Maddie had always thought he was cute.

"Wonder how Jay's doing," Maeve mumbles as she squeezes the bridge of her nose.

"Headache?" Maddie asks quietly.

"Five-day headache. He came over here a few nights ago and ripped into me about Ellie. He's never gone off on me like that."

"Yeah, it feels good, doesn't it?" Maddie asks sarcastically. "He should be okay now. Ellie seems to have settled down."

Maeve eyes her sharply; the wine haze is gone now. "Ellie's settled down, huh?"

Maddie wants to sigh, because she realizes now that Ellie

hasn't talked to her sister since the night of the party for Oliver. But she knows a sigh will provoke Maeve the same as any argumentative words would.

"Yeah," she finally says. "We talked about Rylan. I think I calmed her down a bit. And she's been coming to church the last few mornings."

Maeve raises her eyebrows and gives Maddie a slow, deliberate nod. "Coming to church."

"Yeah. Before she goes to work."

"And what? Are you recruiting?" Maeve lifts a shoulder in a lazy shrug.

"Why do you always have to be such a bitch?" Maddie asks quietly. "I think Ellie is trying to figure herself out. Get past all that stuff she's got going on in her head. Why can't you support her?"

The blood drains from Maeve's face and leaves her looking faint and sick. "I do, Maddie. I just want her to be happy."

"She's got a long way to go," Maddie says as she lowers her feet to the floor. "But she's trying. She's gonna have to get through all of this before she's ready to be with Jay—"

"They've already been together—"

"I know that," Maddie snaps over her shoulder. "I mean before she's ready to commit herself to Jay in any kind of long term relationship."

"Leaving already?" Maeve asks as she follows Maddie to the front door. "Stash is out of town. Why don't you stay for dinner?"

Maddie laughs. "Yeah, I'd just as soon have dinner with a pit viper, but thanks anyway." She glances at Maeve over her shoulder and sees that her words tear a bit deeper into Maeve than they usually would.

Maeve nods and offers her a weak smile. "Thanks."

Maddie wonders why it's okay for Maeve to take shots at

her all day, any day, but whenever she opens her mouth Maeve wears her heart on her sleeve.

"What?"

Maeve shakes her head. "Nothing."

"I'm sorry," Maddie says quietly.

"No, you're not." Maeve shakes her head. "And you shouldn't be. I deserved it."

"Why don't you call Ellie?"

"I'm not calling Ellie." Maeve folds her arms over her chest. "Too old to worry about this kind of stuff anymore." Maddie studies her sister, and it is a jolt to her system to see that Maeve looks a bit rough around the edges today, as if she has aged five years since she last saw her.

"Do you wanna go out? Get something to eat?" Maddie asks, resigned to the fact that her evening has been ruined by the fact that something is on Maeve's mind. It is guilt more than the desire to spend any time with Maeve that forces her to ask.

"No." Maeve holds her gaze steady on Maddie's face. "No, I don't."

Maddie nods and pulls the door open. "You know, I still don't know what this is between us. I know the abortion is a sore spot, but I don't get this twenty-year rift."

"Yeah, you do," Maeve says softly and pushes the door gently shut behind her.

CHAPTER 24

"I MISS THIS." ELLIE AVOIDS HIS EYES. SHE STARES AT THE tennis racket that used to be Rylan's. Funny. She hadn't thought of that at all while they played, but now that they are sitting on her front porch, she can't help but think of Rylan, good and bad.

"Miss what?" he asks her. She feels his sharp blue eyes on her as she watches the sky. There are no stars tonight. The forecast had called for storms. For once, it seems they will be right.

"Just you and me," she answers simply. "Before it got complicated."

"Ellie," he says softly. She turns her head to look at him. "I miss this too, but complicated can be good."

"Storm's blowing in," she mumbles, because she doesn't want to think about things being complicated or Maeve or Maddie or Rylan. This, right now, is what she fell in love with. Jay. Time spent alone with Jay.

"If I weren't here, you'd sit outside in the rain. Wouldn't you?"

She hesitates and finally gives him a reluctant nod. "For awhile."

"Can I sit here with you? In the rain?"

"It's not raining yet," she reminds him.

"Won't be long," he says softly. He leans toward her and kisses her softly.

"Did you guys do this stuff?" She turns her head so he can't kiss her again.

"Who do what stuff?"

"You and Rylan. Play tennis. Shoot baskets," she glances at him again. "Watch the stars."

"Never, never, and never," he answers honestly. "We went out now and then. Movies. Went to eat a lot, because she hated cooking. Hated when I did, because it meant someone had to clean up. Hated sports. Didn't care for my family. Her family was a disaster. Her mom was on marriage number three when Rylan and I divorced."

"See that tree over there?" She nods her head toward the tornado tree. He nods and links his fingers through hers. "I watched it. Last year in May. I watched it, kept waiting for it to snap and fall in pieces in the street. It never did."

"Must be stronger than some trees. Takes a lot of strength to bend with the wind."

"Tell me about it," she whispers.

"Ellie?"

She looks at him from the corner of her eye. "What?"

"I wanna see Luther. I wanna see his room. See his stuff. His picture."

She stares at him in a silence so heavy with sadness, she feels like today is the day Luther disappeared. The distant rumble of thunder makes her blink. She stands up and walks down her sidewalk. Jay watches her when she squats down and tugs at the ever-present weed. When she yanks it from the ground, she turns to him and nods. "C'mon."

Luther's room has a stillness about it, as if in his absence no one can exist inside it. Ellie smothers whenever she steps inside the room, but it is an enticing way to fall apart and feel herself pressed, almost physically, with the memories that she has barricaded inside. She forgets Jay is behind her when she first steps inside. For just a moment, she closes her eyes and pretends that Luther is on the other side of the bed, on his knees on the floor, playing with Legos and building his own little world. It had always been a mystery to her, how Luther had so much trouble with fine motor skills, but he could build the most involved Lego creations she'd ever seen. She'd suspected that his creations were simply a means to an end for him, his escape to some far away world where he could control who he was and the things that happened there.

She opens her eyes when she feels Jay's gentle fingers brush the back of her arm. She knows Jay well enough to know that he wants to say something to comfort her, but he won't. He knows there is nothing he can say that will relieve the pressure building up inside her chest. Her heart swells and breaks every time she's inside his room, only to heal so that it is whole in order to shatter the next time.

With a deep breath, she crosses the floor, knowing the path by heart, and turns on the lamp beside the bed. She catches herself looking down at the pillow, as if she will see his fine blonde hair and his freckled face relaxed in sleep. Desperate to get herself under control, she looks back at Jay.

"He was a Cardinal fan too," she says softly. "Tried to make him a Braves fan, but he wouldn't have it."

Jay's smile is so sweet it hurts. "I think he and I would get along just fine."

"Yeah," Ellie agrees. "I think so too."

She sighs, then turns to the closed door five feet away from the foot of the twin bed still covered with the St. Louis

Cardinal comforter. Her hand trembles a bit as she reaches for the doorknob. Luther's scent tumbles out at her, like toys jammed in a closet in a hasty cleaning spree, as she pulls the door open.

"After he—" She licks her lips and shoots an uncomfortable glance at Jay, "After he disappeared, and I'd walked the whole neighborhood over and over, as much as I dared, I came home and turned the house upside down looking for him. Behind the couch. Under the beds. The cellar." She tilts her head back and looks up at the shelves up above the small assortment of clothes that hang from the rod. "The shelves. The washer and dry—" She buckles inward and drops her head to her hands. Jay's arms are around her in seconds, and she leans against him, grateful that he's there.

For several moments, she stands in his arms, and he smoothes his hand over her back, and she breathes. Finally she lifts her head and takes a step back. Jay allows her the distance, but he keeps his hands loose on her hips.

"You okay?" he asks gently and touches his lips to her forehead.

She gives him a silent nod and then lowers herself to sit Indian style on the floor of the closet. 'Make a pretzel, Mommy.' Luther had scolded her several times not to say Indian style. His teacher had taught them to fold their legs together to make them look like pretzels. Jay sits down beside her and watches her pull a big clear Rubbermaid container toward them.

She takes the lid off and reaches in for a small handful of papers. "He had problems with his fine motor skills," she says softly as she hands him the papers. "Had a hard time learning to write. Holding a pencil or a crayon right. Scissor skills."

"This is a zoo, isn't it?" Jay asks as he studies the top picture. It is drawn in red and blue crayon. Ellie stares at Jay in amazement. On pictures Luther had drawn at home, she would sit with him and have him tell her what he was drawing so she could write what he said on his paper. School pictures never had anything written on them besides Luther's name. Jay looks up in askance, because Ellie is too stunned to answer him.

"How do you know that?" she finally asks.

"This looks like an elephant." Jay traces the long blue trunk with his fingertip. "And this has to be a giraffe. Penguins." He looks at Ellie with a smile.

"Yeah," she answers with a nod. "I never got to take him to the zoo. Not a real zoo. But he loved elephants."

Jay is quiet as he looks through the stack of papers. He reads everything she has written on the papers Luther drew at home, like he wants to learn everything he can about Luther. Ellie finds herself drawn to the look on Jay's face as much as the papers he holds in his hand.

"He was getting the hang of it, wasn't he?" Jay looks up at her. The last paper in his hands is full of big, block lettering that spells Luther, all over the page.

"He'd have one good day out of ten tough days." She raises her eyebrows. "He'd get frustrated. He couldn't think through problems very well. Problem solving, they called it. Had trouble with his thought process."

Jay nods. "I can see the good days just from looking at these papers."

"What's really strange is that he could build really complicated Lego things," she says pensively. "Sometimes I think he used them to escape. To day dream."

"Of course he did," Jay answers with a nod. "Every little boy day dreams about being a hero or some action guy or G.I. Joe when he's building with Legos. Just like little girls play house."

Ellie's mouth tips up in a smirk when Jay looks at her. "You think I played house?"

"I do," he tells her.

"And were you a superhero or G.I. Joe?"

"Depended on what day of the week it was," he says with a little shrug. "My favorite was Luke Skywalker."

Ellie laughs. She jumps when a loud crack of thunder rattles the window panes. "Here comes the storm."

Jay leans toward her and kisses the corner of her mouth. "Are you gonna show me his picture?"

She nods, but she sits still and stares at him for several long seconds. Finally, she pulls another Rubbermaid container away from the wall and pops the lid off of it.

"I had some trouble with his delivery," she says. Her hands rest on a photo album. Jay tears his eyes away from hers and lowers them to look at the gold crescent moon shapes on the album. "I had been pushing for several hours, and he wouldn't budge. The doctor wanted to do a cesarean, but he was too far down in the birth canal. He went a little too long without oxygen—"

"Ellie," Jay says quietly and covers her hands with his. "Stop making excuses for your son. He's part of you, so I love him already. I want to see your little boy."

Her eyes burn with tears, but she nods. She turns her hand over to hold his for a moment. Finally, she digs deep inside like a backhoe tearing through several feet of dirt to create a huge, cavernous hole in the ground. A hole deep enough for a grave. She shakes her head to push the thought away and finds her courage and her desire to see her son's smiling face.

"He's cute," Jay whispers reverently. "So tiny."

"Low birth weight," she says with a nod. "His lungs were underdeveloped too. I didn't smoke as much when I was pregnant with him, but enough to do some damage."

She is startled to realize she is shaking as Jay slowly turns the pages of the album and studies the pictures of her son.

She wonders what he is thinking when he sees Luther's small, widely spaced eyes and flat face. She is about to split with need for Luther; she is desperate to touch his skin or hear his laughter. But she is desperately afraid of what Jay is thinking at the moment. About her and her son.

"Look at those freckles." Jay laughs softly. "God, Ellie, I can feel him just from looking at these pictures." His fingers touch the goofy grin on Luther's face. "I can hear him laughing."

"He loved to laugh." She licks her lips and nods. "He was very friendly. I think—" She looks away when Jay raises his head to look at her. "I think that might be what happened. Luther didn't know a stranger. No matter how often I tried to tell him not to talk to strangers, he did it anyway."

Jay nods. "That makes sense." He turns another page. "He loved you, Ellie. I can see it in his eyes. In every picture."

"But I didn't love him enough—"

"You did," Jay corrects her. He taps the photo album in his hands. "You gave him a good life. You've put your life on hold to wait for him. Tell me how that's not loving him enough."

"Look at what I did to him, Jay," she whispers.

"You made him happy. You made him smile. You made him laugh."

Ellie stares at Jay and shakes her head. "You don't get it."

"I do get it," he answers calmly. "And I'm gonna make you get it if it's the last thing I do."

She goes willingly into his arms. His arms and whispered words quickly go from comforting to arousing. His lips find hers, and he tugs the tail of her shirt from her shorts. She stops cold when she feels his hands on her bare skin.

"Not here," she says and pulls away from him. She rests her forehead against his chin. "Please? Not here. This is all I have left of Luther. I don't wanna make it about this."

~

HE IS VAGUELY AWARE OF THE SOUND OF STEADY RAIN. He could lie like this and listen to the rain and hold her forever. But when he stretches and reaches across her bed, he finds her side empty. "Ellie?" he mumbles as he blinks and tries to focus on the darkness of Ellie's room. When there is no answer, he climbs out of bed and goes to look for her. Carefully he makes his way through her house, growing slightly apprehensive when he doesn't find her on the front porch as he expected to. "Ellie?" he calls as he rubs the heels of his hands into his eyes and moves back through the living room and into the kitchen. He stubs his toe on the kitchen table, bites back a yelp of pain, and notices the back door is open.

She is sitting on the tiny patch of patio covered with a tiny roof watching sheets of rain fall from the sky. He watches her for a moment, touched by the mask of simple beauty she wears. He'd never have dreamed that first day he'd sat down to talk to her that he'd find so much hidden emotion buried beneath her calm surface. He certainly hadn't thought he'd fall in love with her and come to need her as much as he did.

"Ellie," he says softly as he pushes the screen door open and joins her on the porch. She looks up at him with dry eyes and offers him a half smile. "Don't you know how dangerous it is to sit outside alone like this? It's after two in the morning."

"I think I know better than anyone how dangerous it is to be out here alone, Jay," she says quietly as he sits down beside her. The rain has cut through the humidity. Her skin is cold to the touch.

"What're you thinking about?" he asks her.

She shrugs and avoids his eyes and stares at the rain as if she is hypnotized by it. "I just like the rain."

"More than me?" he whispers and leans close to her to nibble on her earlobe.

"I was hoping you would wake up and join me."

"Wake me up next time," he says as he slides his arm around her shoulders. "I don't wanna miss a minute when I'm with you."

"Nothing too exciting out here." She grins at him.

"We could make something exciting happen out here." He raises his eyebrows suggestively. She laughs and shakes her head. "I can't believe classes start tomorrow."

"I know," she groans.

"Got a heavy load this semester?"

"I can't," she answers. "I only go part time so I can work. Can't afford anything else."

"I saw your name on my Russian history class list."

"Is this gonna be hard? Me sleeping with the history professor?"

"We can make it work." Jay shakes his head.

She studies his face for a long moment and then turns to watch the rain again. He pulls her closer to him as thunder crackles around them. "Luther loved storms too. We'd sit out here together and watch."

"Oliver tries very hard to be brave and intellectual about storms. He'll try to explain to me what thunder is, but even as he's saying it, he's shaking in his boots."

Ellie laughs. "He's a doll, Jay."

"Ellie?"

"Hmm?"

"Have you ever made love in the rain?"

She frowns and turns her head to look at him. "Seriously?" she asks with a laugh. "No. And I have neighbors, so forget it."

"It's two in the morning. Do you really think your neighbors are gonna think we're out here making love in the driving rain?" He presses his open mouth against her neck and feels the chills touch her skin as he tickles her with the tip of his tongue.

"Why do they call it driving rain?" She rolls her head back and moans softly. "It's not driving anywhere. Right? Not driving anything."

"I want you." He wiggles around until she is straddling his lap. He pushes her long nightshirt up out of his way and lets his hands roam over her cool, bare skin.

"Jay." His name slips from her lips like a satisfied sigh.

CHAPTER 25

His mother used to tell Maeve that her money must burn a hole in her pocket. Whenever Maeve would babysit or clean her room she would beg Jolene to take her shopping. When she got older, she would simply take her ancient Chevy Impala and go shopping by herself.

Jay had always thought it was funny. Now he understands that something really can burn a hole in your pocket. He'd thought about this for a long time, all summer really. But he'd never mentioned it to his sisters or his mom. They might say he is jumping the gun. But he is certain of this. He knows he has not stepped off the roller coaster ride that is life with Ellie Jordan, but he knows this is where he wants to be when he gets off.

It is a simple, elegant ring, much like Ellie herself. White gold and a round-cut third-carat diamond. It's stunning. Jay cannot wait to see it glitter on Ellie's long finger, but he knows he cannot give it to her just yet. She is still trying to find herself, and until she finds herself and makes peace with who she is inside, she will not take him. She will not promise herself to him, because she feels she is not good for him or his son. One day the timing will be right.

As he unlocks his office door, the burgundy ring box burning a hole in the pocket of his khakis—because now that he's bought her a ring, he can't stand the thought of being separated from it any more than he likes not being with her —he imagines what he will do, what he will say when he asks Ellie to spend the rest of her life with him.

To hell with worrying about Maeve or Maddie or his mom telling him he's jumped the gun with Ellie. This time it's different. When he'd bought the ring for Rylan, he'd been a kid, in lust with a gorgeous woman, who ended up being a child herself. He'd sprung for the biggest diamond he could afford, and they'd had a big wedding, and it had all been a show. This time is staid and certain and eternal. He needs Ellie in his life forever, because he loves her.

Maybe he'll just go by Maeve's house later and see if she wants to grab some dinner. He's always been close to Maeve, and he needs to share his excitement with someone.

ELLIE HATES CHANGE. SHE HATES SETTLING INTO A NEW semester of school. New classes and new faces grate on her nerves until she feels raw inside, as if someone has scrubbed her down inside and out with sand paper. She knows that within a week or two, she will be fine and even get some enjoyment from her classes, but the settling period takes a lot out of her. There is a small part of her that knows these feelings aren't normal. She's young. She should see this time in her life as a challenge, as an adventure. But she feels old inside, and she wants no more adventure in her life. She likes calm and indifferent, and there are days she resents Jay

Bryant for infusing her plain life with excitement and fear and even desperation.

She is learning about religion, and so far, it has been more of an intellectual journey for her. Really, she enjoys comparing what Maddie is teaching her about Catholicism to the other religions she has studied both in school and on her own. She wishes that one day she could see her quest for knowledge as a spiritual journey, a come-to-Jesus journey, because she needs and wants help. She just doesn't know the first thing about asking for it.

Maddie has a dry sense of humor, a trait that Ellie has come to admire. The woman is quiet, but she has loosened up, somewhat, around Ellie. She has an odd, eclectic taste in music, which Ellie also admires and respects. If she hadn't become a nun, Ellie thinks she could probably have been a concert pianist. And if that hadn't worked out, Ellie decided after she'd heard her sing one afternoon, she'd have been a hell of a lead singer for a band.

Ellie learns something new about Maddie almost every time she is around her. And those things she learns never fail to amaze her. The woman likes beer brats, and she can drink her sister under a table, if she wants to. She went skinny dipping in Spalding Lake when she was eighteen, and she loves Howie Mandel. She can also tell Bible stories and make them as interesting as a movie on Lifetime TV, and she has a secret passion for Dean Koontz novels.

The more she learns about Maddie, the less she understands why she and Maeve are not close. She can't bring herself to ask Maddie what is going on, but she's hinted at it. She's tiptoed all around the elephant in the middle of the room and once or twice climbed right up over the top of it, and one day, she'd sat down on it and asked Maddie if she held Maeve's abortion against her.

Maddie had been slightly taken aback, but she'd considered the question thoughtfully rather than hand Ellie a careless answer.

"I guess I do," she'd said softly with a small nod. "But."

"But what?" Ellie had pressed gently.

"If we could talk about it, I could deal with it. I could forgive her."

"But, Maddie," Ellie had asked, "why do you need to forgive Maeve for the abortion? It was her decision. It was her child."

"I was fourteen," Maddie had whispered. She'd stared at her hands, folded in her lap in front of her. "I'd never had sex. Never had a boyfriend. I was educated, Ellie, but I was naïve. Innocent." Maddie had glanced at Ellie then. "Maeve dragged me with her. I sat with her during the whole thing. Holding her hand. Listening to her cry. Crying with her."

Ellie had been too surprised to speak. A long, heavy silence had crept up on them until Maddie had cleared her throat and stood up from her seat on the couch.

"That kind of thing marks a person. Ya know?"

Of course Ellie knew. Torn between Jay's sisters, she'd simply nodded.

She still feels torn down the middle when she raises her fist and taps on Maeve's front door. It is just after five. She's just survived another boring history class, and yes, this one seems like it will be interminably boring. She's not sure what even Jay could do to jazz up the History of U.S. Foreign Relations, but at least he's easy on the eyes. Doctor Prewitt almost reminds her of Granny, in the old Tweety and Sylvester cartoons. The only difference is her dress doesn't quite reach the floor.

"Hey." Maeve answers the door with a big, welcoming smile. Ellie has not talked to her since the night of Oliver's party. She wasn't sure she would be welcome back. Maeve's eyes are sort of sad, but she seems sincere as she steps back and urges Ellie inside.

"Hey." Ellie steps inside and looks back at Maeve. She is dressed in a burgundy suit; the skirt is business sexy with a long slit up the side. Ellie wonders how she can spend eight hours a day on the high heels. "Are you busy?"

"No," Maeve says and looks down at herself. "Just got home. Gimme a sec to change my clothes?"

"Sure." Ellie nods.

"Tell ya what," Maeve says. "On second thought, follow me."

Ellie follows her to the kitchen. She smiles when Maeve selects a bottle of wine from the small wine rack on the counter and raises her eyebrows in askance.

"Sure."

She watches, impressed when Maeve pops the cork on the bottle. Maeve pours them each a glass of wine and then hands one to Ellie.

"Okay." She takes a sip and runs her fingers through her hair. "Now let me go change clothes. C'mere." She tilts her head toward the hall they have just traveled. Ellie follows her back to the living room and then through a door to the left. Her office. It is more like a den than an office, but the room is clearly Maeve's domain. The colors are muted earth tones, like the rest of the house, but there are bookcases along two walls, jammed with all sizes and genres of books. A large desk dominates the far wall. The top of the desk is clear, except for the flat screen Dell computer monitor. "Sit down and make yourself comfortable. I'll be right back."

"Thanks," Ellie says with a smile. She chooses the loveseat that is just inside the door. She sinks low into the cushion and sighs with pleasure. She loves Maeve's house, and the little things that make the house a home, but mostly she loves

Maeve, and now that she's here, she realizes how much she's missed her during the past week and a half.

Again she wonders what is so horrible that Maeve and Maddie choose to live like polite strangers at best. And again, she reminds herself it really doesn't concern her. It's not like her to want to step in and fix things. Once upon a time, she didn't give another person's feelings the time of day. And now thoughts of Jay and Maeve and Maddie consume her.

"So." Maeve's voice curls around her as she strolls into the room. "Did you want to go outside? Or do you mind sitting in here? It's so hot out there. I don't feel like going out."

Ellie eyes Maeve carefully as she sits down on the other end of the loveseat. Maeve's eyes aren't so much sad, as dull and lifeless. The realization sends a jolt through Ellie. She is used to seeing Maeve vibrant and bigger than life. Maeve sips her wine and lays her head back against the loveseat. Even with her sun goddess tan, she looks a bit pale.

"What's wrong?" Ellie is no longer surprised by the things that come out of her mouth. No, she hadn't planned on asking Maeve what is wrong, but she is concerned.

"Just tired," Maeve answers. "Lot going on right now."

Ellie knows that before she stormed out of here the night of the party, Maeve would have told her in detail about what is going on right now in her life.

"I'm sorry—"

"It's not you." Maeve closes her eyes and runs her fingers through her hair.

"No, I mean I'm sorry. About the night of the party. I overreacted."

Maeve slits her eyes and looks at her. "You can't apologize for how you feel anymore than I can apologize for not liking Rylan."

"Still." Ellie shrugs. "What Rylan is or isn't or did or didn't do is really none of my business."

"I think it is," Maeve answers softly. "You're involved with my brother. You're involved with his son. You've become part of this family. I think Rylan is a whole lot of your business."

"You just hit a nerve that night," Ellie mumbles.

"I wouldn't know," Maeve says as she turns sideways on the seat to look at Ellie. "You've told me very little about what happened."

"It's just—" Ellie stops herself and thinks for a moment. "Even if everything you said about Rylan is true, that doesn't necessarily make her a bad mother. Make her love Oliver any less."

Maeve chews on her lip. "Okay, point taken. It doesn't make her a bad mother. It just makes her different from my experience as a child with my own mother. And from how I've raised my children."

Ellie nods, satisfied with Maeve's explanation. "I've missed you."

"I've been right here," Maeve says quietly.

"I know." Ellie leans over and sets her wine glass on the square, glass-topped coffee table. "I just needed some time to clear my head."

"Maddie help you do that?" Maeve asks her. Ellie cuts her eyes straight to Maeve's, stung by the sarcasm. Maeve stands and paces the floor.

"Yeah, actually she did," Ellie answers honestly.

"Good." Maeve turns to look at her and gives her a small nod. "I'm glad."

"You know," Ellie says and pulls her legs up under her. "Before the whole thing about Rylan, something felt wrong."

"What do you mean?" Maeve leans back on the bookcase behind her.

"With us. You were pushing me away."

Maeve opens her mouth to answer her, but she shakes her head and looks away. "You're right. I'm sorry."

Ellie raises her eyebrows and shrugs. "What'd I do? Did Maddie tell you what she knows?"

"No." Maeve laughs sarcastically and takes another drink of her wine. "Why does Maddie know, Ellie? I thought you would talk to me."

"I didn't tell her," Ellie answers. "She recognized me."

"What's that supposed to mean? Are you on *America's Most Wanted* or something?"

Ellie swallows hard. "You never told me why you were playing it cool with me that day."

"Because of something Maddie said. Something stupid. But it hit me hard."

"What'd she say?"

"She reminded me that you're close in age to the child I aborted. And asked me if I was using you to ease the guilt I feel over that."

"So if it bothered you that much, you felt there was truth to it."

Maeve sighs and sits down again on the loveseat. "I had to think about it. Because it wasn't fair for anyone, if that's what I was doing." She glances at Ellie. "Maybe I feel close to you because my child would be close to your age. But I don't think I'm using you to assuage the guilt. I like you. I did from the word go. I'd like to see you ride off into the sunset with my brother. Barring that, I'd like to be friends."

"Do you really feel guilty about it? Even knowing that you might not have been able to provide your baby with a good home?"

"I do feel guilty, and I will for the rest of my life. First of all, my parents would have helped. Yes, they'd have been disappointed, but they'd have helped. And really, I think anything I could have given that baby would have been better than what I did."

"What if he was sick? From the things you did to him when you were pregnant?"

"Are we talking about Luther now?"

Ellie gives her an almost imperceptible nod. "Yeah. Sometimes I think he would have been better off if I'd have had an abortion." This time Ellie stands to pace the room.

"I don't even know what happened, Ellie, but no, I think you did the right thing."

"Yeah." Ellie looks back at her over her shoulder. "Guess we both have to live with our guilt, no matter what it comes from, huh?"

Maeve licks her lips and looks away from Ellie's hard stare. "So why did Maddie recognize you?"

"Because five years ago, when Luther went missing, I was arrested for his murder." Ellie doesn't look at Maeve. She doesn't want to see the look on her face. She doesn't want to see the disappointment. The anger.

"It never went to trial," Maeve says softly.

"No body," Ellie answers, still not looking at her. "No evidence, really, except a young mother who didn't want a kid to begin with. Who happened to be the last person to see Luther alive. Who failed two lie detector tests when the police quit pretending to look for Luther and arrested her."

"So what'd you do? Slice him and dice him? Bury him in your backyard?"

Ellie turns and stares at Maeve in shock. "Are you crazy?" she half shouts. "I never laid a hand on him. Why the hell would you say that to me?"

"Don't be ridiculous, Ellie!" Maeve stands and stares at her. The anger in her eyes is enough to snap Ellie in two. She opens her mouth to say something, but she can't. *What the hell does Maeve mean? Is she serious?* "Would you really think, just for one minute, that I would believe that? Is that why you haven't told me? Because I'm the Goddamned ADA, and I might believe you killed your son?"

"I didn't hurt him, Maeve," Ellie whispers. "I swear to God, I did not hurt my son."

"Ellie," Maeve cries softly. "I know that. My God, do you really think that I'd believe that of you?"

"I thought I had a good life going. I thought I was doing right by Luther, after the way I'd acted when I was pregnant with him. I got my GED. I got a job. I got him into an early childhood program. We played together. We read books together. I loved him so much more than I ever thought I could love a child."

"Of course you did." Maeve wipes at her eyes. Ellie doesn't think about the fact that Maeve is crying. But she feels it. She feels Maeve's concern for her wrap around her like arms that care and want to protect. "You loved Oliver that way. Maddie and I could see it when you were with him."

"Then why did everyone think I was guilty? Why?" Ellie sobs. "Why did my neighbors and Luther's teachers and people we would see at the grocery store point their fingers at me and say 'Yeah, she killed her son'? Why, Maeve? I wouldn't hurt anyone, let alone my kid—"

"I know." Maeve nods and takes a step closer to her. "I know. It's wrong, Ellie, but it's human nature. Please believe that I don't think for a minute that you had anything to do with what happened to Luther."

Ellie rubs her face and looks up at Maeve. "If it had gone to trial, it would have been your job to prosecute me. I'd have been just another Alec Wittmer."

"No," Maeve argues. "No, you wouldn't have. Ellie, his son had been in and out of the ER constantly. With breaks and bruises and injuries. That man killed his son. You didn't."

"But how would you have known that?" Ellie pushes. "We wouldn't have known each other, and you wouldn't have seen me with Luther or Oliver, and you would've done your best to nail my ass to the wall. Because that's what you do."

Maeve's hand trembles as she reaches for Ellie's hand. Slowly, Ellie moves closer to Maeve, until she feels Maeve's arms slide around her waist and pull her against her body. "They had no case against you. They had nothing to prove you guilty of murder, because you didn't kill your son."

Ellie rests her head on Maeve's shoulder and closes her eyes. The tears she's cried are sticky on her face. "Do you see? Do you see now why I'm not right for Jay?"

"No," Maeve answers calmly. "No, I don't. I see someone so real and strong, who would be good to my brother. To my nephew."

"Then you're not looking at me," Ellie says as she pushes away from Maeve. "Because I'm not real. I would have stabbed you in the back the first chance I had back then. I would have slept with your boyfriend—"

"You were a kid!" Maeve shouts. "That's what kids do. Ellie, open your eyes. You've changed—"

"I tried to drink my baby away," Ellie says softly. "I wanted to miscarry him. And instead I made him sick. I made him sick and deformed and—"

"And then," Maeve says and steps close to her again, "You loved him. Didn't you? You loved him. And you held him. And you took care of him. And how many years later? Ten years later, you're still punishing yourself for a mistake you made as a kid."

"You can't call what I did a simple mistake."

"You wanted to miscarry your baby. You wanted to get rid of a problem. You couldn't afford an abortion, so you thought you could force your body to miscarry." Maeve shrugs. "That's a very immature, childish thought. Maybe even selfish."

"Ya think?" Ellie sneers, but she knows the tears that streak her face take the bite out of her words.

"But did you realize how your actions would affect him if you didn't miscarry? Did you know about fetal alcohol disorders? Did you know you could complicate the delivery? Did you know all of that, Ellie?" Maeve's voice throbs with desperation and shared sadness. Ellie cannot answer her. Her eyes are drawn to Maeve's wild eyes and the black shadows her tears have left on her face. It startles her to see Maeve's beautifully made up face wrecked from tears she's cried over her. "Did you know what you could do to your child, Ellie?"

"No," Ellie whispers.

"What?" Maeve snaps. "Did you know what you were doing or not?"

"No, I didn't know." Ellie shakes her head. "I didn't know how much damage I could do. I didn't know—"

"You didn't know, because you were just a kid yourself." Maeve slams her open hand against the top of her desk. "You were a kid, and you needed a way out, and you made a mistake. Let it go."

Ellie shakes her head. "I can't."

"Why? Why can't you let it go? Move on? You have a good man who loves you. You have a little boy who loves you and would do well to have you as a step-mom. You have friends here, Ellie. You have a family here who loves you. Why can't you let the past go?"

"I was good alone," Ellie says softly. "Before Jay. Before Oliver. Before you guys. I was good alone. I didn't need Jay to mess me up like this—"

"He loves you!"

"I can't let go, because he makes me think about it. He makes me remember who I used to be." Ellie sinks down to sit on the loveseat again. She buries her face in her hands. "He brings back all the guilt. The way I hated everyone. The way I hated myself."

"How?" Maeve slumps against her desk. She drags her fingers back through her short hair and stares at Ellie with bloodshot eyes. "How does Jay loving you bring the past back?"

"He's all I think of," Ellie says. "I used to think of Luther. Now all I can think about is Jay. How much he means to me. How he makes me happy. I don't deserve to be happy."

"Jesus, Ellie," Maeve groans.

"I used to be alone," Ellie continues. "Now, when he's not with me, I'm more than alone. I'm lonely. And I want him with me. I want his arms around me. I want to wake up with him. I want to sleep with him."

"You love him." Maeve raises her eyebrows. "What the hell is wrong with loving him?"

"Because it's all about me and what I want. And that's who I used to be." Ellie takes a deep breath. "He makes me feel selfish and demanding." She presses her lips together. "He makes me feel dirty, like I'm still the same little whore I was ten years ago."

"Oh, Ellie." Maeve winces. "Sweetheart, you can't let it be the same. You're an adult now. It's okay to—"

"I can't make the distinction in my heart, Maeve." Ellie forces the words out and swallows hard. "And I don't want to be that person anymore."

CHAPTER 26

He supposes there could be worse things, though at the moment he's hard pressed to think of one. Cancer, maybe. But really, he thinks it might feel the same. Losing Ellie, hell, maybe she was never his to lose, makes him ache all over. It makes him hurt in bones and muscles he never thought about before. It pounds in his head and burns his stomach and takes his breath away, and really, he thinks as he drains his third Bud Lite of the night, he doesn't want to face tomorrow without Ellie.

The shatter of glass snaps him out of his thoughts long enough for him to scoot George away from the shards of the amber beer bottle. He wonders if his neighbors saw him launch the empty bottle at the garage wall. He doesn't care. In fact, he thinks about going back for another beer and drinking it and sending that bottle sailing into the garage wall too. He won't, though, because her ring is on the kitchen table. And with each of the other three beers he drank tonight, he'd stopped and picked up the ring and lost himself in what he'd thought he and Ellie had shared. As much as he wants to drink it all away, to forget the way her lips taste under his, the way she curls up in his arms when they watch TV, the sound of her laughter when she played with Oliver, he doesn't want to see her ring again. He doesn't want to hold the diamond in his hand and think of how it would have looked on her finger and how she would have looked in a wedding dress and how she would have looked in his arms, on their wedding night. He's not strong enough to think of all of that again. He doesn't want to hear her voice in his head again, the same voice that said she loved him telling his sister that he makes her feel dirty. So he puts George back in the house and goes back out to pick up the pieces of the bottle and himself and the way he loves Ellie and throw it all away.

MADDIE WONDERS IF SEX EVER FEELS THIS EMPTY FOR MAEVE. If Maeve ever feels chilled and lonely after an earth shattering orgasm. If Maeve ever wishes that Stash would crawl into bed beside her and slip his arms around her and just hold her. Then again, Maeve's lover is in love with her; Maddie's is not. She'd walked into this sordid affair with her eyes wide open. Not like she can blame anyone but herself for what goes on in her bedroom in the dark.

Robert's touch never fails to excite her; he is an experienced and giving partner, which she has wondered about from time to time. Who else does he sleep with? Who else makes love with a priest and then lies alone and wonders what it would be like to wake in his arms instead of watching him slip away into the night?

She's nearing forty, and sometimes, she hates her life. She hates what she's given up, and she hates that she isn't who she claims she is. She doesn't want to be alone anymore, and yet, there are no other options open to a nun. She could leave. But where would she go? She can't have the only man she ever loved, and she's not sure how she could start over at this age. Sometimes she wishes she could talk to Maeve about this, about the way the fear explodes inside her and suffocates her. Makes her feel like she is breathing lava and reminds her of hell and that most likely, she will find herself there when she dies and how the fear and the unhappiness will never end.

Maeve would probably tell her to go straight to hell and not bother with the rest of her life here. She misses her sister, even though she has found a true friend in Ellie Jordan. She has grown close to her, and she trusts her, and yet she still misses her sister and the way they were close when they were young girls. She wishes somehow the mistakes of the past twenty years could be washed away.

She watches silently as he slides out of bed and dresses in the dark. He doesn't say goodnight. He doesn't tell her he'll call her. He doesn't look back as he disappears through the door, and she turns her head in the darkness to look at the clock. Four a.m. Alone again.

ELLIE COULD COUNT THE NUMBER OF TIMES SHE'S THOUGHT about her family since she left on one hand. Today, she is thinking of her mother. She's not sure why, but she figures somewhere in her head, wires got crossed while she slept, and she's feeling a pseudo mother-daughter relationship with Maeve. Her head pounds as she rides her bike to Maddie's house. She'd had a crying jag hangover kind of headache this morning. Now she thinks she has a plain old headache. It had been a challenge for her to pay attention in class today.

The university might have forked out millions of dollars

on renovations, which included air-conditioned dorms and classrooms, but the powers that be had yet to learn the art of comfortable climate control. Either the air was on so low Ellie had to try to concentrate on former US presidents while she mentally tracked the beads of sweat that rolled over her tailbone or between her breasts, or the air was so high that she couldn't hear her professor speak over the sound of her teeth chattering. Either way, it is exhausting, and that coupled with the heat and the pea-soup-thick air she breathes as she pedals her bike across town to Maddie's gives her one hell of a headache.

She'd heard them arguing. In the hospital corridor. She still doesn't really know how they'd known she was there, that it was time. She'd gone into labor at her friend Kristi's house. Not full-blown labor that would have freaked Kristi out, but some mild contractions. Kristi had whisked her out the door and to the hospital, and Ellie supposes she'd probably called her parents. She'd never been as close to Kristi as she had been to Blair, but then, maybe in a lot of ways that was good.

Her parents had nearly ripped each other's heads off in the corridor as she was being wheeled into the birthing room. She'd heard enough to know where the line had been drawn in the sand and where each of them stood in relationship to the line. She wonders if they are still married. It really wouldn't surprise her to learn they'd split up over that line in the sand. Ellie supposes maybe she should thank her mother, because if she hadn't spoken up, she might be less than a woman right now. Then again, maybe she should be less than a woman, because she hadn't handled the responsibility well the first time.

Maddie looks worse than Ellie feels, and that's saying a lot. She's never seen Maddie look anything other than refreshed and collected, but today she seems tense, and there is a crease in her forehead that screams out loud and clear, headache.

"What's wrong?" Ellie asks as Maddie lets her in.

"Rough night, long day." Maddie dismisses Ellie's concern with a wave of her hand. "You don't look so good yourself," she says as she studies Ellie's face.

"Headache," Ellie mumbles. "I'm fine."

"Yeah? You look hot," Maddie says and leads her back through the house to the kitchen. "Hungry?"

Ellie eyes the makings of a good sub sandwich on Maddie's counter. "Looks good, thanks," she answers with a nod. "Can I do anything?"

"Sure, grab us something to drink," Maddie answers with her back to her. "So how come you have a headache?"

Ellie sighs and takes two glasses from the cabinet next to Maddie's refrigerator. "I don't know. The heat, I guess." Ellie fills the glasses with ice from the bin in the freezer and does a double take at the counter. "Fresh tomatoes? You got more?"

"Yeah." Maddie chuckles. "I have a ton. Take some with you when you go home."

"My mom and I used to eat tomatoes like apples," Ellie says wistfully as she takes the pitcher of tea from the refrigerator.

"Really?" Maddie stops, knife in hand, and turns to look at Ellie. "I think that's the first time I've ever heard you say anything about your mom."

Ellie stares for a moment at the knife suspended above the sub sandwiches and thinks again of the argument her parents had had when she was in labor with Luther. Uncomfortable, even queasy, she pulls her eyes away from the knife and looks up to meet Maddie's gaze.

"I guess I've been thinking about her some today," Ellie

admits. She swallows hard and turns away from Maddie to pour their tea.

"How come?" Maddie asks with practiced nonchalance as she returns her attention to the sandwiches.

"Talked to Maeve last night," Ellie mumbles. "I think that just made me think of Mom."

Ellie sits down as Maddie sets two saucers on the table. Maddie avoids her eyes and then grabs a bag of Lays potato chips from the cabinet. "I'm glad you talked to her."

"You look it," Ellie says sarcastically.

Maddie takes a drink of her tea. Her icy green eyes study Ellie over the top of the glass. "No, I am. She's been upset by that night, the things said. She cares about you, Ellie. I don't wanna see something come between you two."

"She told me what you said to her." Ellie takes a small bite of her sandwich. "About her abortion."

Maddie raises her eyebrows. "I'm sure you won't believe me, but I wasn't trying to be vicious. To either of you."

"Why wouldn't I believe you? I don't think you sit and brainstorm ideas to hurt me."

"But you think I take every shot at Maeve that I can get."

Ellie shrugs. "Seems to me like you two take every shot at each other you can."

"Yeah." Maddie nods. "I guess we do, but that's not what this was about. I was just concerned. About her. Getting too close to you. About you, getting too close to her. If you guys weren't on the same page."

"Still. Wouldn't it suck for Maeve to remind you that I'm around your daughter's age? All in the name of protecting you."

"It would suck," Maddie agrees quietly. "Again, I didn't mean to hurt her or you." She takes a bite of her sandwich and sits back in her chair, a pensive look on her face. "She's eighteen. She turned eighteen last month."

Ellie's gaze flies up to meet Maddie's. "Your daughter?"

"Yeah."

"I thought you don't think about her."

"I do," Maddie says softly. "And you know what I think about most of all? What I pray for?"

"What?"

"I pray that she's happy and healthy, of course. But I also pray that she never tries to find me."

"Why?" Ellie shakes her head. "I don't get that. Maddie, if I could have one more day with Luther, another hour. If I could just see his face again."

"She's Stash's daughter, Ellie," Maddie whispers. "Maeve can't know that I gave birth to Stash's daughter."

CHAPTER 27

SHE HAS NEVER SAID THOSE WORDS ALOUD. NEVER. NOT EVEN in confession, which she finds a bit hypocritical considering she is involved with a priest. Granted, she doesn't go to confession with Robert. But who's to say the priests she does talk to are any more chaste or obedient than she and Robert are?

Her mother knew she was pregnant, yes. In fact, it had been her mother to help her pack her bags and leave town to have the baby on the sly. She'd never asked who the father was. Maddie wonders now if she knew, or if it simply wasn't important to her. She can't really imagine either of those options. Surely, her mother would have had something to say if she'd known Maddie had been pregnant with her brother-in-law's child.

It had mattered to Jolene. Of course she wondered who had gotten her youngest daughter pregnant. But she hadn't asked, and Maddie had been grateful. She'd never told Maeve; she'd never told Stash. Never a soul. And now she sits and stares at this young girl who has just come into her life over the past summer and waits for her to say something about the fact that the daughter she placed for adoption is Maeve's husband's child.

She watches Ellie's eyes, because she knows that she will see the censure first in those eyes. Ellie is thinking hard, that much is obvious. She stares at Maddie, stares so hard that Maddie can feel her eyes touching her. Twice she opens her mouth to say something, and twice she shakes her head and sinks her teeth into her lip.

Finally she shakes her head and raises her eyebrows and lays her head back against the chair. "Wow. I don't even know what to say to that."

"You could borrow a page from my book and tell me you don't hate me for something I did almost twenty years ago."

Ellie nods slowly. "I don't hate you. I'm just stunned." She sighs again and drags her hand down over her face, stopping to rub at her forehead with her fingertips. "You guys are more screwed up than I am."

"Yeah," Maddie agrees with a small nod. "We are, kind of."

"This would kill her," Ellie whispers.

"It would." Maddie pushes her plate away.

"You said you were in love with him." Ellie pops a chip into her mouth. "You're in love with Stash?"

"I was," Maddie says quietly. "I think a lot of the feeling has faded, but I was in love with him when I was younger."

"When he was married. They were married when this happened, right?"

"Maeve was pregnant with Peyton."

"Jesus," Ellie hisses. "I don't know what to say."

"I don't know what I want you to say," Maddie mumbles. "I don't even know why I told you. I feel like I don't know much of anything these days."

"How were you in love with him?" Ellie frowns. "I mean, how did you end up in love with your sister's husband?"

"I don't know." Maddie shakes her head and shrugs. "He

was gorgeous. And he was nice. Yeah, he was Maeve's boyfriend, but he paid attention to me. Talked to me like I was a person instead of looking at me like I was different."

"Why were you different?"

"I was just quiet. I kind of lived in Maeve's shadow. And I was okay with that," Maddie says quietly. "But Stash acted like he cared. Of course I fell in love with him. I didn't know it was happening. I just thought we were friends."

"Are you saying—" Ellie stops herself. She tilts her head and frowns. "Are you saying he was in love with you?"

"No." Maddie shakes her head. "No. He never loved me. Not like that. Maeve was out of town one night. Some kind of seminar. They hadn't been married long. I went over to their house just to hang out. Things between Maeve and me at that point were very tense. I never knew what to say to her after the abortion."

Ellie nods. "Yeah. I guess that would be hard."

"I went over to hang out with Stash. I never intended for it to happen."

Ellie takes a sip of her tea. "How did it happen?"

"We'd both had a few beers. He asked if I wanted to watch a movie. So I was lying on the couch. And he was sitting on the floor. I was kind of buzzing. It didn't take much for me. I came onto him. One thing led to another."

Ellie is quiet, but finally she looks up and says, "He could have said no."

"He could have," Maddie agrees. "I wish he would have. I wish a million times a day that it wouldn't have happened. I never meant to hurt her."

"Does she know?"

"God, no," Maddie answers and buries her face in her hands. "No. I think she thinks it's the abortion that came between us. I need her to believe that's what it is so she never guesses the truth."

"Yeah." Ellie presses her lips together and nods. "You can't let her know the truth, Maddie. Stash is her rock."

"I know."

"She's got so much on her plate right now. She's so down on herself after the Wittmer case—"

"Wasn't her fault," Maddie says softly. "She can't fight the bad guys and win every time."

"And Luke was sentenced earlier this week. Fined and given community service."

Maddie winces. "What'd he do?"

"Marijuana."

"Damn," Maddie groans. "That's good for an ADA's kid."

"Exactly."

"Ellie, I know you're close to her, but you have to promise me you won't say anything about this."

Ellie's eyes grow wide in surprise. "I would never say a thing about this to anyone, Maddie. It's your secret. And I don't want to hurt either one of you."

"I don't know why I told you," Maddie says again. "I just— It's been getting to me. I've never talked about it. And it's been on my mind so much lately."

"Ya know what?" Ellie reaches across the table and touches Maddie's hand. "I'm glad you felt safe enough to tell me."

Maddie raises her eyebrows and wipes at the corners of her eyes. "You won't say anything to Jay?"

"No." Ellie squeezes her hand. "I won't tell Jay."

"I hate to ask you to keep something from him. I shouldn't expect you to keep secrets from—"

"I won't say anything to Jay, Maddie," Ellie repeats. "I promise."

∽

SLEEP HADN'T COME EASY, AND THE BIZARRE DREAMS OF Luther and her family in New York with Rylan had left her wishing she'd never fallen asleep. She'd been haunted in the shower, trying to piece together what the hell the dreams meant and what the hell could ever come of Maeve and Maddie. Was it possible her parents had Luther? She'd never given it a thought before today. Even now, as it nagged at her back in the deepest corner of her mind, she knew it was ridiculous.

Her parents had been hurt, disappointed in her when they'd found out she was pregnant, thanks to her little brother's big mouth. And yes, her father had done his damnedest to have the old battleaxe doctor who delivered Luther to do a hysterectomy on her to prevent her from ruining another innocent child's life. But she didn't see either of them as kidnappers. She's pretty sure that her mother would love to have seen Luther, held him, loved him, but she's just as sure that she wouldn't stalk her grandson and swipe him the second he was alone in the backyard.

Still. These dreams were so unsettling. The dreams that involved her and Luther together were her saving grace. But the dreams that reflected her reality, the dreams where Luther is gone and she's searching, leave her feeling hazy and lost.

She has fifteen minutes before Russian history class, so she decides to drop in on Jay and say hi. She hasn't talked to him since yesterday morning, when he'd left her house after a quiet night together. She misses him.

"Hey." She offers him a smile as she knocks on his open door. She steps inside, but she freezes when she sees the look on his face. "What's wrong?"

He shakes his head and scoots his chair back. "Nothing, Ellie." He lounges in his chair and folds his arms back behind his head. "What're you doing?"

Cold dread coils in the pit of her stomach. Jay has never regarded her with that half-lidded look of disdain. It slips into her veins. She feels the chill deep in her bones.

"Came by to say hi before class," she answers slowly. She feels so insubstantial at the moment, the way Jay is looking at her now, that she thinks the weight of her backpack might pull her over backward. "What? Why are you giving me that look?"

"Were you ever gonna tell me?" he asks as he leans forward. She watches him curiously as he closes the book on his desk and stacks two smaller books on top of it.

"Tell you what?" The panic inside her threatens to drown her, like a tidal wave. What has she neglected to tell him? There's nothing else. She'd slept around when she was a kid, and she had no idea who had fathered her child. She'd tried to miscarry her child, and in so doing, had made him a very sick little boy. She'd lost her son to the unknown, and really, it was the not knowing that kept her tied up in knots most days. What more could she, should she have told Jay?

"How I really make you feel," Jay says quietly. His words are precise and cold.

"How you really make me feel," she repeats with a frown. "What are you talking about, Jay?"

"Let me ask you something." He stands and picks up a pen from his desk. "Where did you intend for this to go? Me and you? Was it fun? Or was this just your sick way of getting off?"

"Jay." She shakes her head and raises her hands, palms up. This is a new side of Jay Bryant, one she doesn't understand. "What's going on? What'd I do?"

"The other day," he says quietly as he slides his hand into the pocket of his khaki shorts, "I overheard you talking to my sister. Imagine how good it made me feel to hear you say I make you feel dirty."

"But—"

"No." Jay shakes his head. "Don't. There's nothing you can say to make me forget what you said."

"Let me explain," she whispers and lays a hand flat against his chest.

"I went to Maeve's to show her this." He pulls his hand out of his pocket and shows her the ring box in his hand. "I thought it would take a little time." He sets the box on his desk and picks up the stack of books. "Now I get it. A little time would never do it, because what was beautiful to me was dirty to you. I'm just still trying to figure out what you got out of it if it was that bad."

She stares at the little burgundy box as he moves toward the door. Her throat is tight with fear and anger and hatred and sadness. She tries to swallow her heart, but it's lodged there sideways and it won't budge. When she glances at Jay he is at the door, but he turns back to her. Eyes bright with tears, she waits for his final blow.

"Shut the door on your way out, would you?" he asks quietly.

She stares after him for a long time before she turns back to the box. Her hand shakes when she reaches to touch it. Her stomach clenches. The box is warm to the touch, and she imagines it is because Jay has been carrying it in his pocket. Jay bought her a ring, and he's been carrying it in his pocket, and now he doesn't love her or want her anymore.

She pulls her hand away from the box, as if it is suddenly red hot, and it burns her. She needs to get out of here. The room is starting to spin and tilt, and she's not sure any distance she puts between herself and Jay and this ring will stand her back upright. She's come so close to being given a second chance, and she's torched it all to hell.

Two steps from the door, she stops again and looks back.

Her teeth chatter as she picks up the box. The office is so quiet she hears the soft cushioned click as she pops it open.

"Oh God," she whispers. The light catches a cut in the diamond, and it sparkles. It was supposed to be hers. She wonders what it would have looked like on her finger, how the name Mrs. Ellie Bryant would have sounded, and how it would have felt to kiss Oliver, her stepson, goodnight as she tucked him in at night.

The ring belongs to Jay. The dreams, her wishes belong to no one. She closes the box and returns it to his desktop and pulls the door closed behind her.

CHAPTER 28

THIS IS A DIFFERENT KIND OF HEARTACHE THAN LOSING Luther had been, a completely different shade of blue. Luther is a pale blue now, faded over the years from all the times she's taken it out and examined it and then folded it to put it away. Losing him had been a deep, intense electric blue, a sharp, keen sense of loss like she'd never known. Like she'll never know again.

But loving and losing Jay is a midnight blue, as dark and velvety as the sky overhead when she sits outside to look at the stars. It is a dull ache that consumes her, twenty-four hours a day. Jay is the shadow that follows her down the sidewalk as she tries to outrun the mistakes of her past. He is the sun overhead as she works in her yard, wishing like hell she could forget. Jay is the heart that beats inside her at night, when she lies awake in the dark.

If only he'd let her explain. If only he'd stayed at Maeve's a moment longer. Then again, maybe it wouldn't matter. And really, maybe it's better this way. Better for Jay and Oliver, certainly.

Her class with him is unbearable. Of course she hadn't

gone the day she'd seen the ring and he'd said his goodbye. She'd left St. Dominic Hall on autopilot and rode her bike home and crawled into bed. Sleep had not come to her rescue. They rarely speak now, and watching him talk with the other students, especially all the gorgeous women, young and old alike, feels like a million little pinpricks in her skin and her throat and her eyes every day. She wishes she could hate him for buying the ring when she definitely wasn't ready. But she can't, because she's been trying to get ready. Trying to get past her guilt so she can give herself to him. She wishes she could hate him for showing her the ring and making her swallow the way her words hurt him and the desperation to fix things and the realization that it's over. But she can't.

It is Maeve that calls her to invite her to Jolene's for Labor Day. Ellie would like to go, but she won't. She is no longer a part of Jay's family, and she doesn't want to be anywhere near him. Just seeing him makes her hurt, makes her ache all over like she's been picked up and slam dunked half a dozen times.

It is Maddie who comes to her house to check on her when she doesn't show up for the Labor Day picnic. Maddie, who finds her—she figures looking like a dead woman—still in pajamas at one in the afternoon. Maddie, who barges in and opens drapes that she has not opened since she saw the ring.

"So I could be nice here and ask if you're okay," Maddie says as she turns to look back at Ellie. Ellie is slumped against the doorframe, the dark kitchen a backdrop against her pale, thin frame. "But I'm gonna do something uncharacteristic of me and be selfish and ask you if you're avoiding my family because I told you about me and Stash."

Ellie raises her eyebrows and lets Maddie's accusation sink in.

"No."

"No what?" Maddie asks irritably.

"No, I'm not avoiding you or your family because of what you told me."

"Then why are you?"

"Why am I what?" Ellie asks. She sighs and rubs her forehead and wishes Maddie would close the drapes and head right back out the door she'd just come in.

"Avoiding me. Avoiding Maeve. What's going on, Ellie?"

"Jay didn't tell you?" Ellie asks with an arched eyebrow.

"Tell me what? Jay doesn't tell me hi, unless I elbow him in the ribs first." Maddie's eyes flash with anger. "Remember? I'm the odd man out with Maeve and Jay. What the hell is going on?"

"Ask Jay," Ellie says softly. She turns her back to Maddie and retreats to her bedroom. She burrows back into bed, but she is not surprised moments later when she hears Maddie's footsteps follow the same path to her bedroom and then feels her mattress give as Maddie sits on the side of her bed.

"What happened?" Maddie asks. Ellie hears the regret in her voice.

"We're done, Maddie," Ellie mumbles into her pillow. "Just leave it at that."

The air is heavy with unspoken words. Ellie lays still, her muscles taut with the tension. She wants to be alone. Alone, like packing up her meager belongings and what she has left of Luther's life and walking out of this town and starting over. Alone. This time she would make damned sure she kept it that way.

Ellie hears Maddie moving, but she doesn't look at her. She doesn't care, as long as it takes her one step closer to the door.

"So that's it?" Maddie finally asks. She is subdued now,

probably careful because she sees the fragile nutcase is coming unglued.

"Is what it?" Ellie sighs.

"You and Jay break up and to hell with me and Maeve? We don't matter?"

"I never asked for this." Ellie sits up. She stares at Maddie defiantly. "I never asked for Jay to come nosing around here. I never asked for him to fall in love with me. I never asked to get involved with you and Maeve and Oliver—"

"Neither did we, but here we are, involved!" Maddie shouts. Ellie cringes and looks away from the fire in Maddie's green eyes. "I don't know what happened between you and Jay, but I thought we had more than something disposable now that that's over."

Ellie combs her fingers back through her hair and takes a deep breath. "I can't see Jay." Her words do not break, but they are small and sad. "It's hard enough to see him at class. To see him having fun with everyone else. Talking to everyone else. He won't even look at me."

"Why didn't you call me?" Maddie asks her. "Or Maeve? Ellie, we'll listen. That's what friends are for."

"I just needed some time," Ellie whispers. "Just needed time to let it sink in."

Maddie nods and waits a moment before saying anything. "What happened?" she finally asks.

Ellie glances at the alarm clock. It is one thirty. She looks back at Maddie. "Aren't you supposed to be at your mom's house?"

"I was," Maddie answers with a shrug. "Maeve said she'd called you. We were worried about you."

"You came because you thought I was avoiding you—"

"Not really." Maddie shakes her head. "Yeah, it's crossed my mind. And I've wished a hundred times that I wouldn't have told you. But Maeve and I were concerned because you weren't there, and Jay didn't say anything."

"Why do you wish you wouldn't have told me?" Ellie licks her lips.

"Because I have the same self-doubts that you do," Maddie admits. "And I can't help but wonder if you look at me differently since I told you."

Ellie considers Maddie's words. "Different, yes," she says with a nod. "But only because I see more of you now."

"Too much."

"Yeah." Ellie's smile is small and bitter. "Sucks when people see so far inside you. I know."

"What happened, Ellie?"

"He overheard part of a conversation between me and Maeve." Ellie meets Maddie's eyes. "The wrong part."

"A conversation you and I haven't had?" Maddie asks curiously.

Ellie shrugs. "I just told her it's hard for me to be with Jay, because he reminds me of who I used to be. And that makes me feel dirty."

"You've never told me that." Maddie raises her eyebrows.

"Kind of hard to talk about sex with you." Ellie grins.

Maddie lifts her legs to sit Indian style on the side of Ellie's bed. She chews on her lip and cocks an eyebrow at Ellie. "Doesn't bother me." She shrugs. "I'm not perfect, Ellie."

"Are you telling me you're sleeping with someone?" Ellie asks from behind her hands.

"Not much sleeping gets done," Maddie says quietly.

Ellie nods. "Okay." She avoids Maddie's eyes.

"That makes you think less of me, doesn't it?"

Ellie lifts her head. "Truthfully? No. It doesn't make me think less of you. It makes me sad for you."

"Why?"

"You're unhappy, Maddie. You can fool yourself, but I see it. You're not happy with this life."

"I don't fool myself." Maddie shakes her head. She stands and paces Ellie's bedroom. "We're not here to shrink my head."

Ellie shrugs and raises her eyebrows. "I care."

"Where would I go?" Maddie stops at Ellie's window and pulls the curtains back. She stares out at the sunny day in silence.

"If you left?"

"Yeah." She nods. "What would I do?"

"Teach," Ellie says simply. "Allow yourself the freedom to be who you really are."

Maddie laughs and glances back at Ellie over her shoulder. "Now that's deep."

"Sorry, my brain's dead." Ellie flops back on the bed. "I hate him, Maddie."

"No, you don't," Maddie says as she turns back to Ellie. She leans a shoulder against the wall. "You love him so much a minute without him makes you feel like your skin is on too tight, and you're gonna burst out of it at any minute."

"Shut up," Ellie says without venom.

"It doesn't have to be over."

"He bought me a ring," Ellie announces. "A diamond ring. He showed it to me as he kicked me out of his office."

"He's hurt."

"I know." Ellie sighs. "I know he's hurt. But he won't let me explain anything."

"How do you explain what you said? Does he really make you feel that way?"

"Not when we're together," Ellie whispers. "It's when he's gone. And I think about him. And what he does to me." She sighs and sits up again. "I was easy in school, Maddie.

Beyond easy. Thinking about sex makes me feel like I haven't changed a bit since high school."

"You've changed, Ellie. If you were the girl you say you were, you've changed." Maddie gives her a lazy shrug. "Open your eyes. See the woman you've become."

"I can't, Maddie. I don't know how."

PART OF THE REASON WHY MAEVE HAS NEVER CONSIDERED herself a good Catholic is because she hates confession. It's not that she hates to be wrong, not even so much that she hates to say she's wrong. She hates knowing she's disappointed someone or angered someone. Today, she hates that what she has to tell Ellie will make her angry. She holds no hope that this is going to be an easy conversation, but it's one they need to have.

Maeve stretches again. Ellie glances up at her from her spot on the floor. "Sorry. My couch sucks," she says with a grin.

"Nah, it's okay," Maeve lies, and they both laugh. "It beats being at the house with all of Luke's friends there."

"I can't believe you're letting him have a college party at your house," Ellie says and shakes her head.

"Stash and Jay are there." Maeve shrugs. She hates the way the smile dies on Ellie's face. It has been nearly three weeks since Jay and Ellie stopped seeing each other. Maeve and Maddie have done their part to keep Ellie connected to them, but neither of them has been able to smooth things over between Ellie and Jay. Maeve hates the way both of them are so unhappy, but she reminds herself every day that it's not her business. Actually Stash reminds her every day that it's not her business. She tries to make herself remember his words, but it's not her nature to stand by quietly while someone she loves is hurting.

Ellie sits up and grabs Maeve's empty popcorn bowl.

"Don't do that," Maeve says softly.

"Don't do what?" Ellie stands and looks back at her.

"Every time his name comes up, you walk away."

"What am I supposed to do, Maeve?" Ellie widens her eyes. "It's survival."

Maeve sighs and nods. Of course Ellie is right. It's Jay who refuses to talk to Ellie. "Sit down for a minute," Maeve says and nods to the couch.

"Why?" Ellie eyes her suspiciously.

"I have to tell you something."

Ellie stares at her for a moment, obviously dreading whatever Maeve has to say. Could she know? Did she know what she'd done? Maddie had been upset with her, but surely she wouldn't have said anything to Ellie about it.

Ellie perches on the edge of the couch and gives Maeve an impatient look. "Shoot."

"Lighten up," Maeve says with a smile. "It's not like I'm a doctor with bad news."

"No, but you look guilty," Ellie answers. "What'd you do? Tell me you went to bed with that gorgeous guy who helped you with the Wittmer case, and I'll clobber you with my bare hands."

"Gorgeous guy?" Maeve frowns.

"Yeah." Ellie nods. "The one who was at your office the other day when Maddie and I stopped in to ask you to lunch. Last Saturday."

Maeve throws her head back with a laugh. "Kody?" she asks incredulously. "Please. He's young enough to be my son."

"He's good-looking, and you look guilty."

"He's cute, but compare him to Stash," Maeve says pointedly. "Really think I'd need him?"

Ellie has to laugh, but she arches an eyebrow. "So what did you do?"

The laughter dies instantly, and Maeve takes a deep breath. "I put out a few feelers on Luther."

Ellie's stare is harsh and hurt and even hateful and hopeful. Finally she looks away and tucks her hair behind her ears. "I asked you not to do that."

"I want to help."

"I specifically asked you not to," Ellie repeats.

"What if we can find him?"

"What if we can't? It's been five years. What are the statistics on that, Maeve? Surely you know. He disappeared five years ago. There was never a ransom note, not that I could have scraped five hundred bucks together if I'd tried. He was probably dead within twenty-four hours from the time I realized he was gone."

"You don't know that," Maeve says quietly.

"I read everything I could find on child abductions when he went missing." Ellie's voice is deadpan now. "Some statistics said he'd be dead within three hours. Some said five. Disabled children are more likely to be abused. There's been a three-hundred-percent increase in child abductions since nineteen eighty. Almost all sexual abusers are heterosexual men." Ellie turns her head to look at Maeve. "Do you know what it feels like to imagine your five-year-old son raped by a grown man? Sodomized. Beaten. Do you know what that feels like, Maeve?"

Ellie's eyes are wild with pain and anger. She swallows hard and looks away again.

"Of course I don't know what that feels like," Maeve finally answers. "But what if there's a chance he's alive somewhere? What if we could find him, alive and healthy, Ellie? Don't you wanna know?"

"I let this go." Ellie ducks her head and rubs her eyes. She drops the popcorn bowl, and Maeve watches salt and unpopped kernels litter the floor. "It took me a long time, but I let this part go. Don't do this to me again."

"How can you sleep at night—"

"I don't!" Ellie stands up. She paces across the floor and stands with her back to Maeve. "I don't sleep much. I have nightmares. I think about him everyday, but I can't go back to hoping he's alive. I can't go back to that hole inside, the one that only Luther can fill. Because every day that I didn't get him back, that hole grew wider and deeper and it was gonna take over who I was."

"It can be different this time," Maeve insists. "I can help you. I have friends—"

"How long have you been looking?" Ellie presses her lips together.

"Couple weeks."

"And what have you found?"

"Three boys that match his age. Two found in the Midwest. Pictures don't match," Maeve quietly admits defeat.

"And?" Ellie shrugs.

"And what?"

"Were they alive?"

Maeve shakes her head. "No. I compared faxed autopsy photos to the picture you showed me of Luther."

"So why are you telling me this?" Ellie asks and throws her hands up in defeat. "I don't wanna know about other dead little boys. I don't wanna know about my own dead son—"

"Because I want you to have closure. I want you to know one way or another what happened to your son. I want you to be able to move on—"

"You want me to be with Jay, and it's not happening, Maeve. It's over. It doesn't matter to Jay what I do now."

"Give him some time," Maeve presses. She stands, but she

keeps her distance when Ellie squares her shoulders and lifts her head in defiance. "You don't love someone like he loves you and then just stop on a dime. You can't. He was hurt. He'll come around."

"He won't listen to me." Ellie shakes her head. "He doesn't even look at me anymore."

"It's more than what I want for Jay," Maeve says adamantly. "It's what I want for you. I want you to be able to put this part of your life in the past, if that's where it belongs, and be happy. With or without Jay."

"This," Ellie says as she rolls her eyes and looks around the living room, "is my life. Without Luther. I have accepted my life without Luther."

"You hold your guilt like a shield in front of you, keeping everyone at bay." Maeve's eyes burn. She has cried so much lately she feels worn down to nothing and no one.

Ellie nods. "Yes, I do. But it's not guilt over losing him—"

"Don't lie to me—"

"I'm not lying," Ellie says loudly. "Yes, at first, I blamed myself for what happened to him. Still do at times. But that's just a shadow of what I feel for what I did to him when I was pregnant. That's the guilt that leaves me paralyzed and hopeless."

Maeve sighs and sinks back to the couch again. "There's something else I need to tell you."

"Great," Ellie mumbles sarcastically. "Let's hear it."

"I called your mother." Maeve watches the color drain from Ellie's face. The color in her eyes fades, as if the blood that rushes beneath her skin sucks the life from the rest of her. She turns without a word and leaves Maeve alone in the living room.

CHAPTER 29

THE CONCEPT OF THE IMMACULATE CONCEPTION HAS ALWAYS intrigued Ellie, but she is even more interested in Mary, the mother of Jesus, now that Maddie has explained it in more detail. Ellie had gleaned from her Catholic friends when she was younger that The Immaculate Conception honored the Blessed Virgin Mary for conceiving Jesus without sin. According to Maddie, and she's pretty sure Maddie should know what she's talking about, the Catholic feast is actually a celebration of Mary's conception and the fact that she is born without sin, Original Sin.

"So God singled her out to carry His child and wiped the slate clean, huh?" Ellie asks softly. There is an open bible in her lap. She feels Maddie's intense gaze on her as her eyes devour the details in the vividly colored pictures in Maddie's bible pages. She is drawn to Mary's simple beauty. It's more than that. Serenity. She watches her own fingertip trace the curve of Mary's head bent over her newborn son.

"Singled her out, yes," Maddie agrees. "Before she was born."

"How can He know someone before she's born?" Ellie looks up.

"He creates life, Ellie," Maddie says softly. "Of course He knows you before you're born."

"Do you really believe that?"

"Yes, I do." Maddie's answer is firm. "I know I've made mistakes, but I don't question my faith or the doctrine of the church."

"Is that how forgiveness works for Him? He just erases the past and sets you back on track to try again?"

"Yeah." Maddie nods and shrugs. "If you ask Him for forgiveness."

"What if you don't know how?" Ellie whispers. Her fingers still smooth over Mary's blue gown.

"You just ask. You just talk, Ellie, the way you talk to me." Maddie raises her eyebrows. "It's not God who needs to forgive you. God can see the way you live now. The way you shoulder your regret about Luther." She touches Ellie's hand. "You need to learn to forgive yourself."

Ellie's mouth works to answer her, but she can't find her voice. Finally, she looks away and shakes her head. "I don't know how."

"You're learning," Maddie says softly.

"No." Ellie lifts her gaze to look at Maddie. "When I go home at night, and it's all said and done, I still feel like the person I used to be."

"Can I ask you something?"

"What?"

"Are you ever going to forgive Maeve? She's only trying to help."

"I didn't ask for her help," Ellie mumbles. She closes the bible and sets it on the couch, effectively distancing herself from Maddie.

"But it's her nature to want to help. How can you fault her for that?"

"I asked her not to get involved." Ellie stands up and crosses to the window. It is a bleak fall day. The sky is gray and heavy with rain. Ellie imagines she can see the wind, streaks of cool gray that paint the houses and the trees and make them fade into the horizon as if they are miles away, instead of just across the street. "She did it anyway. I can't live like that again, Maddie. I can't wake up each day and think it might be the day I get my son back. I can't."

"I understand that," Maddie says gently. She nods when Ellie looks back at her. "I do. Maeve doesn't. You're angry with her for something that is part of who she is. She loves you, and she wants to help you."

"She called my mother." Ellie spits the words out and turns back to the window. The leaves are just starting to turn colors. She thinks of the tree in her neighbor's yard; it's made it through another season of storms. Will it hang on another year?

"I know she did, and I'm sorry," Maddie tells her. "I asked her not to. I told her I thought she was overstepping, but she's a fixer. She wants to fix it for you."

"And she just assumed reuniting me with my parents would do that." Ellie licks her lips and turns to look at Maddie. "When I was in the hospital, I heard my father demanding that the doctor do a complete hysterectomy on me." Her lip quivers, but she continues. "I was sixteen. He wanted to take away my right to have children, because I was irresponsible. He didn't even know at the time that Luther would be so messed up."

"He can't do that," Maddie says softly. "He had no legal right to do—"

"No." Ellie chews on her lip. "The doctor didn't do it. But that's not the point."

"The point is that your father demanded him to do it." Maddie nods.

"I used to go fishing with my dad," Ellie whispers. "I baited all of his hooks." She laughs softly, but tears streak her face. "We used to play pitch and catch every day when he came home from work. He taught me how to shoot a jump shot."

Maddie waits for her to go on. She slides her hands in her pockets and stares at Ellie, shared sadness in her eyes.

"I was Daddy's girl." Ellie's voice is hollow.

"I'm sorry."

"I can't go back to him now, Maddie," Ellie cries quietly. Maddie takes a step closer to her.

"Ellie, what about your mom? Remember how you felt when you lost Luther?" Maddie bends her knees and dips a bit to look Ellie in the eye. "What if she feels the same way?"

"Does she?" Ellie asks hesitantly. She feels a flicker of something warm in her belly, but she is quick to push it aside.

"She lost you ten years ago," Maddie reminds her. "For ten years, she didn't know where you were. If you were okay. If you were alive."

"What did she say?" Ellie holds her breath.

"Maeve said she cried," Maddie answers. "But, Ellie, you should talk to Maeve. Ask her what your mother said."

Ellie gulps in a huge breath and wipes at her eyes. "I don't want Maeve involved in this. I don't want to go home, and I don't want you guys to pressure me."

"You just said you wanna know what your mom said. At least ask Maeve that."

"She'll take it as a green light to keep looking for Luther." Ellie shakes her head. "I don't want her—"

"Ellie, you've shut her down cold. Twice." Maddie squeezes her hand and then lets go. "Give a little, will ya?"

～

SEEING HER HANDWRITING, OUTSIDE OF CLASS, HAD GIVEN HIM quite a jolt. Seeing her handwriting on a small envelope in his mailbox was like a big hand had reached down his throat and grabbed his heart and squeezed it painfully hard. The check inside, written for the amount of the starter he had put on her car, had been that same, big hand ripping his heart out and dragging it up his throat. Had it been the check inside? Or the absence of a note? Of anything personal? He'd stared at her signature forever, and he figured he'd probably looked like an idiot, standing there on his front porch, staring at something he'd retrieved from his mailbox.

She had small, neat handwriting. Small enough that it often gave him a headache when he read her test papers. But it didn't matter. Even now, after they'd stopped seeing each other, her handwriting never failed to touch him. Make him remember the sound of her laughter. Her whispers as he made love to her and held her close against his body.

Like a fool, he'd taken one glance at the envelope with her handwriting on it and thought... thought what? What had he thought? That she'd written to him, begging him to take her back? That she'd written a long love letter and said she missed him and she wanted his ring and she wanted to marry him? Ellie is too prideful to do that, and he knows that. But there had still been a flicker of hope when he'd seen the envelope. And now there is a huge wave of disappointment drowning him, and he hates the helpless feeling and the fact that he'd lost her and that he still loves her.

Instead of going inside, he turns and marches back to the curb and climbs up inside his truck. He doesn't really know how to handle helpless or desperate so he churns the feelings in his gut until finally, when he pulls the truck to the curb in front of Ellie's house, he's good and pissed. He can do pissed;

he can wing any scenario by the seat of his pants, if he's good and pissed off.

She's on the front porch, and for a moment her vulnerable pose catches him off guard and all he wants to do is take her in his arms. She's casual in her faded jeans and oversized sweatshirt. He notices when he sits down beside her that her feet are bare. Her knees are pulled tight to her chest, her arms tight around them. In the thick of the night, he can't tell what color her toenails are, but the fact that they're painted touches him.

"What're you doing here?" Her voice is gruff. She doesn't look at him. She's not looking at the stars either. She's staring at the tree across the street, watching it as if she expects it might come crashing down at any second. He wonders why she's not looking at the stars, and that makes him think of the conversation he and Maddie had had just the other day. Maeve had begun a search for Luther, and Ellie had sort of banished her from her life. He hurts for both of them, but before he can slide his arms around Ellie's shoulders, he remembers the hope he'd had when he'd opened the envelope with her handwriting on it. And the way the hope had drained out of him and left him empty when he had realized what she'd mailed him.

"What is this?" he asks, pulling the envelope out of his back pocket. She glances at it, but she won't look at him.

"The money I owe you for fixing my car," she answers simply. "I'm sorry it took me so long to pay you. I forgot about it."

"Ellie, I don't want your money."

This time she did look at him. "I owed you the money for the part you put on my car."

"It was a favor. I didn't expect—"

"Yeah, I know it was a favor," she says with a nod. "But I didn't expect you to buy the part."

Jay sighs and shakes his head. "I don't want your money."

She watches in silence as he rips the check in half. "What do you want, Jay?"

"Nothing." He looks away from her heavy stare. He wants to put his arms around her. He wants her to say she loves him. He wants her to explain to him how something he had seen as beautiful was dirty to her. He wants to rewind time and find himself somewhere else while Ellie was saying those horrible words to Maeve.

When he glances at her again, her head is turned away from him. He wonders what she's looking at.

"I hear you're going to New York next week," she finally says. Her voice is neutral, and it makes him wonder how she feels about him going to New York and seeing Rylan. Granted, he's not going to visit Rylan. He's picking up Oliver and bringing him home for the fall break. But he wants her to be jealous. If she's jealous, doesn't that mean she still loves him?

"Yeah."

"Say hi to Oliver for me," she tells him.

"I'm bringing him here for fall break," he tells her and wonders why he feels the need to explain himself to her.

"Still," she mumbles.

Again silence creeps in on them. It's dark and thick, and it breeds a fear inside him like he's never known. What if she'd never loved him at all?

"I hear Maeve's—" He cuts himself off, because he doesn't want to hurt her and just saying Luther's name seems to hurt her.

"Yeah." She shrugs. "She is. And I asked her not to."

"She wants to help."

"It's really none of her business," Ellie says quietly. "Nor did she have any right to contact my mother."

Jay lets those words sink in for a moment. Maddie had

told him that too, and he agrees with Ellie, that Maeve had overstepped her bounds by calling her mother. And yet, he still understands why Maeve had done it.

He clears his throat. "Have you heard from her?"

"Maeve?"

"Your mother."

From the corner of his eye, he sees Ellie swallow hard, working to keep her emotions under control. "No. I don't want to."

"But she must have been relieved to know where you are. To know you're okay."

"Am I, Jay?" she asks as she turns to eye him again, with accusation, he thinks. "Am I okay?"

Her eyes bore into him as she waits for an answer. His heart is tight, and he feels his stomach clench. Maybe she's not okay, but she was just right for him. Until he'd realized he hadn't meant anything to her.

He stands up and glances down at her. "Look. I just..." He shrugs. "I'm glad you're still friends with Maddie and Maeve." He makes the mistake of looking her in the eye before he walks away. He expects her eyes to be cold or empty, because he can still hear her words in his head. He can still feel the sharp pinpricks of pain he'd felt when he heard her say them, all over his body, as if he were a voodoo doll and someone had stuck him good.

But her eyes are warm and dark and sad, and before he turns to walk away from her, she loses her control and tears wet her long, thick eyelashes. Slowly, she closes her eyes and turns her head, and he knows he's been dismissed. He turns and heads to his truck and doesn't look back again.

CHAPTER 30

RUSSIAN HISTORY IS A BITCH WHEN ALL YOU CAN THINK OF AS your professor talks about the czars or the wars or society is how it felt when he used to slide his fingers up your arm to cover your hand as you pointed at the stars. The sound of his voice next to your ear as he told you a story about a star named Maladorny. It's a bitch to study in the evening when you've pissed away all your class sessions remembering Jay the man and not listening to Jay the professor and even when you have an exam the following day, your mind is still focused on sharing ice cream with Jay and Oliver, and your heart is so full inside it feels like it's going to burst, and you think you might die. For the first time since she went back to school, she hates the itch between her shoulder blades that reminds her that she needs to study but distracts her from her pages of notes and the textbook that's been open to the same page for over an hour now.

She welcomes the small tap on her door and hurries to the screen to find Maeve standing on her porch. Surprised, she pushes the door open and steps back. The cold and the damp creep in around her bare feet as she watches Maeve consider coming in.

"I'm looking for Maddie," she says instead. "She's not here, is she?"

"No." Ellie shakes her head. She curls her toes under in a useless attempt to pull them out of the cold. The rich colors of autumn have decorated the tree across the street, and she can't help but look past Maeve and catalog the flaming orange and crisp, spun gold. A light wind touches the leaves. Ellie shivers at the sound of the leaves kissed by the wind.

"God, I wish she'd get a cell phone," Maeve groans. "Know where she is?"

Maeve, Ellie sees when she looks at her again, is decked out in office professional. She wears a chocolate brown pantsuit and an adobe silk tank under it. Ellie loves her presentation, from her expensive looking clothing to her richly colored sable hair.

"No," Ellie says softly. "I don't. I'm sorry."

"Thanks." Maeve nods and turns to walk away.

"Maeve?" When the woman looks back at her over her shoulder, Ellie raises her eyebrows and chews on her lip. "C'min?"

Maeve dips her hands in the pockets of her slacks and studies Ellie's face for a moment. Finally she turns back to the door and steps inside. Ellie can feel the cold air seeping from her suit. She smells the dampness, the fresh, earthy smell of autumn mixed with Maeve's perfume.

"How ya doing?" Maeve asks her quietly. Ellie hates the way they keep replaying this awkward scene over and over. "Haven't talked to you for awhile."

Ellie frowns and shakes her head. "Okay, I guess. Jay came by the other night."

"Yeah." Maeve nods. "He told me."

Ellie clears her throat. "Can I get you something to drink?"

"Coffee?" Maeve asks with a small shiver. "It's kind of cool out there today."

Ellie winces apologetically. "Hot chocolate?" she offers.

"Sounds good."

"It's not the good kind. I don't have any milk."

"I don't care," Maeve says simply. She follows Ellie to the kitchen and sits while Ellie fills the teakettle with water. "You don't have a microwave?"

"Nope." Ellie laughs and shrugs. She sets the kettle on the stovetop.

"What were you working on?" Maeve looks down at Ellie's books.

"Test in Jay's class tomorrow," she answers.

"Jay says you could breeze through all of it without cracking a book."

"Well, we'll see if he's right tomorrow," Ellie mumbles. "I can't concentrate anymore." She sits down and turns her eyes to Maeve. "Hard to give a damn about this when all I can think about is Jay."

"Do you still love him?"

Ellie laughs bitterly. "Yeah. I do." She stands up again. "Too bad for me, huh?"

When Maeve doesn't say anything, she glances at her. She is staring at Ellie's notebook, but she is a million miles away.

"Kind of a whirlwind romance for everyone involved, I guess," Maeve finally says. Her words are flat, but Ellie sees the sharp edge of pain in her dark eyes when she looks up at her.

Ellie turns away and stares at the kettle. She knows she can't will it to boil any faster. To busy herself, she takes out two mugs and the Nestles Quick. "Luther loved hot chocolate." The words slide out of her mouth with ease. "I think he'd have made a good cowboy, always wanted to be outside. Even when it was cold and damp like today." She glances at Maeve and sees that she is hanging on every word. "I made it with milk then. Loaded it down with marshmallows. As soon as it was cool enough, he'd take a big drink and get all that milky, sticky frothy stuff all over his face like a moustache. Then I'd call him Mister Jordan. It made him laugh."

Maeve smiles when she looks at her again. "Peyton drank coffee with me. I'd give her a cup of milk and sugar and add a drop of coffee, and she'd climb up in her chair. Sit on her knees and sip her coffee with me, while I read the paper."

It's Ellie's turn to smile. "There's something I want to talk to you about, but—"

"But what?" Maeve asks gently.

"I'm afraid I'll give you the wrong idea," Ellie says as she spoons heaps of chocolate into the mugs.

"I've looked at four more autopsy photos," Maeve tells her.

The words hit Ellie like shots from an M16 rifle. She takes a moment to catch her breath and then reaches for the kettle when it starts whistling. "No, that's not what I need to talk to you about," she says as she shakes her head.

"What?" Maeve prods her.

"My mother." Ellie's words hang between them for a few awkward moments.

"I know how you feel about what I did," Maeve finally says. "I'm sorry that I hurt you. But I can't apologize for letting a mother know her daughter is alive and well."

Ellie hands Maeve her mug and then sits down again. She avoids eye contact by closing her books and setting them aside. "What you did is make me feel like I'm out of place with your family."

"Ellie!" Maeve sloshes hot chocolate over her mug as she sets it down. "That's not true. You know—"

"I do," Ellie says simply. "In my head, I know you didn't mean it that way. But that's how my heart took it. I've made a mess of my life. And now I've hurt your brother. And maybe you'd like to wash your hands of me and move on."

"Has it ever occurred to you that I admire you?" Maeve's eyes are heavy and intense on Ellie.

Ellie laughs. "Why would you admire me? You're a successful attorney with a great family. Great house. Financial security. A husband who loves you."

"You got pregnant at sixteen. And you had the baby. And you kept him. I took the easy way out."

"I gave birth to him after I—"

"That's water under the bridge, Ellie." Maeve shakes her head. "Especially with me. You loved your son more than anything else, and you took good care of him. You gave him a home. You made a life for yourself. You're working. You're going to school."

Ellie nods, but she says nothing.

"Look," Maeve sighs and runs her fingers through her hair. "I know I overstepped with you. And I know better than to tell you I won't do it again, because most likely, I would. But I certainly didn't do it to get rid of you."

"What'd she say?" Ellie whispers. Her eyes burn, but she blinks to hold all those long dead emotions inside.

"Not much, El," Maeve admits. "She cried. I just told her that you'd become a part of our family. That you were safe and healthy. That you were going to school."

"Did she ask about Luther?"

"Yeah." Maeve nods. "That was hard."

Ellie swallows hard, but she draws her knees up to her chest and rests her forehead against them.

"She thanked me." Maeve takes a drink of her hot chocolate. "And then she asked me not to call again." Ellie raises her head to look at Maeve. "I got the feeling she didn't want your father to know I called."

"I'm sure she didn't." Ellie decides they must still be together, but she doesn't doubt that their marriage staying together is contingent upon her mother pretending like she never existed.

"I asked her not to contact you," Maeve continues. "But I gave her my phone number in case she ever wanted to talk."

"And has she called you?" Ellie asks. She tries not to hope that Maeve will say yes. When that doesn't work, she tries to hide that she wants Maeve to say yes. She knows she's failed when Maeve's eyes fill, and she turns her face away before she says very quietly, "No."

OLIVER WANTS TO VISIT ELLIE, AND JAY CAN'T MAKE HIM understand why they can't just drop in on Ellie unannounced. It's simple when you're a kid. If you love someone, you tell her. End of story. Hell, even Rylan made it sound that simple. Granted, he hadn't given Rylan too many details, but she'd put him in his place when he was in New York.

She'd stopped him cold when he'd come onto her after she'd tucked Oliver in the night he'd arrived. Actually, in hindsight, he was glad she had. He'd fallen into habit with her, and it had seemed like a good idea at the time. Use sex with Rylan as a way to forget about Ellie. Except he knew when he kissed her that he didn't want her. He knew he wouldn't be able to get it up for her. Thank God, she'd shoved him away and asked him point blank what was going on with Ellie.

He'd told her they weren't seeing each other and simply said that Ellie was using her past as a way to hold him off. Rylan had floored him then by crying. He still doesn't know what to make of everything she'd said, as they sat in her living room and talked about the future and more importantly, Oliver's future. Doesn't matter anyway, not as long as Ellie feels the way she does.

"Hey, someone said there's a good looking guy here!"

He smiles when he hears his sister's voice boom in through the kitchen door. Oliver, who is curled on the floor playing with George, looks up with a sloppy grin. Jay watches as Oliver climbs to his feet and throws himself into Maeve's arms when she enters the living room and gives her an even sloppier kiss on the cheek.

"Long time, no see, shortstuff." Maeve kisses him back.

"Daddy says I can't go see Ellie," Oliver whines. Jay rolls his eyes as his son uses his first weapon in a long line of defenses. He's told Oliver often that men don't bat their eyelashes to get what they want, but as long as it works for the kid, he's not going to quit.

"I'll take you to see her," Maeve says with a smile.

"You will?" Oliver asks excitedly. He cups Maeve's face in his hands and gives her a smacking kiss on her lips. "Thanks, Aunt Maeve!"

She laughs and sets him down. "You bet." She flops down on the couch by Jay. "You look like you've been hit by a train."

"Worse," Jay mumbles.

"Wanna talk about it?" She offers.

"Not now."

"Aunt Maeve." Oliver tugs at her hand.

"What, honey?"

"I wanna go see Ellie."

Jay has to smile. His son is in love for the first time. And why not? What is there not to love about Ellie Jordan?

Except maybe her fatalistic attitude about herself. He can accept her flaws, her mistakes of the past. It's the way she uses them to push him away that drives him to distraction. Not to mention that what they had never meant as much to her as it did to him.

Oliver's hair is still longish and curly. He wears carpenter jeans that make him look even shorter and a bright orange Nike sweatshirt. Jay finds himself in awe of his son. He wonders what it would be like to lose him. To wake up one morning and lose Oliver and never see him again. When his heart misses a beat and he feels like he's clawing his way out of a plastic bag, he shakes his head to push the thought out of his mind.

He wonders what it would be like to have a baby with Ellie. To touch her again. Afraid Maeve will guess the direction of his thoughts, he jumps up from the couch and tousles Oliver's hair as he walks by on the way to the kitchen. "Not today, buddy."

"Why not today?" Maeve follows him.

"Because you're working," Jay says automatically, because as excuses go, it's a good one. But he realizes then that Maeve isn't dressed for the office. She's in blue jeans and a faded blue sweatshirt and Keds.

"No, I'm not," Maeve answers. "I'm running errands. It's dinner time. Let's go get Ellie and go somewhere to eat."

"I'm not going out to eat with Ellie," he says firmly.

"How are you going to patch this up if you don't take the first step?" Maeve asks him. The fire in her eyes tells him she's cleaned the sentence up from what she's thinking. They are both very aware of Oliver watching them and listening to them.

"Why do I take the first step? Why is it my problem?"

"It's your problem because she's trying, and you shut her down."

"She said—"

"I know what she said, Jay." Maeve nods. "And I know she has more to say, and I know you won't listen."

"I don't think she loved me," Jay says quietly when Oliver leaves the room, bored with the adult conversation. They hear Oliver giggling, and George barking.

"Then you're a damned fool," Maeve answers simply.

"I need to talk to you, Maeve." Jay shoves his hands deep into his pockets. "About Rylan."

"What'd she do now?" Maeve asks with a shake of her head. "And how is that important when we're talking about Ellie?'

"Oh, it's important." He nods.

"So tell me later," she says with a shrug. "Let's go get Ellie and go out."

Jay hesitates, but Oliver is chasing George through the house, and he stops when he hears Maeve's suggestion.

"Can we, Daddy?" His eyes are so big and blue and full of hope, Jay cannot say no.

Ellie is home, but it is obvious she has just gotten home from work. She is still wearing her khaki pants and black knit shirt when she opens her door to them. She greets Maeve with a smile, eyes Jay suspiciously, and then grins when she sees Oliver standing by Jay.

"Hey!" She pushes the door open and opens her arms to his son. Jay's chest is uncomfortably tight when Oliver rushes into her embrace, and she picks him up to swing him around in circles. "I missed you, Oliver!"

"Me too," he says and squeezes his arms tight around her neck.

"What're you guys doing?" Ellie addresses this question to Maeve, and Jay assumes she doesn't plan to talk to him at all.

"Came to see if you wanna go out to eat with us," Maeve answers.

"Sure." Ellie grins, but still she avoids Jay's eyes. Oliver still in her arms, she hurries to the kitchen and grabs her keys and her small purse from the table. She glances at Jay as she pulls her door shut behind her. Jay is driving, so Ellie and Oliver climb into the backseat of his truck. Ellie straps Oliver into his car seat and talks to him, but Jay tries to ignore her and listen to Maeve as he drives to Kasey's, a local bar and grill where Oliver likes to eat.

Inside the restaurant, they are seated at a booth and Oliver clings to Ellie. Jay watches her face closely, and he knows she has to feel the way he's looking at her. She will not give an inch, but she doesn't seem to mind Oliver's atten-tion. They order, and Ellie plays tic-tac-toe with Oliver, while Jay watches her and pretends to be listening to Maeve. He thinks again about Rylan and sighs, weary and tired. Ellie looks up at him then, and their eyes lock.

She chews on her lip, and he remembers her soft kiss, and he wishes she would let him just stroke his thumb over her lip. Afraid she is going to look away when Oliver taps the back of her hand, he searches for something, anything to say just to hold her attention for a moment longer.

"I graded your test last night on the plane." It's lame, but it's all he can come up with. Still she glances at Oliver, smiles, and then looks up at Maeve.

"Did I bomb it?" she asks and looks back at him. She did score lower than she usually does, but she'd scraped by with an A minus. He wonders what thought she and Maeve had shared with that look.

"A minus," he answers. She glances at Maeve again.

"Told ya," she mumbles to Maeve.

"Yeah, horrible grade," Maeve agrees. She takes a drink of her tea. "What're you planning to do with all of your history, Ellie?"

"I don't know," Ellie answers. She pencils in an O on the

grid and watches Oliver study the progress of the game. "I guess I haven't thought about it."

"Ever thought about law school?" Maeve asks her.

Ellie looks up with a sharp frown. "No."

"I thought you wanted to teach." Jay drums his fingers on the table. "History."

"I don't know what I want, Jay," she answers in a lifeless voice, eyes back on the tic-tac-toe grid.

Their food arrives, and Jay watches Ellie pull Oliver's chicken strips apart so they will cool quicker. He listens to her talk to Maeve about a TV show they have apparently watched together on occasion. He talks to Maeve about his mother when she tells him she is concerned again about her health. He and Ellie have nothing to say to each other. Thankfully, Oliver doesn't seem to notice.

She pays for her own meal, and though he wants to argue, he doesn't. She kisses Oliver goodnight when he pulls up in front of her house, tells Maeve goodnight, and climbs out of the truck and then looks back at him and mumbles a good-bye. He catches the evil look Maeve shoots at him and then slides down from his side of the truck to walk Ellie to the door.

"You don't have to do this," she says without looking at him. He follows her to the door.

"I want to," he says automatically.

"No, you don't." She turns to him when she reaches the door. "Maeve told you to."

She unlocks the door and frowns at him when he follows her inside.

"I hate that we can't even be civil to each other," he says quietly. He stares at her boldly, but his hands feel superfluous so he tucks them in his pockets.

"Hard to go back to being friends after what we had." She licks her lips.

"Did that guy really ask you out?"

"What?"

"I heard you tell Maeve some guy asked you out the other day after your US foreign history class."

"Yeah," Ellie says softly. "He did."

"Are you gonna go out with him?" He hates that his voice is thick with jealousy, but he hates the thought of her with another man even more.

"No." She crosses her arms over her chest.

"Ellie," he says her name and it feels like cotton candy, so soft and sweet on his lips. He takes a step toward her and pulls his hands from his pockets. He wants to kiss her. Slide his arms around her and hold her.

She raises her hand and skims her fingertips over his jaw. "Did you sleep with Rylan? Did you make love to her last night?"

It matters. He is stunned by her question. It matters to her if he slept with Rylan. She's jealous. She wants him. But does she love him? Rylan. Oh God. He'd thought about making love to Rylan last night, because he'd been desperate to get Ellie out of his mind. He'd thought about it. He'd kissed her. He'd closed his eyes as he kissed her and wished with all his might that Rylan was Ellie and that he could be with the woman he loved while he loved the woman he was with. Instead, his ex-wife had sat him down and talked to him and what she'd said had left him shell shocked, and he had yet to get a grip on the way his life could change.

"No—"

Ellie shakes her head and touches her fingers to his lips. "Never mind."

"Ellie, nothing happened," he says desperately.

"Took you an awful long time to think of an answer." She backs away from him and folds her arms across her chest again. "Goodnight, Jay."

He licks his lips and imagines he tastes her touch there. She presses her lips together and looks away, but not before he sees the sadness in her eyes. Outside, he glances at the sky as the door clicks shut behind him. The night is overcast. There's no comfort for him in the stars.

CHAPTER 31

ELLIE IS LEARNING TO WORSHIP THE BLESSED VIRGIN MARY IN anything but a typical way. Maddie knows Ellie is enthralled by the pictures of Mary in her bible and the stories of the Annunciation and Nativity. Maddie can't imagine sitting Ellie down with a religion book and trying to teach her the doctrine of Catholicism in an ordered way. She loves the fire in Ellie's eyes as the girl listens to her talk about Mary and the explanations behind the Holy Days of Obligation devoted to her. Ellie had been especially intrigued by the concept of the Immaculate Conception. Today she is hanging on Maddie's every word about the Assumption, mouth open in wonder when Maddie tells her that Mary's body was taken to Heaven and that Catholics now pray to Mary in petition.

Ellie believes, whether she knows it or not. It may be out of sheer desperation, but Maddie is confident that Ellie's interest has fostered a strong belief in God and the powers of prayer. Maddie has not considered pressuring Ellie to make a commitment to the church, to take a formal religion class or to be baptized into Catholicism. She is just happy to see Ellie sliding gracefully into the faith and at the same time becoming more comfortable in her skin. Maddie sees Ellie at mass often, though Ellie never ventures far into the church. Most days, she appears lost inside herself, and Maddie believes this is the religion she needs most right now. Self-discovery and forgiveness.

"My mom gave it to me when I took my vows," Maddie says now. Ellie is holding her rosary, fingers curled slightly around the emerald jewel beads.

"It's beautiful," Ellie says reverently. She looks up at Maddie, but her eyes are hazy and distant. "This is the color of your eyes."

Maddie smiles. She is touched by the comment, but Ellie is already looking at the rosary again. "I'm not very good at what I do, Ellie," Maddie says softly. "But I do believe with all my heart that she listens."

"How often can you be forgiven for something you know is wrong?"

Maddie raises her eyebrows; Ellie's words hit home. She sighs but finds she doesn't trust her voice to answer her.

"I'm sorry," Ellie says and shakes her head. "I shouldn't have said that. It's none of my business."

"I've made it your business," Maddie says simply. "And you're right. I'm just scared to leave."

"Why? If it would make you happier to leave, why does it scare you?"

"Leaving my home. Being out on my own. Wondering what my mother would think. What Maeve would think."

"Who cares what they think? This is about your happiness." Ellie touches Maddie's hand. "Maddie, maybe it's about your eternal life, if you believe that. And I think you're strong enough to do whatever you want."

Maddie climbs to her feet and moseys over to her window. It is hard to believe Halloween is just days away. Some people are so strict they don't allow their children to partake in the superstitious holiday. Maddie loves it. She loves the stream of children who ring her doorbell and chime trick or treat when she answers and practically sing thank you when she gives them candy. Every year she sits alone and hands out candy and wonders what her daughter dressed up like each year of her childhood.

She rests her forehead on the glass. She's never told anyone that. She's never been able to tell anyone the way she's thought of her daughter through the years. Not until Ellie. The glass pane is cold against her skin. She longs to be outside, to feel the crisp air against her skin and smell the decay as the last of the leaves fall, and the trees stand barren, like skeletons lined up and down her street. She longs to be free, to walk away from all that she is supposed to be and find who she is deep inside.

"I'd have to leave town," Maddie says to Ellie, but she still stands with her back to her.

"I don't think so," Ellie answers. "But so what if you did? You could start fresh anywhere."

Maddie turns to look at Ellie, who still holds the rosary. "Do you remember the Hail Mary?"

Ellie nods. She looks up as Maddie comes back to sit by her again. She hands Maddie the rosary and watches her with sharp eyes. Maddie takes the crucifix in her hands.

"The Apostles Creed," she says softly. "It's a prayer that sort of enunciates all of the Catholic beliefs."

"Is that like the Nicean Creed you say at mass?" Ellie asks with a look of sincere concentration.

"It is, kind of." Maddie nods. "That came from the First Council of Nicea in A.D. 325. It was an attempt to combat the heresy of Arius. Arianism denied Christ's divinity."

"You know, the history alone is very interesting," Ellie says thoughtfully.

"It is," Maddie says with another small nod. She moves

her fingers to the next bead, the first emerald bead, set apart from the next three. "The Our Father."

"Which you say at mass, before communion." Ellie nods.

"Right." Maddie moves her fingers again and holds the next three beads loosely over her fingers. "These are Hail Marys. And then a Glory Be."

"I've never heard of that." Ellie looks up at her.

"Very simple. Glory be to the Father, to the Son, and to the Holy Spirit. As it was in the beginning, is now and forever shall be, world without end. Amen." Maddie's heart slows a bit as she settles into the familiar. Yes, she wants her freedom, but she is still comforted by the familiar. "Then the first mystery. Lots of mysteries. That used to confuse me when I was a kid. The Sorrowful. The Joyful. The Glorious. Now they have the Mysteries of Light."

"You had to know them when you were a kid?"

"Yeah," Maddie says with a smile. "When they're written down, though, it's just a matter of memorization." She looks at the rosary again. "The Our Father."

"What about this?" Ellie touches the small silver piece that connects the beads that make the loop of the rosary. On Maddie's rosary, it is a small, metal depiction of Mary.

"The Fatima Prayer when you start. And then when you finish the decades, which are just Hail Marys, the Hail Holy Queen."

"Sounds harder than Jay's tests." Ellie laughs softly.

"It's very simple once you try it," Maddie tells her. "But I'm sure it sounds complicated."

Ellie lays her head back on the couch and closes her eyes. "Maeve said Rylan is flying Oliver here for Halloween."

"Yeah. She's going to Las Vegas, I think." Maddie glances at Ellie.

"I think Jay slept with her when he was there a couple of weeks ago."

Maddie sighs. She starts to deny it, because she doesn't want to think her brother could be such an ass. But she stops herself, because she knows Jay can be an ass, and he might have slept with Rylan. Then again, how does that make him a bad guy? No worse than the rest of them anyway.

"I wish you would just tell him you still love him," she says instead.

Ellie shrugs. "He doesn't listen."

"Oliver is so crazy about you," Maddie says softly.

Ellie shakes her head and sits up straight. Maddie knows that look. The conversation is over. Ellie won't talk much about Jay, and she's just reached her limit. "How's your mom doing? I worry about her."

"Yeah, I know," Maddie agrees. "She always seems to be under the weather these days."

This time Ellie stands and wanders to the window. Maddie wonders if Ellie loves the cold bite of the wind and the skeleton trees that reach to skim the dark gray skies.

"I think you should think about it," Ellie says quietly.

"Think about what?"

"Leaving."

ELLIE KEPT TO HERSELF SO MUCH WHEN LUTHER WAS LITTLE, she'd never actually taken him trick or treating. She regrets that now. Yes, she'd pieced together costumes for him, and they'd had their own little Halloween party, complete with far too much chocolate for either of them. And one year, she *had* taken him to the mall to trick or treat, the year he was four. His last Halloween with her. She wonders, for just a moment, if he's ever trick or treated since he's vanished. Wishful thinking. Before she can dwell on the thought, before the antithesis of that thought can get a nasty grip on her throat and make her hurt from head to toe, she hears a light tap on her door.

Oliver's trick or treat socks her in the gut and leaves her breathless. She'd been expecting Oliver and Jay to come by; she'd been hoping they would come by, but now that they are here, she thinks she might melt like the big Hershey bar and the King-Size bag of M&M's she got for Oliver would if she left them sit on the dash of her car in the middle of July.

She smiles, even though her stomach hurts, and she wants to cry. She flicks her eyes up to look at Jay and fights the urge to reach out to him. She thinks a smile plays at the corner of his lips, but she looks away too quickly to be certain. Oliver grins at her as she squats down in front of him.

"If it isn't the king of the jungle," she says and holds her hand out so he will give her five. When he does, she closes her fingers around his small hand and pulls him close to hug him. "Cool costume, Oliver," she says as she smoothes her hand down over the wild fur on the back of the lion costume.

"Thank you, Ellie." He squeezes her tight and then backs up, eyes bright with anticipation.

"What?" She grins. "You think I have candy for you?" She stands when he nods and motions for them to come inside.

"Just what you need," Jay says with a groan when she hands Oliver the chocolate. Oliver beams and shows her his pumpkin. Already the bottom is full of small candy bars. She sees several Tootsie Rolls and wonders if he has already been to Maddie's house. Maddie had told her Oliver loves Tootsie Rolls.

"Been to Aunt Maddie's?" Ellie arches an eyebrow.

"Not yet," he answers and shakes his head.

"Where'd you get all this candy?"

"Been around to a few friends' houses," Jay answers for him. "Some of the teachers over at the college."

"I see." Ellie glances at Oliver again. He is still looking at her, eyes still bright with excitement. "What?" She leans over and picks him up. She can't nuzzle his neck because of the costume. Luther had dressed as a Cardinal baseball player the last Halloween he'd been with her. She rests her forehead on Oliver's lion's mane, closes her eyes and presses her lips together.

"Will you come trick or treating with us, Ellie?"

She has no desire to walk alongside Jay and not talk to him or touch him. She can't say no to Oliver, because she wants to spend tonight with him and Jay. Missing Luther has become a full-time obsession again since she has fallen in love with Oliver.

"I don't think it's a good idea," she says softly. She lifts her head and looks at Jay as disappointment paints his face.

"Please, Ellie?" Oliver whispers.

"Come with us, Ellie," Jay says with a nod.

She swallows hard and tries to breathe. All the hope inside her is lodged just under her heart, and it hurts to breathe too deep or hope too hard.

"Are you sure?" she asks Jay.

He answers with a simple nod, which is not enough but at the same time, more than she'd hoped for.

It is almost like old times being with Jay's family. Almost, except that Jay does not touch her. He does not hold her hand or put his arm around her or even touch his hand against her back or her arm when he speaks to her. Actually, he doesn't have all that much to say to her. She longs for him to hold her hand, just that small skin-to-skin touch would mean so much to her right now. But she makes herself content just to be in his company. They go to Maddie's house first, and Ellie notices that Maddie wears that same lost look that she's seen in the mirror on occasion. Loss marks a person, changes the landscape of her face and colors her faintly blue. Maddie, Ellie knows, is handing out candy and thinking of all the years she has missed out on in her daughter's life.

She can't say anything to Maddie, so she simply slips her arm around her and squeezes and feels the sadness in her shoulders, which are usually strong as steel. Oliver hits the jackpot and squeals with delight when Maddie pours a bag full of Tootsie Rolls into his pumpkin. Jay groans again, and Maddie and Ellie share a laugh.

Jay asks Maddie to go with them when they leave, but Maddie begs off, and Ellie understands that she just needs to be alone. She feels Jay's eyes on her as they buckle their seatbelts, and he pulls away from the curb.

"You know, don't you?" he asks quietly.

"Know what?" She looks at him, surprised by his question.

"Something about Maddie," he says without looking at her. "Something about Maddie and something about Maeve and why they don't get along."

Ellie raises her eyebrows in acknowledgement, but she says nothing. She has no intention of telling secrets that belong to someone else.

"It's okay," Jay says as if he senses her discomfort. "It just seems like you're pulling them back together."

She stares at him in silence. It is an awesome responsibility to be charged with, putting the Bryant sisters back together after all that has ripped them apart. There are a million things she could say; she could tell him she loves both of his sisters. She could tell him that inside Maeve, the protector, is a woman who is fragile like the rest of the world, who sometimes needs to be protected and loved. She could tell him that his sister who is a Catholic nun is so much more. She is a mother who suffers from the loss of her child. She is a woman who wants to love and be loved in return.

She says nothing. She's not sure words could do justice to the way she feels about Maeve and Maddie.

They end the night at Maeve's house. Luke and his buddies are eating pizza and candy and talking and laughing and oddly enough, the party atmosphere soothes the rough edges Jay has put around Ellie's heart. She is not close to Luke, and she sees herself in the three girls Luke and his buddies are flirting with, but she reminds herself not to linger on those thoughts because it was a lifetime ago when she was the party girl who found herself pregnant and alone. She is at home in Maeve's house. She can't imagine her life without Jay's sisters.

She wishes she didn't have to imagine her life without Jay and his son.

NOVEMBER MAKES HER FEEL ALIVE INSIDE, ALMOST AS IF WITH the decay of natural life she's reborn inside. Maeve has always loved this time of year. Then again, as each new season creeps up on her and unfolds around her, she always decides it's her favorite season. She supposes some would call her fickle for less than that, but she doesn't care. She loves the naked trees that reach to the gray sky and the damp chill of fall that settles into her bones. She loves the hush of the first winter snowfall, but she is always happy to see the dogwoods bloom when spring comes, and she always looks forward to the long, sultry summer nights.

This winter will be different; she feels it in her bones. Jay has brought Ellie into their lives, and Maeve now looks at her sister through Ellie's young, but jaded, eyes. Maddie isn't perfect, but then neither is she. There is a depth to her sister that she has never cared to notice before. She cannot help but stumble into it when she's in Ellie's company. Maddie is a gorgeous woman, and Maeve can finally admit, to herself at least, that she feels threatened by Maddie's looks. Lately she sees a desperation in her sister; Maddie's not happy with her life, and there's a part of her that wants to fix whatever it is that hurts her little sister. And yet, even the magic of Ellie Jordan cannot grease the cogs that broke several years ago between Maeve and Maddie. If ever she and Maddie are to put the past behind them, it will be she or Maddie to make the first move. Not Ellie.

Maeve glances again at the autopsy photo of a young boy she'd once again thought might be Luther. At first glance, he does resemble Ellie's son. But upon closer inspection Maeve had noticed a birthmark nearly hidden in his hairline. Luther wore the marks of his birth much more prominently, the features of Fetal Alcohol Syndrome obvious. She'd wanted so badly to find Luther, or at least find his body so that Ellie could find closure. But Ellie is right. This is killing her. Not only is the disappointment of not finding Luther alive and well killing her, the constant barrage of autopsy photos of young boys makes her heartsick. The stop and start hope and despair she rides like an old, rickety roller coaster has jerked her around and left her bruised and sore. She cannot imagine how living this way has hammered away at Ellie all these years. Maybe she should call it quits and let Luther fade back into the woodwork. She won't be able to bring Ellie happiness or even peace of mind, but backing off may save her own sanity. She knows Ellie will understand. In fact, she and Ellie do not speak of finding Luther. For Ellie, the boy is dead and gone. Once again, it appears that she can learn something from Ellie Jordan.

CHAPTER 32

JAY LIKES TO BE IN CONTROL OF HIS LIFE. SINCE HE MET ELLIE, he's careened off the nice, comfortable path he'd been walking, and his life has gone crazy. He knows this is one thing Ellie has said to his sisters about him. She was doing fine until he came along and upset her applecart. He wonders if she realizes that falling in love with her has done the same thing to him.

"Don't bullshit about this, Jay," Maeve tells him. She plays with the brown bottle on the table between them.

He stares into his mug of Bud Lite and thinks about how Ellie used to trace circles in the condensation on her soda glass when she wanted to avoid his eyes. "I'm not bullshitting, Maeve," he says quietly. His rib basket sits in front of him, untouched. Up until a moment ago, Maeve had been happily working her way through a grilled chicken sandwich. She'd swallowed his heavy words with a healthy bite of the sandwich, taken a long pull from her bottled Bud Lite, and stared at him in shock.

"Rylan wants to give you custody of Oliver," she repeats

his words. "She just up and decided that it'd be best for Oliver to live with you."

"If I'm with Ellie."

Maeve sighs. "I still don't get it."

"Well, maybe not Ellie. But she said she saw something between me and Ellie. And she thinks he would be better off here, in a smaller town, with a close-knit family around him. A backyard to play in. A dog to play with."

"But her giving you Oliver depends on you being with Ellie?"

"I don't know," he answers with a shrug. "She said she thought Ellie was very real and that she obviously loves Oliver, and she wanted to see us together as a family."

"Wow." Maeve rubs her fingertips over her forehead.

"Wow what?" Jay downs half of his beer and then sets the mug down with a thud. "What're you thinking?"

"First of all, I'm thinking you need to slow down on the beer and eat something. I don't feel like dragging your drunk ass outta here—"

"I've only had two," he reminds her.

"And nothing to eat." She shoots back at him. "Jay, this is huge."

"I know."

"Your ex-wife bought a heart in New York."

"I can't ask Ellie to live with me or marry me so I can have Oliver."

Maeve stares at him thoughtfully. She purses her lips in concentration and then leans across the table. "No, you can't. I thought you were in love with her."

"I am," he answers simply. "But she's not gonna believe me if I drop this in her lap."

"No, not after the way you've treated her."

"The way I've treated her." He takes another drink and

then picks at the barbequed ribs before Maeve can chastise him again. "How about what she did? What she said?"

"Taken out of context, yeah, I see how it hurt you," she says with a nod. "But she said a helluva lot more that night that you didn't overhear."

"Like what?"

Maeve shakes her head. "Things that need to be said between you two." She pushes her plate aside and picks up her beer. "Look, as your sister, I wanna go get her and drag her ass out here and tell her everything you just told me. Of course I want this for you, I want Oliver here. I want Oliver to have his daddy and to be close to his grandma. And to have George to play with. Hell, I want him to have Ellie for a stepmother."

"But."

"But Ellie's my friend, Jay, and you're letting this go way too far. She hurt you, but it wasn't her intention. She's trying so hard to work through all that baggage that she's been dragging around since you've known her. You have to give her credit for that. I don't wanna see you drag her into this and see her end up getting hurt. I don't want any of you to get hurt any more than you already have been."

"So what do I do, Maeve? Do I tell her what Rylan said and ask her if I can come back? I don't want to think she'd reconcile with me just for Oliver."

"That's like a pregnant woman hesitating to tell the man who got her pregnant about the baby. Because she's afraid he'll stay with her only because of the baby. You need to talk to her. Listen to her. And go from there."

"You tell her your secrets, don't you?" he asks after a lengthy silence.

"I don't have any secrets."

"I think we all have secrets, Maeve."

"Okay, share one with me. Did you sleep with Rylan when

you were with her back in October? Ellie's convinced that you did."

"No, I didn't. That's when we had this talk about Oliver."

"Why'd you wait so long to talk to me about it?" Maeve asks him curiously.

He lifts a shoulder in a lazy shrug and glances around the nearly empty bar and grill. It is a late Wednesday evening, and the wind outside is so cold, Jay nearly shivers just thinking about the way it cut inside his leather jacket and sliced right through his lungs. "Just needed time to process everything."

"Do you want Oliver, Jay?" She is dead serious; her bottle hovers near her lips.

"I want 'em both, Maeve," he answers simply.

"LIFE IS WHAT YOU MAKE IT, ELLIE," MADDIE TELLS HER AS SHE stretches her fingers over the keys on the church piano. "What do you want?"

Ellie sighs heavily and sinks down on the piano bench beside her. "I could say the same to you, Maddie," she answers.

"What do you want?" Maddie asks again.

"What do you want?" Ellie turns the question around and stares boldly into Maddie's emerald eyes.

Maddie surprises her. Instead of insisting Ellie answer, she narrows her eyes and looks down at her fingers on the keys. Instead of saying she wants to be free of her vows or that she wants to find love or at least a relationship with a man, she finally raises her gaze back to Ellie and says simply, "Forgiveness."

Ellie stares at her silently, taken aback by what she's said. "You told me God is forgiving."

"Maeve's forgiveness," Maddie explains.

"Oh God," Ellie mumbles as the cold fingers of dread grip her stomach and squeeze uncomfortably hard.

"I'm stuck, Ellie," Maddie whispers. "I can't go anywhere with my life until I get this out of the way. What I did, what I did with Stash, it's like a brick wall between us. It's like a huge brick wall, and now and then one of us can peck through the mortar between the bricks to get a look at each other. And remember what we used to be like. But neither of us can climb the wall or tear it down."

"Maddie," Ellie says softly. She touches the back of Maddie's hand. "Think about this." Ellie searches Maddie's face for understanding. "I know you need forgiveness. But think of how you'll hurt her just to get what you need."

"She knows something is wrong between us." Maddie turns her body toward Ellie and cocks her head to the side. "You knew something was wrong between us. I can't let Maeve go on thinking that I've spent the last eighteen years resenting her, hating her, because of her abortion. She needs to know the truth."

"What if you tell her the truth? And she can't forgive you? What if you split her marriage up?"

Maddie presses her lips together and raises her eyebrows. "I know you care about Maeve, Ellie," she whispers. "But I need you. I need your support."

"I'm not going anywhere." Ellie's quiet but firm voice seems to calm Maddie. The tension that had lodged between Maddie's eyebrows eases a bit, and her fingers move gracefully over the keys. The song climbs inside Ellie and sinks to her heart and her soul and her fingertips where she used to feel Luther's hand when they walked together. "Amazing Grace" is a beautiful song, but really Ellie hates it when Maddie plays it and sings and tears her down to less than she is. She feels unwanted chills climb her legs and her backbone under her warm jeans and sweater, but she refuses to let the tears come.

"Stop," she says loudly as she climbs to her feet.

"What?" The music stops instantly, and Maddie spins on the piano bench to look up at her. Her face is a mix of surprise and concern. "What's wrong?"

"I hate it when you play that song," Ellie says quietly. She drags her fingers back through her hair and then turns her back to Maddie.

"Why?" Maddie stands, but Ellie senses her approach and makes a quick shot for the side door of the church. She knows she can't get away; Maddie will be on her tail and follow her right outside. But it is close in the church; the same pervasive calm that sometimes comforts her can also seep into her skin and slide down her throat and suffocate her. At least outside in the cold, sharp wind she can breathe.

"I just do," Ellie says when she is certain Maddie is outside, behind her on the stone steps.

"What do you want?" Maddie asks her again. Ellie pretends she doesn't hear her. She glances back at her and sees her huddle deeper into her thick black sweater. "It's a simple question, Ellie. What do you want?"

"I wanna be normal, Maddie," she finally answers. "Normal. And safe. And happy."

Maddie considers her answer and then studies the cold November sky. Ellie lifts her eyes to see what has Maddie's attention, but she looks away when she sees the bare tree limbs set against the backdrop of slate, gray sky.

"You and me both, Ellie," Maddie says softly. "You figure out how to get there, you let me know."

Ellie jams her hands deep into the front pockets of her jeans and stares at her tennis shoes, the same shoes she'd dripped paint on last summer. There's a huge gash in her side since Jay is gone from her life. She bleeds for Jay and Luther, and she thinks that one day she will simply bleed out and fade away and no one will even remember who she is.

"I'm going home," she says abruptly. She looks up at Maddie without apology; even outside in the biting cold and the endless sky of gunmetal gray, she finds she can't breathe. As much as she loves Maddie and Maeve, there are days when she simply wants to be alone. Sometimes solitude is constructive, and she gets a paper written or the house cleaned. And sometimes, it's sheer hell, and she simply watches the hours crawl by, slower than the lumbering freight trains that used to stop traffic back home when she was a kid.

Sometimes she thinks she's like a sponge. She absorbs Maeve's and Maddie's feelings and, even knowing she shouldn't, she lets the way they feel override her feelings, and now she's sick with dread over what will happen between Maeve and Maddie. Maybe it will be like a volcanic eruption, and once they get it all out in the open, the ashes will settle to dust, and they can start over. But volcanic eruptions can be violent, and Ellie worries that someone will be burned by lava or at the very least, suffer some sort of lingering damage from smoke inhalation.

MAEVE HAS VOWED TO HERSELF THAT SHE WILL STOP THE search for Luther. She has made this vow several times in the last six weeks. Each time she does, she gets another email or fax from a far-reaching friend or colleague, and she sees another picture of a missing boy or worse, another autopsy photo, and she falls back down into that black pit of muck and sludge, and she's sort of wallowing in it. It's hard to look at the pictures and imagine the horrors these boys have suffered. It's harder to imagine Ellie, as a mother, imagining all the horrid things that might have been done to her little boy.

She worries about Jay and Oliver. Once or twice, she's stopped to wonder about Rylan, more specifically about what had changed Rylan's mind about raising Oliver. She hopes it is just as Rylan told Jay, that she saw something special in Ellie and wants her son to be happy with two loving parents. But Maeve is suspicious by nature, and she loves her family fiercely, and she won't stand by and watch them be pushed around like small wooden chess pieces over a game board where someone is bound to lose.

She worries about her mother; she seems to have aged five years just this past summer. Maeve suspects something is brewing there, but she hopes that she's wrong. She supposes she loves Maddie too, though she'd be hard pressed to find her voice and actually say those words. It's because of Ellie that she sees it so clearly now. It is Ellie who facilitates the shared afternoons or evenings between her and Maddie. It is Ellie who makes her want to talk to Maddie.

Her stomach still drops at the thought of that conversation, like when you're on a roller coaster and the cars are slowly clicking their way up the biggest incline on the track, and you know you're about to drop straight to the bottom, and you wonder for the briefest of seconds if your car will jump the track and you will go on racing straight to hell and if death will be a heart attack or a broken neck. Only this is worse. The thought of talking to Maddie scares the hell out of her. But anymore, not talking to Maddie hurts like hell and scares her because they're all getting older and really, aren't they wasting time they could spend as friends?

She almost doesn't answer the phone. Luke is at the library, and that's another thing; she knows damned well he's not at the library and if she were to wait up for him he'd come home falling down drunk at dawn or not come home at all. Stash is home, but she has no idea where in the house he is. He could get the phone though. She's tired, and she doesn't want to talk to anyone.

But it could be someone about Luther. As she curls her fingers around the cordless handset, her heart skips a beat, and her eyes burn as she realizes this is how Ellie has lived for the past five years. She is bound to her home, this town, this life forever on the miniscule possibility that Luther might come home. The not knowing is her cross to bear, and Maeve knows now that it's heavy and it's hard and it's very tempting to let it fall and walk away.

"Hello?"

"Ms. Taylor?" The voice is slightly familiar, but Maeve cannot place it. She's working a new case, the attempted murder of a young meth dealer, shot in the back outside a bar on Third Street. The kid had survived the shooting, but any further dealing he did would be from half-mast on two big wheels and two small wheels and a slick little hand brake. Best guess, this voice had nothing to do with the Manny Rantoul case.

"Yes, this is she," she says with a tightly controlled sigh. It's a Sunday afternoon, and she's tired and her head hurts, and she thinks, when she looks out the window in her office, that it is spitting snow. She doesn't want snow right now, not when she's in this mood. Snow is for Norman Rockwell paintings and those sickeningly happy Norman Rockwell painting looking families, and after all the years of pretending, she can no longer deny that her family is not one of them.

"This is Donna Jordan," the woman practically whispers. "Ellie's mother."

Maeve is suddenly so cold it's as if she is standing outside, naked and wet from the shower, in the middle of the harsh wind and the tiny snowflakes that touch the barren ground outside and disappear. "Donna." She can't say anymore. She doesn't know what to say, and as she drops back into the chair behind her desk, she's overcome with a guilt so strong it must rival that of a dead man walking as he is taken to the death chamber. To the needle. It must rival that of a woman who is too selfish to give birth to an unwanted child so she aborts the baby, unwilling to make sacrifices in her own life. Ellie does not want any contact with her parents, and now Maeve has opened a big can of worms, a big pit of snakes, and both Ellie and her mother could end up further damaged by what she's done.

"I just." Donna hesitates, clears her throat, and tries again. "I just can't see her. But I don't want you to think I don't think about her."

Maeve presses her lips together. Why does everything have to hurt? She's not worried about herself now; she just hates that this woman has to hurt, and Ellie has to hurt and Luther probably had to suffer. "It's okay." She is surprised to hear herself speak. "Frankly, Ellie is adamant that I not contact you again. I just—" It's Maeve's turn to struggle for words. "I hate to see the way Ellie wonders about Luther. I just wanted you to know that she's okay."

"We don't talk about Ellie," Donna explains. "My husband."

Maeve manages to quell a desire to tell Donna what she thinks about her husband, the man who insisted a doctor perform a hysterectomy on a sixteen-year-old girl. "It's very hard," she says instead. "I understand."

"Is she happy?"

In their first conversation, Maeve had really said very little about Ellie. It had been a short talk in which Maeve had told her that Ellie was alive and well, but that Luther had vanished when he was five years old. Donna had said precious little, but her tears had spoken a thousand words from one mother to another. Maeve suspects that mostly everything she'd said about Ellie after the fact that she's alive bounced off her mother like a tennis ball off a racquet. Donna had probably heard nothing after Ellie's name.

"She's getting there," Maeve answers. "She's been content, accepting of things for so long that it's like she has to learn how to be happy all over again."

"I just needed to know that," Donna whispers. "Luther—"

Maeve waits for her to go on, but a thick silence creeps through the phone line. "She was a good mother to him. She loved him."

"My daughter Natalie is studying communications," Donna tells her. Maeve closes her eyes. She really could not care less what Natalie is doing, because Ellie is here rebuilding a life that never really had a chance to shine before she was cut off at the knees. Maeve is proud of Ellie for every tiny effort she puts forward. She's willing to bet that neither Natalie nor Nick has lived with the kind of oppressive guilt and sorrow Ellie fights to overcome. "Nick is a marketing major." Maeve says nothing. "What does Ellie do?"

Maeve takes a deep breath and purses her lips as she blows it out. "She works at the library. She loves books. She used to read to Luther all the time." She's not lying; Ellie has told her this. "She studies the stars at night, and she thinks about Luther and the stories they used to tell each other about the stars."

"So she's a librarian," her mother says quietly.

Maeve bristles. Ellie is not a librarian and damned if she will let her mother get away with thinking that, much less saying it. "She's studying history. She takes part-time classes at the university. She does very well. In fact, my brother has asked her to work with him on a book he's considered writing."

Donna is quiet now. "And you're her friend?"

I'm so much more than her friend, Maeve wants to say. *I am her friend, her sister, her confidante, her mother away from home. I give her friendship, but she gives me just as much, if not so much more, in return.*

"I am," Maeve answers simply.

CHAPTER 33

IN HIGH SCHOOL, ELLIE OFTEN FOUND HERSELF CAUGHT between two friends. Just as she is the go-between now with Maddie and Maeve. In high school, it was petty and sopho-moric. Though it sometimes feels like the same game now, the stakes are much higher. This is a family bond that she sometimes feels rests on her shoulders. Since Maddie had told her that she wants forgiveness, she's afraid each time she sees Maddie she'll have something horrible to tell her. No matter how hard she tries, she can't imagine a happy ending with Maeve and Maddie. She hates that she feels that way; it makes her feel guilty, as if she's letting Maeve and Maddie down. As if she does not see them as capable and forgiving adults. It's not that; it's just that she knows how deep that sort of hurt runs and forgiveness, though very hard, is only the tip of the iceberg. Suppose they talk, and they can forgive. What if they can't forget? It's hard to love when you can't forget the way you've been hurt. She ought to know. She's done a bang-up job on herself.

It is still November, and it's cold, but it is warmer today

than it has been in several days. Ellie puts on a pair of gray sweatpants, an oversized navy sweatshirt, and heads out on foot to Maddie's house. She takes a glance at the tree in her neighbor's yard and feels an instant smack of guilt for thinking that it's ugly. It is. Without its gorgeous head of green leaves or its autumn crown, it is just a plain tree, with bleached, pale limbs reaching out in a hopeless effort to scrape the winter sky. She forces herself to look again, look harder, and see the tree bent and sweeping the ground, in an effort to survive. Sometimes survivors are ugly and small, but when you look closer you can see something special. Without Luther, without Jay, she has no smile. Sure, she has that pretend thing she can conjure up as if from a Crayola box, but there is no real joy inside her. Some might say she is a survivor. And some might say she is ugly. But maybe someone might look a little closer at her and see something special. She has never given up. She is fighting to survive.

"What are you doing?" Maddie asks her fifteen minutes later when she opens the door to her. "It's cold out there."

"It's not so bad." Ellie shakes her head. "C'mon. Go for a walk with me."

"I'm old," Maddie argues. "I could have a heart attack out there."

"It's forty-five degrees," Ellie tells her. She asks Maddie if she's talked to Maeve yet, while she waits for Maddie to change her clothes.

"No," Maddie says and pulls her door shut behind them. She shoves her keys into her pocket, and the two of them set off at a fast pace. "One day I wake up, and I want to just call her and see her and get it all out in the open. The next, I get sick at the thought."

Ellie nods.

"Maeve's out of town right now anyway," Maddie says

distractedly. She waves at a passing car and then watches the brown leaves crunch under her feet.

"She is?" Ellie's surprised. She'd talked to Maeve two nights ago, but Maeve hadn't mentioned any trips. "Where'd she go?"

"I don't know." Maddie shrugs. "Maybe she had to go out of town to get a deposition or something on the Rantoul case."

Ellie considers this for a moment. "Do you think her job poses any danger to her?"

"Not in the way you mean," Maddie answers immediately. "Maybe in a big city it would. But not here. I think her biggest danger on the job is that she feels too much. I think it's all starting to get to her."

Ellie loves that Maddie answered her without having to think about it. Seems that must mean Maddie thinks about it at other times, which seems to mean that Maddie cares for Maeve.

"Sounds like you," Ellie says after they've walked several steps in silence. "It's all starting to get to you."

"What do you want for Christmas?" Maddie asks her. Ellie frowns. She knows Maddie simply wants to change the subject.

"Nothing," Ellie answers honestly.

"Really?"

Ellie sighs and shrugs and looks Maddie in the eye. "No. That's a lie."

"So what do you want for Christmas?" Maddie asks again.

"I want that ring that Jay showed me. I want it on my finger. I want his name. I want his son." She stares at Maddie boldly. "I want him."

Maddie's smile lights up the gray day, and for a moment, it's like the street is bathed in springtime sunlight. "I want that too. I want that for all three of you."

"Jay doesn't," Ellie says and dims the light.

"How can you know that for sure?" Maddie stops walking and lays her hand on Ellie's arm. "How can you know that? You let him walk away—"

"I didn't—"

"He got mad, and you let him walk away." Maddie shrugs and drops her hand from Ellie's arm and starts walking again. Ellie stares after her for a moment and wonders where she hides the mirror she's always holding up so she can see herself so clearly. "Stop looking at me like that and get up here by me," Maddie calls over her shoulder. Ellie laughs softly and hurries to catch up with her.

"Do you ever get tired of me and the ball and chain around my ankle?" she asks as she falls into step beside Maddie.

"You ever get tired of me and all the baggage I drag around?"

Ellie glances at Maddie. They are not Abbot and Costello. They are not Bartles and Jaymes. She and Maddie and Maeve are not The Three Musketeers. And yet, she feels as if they are all somehow attached and losing either of them would be life threatening. "No."

Maddie laughs and arches an eyebrow. "You had me worried there for a minute."

"Just thinking," Ellie answers with a sad smile. "I don't know what you call it, but whatever it is, I need you guys."

"I think it's family," Maddie says as she studies Ellie's face. She looks away before Ellie can answer her. "Maeve tell you that your mother called her the other day?"

"Yeah."

"I think she cares."

"Yeah, just so long as my father doesn't find out." Ellie hears the sarcasm in her voice and cringes. "Dear old Dad's probably threatened to divorce her if she so much as speaks my name."

"You have to deal with it, ya know."

Ellie looks at Maddie from the corner of her eye, but she says nothing.

"You've changed, Ellie," Maddie explains. "You fit inside your skin now. You didn't when I first met you. But your parents. Your family. You're going to have to face them and deal with all of that before you're free of your past."

"Just because you wanna walk through fire, doesn't mean you have to drag me in with you."

"You know I'm right," Maddie says quietly.

Jay itches to get the hell out of class. He dreamt last night of Ellie, and it was so realistic and so perfect, he'd gotten up feeling good today. It feels as if he really spent the evening with Ellie last night. As if he'd really held her in his arms and breathed in her soft, clean scent and really heard her say she loved him. Damn his luck, but it's Tuesday, and he doesn't have her in class today. He's dying to see her, just catch a glimpse of her in the hallway. Her dark blonde hair, soft as silk. Her warm butterscotch eyes. Naturally, he hasn't seen her all day.

He watches the hands on his watch crawl slowly by as his students discuss something about Alexander the Great. Hell, he doesn't even remember what he's teaching right now. He's as ready to bolt as the jocks in the back row of the classroom. The difference is they're most likely hankering to get to the dorms and down a beer or another alcoholic beverage of choice. He's ready to hit the streets and find Ellie. It's late November, and he thinks he should go Christmas shopping.

He wants to go out with Ellie and look at the millions of toys that Oliver has not so quietly hinted that he wants for Christmas. He wants to hold Ellie's hand and walk through the mall and share a cup of hot chocolate with her. He wants to see her eyes light up as they talk about Oliver.

He wants to know what else she said to Maeve that night he'd overheard part of their conversation.

Her house is closed up when he drives by after class. She's probably working, and it takes all the self-restraint he's got not to go barging into the library looking for her. Instead he goes home and takes a shower. Reads a bit of the Ridley Pearson book he'd picked up the other night at Wal-Mart. Watches the clock. At five on the dot, he tosses his book aside and grabs his keys and then tells himself he's got to give her some time. She would probably be irritated to get home from work only to find him waiting on her front porch. He calls Maeve to kill some time, but there's no answer. He considers calling Maddie, because he knows she and Ellie are very close and that means that beneath her cool surface Maddie must be very approachable. But he doesn't really know what he'd say to her.

Finally, when it is nearly six o'clock, he grabs his keys again and heads out. Part of him hopes to find her on the porch. God, how he misses those nights they'd spent on her porch, talking about the stars. Then again, it's cold and windy, and clours are beginning to step in and set up camp, so there are no stars for her to watch.

Her house is closed up, still, but he stops this time. Surely she's home by now. He hesitates once on his way to the front door. What if she doesn't want him here? What if she doesn't want him? What if she decided to go out with the guy who'd asked her out after her American Foreign History class? He takes a deep breath and reminds himself a lot of time has passed since they were last together, since they stopped seeing each other.

She answers the door wearing old Levis with a hole worn through in the knee. Her gray sweatshirt is long and faded, but she looks cozy. Her feet are bare, her toenails painted a dark purple. Her bare feet and her ponytail remind him of the night he'd first come here to talk to her. She looks vulnerable, yet tough all wrapped up together. It's all he can do to keep his hands in his pockets.

"Hey."

"Busy?" he asks and glances over her shoulder. What if she's not alone? He'd thought about using sex to get her out of his mind. What if she's done the same? What if he'd never really been in her mind, and she's over him, and she's had several boyfriends since they broke up? Wouldn't Maeve had told him that?

"Working on a paper," she answers with a shrug. She pushes the door open, which is as close as he'll get to an invitation inside. He takes it before she changes her mind. "What's up?"

He feels Ellie's home settle in around him. He's missed the feeling. For a long time, he'd felt more at home here with her than he did in his own house. "Missed you." His answer is short and quiet, and he wonders if she heard him.

When he meets her gaze, she blinks and runs the tip of her tongue across the bottom of her teeth. Finally she raises her eyebrows and turns to head back to the kitchen. He follows her, again knowing she will not ask him to join her. She stands in front of the open refrigerator door. He drops into a kitchen chair and glances at her open notebook. The page he sees is two thirds full of her small handwriting. There are two other books open on the tabletop. She is, indeed, working on a paper.

"Don't read that," she says crossly when she catches him.

"I read your papers all the time," he reminds her as she closes her notebook.

"Yeah, when I turn them in to you." She takes a bite of a big red apple. "This is different."

"We never wrote that book," he says and remembers the night he'd first asked her to work with him. She ignores him, takes another bite of her apple, and takes a glass from the cabinet above the kitchen sink.

"Want something to drink?" she asks without looking at him.

"No, thanks." He watches her fill her glass with ice and water. "Supper?"

"Yeah," she answers when she sits down at the table with him.

He stares at her boldly as she eats her apple and avoids his eyes. Now that he's here he can't seem to find the words he was so desperate to say to her earlier today. She is distant and cool, and it hurts him to think maybe she doesn't want things to be as they were.

"Do you remember making love out there? In the rain?"

She looks at him, clearly shocked by his question. Her eyes are dry. She sighs, stands, and throws her half-eaten apple away, and keeps her back to him. "What do you want, Jay?"

"I just needed to see you," he answers after too much quiet has passed.

She turns to look at him and folds her arms across her chest. "So it's just okay for you to blow me off when it suits you and to barge in here when you need to see me?"

"I don't blow you off—"

"No, you're right. You don't," she says with a small nod. "You don't even give me that much. I don't exist until you need something."

"I didn't sleep with Rylan—"

She holds up a hand to stop him. "I don't care. I don't wanna know."

"Sit with me?" he asks. He stands and reaches for her hand.

"What?" She takes a step back from him.

"Outside. Can we just sit for awhile?"

Without answering him, she pushes past him and disappears down the hall to her bedroom. She returns a moment later with socks on. He follows her outside and sits beside her on the porch.

"Do you do this? In the winter? Do you watch the stars?"

She nods. He sighs and looks at her. She sits as far away from him as she can and still be on the porch. She draws her knees up to her chest and wraps her arms tightly around them.

"I watch the stars, because I think—" She swallows hard, but she doesn't look at him. "I think he's dead. And maybe." She shrugs, eyes still turned to the starless sky. "Maybe he's up there. Maybe my little boy is a star now, and maybe he watches me, and I want to find him there. Because I can't find him here."

"Ellie—"

"I know, Jay. I know Catholics don't believe that. Maybe he's in purgatory. Maybe he's an angel. I don't know. It just helps to think I might find him up there in the sky."

"I was just going to say that I want him to be there. In the sky. For you."

She glances at him. Her eyes fill, but she blinks the tears away.

Life is all about risks, he reminds himself. Going out on a limb. Taking chances. How's he ever going to know if they have a chance if he doesn't try something? He thinks there is probably something he should say, but he doesn't know what it is. Instead, he reaches for her and touches her face and strokes the pad of his thumb over the hollow of her cheek. She closes her eyes and turns her face away from his touch.

"Ellie."

"I have a paper to write, Jay," she says quietly.

He sighs. Instead of arguing, he simply nods and stands and studies his boot-clad feet. "Okay."

CHAPTER 34

MAEVE LOOKS LIKE HELL, AND ALL SORTS OF HORRIBLE thoughts cross Ellie's mind. What if Jolene is sick again? Since the bout with pneumonia last summer, she's not been truly healthy. What if Maeve is sick? She looks like she's lost weight. Her skin is pasty, and her eyes are dull and lined with red like a road map. Ellie thinks if she looks at them long enough she might find the highway to hell there.

Ellie glances at Maddie. She's not sure if she feels relieved when she sees that Maddie has noticed that something is definitely wrong with Maeve or if the fact that someone else has validated her worries should make her worry more. As she drops her coat on the loveseat in Maeve's sitting room, she looks around. The house looks the same. No clues here. She's not sure what she'd hoped to find. Luke's grounded ass in the rocker in the corner? Peyton running scared and home after shacking up with the professor twenty years her senior? A billboard sign saying "Maeve is suffering from" with some-thing concrete filling in the blank.

"Are you sick?" Maddie asks quietly. "Maeve, you don't look good."

Maeve sighs and narrows her eyes at Maddie. "Do you always have to be such a bitch?"

"I'm not," Maddie answers defensively. "What's wrong? If you're sick, you should have called. We could have put off lunch till you feel better."

"I'm not sick," Maeve says simply. Ellie and Maddie follow her into the kitchen. "Just tired."

"Still," Ellie says softly. "We didn't have to do this today."

"I can't believe next week is Thanksgiving," Maddie mumbles.

"I'm ready for a break in classes," Ellie says as she slides onto a stool at the counter.

"You want me to bring anything?" Maddie asks Maeve. But Maeve is staring at the counter with a surgeon's concentration. "Maeve?"

"Huh?" Maeve looks up at Maddie and quickly pulls herself together.

"What's going on?" Maddie asks. "Really. Is it Mom? I talked to her last night, and she seemed fine."

"No, Mom's fine," Maeve assures her.

"Okay. What then?" Maddie raises her eyebrows. "Luke? Peyton?"

Maeve sighs and turns her eyes to Ellie. "I was in Wisconsin," she says quietly.

"What?"

"When I was out of town," Maeve explains. "You thought I was out of town getting a deposition. I was in Wisconsin."

"What's in Wisconsin?" Maddie asks with a frown.

Again Maeve looks at Ellie. "I thought I found him."

"Oh God." Ellie's words break over the knives in her throat.

"I thought." Maeve swallows hard and starts again. "I have a friend there. He's a detective. He faxed me a picture, and it looked like Luther."

"Enough that you went there?" Maddie whispers.

Maeve nods. "It was an autopsy photo." Her hands shake so she balls them into fists and rubs them hard into her eyes. "I had to know. I had to know if it was Luther."

Ellie burns inside, like she's swallowed hell. Chills make the hair on the back of her neck stand on end. "Was it?" She asks calmly. "Was it Luther?"

"No."

"How do you know?"

"This boy had an appendectomy. I saw the scar. He'd been found three years ago, but there were several pictures."

"Did Luther—?" Maddie glances at Ellie, but she stops when Ellie shakes her head.

"I didn't tell you, because I wanted to be sure first." Maeve takes a step toward Ellie, but she stops suddenly. Ellie doesn't know what Maeve sees in her eyes, because she doesn't know what she feels. Relief? Disappointment? Sorrow? She doesn't know anymore, and it's that flux that makes her feel like she's going crazy. Like she's ten thousand leagues under the sea and her lungs are going to explode, and her mind is taking on water, and she itches, and she wants to claw her skin off her bones. "I just. I thought this was it. I didn't want it to be him, because God knows, Ellie, I'd give anything in the world to bring him home safe and healthy."

The silence in the kitchen is charged with an electrical current. Ellie bites her lip to keep from screaming. Screaming that it isn't fair. That she would give her life to find Luther safe and healthy and happy. Screaming at Maeve for digging back through the layers of scar tissue. Screaming at her to back off and mind her own business. Screaming at Maeve for hurting her because there is no balm for this sort of wound. There is nothing that can take away this hurt.

"But I thought at least…" Maeve stops for a moment, and Ellie, who now hides her face behind her hands, assumes she is struggling to control herself. "If it was him, it would be closure for you. I just want to do something for you—"

"You can't," Ellie says softly.

"Maybe I can—"

"You can't," Ellie repeats. She looks up and drops her hands to the counter. "You can't do anything for me. You can't change the way I messed everything up. You can't do that. You're used to getting what you want, Maeve, but you can't get this. No matter what you do, you can't do anything for me."

"Ellie," Maddie says softly. Ellie recognizes the tone. Maddie is warning Ellie not to cross the line. Not to say something she might regret.

"This is why I asked you to stay out of it," Ellie says as she stands. "It doesn't matter what you do. You can't fix this. You can't change what happened. You can't bring my son home to me. Even if he's alive and well, you can't bring him home to me unchanged."

"If there's a chance that he's alive, how can you turn your back on him?"

"It's been five Goddamned years!" Ellie shouts. "He's dead, Maeve. I can't think anything else. I can't imagine the torture he might have been through. The chance that he was sexually abused. I can't deal with that. I have to believe he's gone—"

"Then let me be the one to hold out hope for him." Maeve reaches for Ellie, but Ellie ducks out of the way. "I understand, Ellie," she whispers. "God, I do. This has taken a piece of me. This has changed me. It's not just that I haven't found your son. It's all the missing boys and murdered boys I have found, El, that are killing me. But as long as he isn't found, there's a chance that he might be alive."

"I can't live with that, Maeve." Ellie's throat throbs with the force of her words. "I can't live like that anymore—"

"Then let me do it for you," Maeve says again.

"Maeve, you can't do this to yourself," Maddie says quietly. She moves around the counter to stand beside her sister. "It's tearing you down. You have to let this go."

"It doesn't matter what this does to me." She reaches again for Ellie. Her fingers skim the back of Ellie's hand. "I've promised myself a million times since I started this that I would back off and let it go. But I can't. I know you can't live with the hope that he's okay." Maeve presses her lips together. "But I'm stronger than I look, and I need to do this for you."

"Why do you need to do this for me?" Tears burn in Ellie's eyes and her throat and her stomach. She swipes at her eyes and stares at Maeve suspiciously. "No one else has ever wanted to help. Why start now?"

"Because I love you." Maeve's voice is thick and desperate.

"Don't make me promises." Ellie shakes her head and looks away from Maeve's wild eyes. "I don't believe in them."

"It's not a promise," Maeve answers quietly. "It just is."

"I don't wanna see you go to pieces," Ellie tells her. She takes a deep breath and turns to pace the kitchen floor. "This is too hard, Maeve. You've got your own family. Your own things to worry about—"

"If you could change the past for me, would you do it?" Maeve asks her. Ellie looks back at her. She glances at Maddie and then back at Maeve, and nods.

"Of course I would," Ellie answers, though she is not sure what past Maeve is talking about. The abortion? Maddie's affair with Stash? The baby Maddie gave birth to? The baby that Stash fathered? She has to be talking about the abortion, of course. Maddie has yet to make the big confession.

"Let me do this." Maeve raises her eyebrows. "Let me do this for you."

⁓

THANKSGIVING WITH JAY'S FAMILY IS REALLY A LOT LIKE ELLIE remembers Thanksgiving with her family was. The smell of turkey and pies and homemade rolls permeates Maeve's house. Stash and Jay drink a few cold beers, but Ellie joins the women in a glass of wine. She'd been a bit nervous about meeting Peyton, but it had been for nothing, as Peyton had proved to be as warm as Maeve.

Football blares from the TV, the noise of the game occasionally interrupted by groans or cheers from the guys watching. Ellie eats more than she's eaten the entire month of November. She and Maeve have passed the baby-steps phase of their relationship yet again, and it's comfortable and even fun cleaning up and washing dishes when dinner is over. Now and then she catches Maddie watching Maeve, with a wistful look in her eyes, and she feels her stomach start a slow slide to her knees. When the kitchen is sparkling clean, she sits with Jay's sisters and mom and niece and mostly listens to the conversation around her. Peyton asks her about the classes she's taking, but she seems a bit distracted when Ellie answers. Ellie notices that she is missing her significant other. She'll ask Maeve about that tomorrow when they go shopping. She has never done the day after Thanksgiving shopping spree as an adult. When she had Luther, she'd done her shopping early and taken advantage of the layaway department at Wal-Mart, paying a bit at a time, when she could. Even now, she doesn't really have that much shopping to do, but the thought of a festive day of holiday shopping with Maeve and Maddie appeals to her. She knows Maeve was hoping Peyton would join them, but Peyton has announced that she has to get back tomorrow. Maeve is disappointed; it's a look other mothers know, but she hides it well.

Several hands of gin rummy and two glasses of wine later, Ellie decides it is getting late, and she should go home. Really, though she's enjoyed herself, she can't help but think that Jay is in the other room and aside from asking her to pass him the salt at dinner and a soft sort of smile for her as he'd left the kitchen, they haven't even really looked at each other. Maybe she should have been a bit more open to talking to him when he'd last come to see her.

Maddie walks her out to her car and reminds her that she doesn't have to go. The night is young, Maddie tells her, though it is well past ten, and she is exhausted from the effort to be impartial to Jay. She hugs Maddie goodbye and says a silent prayer that Maddie will not pick tonight to talk to Maeve.

It's mild for Thanksgiving. She sits on her porch and watches the stars, but she is not thinking about Luther. Or Jay, even. She remembers a Thanksgiving when she might have been eight or ten and Blair came over late in the afternoon. There had been snow. At least two feet of snow, and she and Blair and Natalie and Nick, all bundled up in snowsuits that left them no room to move, had made a snowman and snow angels. She wonders what would have become of Blair, had she lived. What she would have done if she hadn't gotten the wake-up call and gotten pregnant with Luther. Nothing good, she's pretty certain of that.

She catches her breath when Jay pulls up in front of her house. She's not surprised to see him. She just hopes this visit works out a bit better than the last. He buries his fists in his coat pockets as he approaches her and then sits next to her on the porch.

"Kind of cold out here," he says quietly.

"Why'd you leave Maeve's?" she asks him.

"Because you did," he answers. He looks anywhere but at her. "Went by the house and let George out."

Ellie smiles. "I miss George."

"I miss you," he says, but he still doesn't look at her.

"You said that last time you were here." She waits for him to turn to her. His eyes touch her when he does.

"I'm glad you were at Maeve's today."

"Me too."

"Maeve and Maddie. They seem to talk to each other more now," he says after a moment.

She considers this and remembers the day Maddie told her she wants forgiveness. "They're scaling the wall," she mumbles. "They need to just knock it down."

He eyes her curiously. She feels a flash of heat flood her, afraid that he will press her for details about his sisters. "You're good for them."

She raises her eyebrows and shrugs. "They're good for me." She wants to move closer to him. Lean on him. He feels too far away. The tree across the street mocks her and reminds her that maybe she's ugly, and this was never supposed to work out. When she looks back at Jay, he's dangerously close to her. His breath tickles her lips. His kiss is cautious. She doesn't move, except to kiss him back. Wanting to make sure he never moves away from her and wanting more of him, she opens her lips and brushes the tip of her tongue over his.

He tangles his fingers in the hair at the nape of her neck, and his tongue dances over hers and over her lips and into her mouth. She moans appreciatively. Hungry for more of him, she lifts her hand and lets her fingertips graze his chin. His five o'clock shadow ignites a fire in her hand that spreads low to her belly.

Her teeth chatter when he pulls away from her. She sobs and drops her forehead to his chest.

"Jay," she says against his coat.

In the dark he finds her hand and links his fingers

through hers and stands up. She lets him pull her to her feet. The house is warm. She shrugs out of her coat, but Jay stops her when she pulls her shirttail from her jeans. She looks up at him, scared he is going to walk away.

"Let me," he says simply. She sighs contentedly as his fingers slide inside her waistband and pull the shirt out. She'd splurged on the outfit because she'd wanted to look nice for Jay and his family. Silver brand jeans and a pink knit shirt. A touch of makeup. She wants to cry and laugh and say I love you as he pulls her shirt over her head, and his fingers skim down over the silver chain and Luther's Cross and her breasts. He hesitates, but she nods when he meets her gaze.

They leave a trail of clothing from the dark living room to the bedroom. His skin is warm against hers. His hands move slowly as he reacquaints himself with her body, but when she closes her eyes, it's as if he's touching her everywhere at once. He lays her down and slides his body over hers, his mouth touching hers gently.

"Oh my God," she whispers as he drags his open mouth down over her neck and closes his lips around her nipple. "Jay."

He strokes his hand low over her belly and takes her hint when she draws her knees up and opens herself to him. He kisses her and swallows the desperate way she says his name.

"Ellie," he says as he settles himself between her thighs.

"Please?" She bites her lip. He pushes gently inside her, but he doesn't move.

"How can you think this is dirty?" he asks her. She hears the hurt and the sadness in his voice. She hates that he'd only heard this much all those months ago. "El, this is the most beautiful thing I have in my life. You and Oliver."

She moves a bit under him and closes her eyes. "It's not making love to you that made me feel that way," she says the words that she should have insisted he hear that day in his office. "It was the way you made me feel when you were gone. The way I wanted you. The way you just sucked me up and made me want you when you were gone again."

"But why is that wrong?" he asks her. He cups her chin in his hand. "I wanted to marry you, and you labeled what we had as wrong."

"I wasn't ready, Jay." She drags her nails up his back. "I didn't understand that this is good. I was just scared."

"Scared of me?"

"No." She lifts her head and touches her lips to his. He allows her to draw him into a deep kiss, but he shakes his head when she shifts again and pushes her hips against his.

"Scared of what?"

"Sex. I was afraid that wanting to be with you this way meant I was still the person I used to be. I don't ever want to be that person again. I don't want to be selfish."

"We've never had sex, Ellie," he tells her. "We've made love."

"I know that now," she says with a nod. "God, I know that now." She feels tears slide from her eyes and leave a trail and then disappear in her hair. "I'm so sorry. I never meant to hurt you."

"I hated you when I heard you say that."

"I know." She sinks her teeth into her lip. "I know, and I'm so sorry."

She cries as they make love, and she holds on to him afraid she's dreaming and when she opens her eyes she will find herself alone. He seems as desperate to keep her skin to skin, in his arms. She fights sleep because they have really settled nothing, and she doesn't want this night to end. What if he's had too much to drink? What if when morning comes and they see each other in daylight the magic of this moment is gone?

As hard as she fights, she curls up in his arms after the

second time they've made love and lays her head against his chest and presses her lips against his neck. Luther is gone, but she has a chance to be happy with Jay and Oliver. It matters so much to her that she is crying again when she falls asleep.

CHAPTER 35

ELLIE HAD FORGOTTEN HOW MUCH SHE LOVES TO MAKE SNOW angels. It's so much more fun with Jay. She rolls over on top of him and thinks maybe their kiss could melt the snow. He's laughing too, and she's happy to taste his laugh and swallow that part of him. There's a loud noise, and she shivers, suddenly chilled in the snow.

"What the hell?" Jay groans.

Reality crashes in all at once. They are not making snow angels. They've spent the better part of the night making love. The sheet covers them, huddled together in each other's arms, but the quilt is tangled around their feet. Someone is knocking on her door.

She manages to pry one eye open. He's here. It's real. He made love to her last night. Relieved that it wasn't all a dream, she turns her concentration to the obnoxious banging on her door.

"Oh shit!" She climbs over him and out of bed. His hand cups her breast as she does so, and she wishes she could slip back between the sheets beside him. "Maeve and Maddie," she explains and glances at the alarm clock. "We're going shopping."

He stretches and rolls his eyes, but she sees the hint of a smile on his lips. Unable to resist, she leans over and licks them and coaxes a smile out of him. "Will you get that? I gotta get a quick shower." She smacks her lips against his and hurries to grab panties and a bra from her dresser.

"Sure," he mumbles. She hears him rustle around to get up, but she rushes naked to the bathroom and turns on the shower water. Her body is deliciously sore and tender from last night. It's a feeling she's missed more than she realized. As she lathers her hair with shampoo, she thinks about last night. It's almost enough to make her holler an invitation for him to join her and his sisters to go back home.

Only fifteen minutes have passed when she steps out of the bathroom and hurries to her bedroom to get dressed. She stops dead in her tracks when she sees Maeve and Maddie perched on the edge of her bed. Jay is conspicuously absent. She glances down at her white panties and bra.

"Eh." Maddie lifts a lazy shoulder. "Nothing we haven't seen before."

"Dish," Maeve says sweetly. She smiles, but it is the predatory smile of a jungle animal about to pounce on innocent prey.

"Did he leave?" Ellie can't hide her disappointment.

"Of course he left," Maddie answers with a soft laugh. "We're his big sisters, and we just caught him in bed with you. Do you think he wanted to answer our questions?"

Ellie knows Maddie is right, but he didn't say goodbye. It hurts that he didn't tell her goodbye.

"He didn't say goodbye," she says softly.

"Get some clothes on," Maeve urges her. "And then we'll get coffee and head out of town, and you can tell us all about what you did last night when you left my house."

"I don't want coffee." Ellie snaps. She pulls a pair of Levis out of her drawer.

"No." Maeve shakes her head. "Wear those." She points to the Silver jeans that lay on the floor at the foot of her bed. She blushes when she remembers Jay sliding them down over her hips.

"I wore them yesterday," she argues.

"I know, but they're cute," Maeve tells her. "C'mon. I want coffee. You can have hot chocolate."

Ellie sighs and picks up her jeans and steps into them. She disappears into her closet, grabs a black ribbed turtleneck and pulls it over her head as she walks back out.

"Very nice." Maeve gives her a thumbs up. Ellie rolls her eyes, grabs black socks from her top dresser drawer and then sits on the edge of the bed by Maddie to pull them on.

"Want me to throw your sheets in the washer while you brush your teeth?" Maddie gives her a nudge with her elbow.

Ellie has to laugh. "Will you shut up?" She glances at them. "I already brushed my teeth anyway." She leads the way out of the bedroom, stops at the bathroom to brush her hair again and trace her lips with Strawberry Frost lipstick. "You ready?" she asks as she steps into low-heeled black boots.

"God, you're hot," Maeve says appreciatively.

"If you'd have hit me up ten years ago, we'd be in bed by now," Ellie says with a small grin. "I don't do that anymore."

"Seriously?" Maeve asks.

"Couple times," Ellie answers as she picks up her purse. She stops and stares at them. "Oh my God. I can't believe I just told you that."

"Experimenting is half the fun," Maeve says in a way that suggests she's tried a few things too. "Don't you think, Maddie?"

Ellie pulls on her black jacket and glances at Maddie.

Maddie stares at Maeve, obviously surprised at Maeve's remark.

"I saw you once," Maeve says softly. "After a pool party at the house."

"Oh God," Maddie groans and looks away. "You never said anything."

Maeve shrugs. "Let's go," she says and flashes a smile at Ellie. Maeve is driving Stash's white Durango today. Maddie climbs into the backseat, leaving Ellie to sit with Maeve. "Are you pissed at me now?" Maeve looks at Maddie in the rearview mirror.

"No." Maddie sounds sincere. "But I thought we were going to grill Ellie about what Jay was doing at her house at seven o'clock this morning. Not pick on my past transgressions."

Ellie laughs.

"That's right," Maeve agrees. "What happened?"

"What do you think happened?" Ellie grins. She feels a blush creep up her neck.

"But how?" Maddie asks. "I saw him leave Maeve's and wondered what he was doing."

"He just showed up here. We were sitting outside. He kissed me. One thing led to another."

"Is he good?" Maeve asks. Ellie shakes her head, certain she will die of embarrassment before the day is over.

"Will you shut up?" She laughs.

"Well?" Maddie raises her eyebrows.

"Yes," Ellie answers. "Yes, he is. It was. It always is."

"Then why do you still look sad?" Maddie asks her.

She opens her mouth to protest, but she can't find the words or the heart to do it. Instead she licks her lips and looks back over the seat at Maddie. "We didn't get things figured out. Not really. And he didn't say goodbye this morning."

"Did you tell him?" Maeve asks. "The things he needs to know?" She knows Maddie knows about the conversation Jay had overheard.

"Yeah," Ellie says softly. "But."

"But what?" Maeve pushes her.

"What if it wasn't real? What if he had too much to drink? What if he regrets it now?"

"He wasn't drunk," Maeve says firmly. "He was with you because he wanted to be with you."

She bought Oliver a life size Spider-Man doll and a Spider-Man Lego set. She wanted to find the perfect gift for Jay, but nothing touched her. Maddie picked up a few things, but she didn't really buy much more than Ellie did. Maeve, however, had enough bags for the three of them to carry. After the initial sadness at Jay leaving without telling her goodbye, she'd found herself enjoying the day. Her hot chocolate had tasted that much better because she sipped it in the company of friends. Lunch, which Maeve had insisted on buying, was a delicious and relaxing hour and a half in a bar and grill. Ellie didn't know how she could eat after she'd eaten so much the day before, but she put away enough food again at lunch to last her a week or two.

She hopes there is a message on her machine or a note or something when Maeve drops her off. But there is nothing. Just her empty bed, sheets and quilt the tangled evidence that she had really spent the night making love to Jay. It hadn't been a dream. Tired, but knowing she won't sleep much anyway, she peels her sheets off the bed and throws them in the washer.

She curls up on the couch with the phone in her hand. It's not too late for him to call. At least she hopes it isn't.

Maddie feels like a liar. Like a thief. The closer she gets to Maeve, thanks to Ellie, the more she hates herself. She has to tell her. If there is ever to be a chance that they can regain any ground they've lost over the past eighteen years, she has to tell her. But she hates to risk what they have started to rebuild. She feels like she and Maeve stand on a swinging footbridge, and each day they tack on a new board where an old one has weathered and fallen away. They scramble to patch the little holes in the pool liner, all the while water is gushing out over the top. They're treading water, but they can't swim.

She thinks about Maeve often these days. Prays for her, although she knows Maeve would call her sanctimonious and arrogant if she knew that. It's not at all that Maddie believes herself holier than anyone. It's simply that Maeve's devotion to someone else, namely Ellie and Luther, touched her so deeply that the whole scene about Maeve thinking she'd found Luther in Wisconsin is permanent in her mind. She's in awe of her sister, that she would go to such limits to find happiness for someone else. Maddie wonders if she could do the same if she were in a position to help someone. She sort of doubts herself, and that makes her feel low.

"What're you thinking?" Ellie asks her. Maddie glances at Ellie, who is sprawled out on her couch. Ellie has finished final exams for the semester. She has been at Maddie's house all evening. Maddie has been alternately filling out student assessment forms and staring at the blank TV screen. Ellie has had her nose in a LuAnne Rice book most of the evening. Apparently she has been watching Maddie pretend to be engrossed in work too.

"Thinking about Maeve."

Ellie winces. Maddie hates that she has put Ellie in this position. Ellie will suffer the brunt of it if she talks to Maeve about the past. When she talks to Maeve. She believes Ellie is strong enough to shoulder them both, but she finds herself wondering if Ellie wants to be there for both of them. Maybe if there is a division among them, Ellie will fall on Maeve's side of the equation. She hates herself for doubting Ellie. But she can't help it. Maeve has always been the popular sister. Why wouldn't Ellie choose to remain friends with her? It surprises her, the depth of the sadness she feels at the prospect of losing Ellie.

"No," Maddie says softly. "Not that. I was just thinking of how she went to Wisconsin. Looking for Luther."

Ellie closes her book and stares at Maddie in silence.

"Selfless," Maddie mumbles and looks away.

"I don't expect acts of selfless bravery in exchange for my friendship."

Maddie raises her eyebrows, hating that Ellie sees inside her this way. "I'm afraid of losing you to her. It's happened all my life."

Ellie sits up, obviously surprised at the raw honesty in Maddie's statement.

"I don't qualify people that way." She draws her knees to her chest and loops her arms around her legs. "I'm not going anywhere."

"Peter denied Christ—"

Ellie shakes her head. "Don't spout off the bible to defend the way you're thinking. You've given me a safe place to land. You've given me hope. You've helped me to find self-acceptance. You've prayed for me, and you've taught me to do that for myself."

"I've sacrificed nothing for you."

"And me for you," Ellie says with a shrug. "I would though. If I had to, I would do anything to make you happy."

"You would?"

"Maddie, I had a brother and a sister, and I lost them. I let that go, and it's too far gone to ever go back. You know that, as well as I do. You and Maeve are my family now."

Maddie sighs. "I guess it's just old insecurities. I've always felt second best to Maeve."

"You told me once that you never let that bother you."

"I lied," Maddie says boldly. "Does that make me a horrible person?"

"No," Ellie answers with a small smile. "It makes you real."

Maddie drops her pile of papers on the floor and stands up. She feels Ellie's eyes on her as she leaves the living room. The small package is on her dresser, where it has been since she'd wrapped it a few days ago. Her hand shakes a bit when she hands the small box to Ellie. Ellie eyes her suspiciously as she sits down beside her.

"What's this?" she asks as her fingers rub over the shiny silver paper.

"It's just something small that I wanted to give you," Maddie answers, never taking her eyes off the red bow. Ellie unties the bow, but she stops and looks up at Maddie again.

"Is this for Christmas? Because maybe it should wait. I don't have anything for—"

"It is for Christmas," Maddie tells her. "And I want you to open it now. There's only one thing I want from you for Christmas."

"What?"

"I want you to stand by me when I tell Maeve what I did. I know she's gonna need you. But I will too."

Ellie opens her mouth, but Maddie shakes her head.

"Don't make me promises," Maddie whispers. "Just do it."

Ellie nods. She looks back at the package in her hands and pulls the wrapping off the box, careful not to tear it. She folds the silver paper and lays it beside her on the couch. Her hand shakes as she opens the box. Maddie watches her eyes as she reaches in and gently takes the rosary from the box.

Ellie's eyes are bright with tears when she lifts her head to look at Maddie.

"Blue," Maddie says quietly. "Like Jay's eyes. Oliver's eyes."

Ellie is quiet for so long that Maddie wonders if she's offended her. Ellie covers her mouth with her hand and works to push the tears back into the well inside her. Finally, she looks again at Maddie. "This is the first present I've opened. Since I left home."

Maddie blinks but says nothing.

"Thank you." Gently, she wraps the shiny blue beads around her fingers, eyes never leaving Maddie's face.

JOHNNY MATHIS IS MR. CHRISTMAS TO ELLIE. HER MOTHER had two or three of his Christmas albums. "Sleigh Ride" has always been her favorite Christmas song. Sitting in Maeve's living room, in front of a card table, wrapping presents, goose bumps raise on her arms when the song starts. She stops and sits back and listens. The music washes over her; it's as if someone is standing over her, pouring a bucket of memories over her head, coloring her just as if it were paint rather than memories, in the bucket.

"What?" Maddie asks. Ellie hears the concern in her friend's voice. She glances at Maddie and smiles. Maeve stands and goes to the fireplace. She glances back at Ellie and then turns to throw another log on the fire. Something swells inside Ellie, swells so big and tight she cannot breathe. But she isn't afraid. She is going to share Christmas with a family. With a new family who loves her and accepts her for who she is. She has grown so close to Maeve and Maddie over the past several months that at times she is not sure where she ends and they begin. She trusts them enough to say anything to them and know that she cannot push them away. She and

Jay had dinner together two nights ago. It's not marital bliss, but it is enough to give her hope that maybe someday they'll be together.

It's hope that swells inside her now. Hope that drives her to stand and makes her struggle for a deep breath. Hope that allows her to fold Luther up and slip him inside her heart and look forward to Christmas with another little boy. She will never forget Luther. But she has plenty of love left over for Oliver Bryant.

"My mom had this album," she tells Maddie. "We used to do this at home."

"Do what?" Maeve asks as she pokes at the logs in the fireplace. Satisfied with the flame that results, she puts the poker away and joins them again at the table. The guys are at a basketball game. Maeve had invited Jolene over too, but she'd stayed home to play cards with an old friend who is in town for an early holiday visit.

"Listen to music. Drink hot chocolate. Wrap presents."

"They love you," Maeve whispers. She looks up, her face twisted with guilt, apparently surprised she'd said the words aloud. "You don't have memories like that if no one loved you."

Ellie doesn't argue with her.

"Are you ever going to go back, Ellie?" Maddie asks her quietly. "Go back and show them how strong you are. Show them who you've become."

"No."

"It takes a damned strong person to go back and face the past, Ellie," Maeve says quietly. "You're strong."

Talking about her family does not make her feel strong. It makes her feel weak and stupid and ashamed. This is one thing she can never make them understand, her need to be free of her family.

"Do you really believe that, Maeve?" Maddie asks softly.

"Believe what?"

"That it takes a strong person to go back and face the past?"

"Of course I do," Maeve answers with a shrug.

Maddie licks her lips. "There's something I've wanted to tell you. For so many years, I've watched you and wanted to tell you. But I didn't know how. I was afraid you'd judge me. Afraid that you would hate me."

Ellie winces and drops back into her chair. This is it. Maddie has just pried free the boulder that will become an avalanche that will leave them all buried. She hadn't planned to be along for the ride. She glances at Maeve, who is staring at Maddie expectantly.

"I want to leave." Maddie's voice shakes. "I want to be free of my vows."

Maeve is quiet for a long time. Finally she arches an eyebrow and looks directly at Maddie. "I know you've been unhappy for a long time, Maddie. I know you're searching for something, and you're not finding it."

Maddie sighs.

"But I hate to see you just give up."

"I never really wanted to do this," Maddie tells her. "Just sort of something I did by default."

"What do you mean?"

"I was pregnant," Maddie whispers. "Mom sent me away to have the baby quietly. I couldn't come back and just pretend nothing happened."

Maeve closes her eyes. Ellie's touched by her tears for Maddie.

"Maeve." Maddie's voice breaks. "I'm so sorry. God, I'm sorry, but I have to tell you this—"

"I know," Maeve says softly.

"When you were pregnant with Peyton, you went out of town—"

"I know," Maeve repeats.

"And I went to your house." Maddie does not hear Maeve's words or her soft cries. Ellie feels like a voyeur. If there were an easy way out of the room right now, she'd be on it. "I liked him. I thought I was in love with him. I never—"

"I know." Maeve snaps. She shoves the table away and stands up. "Goddammit, Maddie, I know. You slept with Stash. I know that. I know what you did. Why do you have to bring it up now?"

Maddie stares at Maeve, stunned by her admission. "You know? How do you know?"

"He told me," Maeve whispers. She runs her fingers through her hair and then holds her head in her hands and paces away from the table. "He told me, Maddie."

"When?"

"When I came home." Maeve turns to look at Maddie. She cries in earnest now. "When I came home, pregnant and feeling unattractive and clumsy, my husband told me he'd been with you. Pretty, young, sexy you." She shudders and rubs her eyes. "He begged me to forgive him." Maeve glances at Ellie now, and Ellie wishes for an earthquake to split the living room and swallow her to safety. "I loved him. God, I loved him with all my heart. I hated you, and I loved him."

"Why did you always hate me?" Maddie stands and reaches for Maeve. Maeve evades her hands.

"You had something I didn't," Maeve says softly. "You were innocent. And I lost that when I had the abortion. You never let me forget it. Every time you look at me, even now, I see the way you looked at me that day—"

"I was a kid." Maddie's voice is desperate. "I was scared. What I saw that day scared the hell out of me. I didn't really even know anything about sex, Maeve. I lost that same innocence right there with you."

"You've made me feel like a whore. Like a murderer. Since the day it was done, you've made me feel that way."

Maddie shakes her head. "No, I haven't. I've never meant to make you feel anything like that. But it marked me too, Maeve. You shut me out. You dealt with the abortion, and you moved on, but you shut me out and left me to try and understand it on my own."

"It's your own guilt, Maeve," Ellie whispers. She stares back at Maeve when the woman looks at her with angry eyes. "You pushed your own guilt off on Maddie, so you could justify hating her. She let you go through with it. Maybe you wanted her to stop you. Instead she was with you. That gave you the perfect opportunity to shift the blame."

"You've known all along, haven't you?" Maeve finally asks her.

Ellie considers asking her to clarify what she's known all along. But she doesn't. There's no room for coyness here. This is hard, in your face, truth time, and they've included her in their secrets, and now she is part of this. "For awhile." She nods.

"For years"—Maeve turns to look at Maddie—"I was afraid he would leave me for you. When he made love to me, I wondered if he was thinking of you. When he slept, I wondered if he dreamt of you."

"Maeve, if anything is painfully obvious it's how much that man loves you," Maddie mumbles. She pushes her hair off her face. "I would give anything to have someone in my life like you do. To have someone love me the way Stash loves you."

"I know he loves me." Maeve leans over the table, pushing into Maddie's personal space. "I know that. But it doesn't stop me from thinking of you and him and what you did. It doesn't stop me from being afraid of you every day of my life."

Maddie shakes her head. "I'm sorry. Please, Maeve, please know that I'm sorry, and I know I was wrong."

"I wanted you to tell me. I wanted to break you. I wanted you out of our lives."

Maddie nods. "Yeah, I've always known you felt that way about me." She sits again. "I just never knew why."

Maeve wanders to the fireplace again. "Oh my God."

Ellie watches the truth break over her like water gushing through a dam. She folds in on herself and slowly sinks to sit on the hearth. "Oh my God. You were pregnant."

Maddie reaches for her boots. She glances at Ellie as she pushes her feet into them. When there is silence, except for Johnny Mathis singing "Silent Night" in the background, Maddie looks up to meet Maeve's gaze. She simply nods.

"You were pregnant by Stash?"

Again, another small nod.

Maeve takes a deep breath. Ellie watches the war of emotions play over her face. "Did he know?"

"Of course not," Maddie answers. "I knew I'd done enough damage. I had no desire to wreck your family."

"No, just to fuck my husband."

"I gave her up for adoption, Maeve," Maddie says quietly.

"Oh God." Maeve covers her face with her hands.

"She's gone. It's over." Maddie stands and picks up her coat. "I just wanted you to know."

"Wait." Maeve stands. "I have to know, Maddie."

"Know what?" Maddie asks. Her face is pale and gaunt. Sorrow has etched a few new lines around her eyes.

"Is this why you want to leave the sisterhood? To find your daughter?"

"Of course not," Maddie answers. "I told you I have no

desire to wreck your family." She glances at Ellie. "I want to leave to find myself."

Ellie watches her walk to the front door. She looks at Maeve, broken and scared, perched on the arm of the sofa.

"Maddie!" Ellie calls as she jumps up. She hurries to the door and puts her arms around Maddie. "God, I'm sorry. I'm sorry everything's so messed up."

Maddie holds her tighter than a pirate holds his chest of gold. She cries quietly on Ellie's shoulder. Ellie hates being here in the middle. She loves them both, and they are both in pieces, and she only has two hands to put them back together.

"Let me go," Maddie pleads.

Ellie kisses her cheek and lets her go. As Maddie hurries out the front door, Maeve rushes by her and climbs the steps two at a time. Ellie turns to the empty living room. Johnny Mathis has finished singing. Alabama is singing "Santa Claus, I Still Believe in You." The words cut through Ellie like broken holiday crystal. She leaves the music on, but the bad feelings expand inside her, metastasizing like cancer cells. Her mother had this album too. She cannot handle thoughts of her own past on top of the past relived in this room tonight.

She cleans the living room and kitchen for Maeve. Later, when the house is put back in order, she turns off the music and lets herself out. Blue Christmas, she thinks, after all.

CHAPTER 36

It seems like she should care that her only sister gave a child up for adoption. Of course the fact that it was her husband's child puts a lid on how much sympathy she can drum up. She finds it sort of amusing that the loss of a child is the tri-bond between herself and Maddie and Ellie. As she holds her coffee mug in her hands, she thinks of the board game, Tri-Bond, that she and the family used to play. Three things. Find the common bond. The loss of a child. Of the three of them, she is the most pathetic. She killed her child. And she'd never even told the man she'd given herself to, forsaking all others. As lies of omission go, she guesses this is a pretty big one.

All of the fear and the hatred had roared back to life inside her last night when Maddie started talking. It hurts her now, because she was beginning to like her sister again. What if Maddie finds her daughter? Will Stash want to be a part of her life? How will her children deal with the fact that they have a cousin who is also their sister? This is worse than Rylan and Joe. Maddie and Stash created a life together. She doesn't know how to let this go.

Seeing Ellie rush to Maddie had felt like someone had shoved bamboo shoots up under her fingernails. Ellie is her friend. Ellie was her friend first. Why is Ellie defending Maddie? She looks around the kitchen again. When she'd rushed upstairs last night, she'd assumed Ellie would leave with Maddie. Apparently Ellie had stayed and cleaned up. Stash had come home just after eleven, but he hadn't come to bed till midnight. She'd showered and washed away the evidence of crying, and when he came to bed, she'd pretended to be asleep. It wasn't the first time, but it was unusual. They had made a pact early on to talk everything through when one of them was hurting over something. Maeve had wanted nothing to do with him when he'd come to bed. Not when the hurt from eighteen years ago had just been exhumed.

She is glad it is Saturday, because there is no way in hell she could have put her game face on and gone into the office today. She pours herself another cup of coffee, checks the caller ID on the phone when it rings, and sets it down without answering it when she sees Ellie's number.

JAY DOUBLE-CHECKS THE CHICKEN IN THE OVEN. HE'S NEVER baked a chicken before, but it looks okay. Oliver has insisted he play Chutes and Ladders for two hours straight, but he's been like a caged tiger, pacing the floor. Bouncing from the oven to the game to the bottle of wine that is chilling in the refrigerator.

She will be here at any moment. He had offered to pick her up, but she'd insisted that she could drive. She'd sounded genuinely happy to be invited over for dinner with him and Oliver. But under that happiness, he'd heard sadness. He intends to find out what is bothering her. His stomach has been in knots all day. He and Oliver had wrapped Ellie's presents earlier. Most of them they will save for Christmas Eve. But there is one Oliver wants her to open tonight. It is a hand-drawn picture, done with exquisite care. The medium is crayon, the artist is Oliver, and the theme is love. It is a family portrait. The family is Ellie, Oliver, and himself. They'd put it in a shirt box and wrapped it with green paper, and then Jay had laced silver ribbon through the diamond ring and tied a bow on the package.

Jay had discussed it with Oliver. He would not ask Ellie to marry him if Oliver did not approve. If Oliver would not be happy, he would not be happy. As he had expected, Oliver had danced with glee when he'd asked him what he thought about marrying Ellie. It isn't that he wants to use Oliver as a trump card to lure Ellie in. It's simply that Oliver is a part of this.

He'd proposed to Rylan over champagne, starlit sky in the background. Their relationship had been as deep as a rain puddle. He and Oliver will do this together, after a family dinner, curled up with Ellie by the Christmas tree. If she says no, it will break him. It might break them both, but Oliver is young and resilient. At least that's what he thinks Maeve would tell him if she would answer her phone so he could share his plan with her. If Ellie says no, he will tell Rylan he still wants custody of Oliver. He will give her visitation rights; he won't be an ass about dates and schedules. She has admitted that Oliver would have a better childhood here in a smaller town, with a family around him. Jay will push her on this, if today falls through with Ellie.

Oliver grins when they hear the knock on the door. Jay swoops him off his feet and tosses him over his shoulder. "Not a word until after we eat. You hear me?"

"Yes, Daddy," Oliver says with a giggle.

Ellie offers the two of them a tentative smile when Jay

opens the door. Oliver wiggles away from Jay and falls into Ellie's awaiting arms. Jay waits for the words to tumble out of his son's mouth, but Oliver simply grins so big he nearly knocks his ears off.

"Hi, handsome," Ellie says to Oliver. She plants a big kiss on his cheek. Oliver, the ladies' man, cups Ellie's cheeks in his hands and smacks his lips against hers. Ellie laughs and hugs him hard and leans over to set him down. "I love your tree. Did you help Daddy decorate it?"

"Yes." Oliver beams at her. "Maybe you could help next time."

Ellie raises her eyebrows, glances at Jay, and chuckles. "Wow. Next Christmas already. Maybe."

"Let me take your coat," Jay says and reaches for it as she slips it off. She is wearing those Silver jeans she'd worn Thanksgiving Day. The night he'd slipped his fingers inside the waistband and skimmed his knuckles over her belly. The night he'd pushed the denim down over her hips and then hooked his fingers in the elastic of her panties and pushed them out of his way. He takes a deep breath and looks up to meet her gaze. She looks breathless, and he knows from the color in her face and the heat in her eyes, she is thinking of the same thing. "I love that sweater," he says. He touches the red sleeve. It is a cashmere sweater, with a deep V neck.

"Thanks," she answers. She lets Oliver take her hand and lead her into the house.

"Daddy fixed your chicken," Oliver tells her. Jay snorts softly and lays her coat on his bed. He follows them to the kitchen. "And he got some wine. Says you like it, but Mommy hates when I whine. She said so."

Ellie laughs and bends to drop a kiss on his mop of curls. "I've missed you."

"Are you hungry?" Jay asks her.

"Yeah." She looks up at him. A tiny smile curves her lips. "Can I have some wine?"

Her eyes shine, and he smells a soft, sweet perfume. He leans toward her and touches his lips to hers. "Yes," he says as he kisses her again. "You can have some wine."

Dinner is cozy and fun. Where things might have been a bit quiet between the two of them, Oliver chatters nonstop. Jay holds his breath, hoping his son can hold his excitement in until later, when they give her the ring. The chicken is surprisingly good. Baked potatoes and green beans round out the meal. Ellie strokes her fingers over the back of his hand when Oliver isn't looking. He fills her wine glass again.

Oliver disappears to the living room. They hear him playing with George. When the zany music of cartoons fills the house, Jay leans toward her and brushes her lips again with his. She kisses him back. Before he loses control, he eases away from her. She smiles, but she looks tired.

"What's wrong?" he asks.

"Nothing. Why?"

"You look tired," he tells her. He twirls a lock of her hair around his finger.

She sighs. "Maeve and Maddie."

"What happened?"

She shakes her head. "They dug up some skeletons the other night."

He studies her face for a long moment and then nods. "You okay?"

She closes her hands around his fingers and smiles sadly. "I'm okay, Jay, but I'm worried about both of them."

"Can you tell me?"

"No," she whispers. "I'm sorry. But I can't."

"Okay."

"I don't like keeping things from you, but this isn't about me, Jay."

"I know."

"Let's clean the kitchen really quick."

"No." He stands and takes her hand. "Let's go play with Oliver and George."

She follows him to the living room. Oliver is hanging upside down over the edge of the couch watching Sponge-Bob. Ellie laughs and sits down beside him. "Aren't you gonna be sick doing that?"

"Me and Mom watch cartoons like this all the time," he tells her. She looks up at Jay and then back at Oliver. His long curls hang from his head. His smile is bizarre upside down.

"Really?" she asks.

"Don't even think about it," Jay says and sits down by her.

"Can we do a puzzle?" Oliver asks. He flips off the couch and lands on the floor with a thud. George lets out a lazy yap and saunters over to sniff Oliver's hair. Oliver giggles and rolls over with the dog.

"Sure," Ellie answers him. "Got a Christmas puzzle?"

Together they work on a simple Santa Claus puzzle. When they finish it, they watch Jimmy Neutron. Jay is amazed that Ellie appears to like the cartoons. Oliver is glued to Ellie's lap. Jay knows it's time to move when Oliver sticks his thumb in his mouth. It's after eight. Oliver is getting tired.

"Ellie," he says and turns off the TV. "Oliver and I have a present for you to open."

Oliver springs off her lap like a jack in the box. Ellie laughs. "It's not Christmas yet."

"But this is cool," Oliver assures her. "For real."

Ellie cuts her eyes from son to father. Jay shakes his head with a shrug. "Don't ask me."

"I didn't bring you guys any presents tonight, though," she tells them.

"Humor us," Jay says. Oliver slithers under the tree and then backs out on all fours, pulling the special package with him. He pushes it close to Ellie and then scoots back to sit in Jay's lap.

"To Ellie," she reads the tag. "From the boys." Jay sees her eyes fill and sees her fight to stay in control. She doesn't notice the ring when she breaks the ribbon and unwraps the present.

"I drew it," Oliver says proudly when she lifts the drawing from the box. She smiles, but a tear drops on the picture. She laughs and holds the paper out and wipes at her eyes. "You don't like it?"

"I love it, Ol," she answers. "I'm gonna put it on my refrigerator."

"It's us." Oliver leans close to her. He points each of them out to her and then claps his hand over his mouth. "I forgot George."

"You can add him before I leave," she tells him. She kisses Oliver again and brushes his hair off his forehead.

"That's not all, Ellie," Jay says quietly.

"What's not all?" she asks. She looks in the box again and then picks up the paper. She freezes when she finds the diamond ring. "Oh my God," she whispers. She looks at Oliver, who is beaming, and then at Jay.

"Will you marry us, Ellie?" Oliver asks her. Jay can practically see his son vibrating with anticipation. She looks at Jay again.

"I know we hit a rough spot," he says. "And I know this might feel—"

"Yes," she whispers.

"—sudden to you. I know it's a big step—"

"Yes," she repeats.

"But we've wasted so much time and—"

"Daddy!" Oliver throws himself into Ellie's arms. "She said yes."

"You did?" Jay asks.

"I did." Ellie giggles and with Oliver in her arms, climbs closer to him, into his lap and presses her lips to his. "Yes, I did say yes."

"Put the ring on her, Daddy!"

Jay's hands shake as he finds the ring, unties it and takes her hand in his. Oliver touches her hand when the diamond glitters on her finger. "You'll be my stepmom, Ellie." He grins. "You'll be my mommy here."

Ellie nods and laughs and cries. She looks at the ring on her finger again. It was gorgeous last summer when she'd seen it in the box. It looks even better on her finger.

"I love you, Ellie." Jay cups her chin in his hand.

"I know." She turns her face and kisses the palm of his hand. "And I love you."

LATER WHEN OLIVER IS ASLEEP, ELLIE CURLS UP IN JAY'S ARMS at the end of the couch. Jay rests his cheek against her head and smells her perfume and closes his eyes.

"I didn't mean to use Oliver as a pawn. He just got really excited about what I was going to do."

"It's okay," she says softly. "I think it was the best moment of my life."

"There's something I need to tell you."

She stirs in his arms and sits up straight to look at him. "What is it?"

He sighs. What if this puts her off? What if she thinks he's using her to keep Oliver? "In October, Rylan told me she wanted me to have custody of Oliver."

"Oh my God!" Her smile is so sincere it makes him hurt inside. "Jay, that's incredible."

"But I want you to know she had a condition. I didn't push her to see how far she would bend, but you need to know this."

"What?"

"She wanted me with you. She wants us raising Oliver. Together."

Ellie laughs softly and raises her eyebrows. "And you're afraid I think you're using me to get Oliver?"

"Do you think that?" he asks. "I don't want you to think that for a minute."

She lays her hand over the back of his. "I don't think that, Jay. You and I started long before I even met Oliver."

"Are you okay with this? I mean, getting married. Instant family."

"I'm good with it. I'd marry you tomorrow, if it meant we could skip all the hoopla and just be together."

"No way," he says with a small smile. He brushes her hair off her face. "I want a beautiful bride. I want to show you off to my family and friends."

She grins, but she ducks her head. "I don't want anything too big."

"Okay." He nods. "That's fair." He slides his arm around her again and draws her against his chest. "How do you feel about having a baby with me?"

She sits up straight again and shakes her head. "I can't replace Luther. I can't—"

"I would never ask you to replace Luther. Or forget about Luther. I want you to remember your son every day. I want you to share those memories with me and Oliver and my family. I want that little boy to be mine, if we ever find him."

She sucks in a deep breath and turns her face away from him to hide her tears. "Do you mean that?"

"Yes."

She stands up and wanders to the Christmas tree. "Thank you."

"But," he says and stands up to join her by the tree. "I want to have a child with you. I want to share that bond with you, Ellie."

She nods, but she is slow to answer him. "I'm scared."

"It would be different this time," he reminds her gently. "We'd be together. I'd be with you through everything."

She smiles, but her eyes brim with tears, and there is a look of sheer panic on her face. Jay rubs his thumb over her lip.

"I don't mean right now," he tells her. "I don't mean to rush things. But one day, I want to do this. I want a beautiful baby girl, with her mother's eyes."

She goes willingly into his arms and rests her head against his chest. After several minutes of silence pass, she lifts her head to look up at him. "I'm a little bit afraid this is just a dream, and I'm gonna wake up and I'm gonna be alone."

"You and me both, Ellie." He presses her head back against his chest and kisses the top of her head.

"Is this real, Jay?"

"You and me and Oliver," he says. "We're real."

CHAPTER 37

CHRISTMAS SHOULD BE LIKE THANKSGIVING, BUT IT'S NOT. Ellie walks the fault line between Maeve and Maddie and wonders why no one else senses it. No one else sees the warning signs or feels the tremors. When the two of them are in the room together, the seismic activity is off the charts. Ellie fears for all of them when the ground will finally break.

Peyton is home, and this time she's brought her professor with her. Though Maeve has said precious little to Ellie all day, precious little to her since Armageddon actually, Ellie knows Maeve is on edge with her daughter's older man. The guy seems nice enough, Ellie thinks, but it blows her mind that Peyton is living with him. She's a beautiful young woman, and Ellie knows it's cliché, but there is so much world out there waiting to be explored it's a shame to see someone like Peyton waste herself on this man.

Luke and Joe are obnoxious and more so as the day wears on. Ellie has learned to ignore them. But she knows they are walking on Maeve's last nerve. It amazes her that Luke can't see it in his own mother; she's ready to break down. Then again, maybe it's because he's a guy, and guys don't notice these things. Although Jay has noticed. Many times today, Jay has caught her eye in askance, and she can only shrug. Maeve had barely reacted to the ring on her finger or the announcement Jay had made when the whole family had gathered at Maeve's. She'd not spoken much to Jay all day. She hasn't really given Oliver ten minutes of her time. Somehow she's managed to look busy and harried each time Ellie has caught her eye.

Maddie had hugged her and held her for a moment and congratulated her and apologized to her, and Ellie had wanted so badly to sit down with her and talk. But Christmas Day is not the time for those much-needed, come-to-Jesus talks, most especially not with an audience.

Ellie and Maddie help in the kitchen, insisting that Jolene stay off her feet. Ellie notices both Maddie and Maeve keeping a close but sly eye on their mother, who has been complaining about a severe headache for the past couple of days. Ellie had enjoyed Thanksgiving at Maeve's so much, she is disappointed in how hard this day is. Dinner is over, and the present exchange is over, and Ellie and Maeve have cleaned the kitchen, because Maeve had asked Maddie very quietly when just the three of them were alone there to let her worry about her kitchen and the details.

Ellie is ready to go home. To shut out Maeve and Maddie and their problems. To be with Jay. To tuck Oliver in and sit with Jay and think about what next Christmas might bring for the two of them. She folds the dishtowel, but as she lays it on the counter, Maeve touches her hand. It is the first time since the night all hell broke loose that Maeve has touched her.

Ellie stares at Maeve's fingers on hers, Maeve's thumb when it brushes over the diamond. She steels herself when

Maeve looks up at her. This is Russian Roulette. She has no idea what to expect from Maeve, anger or sadness or hatred.

"Why didn't you tell me?" Maeve asks quietly.

"I've called you twenty times or more since that night," Ellie tells her. "I can't talk if you're not listening."

Maeve licks her lips and takes a deep breath. Her eyes scale over Ellie's face and then slide shut for a moment. "She took him. She took Stash. I've always known, and now she's got you—"

"No." Ellie shakes her head. "She didn't take him. What they did was wrong, Maeve, yes, I agree with you absolutely. But she's lived with that regret for eighteen years. Stash confessed to you and asked you to forgive him. He loves you. He loves you, and he belongs with you, and she did not take him. You know that. You know the way he loves you." Ellie taps Maeve's chest with her finger. "Inside. You know that. You and Stash squared this away eighteen years ago. It's time you get it taken care of with Maddie."

"I can't."

"You can," Ellie corrects her. "And as for me. Bullshit. You know how I feel about you. We have some variation of this conversation once a month. I am not yours for her to take. I am your friend. I am always your friend." Ellie stares hard at Maeve. "You'd know that, if you'd stop wallowing in self-pity and look beyond yourself—"

"You defended her—"

"I care about her!" Ellie snaps. She looks up, but she and Maeve are still alone in the kitchen. "Yes, I care about Maddie. Yes, she is my friend. You're both a part of me. Why does it have to be a competition?"

"When you walked away that night, I felt like I meant nothing to you—"

"I did not walk away." Ellie shakes her head. "I held her

for a minute, because she's completely alone, and she's hurting, and she needs you. But I did not walk away from you. I was here, long after you walked out."

Maeve buries her face in her hands. "She could take him in a heart beat. She's beautiful. She's sexy. She had his child—"

"She doesn't want to take him. He doesn't want to leave you. It's over, Maeve. It was over eighteen years ago." Ellie looks around again and heaves a sigh of frustration. "You're gorgeous. You're sexy. You're his wife. How can you let her be a threat to you after all these years?"

"But what if she searches for her daughter?"

"She has no intention of ever doing that. She just wants to find a little peace of mind, Maeve. She's driving herself crazy trying to be someone she's not."

"I'm sorry," Maeve whispers. She wipes her eyes and looks at Ellie through tear-spiked lashes. "It's hard to go through this again."

"I know it is." Ellie is sincere. "Of course it is. It's supposed to be, because it matters to you."

Maeve laughs softly. Her eyeliner is smudged under her eyes. "When'd you get to be so smart?"

"I've learned a lot about family from you and Maddie," Ellie says quietly. "You've already lost the last eighteen years, Maeve. Don't wait much longer."

"I could remind you that you've lost the last ten." Maeve clears her throat. She turns to the sink and runs water in it to rinse it out, even though Ellie had just done the same thing ten minutes ago.

"You could, but we're talking about you, not me."

Maeve's hands shake as she dries off the counter again. Ellie senses she still has something to say. Finally, Maeve slants a glance at her from under her bangs, timid and unlike

Maeve. "She really hasn't said anything to you about finding her daughter?"

"She told me she won't look, because she doesn't want to do any more damage to you and Stash."

Maeve sniffles and nods and rests her hand on Ellie's again. "Congratulations, Ellie," she whispers. Ellie thanks her and turns her hand upside down and links her fingers through Maeve's.

ONCE, WHEN MAEVE WAS EIGHT OR NINE, SHE AND HER FRIEND Julie had gotten into a knock-down, drag-out fight. She'd been so mad at Julie, she'd called her a bitch. It was a word she hadn't heard all that often, and she had no idea what it meant, only that it was usually used in a bad way, and she'd wanted to hurt Julie. She'd gone home, but she'd been so weighted down with guilt, she'd probably appeared six inches shorter to her mother. Jolene had fixed her an after-school snack, apple slices smeared with Jif peanut butter, and asked her how her day had been. Maeve had come undone and confessed to her mother what she'd done and what she'd called Julie and that she felt really bad inside now that it was over. Jolene had suggested, in a motherly tone that had told Maeve it wasn't really a suggestion but an order, that Maeve go to Julie's house and apologize.

She doesn't remember now what she and Julie had been fighting about; that's how important it was. In fact, it had probably been forgotten within a week. But she recalls the way her stomach had quivered with nerves as she'd walked up the Watkins' front walk and then stuck her index finger on the doorbell and jumped when she'd heard it ring. She recalls that feeling now because she feels the same way as she eyes Maddie's house and climbs reluctantly from her car.

Maddie is dressed in faded jeans and a faded red T-shirt when she opens the door. Maeve realizes it is a Chicago Bulls shirt, and she wonders when her sister picked up a taste for professional basketball. And all at once, it hits her that she really doesn't know this woman who is her flesh and blood. She only knows the bare bones, and even that has changed now.

"What're you doing?" she asks as she watches Maddie stack books in a big box.

"What does it look like I'm doing?" Maddie asks, but her voice is flat. Her words don't carry the sarcastic punch Maeve is used to.

"Packing."

"Give the lady a prize," Maddie mumbles.

"You're leaving?"

"I talked to Sister Kathleen. She's my mother superior." Maddie stops what she is doing and looks directly at Maeve. "I've been released from my vows."

Maeve opens her mouth to respond, but she doesn't know what to say. Sister Madeline. She's just Maddie now. That barrier of religious dogma and faith is gone, and now they are just two women, two blood sisters staring each other down across this small room in a house she has visited only a handful of times.

"But you're leaving?"

"I have to get out of this house, Maeve," Maddie tells her. She rolls her eyes. "The church pays my rent."

"Where will you go?" Maeve perches on the arm of the couch and folds her arms over her chest.

"I don't know," Maddie answers distractedly. "I'm thinking about Chicago. Or St. Louis. For now, anyway."

"Why?" Maeve asks quickly. "Why leave town?"

"Because I need a break."

"Maddie, you can't just move away. I mean, your family is here—"

Maddie laughs and shakes her head. "You and I have nothing left. And Jay and I have never been close. Joe probably doesn't even know my name—"

"Don't say that." Maeve shakes her head and frowns. "Don't say we have nothing left."

"What, Maeve? Am I your New Year's Resolution? Make up with Maddie? Go home and cross that off your list. And then live guilt-free for a few months. There's nothing, Maeve, between us. Ellie made us polite strangers—"

"Bullshit!" Maeve stands and paces across the room. "Bullshit. Yeah, so things are messed up right now, but nothing's gonna change. Nothing's gonna work out if you leave."

"I've been waiting eighteen years for things to work out with you. For you to tell me why you hated me. For you to remember who I am. To see me behind the title." Maddie stares at Maeve for a long time and finally turns and walks out of the room. Maeve follows her. "I'm done waiting, Maeve."

"I've always seen you—"

"You never saw me," Maddie sneers. She turns to Maeve in the kitchen now. "This life was the perfect excuse for you to ignore me. And now that I'm leaving that life, you feel threatened."

Maeve sinks into a kitchen chair and stares at her feet.

"I'm not leaving to scare you," Maddie says quietly. "This has nothing to do with you."

Maeve hangs her head when Maddie walks calmly from the kitchen. She hadn't expected this to be easy. But she hadn't expected to hurt like this either. She doesn't want Maddie to leave. But Maddie's right. This isn't about Maeve; it's all about Maddie. Her sister is a person. A real person whom she's avoided for almost twenty years.

~

ELLIE MISSES MADDIE, AND SHE'S NOT EVEN GONE YET. SHE knows of her plans to get in the car and drive. And find herself in a new world, a new life when she stops the car. Ellie can't disapprove. She'd done the same thing nearly eleven years ago, when she'd started over with her baby son in tow. But she still misses her. She still winces when she hears the sadness in Maddie's voice over leaving the church and the school and Robert. Starting over is sometimes the only way, but it is so hard to walk away from the familiar. Ellie knows this, and she tells Maddie that, and they promise to write and call every time they talk. But today is it. Today Maddie had gotten out of her bed for the last time in her little yellow rental home and showered and dressed and got in her car and driven away. Ellie tries to imagine the little house empty of Maddie's touch, of her life. The furniture will stay, but all of Maddie's personal belongings, her books, her puzzles, her special mementos of childhood, are all packed away in storage.

She sighs and tries again to read the open textbook in front of her. She simply cannot work up enough interest to read more about the US in the early 1900s. Classes have started again, but she is no longer in any of Jay's classes. Conflict of interest, with them being engaged and all. He's mentioned writing that book again, and Ellie finds herself sort of tingly with anticipation. She wants to work with Jay.

She wonders how far Maddie has gotten in one day of driving. If she is lonely or if she's found strength in being alone. She wonders if the hard, dark music of Evanescence pounds the interior of the car as Maddie drives. If she's singing along, as usual. She'd considered, for just a moment, giving Luther's Cross to Maddie to wear as a talisman of sorts. Against whatever bad things she might find, whether they be real or those imagined demons she and Maeve and Maddie share. But she couldn't do it. As much as she loves them all, she cannot let Luther go. He is the seed that created this new life she now lives, and she keeps him close any way she can.

CHAPTER 38

"How is she?" Maddie asks as she rounds the corner of the hospital corridor and slips into her mother's room. It is early evening, but it is still winter, and darkness has already gathered outside the only window in the small, private room. Her heart pounds so hard she thinks it's going to push right through the layers of muscle and skin and fall out on the floor and make her trip and misstep. God, she's so afraid right now that she's going to misstep.

She has not seen her family in nearly six weeks. She'd left her sisterhood and her family all in one big whirlwind, never taking the time to look back and see whom she'd left standing. She knows Maeve is wounded, and she fully expects the war to wage onward while she is here. But she wonders where she stands with her brothers. With Ellie. And with Jolene, of course. What if they all hate her, like Maeve does? What will she do then?

Maeve is perched on the side of the hospital bed, holding her mother's frail hand. Jay leans on the wall in the far corner of the room. His ankles are crossed, as are his arms over his chest. Ellie sits in the chair at Jolene's bedside, but the chair is pulled back a good distance, as if she'd wanted to give Maeve some time alone with Jolene. Maddie notices the blue beads wrapped around Ellie's fingers. The rosary. She's holding her rosary. She is touched that Ellie uses it, but it scares the hell out of her that Ellie, a non-Catholic experimenting with prayer and symbolism, is praying the rosary for her mother.

"How is she?" she repeats, louder this time. She steps around Maeve to get a better look at her mother. She looks frail and old. She breathes with the help of an oxygen tube in her nose. There is an IV in her hand. Maddie wonders what drug is dripping into her mother's bloodstream.

"Sleeping," Maeve answers. She slips off the bed and turns to look at Maddie. "Took you long enough."

"I left as soon as you called." Maddie's words are riddled with irritation. "It's a long drive, Maeve."

"She's doing a little better," Jay tells Maddie. He pushes off the wall and comes toward her. She gives him a curious look as he puts his arms around her. She's not sure he's ever hugged her before.

"What happened?" she asks as she returns his hug. "What's going on?"

"She had a headache," Maeve answers. "She was just acting strange. Didn't know who I was."

"They think she had a stroke," Jay says quietly.

"Oh God," Maddie cries. "Is she going to be okay?"

"It was a mild stroke," Jay tells her. "She was awake earlier today. She seemed fine."

"I shouldn't have left," she whispers.

"What? Your being here would have prevented it?" Maeve snaps.

Maddie sighs and looks at her hands. When she notices they are shaking, she pushes them deep into the pockets of her jeans. "No. But maybe I should just be here." She shrugs.

"She's okay, Maddie," Jay says gently. He lays a hand on her shoulder.

Maeve stares at them silently.

"How's Chicago?" Ellie asks her with a small, tired smile.

"I like it," Maddie answers.

"It suits you," Ellie says as she stands up. She stretches and groans when her bones pop and crack. "You look great."

"Thanks."

"Still teaching?" Jay asks her.

"Yeah," Maddie answers Jay, but she turns her eyes back to Jolene. Maeve has moved away from the bed. She stands on the far side of the room, huddled into herself. Maddie feels a pang of regret slice through her. To push it away, she sidles up to the bed and perches next to her mother, as Maeve had been when she'd walked in.

"You left a teaching job."

Maddie glances at Maeve. "I left a teaching job where I was known as a Catholic nun. I'm still a teacher, Maeve. I still enjoy it. I'm just different inside."

"Let's get some coffee, Ellie," Jay suggests.

"Buy me a Coke and I'm right there with ya." Ellie grins and gives him a peck on his lips.

"You guys married yet?" Maddie asks. She reaches out and takes her mother's hand in hers. She'd hesitated, fearing touching her would be like touching death. That she would be cold. She sighs with relief when she curls her fingers around Jolene's warm hand.

"September," Ellie tells her.

"Really? You set a date?" Maddie can't help but be excited.

"We'll be back in a bit," Jay says as he ushers Ellie out to the hall.

Maddie studies her mother's face when they are gone. Her throat aches with pent up emotion. She had not allowed herself to cry the whole drive home, as if by some magic, she could control her mother's fate if she could control her own emotions.

She doesn't look up when she hears Maeve step up beside her. "Is she really gonna be okay?" she whispers, hating the rough edge in her voice, the one that will tell Maeve she is ragged and ready to break down.

"I think so," Maeve says quietly. "The doctors say she's lucky. This was just a warning sign."

Maddie looks up then and meets Maeve's eyes. "What're they doing for her?"

"Got her on some brand new medication. They want to keep her here for a few days to watch how she does on it."

Maddie nods and wipes her eyes. She looks back at Jolene. "Reminds me of Daddy."

"I know."

Maddie doesn't move when she feels Maeve's hand on her shoulder. She feels like a kid again, a scared kid, and she wishes she could cry to her mom. She feels her rosary pressed tight against her thigh in the pocket of her jeans. If she can't talk to her mom to feel better this time, she can pray. She hasn't abandoned what she believes in.

"I haven't seen you in a ponytail since you were about thirteen," Maeve says softly. Maddie turns to look at her when she feels Maeve's fingers playing with her hair.

"Fourteen," she whispers. "I never wore it up after—" She glances at Maeve and shakes her head. "Just felt like I'd seen too much to look that innocent."

"I did that to you." Maeve drops her hand to her side.

"We should have talked," Maddie says with a shrug. "A part of my big sister was gone after that. I was scared."

"I'm sorry," Maeve says sincerely. "I'm sorry, Maddie."

Maddie takes the hand that Maeve offers her. She squeezes back and holds on even when Maeve reaches behind her to pull the chair up next to the bed.

~

"You should go home," Jay says softly. He squeezes Ellie's fingers. "Get some rest."

"I'm fine," she answers. "I wanna be here with you."

They look at each other as they wander down the hospital corridor, back toward Jolene's room. A small smile plays at the corner of his lips. "I never thought we'd be here." He rubs his thumb over the ring on her finger. "I never thought you'd fall in love with me."

He stops and draws her into his arms. "Where else would I be, Jay?" she whispers. "This feels just right to me."

"I know." He kisses her forehead.

"I never thought—" she stops and shakes her head.

"What?" Jay cocks his head and gives her what she knows he considers his sexiest smile. "You never thought what?"

"That I'd get a second chance." She raises her eyebrows and presses her lips together.

"Looks like we're both getting a second chance." He takes her hand again, and they continue down the corridor.

"Maddie looks good."

"She does," Jay agrees. "It's just hard to get my head around her leaving the way she did."

They round the corner and step into Jolene's room. Ellie feels her heart in her throat when she sees Maddie sitting on Jolene's bed, stretched forward, her hand tucked safely away in Maeve's folded hands. Maeve sits in the chair, pulled up close to the side of the bed, head bowed. The silence is thick and slow, like honey on a hot July day. Ellie pivots on her toes and drags Jay back out of the room.

"Let's give them a few minutes," she says softly. He nods and follows her back around the corner. They stop at the window closest to the corner and stare out into the bleak winter night.

"You did that." Jay watches her closely.

"Did what?"

"Put them back together."

"No." Ellie shakes her head. "They're doing all the hard stuff."

She feels Jay's heavy gaze, but she avoids his eyes. Engaged or not, she still does not feel it is her place to share their secrets. "It was a guy, wasn't it?" he asks her.

Ellie licks her lips but says nothing.

"And for a guy to stay between them that long, I'm wondering if it wasn't Stash." He looks away from Ellie and out the window. He watches a pickup truck creep slowly through the visitors' parking lot. "You don't have to say anything. Guess what matters is they're in there together right now."

Ellie reaches for his hand and links her fingers through his. She steps closer to him and turns to look again out into the night.

Ky's acting weird. Like, even this morning, when Dad hollered goodbye as he walked out the back door with his travel mug full of coffee and Mom was scrambling eggs with spinach and tomatoes in them, dressed in her yoga pants and running shoes, he was in the living room acting strange. He was quiet, kind of agitated, and when we got home from school, he bailed out of the car even before I had it in park.

When we first got him—Mom would lecture me, because that makes him sound like a dog—and he had those moments of rage, and he kicked and screamed and cried until he would just wear himself down completely and then sleep for days, I would hide. I didn't get it. Didn't get him. Why he had to be here.

He scared me. Everything about him scared me, even when he was crashed out hard on the other twin bed Mom and Dad had squeezed into my room. I didn't get close; getting close to him creeped me out, but I would sit, mesmerized on my bed—scrunched as far back into the corner as I could get—and stare at him. He never moved. When he slept, he never moved an inch. Like, when he first came here and he'd go through that whole melt down thing and then sleep, I would panic because I thought he was dead.

I didn't care. I didn't know the kid enough to give a damn if he was dead.

I just didn't want any dead things or bad vibes in my bedroom.

Kyler is freakishly pale, and he has a lot of freckles on his face, and when we first got him, there were times his skin was translucent, and his freckles looked like black bugs on his face. Not that I knew the word *translucent* then; I just knew that when I grew a pair and finally walked over to stand beside his bed, I could see the veins in his face. Dark purple, like worms under his skin.

I didn't hate him. Not then, anyway. I mean, I didn't love having to share a room with him, and I didn't defend him when my friends called him a freak. And even then, I kept him away from Layla. But I didn't hate him. Yet.

"Where's Ky?"

I gulp the rest of the milk in the gallon jug and swipe the back of my hand over my mouth as Mom follows her question into the kitchen. She eyes the empty jug and then my face and rolls her eyes as she looks away.

"Move, Jason." She throws a hip at me as she swings her hands up and then rests the grocery bags hanging off her wrists on the counter. "I could've used some help carrying these in."

"Didn't know you were out there."

I left my *Call of Duty* game on pause a few minutes ago, but I know there's no escaping her right now. Instead, I help her unpack the bags and put stuff away.

"Where's Ky?" she asks again. Back to her, leaning into the fridge to put away all the produce she insists Kyler and I eat, I shrug. When I straighten and twist around to grab more— Layla eats this crap now with her, but Kyler and I hate it—I figure she'll badger me about him, but she's already squatting in front of the cabinet and pulling a skillet out so she can start dinner.

"Dad's got a meeting tonight."

I watch her as she stands, sets the skillet on the island cooktop. The big grates on the burners look commercial, like Mom's kitchen could be something out of a five-star restaurant. Maybe at one point, she was a good cook. Not sure anything she fixes now is edible, much less tasty. Not sure it can make any sort of difference for Kyler when he pushes it around on his plate and gags on the rare forkful he actually puts in his mouth.

"I need you to get Layla from softball."

"I don't want to."

"Tough, Jason."

I get that tough-as-nails mom look over her shoulder. When I was little, I thought she was pretty. Then after Kyler, I thought she was crazy. A little bit mean. She's still pretty, I guess, but she wears her age and her wisdom in her face. My friends still stare at her when she walks into a room—she has those lines around her eyes and mouth, but the rest of her body is proof that she still works out religiously—and I still get seriously creeped out over that.

I mean, Eli's stepmom is hot, but she's his stepmom. And younger.

Layla is a pain in the ass, and I have geometry to do. But if I say so, Mom will march into the den to look at the TV—the video game paused on the screen—and back at me, just to make a point, before turning the game off.

Layla's friends flirt with me, and that weirds me out just as much as my friends calling my mom a MILF. Four years isn't a big age difference, except when you're talking about twelve year old girls. She's a badass softball player, though, so even now that Dad got promoted, and he travels a lot and has meetings all the time, Mom makes me help with drop-off and pick-up.

Kyler doesn't drive. I don't know if he could, but Mom and Dad have always just avoided the subject. He doesn't seem to care one way or another. Sometimes, if you aren't looking closely, you might assume his leg is connected to his bike pedal. He rides everywhere. You would never believe it if you had seen Mom outside with him when we were kids, trying to teach him to ride. Sometimes I doubt my memories, because it seems like after a few crashes, it all clicked for me and I was flying through the backyard and begging Mom to take me over to the park where I could ride, and Kyler was wobbling around on training wheels, with Mom walking behind him, holding him up like back up training wheels.

Pretty much everything is like that for Kyler. He gets it, eventually, but it takes him a lot longer. That's why I wonder if he could drive if someone taught him. Then again, he might kill a few cars and people before he got it right, so maybe Mom and Dad are right about this one.

When Mom pulls the pantry door open, I steal a cookie from the jar on the counter and shove the whole thing in my mouth.

"Really, Jason?" Mom says without turning to look at me. "I'm starting dinner."

I don't tell her Kyler ate a whole bag of chips before she got home. She wouldn't care anyway. Not that they favor him, but she rips on us—sorry, *scolds* us for our behavior—and rarely punishes us. Without another word, I go back to the den, turn the TV off, and then run upstairs to my room. We have a different house now, so Kyler and I don't have to share a room anymore. I'm glad to have my own space, but I'm not, like, afraid of him anymore.

He's still a freak, but mostly, he's a likable freak.

My backpack is on the floor by my bed, so I grab it and

dig my keys out of the front zipper pocket. I thought I left my phone in the same pocket, but I can't find it. I pat the pockets of my pants down, come up empty-handed, and decide I must have carried it downstairs with me when I got home.

I don't text much. Which isn't to say I don't *get* a lot of texts. Girls—especially Corie and Meredith—text me all the time. In fact, Mom saw some of Meredith's texts once. That was the one time she did punish me. She opened up a can of parental whoop-ass and let me have it, even though I told her a hundred times I wasn't into Meredith and didn't ask for the pictures she sent. She took my phone for a week. I didn't bother to tell her I didn't care. Taking the video games away would have been a much stiffer punishment. I'm not a bad kid, but I'm not stupid.

Ky's not, either, but he's not as smart as I am.

I drop my backpack to the floor and turn to go after Layla before Mom starts yelling at me to get moving. Dad has that meeting, but he should be home by six, so we'll be eating dinner soon. I'm hungry, but I suspect dinner will be something green and plant-based, and so I'm not too excited about getting home to eat. Just don't want to put Mom in a bad mood before we all sit down together for dinner.

That's a thing. We're all expected to be at the table for dinner. If Layla has practice or a game, Mom adjusts dinnertime, and our asses better be there. If Dad has a meeting, we eat dinner later. If Ky has a robotics competition at seven, then we eat earlier, and our asses better be in our chairs when the plates touch the table. One thing Mom has always insisted on. Even when we got Ky. Before, really.

He's standing in my doorway when I turn around. He's slight, like a foot shorter than me, and skinny. But then again, I apparently got my paternal grandfather's height, and at sixteen, my doctors tell me my growth plates are still open.

For Dad, that translates to big basketball scholarship money —I have a pretty shot, and I'm on par to tie the three-point record at my high school. For Mom, it means I've always been a pain in the ass to buy pants for. Skinny, scrawny, and tall when I was younger—which was a real pain the ass. Now that I'm in high school and playing ball, I work out, and I eat more (well, I used to before our meals started looking like berries and leaves) so I'm bigger and broader, and my waist size is easier to find.

"What?" I ask him, because he's frowning, and mostly, he's not *that* guy anymore. The first years he was here were a bitch. That's when I hated him. But for a long time now, he's been pretty cool, mostly.

A teacher called him jovial once. I'm not sure I would say that, because it makes my brother sound like a freak dick, and it's different when your classmates or friends say something like that and when a teacher or an adult in a position of authority says it.

His bony shoulders do a quick shrug. Propped in the doorframe, he watches me for a second and then backs away. His hands—like always—are shoved deep into the hip pockets of his jeans. Like, Garrick—this guy I've known since before we got Ky, like, from preschool—used to tease him and ask him if his elbows were cold, because it looked like he wanted to push them down into his pockets, too. That used to set Ky off. The little shit busted Garrick's lip open once with his bony, little fist.

Not that any of us were beefy back then.

"Mom's trying a new recipe," he mumbled. His voice is deceptively deep for how little and wiry he is. I don't hear the apology in his voice anymore, but then I stopped listening for it a long time ago.

"We could sneak out later and get burgers," I suggest, because we've done it a few times. But the last time we did,

Layla caught us. She threatened to tell Mom if we didn't do something for her. We told her to tell Mom, but then she just got more bent out of shape. She's nosy, so mostly, she just wanted to hang out in his room or mine and ask us stuff. Neither of us was too excited about the idea, and we told her again to tell Mom, but then she upped the bargaining and told me she knew I had watched porn the weekend before on my laptop. God only knows how she found that out, but she got my attention.

So she hung out with us one night, and she asked me, like, five million questions about Braden Bartell. Braden is the starting senior point guard, and all the girls have a thing for him, including my little sister. I showed her the door when she asked me if I'd seen him naked in the locker room.

Kyler spins around in the hall outside his room and rolls his eyes. Yeah, not a good option. If Layla caught us again, I'd have to do something horrible to make her want to tell Mom so we wouldn't have to play twenty questions with a love-sick seventh grader.

For the record, Braden Bartell is an okay guy; I've seen a lot of him in the locker room, though I don't go looking for it, but no way in hell would I want my little sister around him, even if she was sixteen, instead of twelve.

"Oh." Ky shakes his head as if he's upset with himself or maybe just remembered something. "Here."

When he pulls his hand from his pocket, I look down to see he's offering me my phone.

"Why do you have my phone?"

If Layla had my phone, I would be beyond pissed. I'm not excited that Ky had it, but I'm not really too concerned about it, either.

"Just wanted to look something up," he mumbles and dismisses me with a slight frown. He's notorious for losing or dropping his phone, and half the time, if he knows where it's at, it doesn't work, or he can't read the screen. He shuffles into his room, though he doesn't close the door in my face. Not anymore. Still, he's in his own world now, as if I don't exist, and to him, at this moment, I don't.

Ky's weird about that. His attention span is so short, sometimes you blink and you miss it. But when he is focused on you, it's intense, and sometimes it can be ridiculously uncomfortable. His eyes are small, but they're shark-like, and he sees everything. Not gonna lie. There are times even now when that creeps me out.

He stretches out over his bed, the sketching pencil in his hand flying over his art pad. That's kind of creepy, too, the way Kyler draws. It's almost like he's gone—like he mentally checks out—and he's somewhere else, and his hand creates incredible, intricate artwork. I don't know; maybe all artists work that way. But sometimes I wonder what would happen if someone picked him up and moved him when he was in that zone. Would he ever come back to himself? Or would his brain or whatever just float around in some other dimension?

Mom discovered his talent when he was, like nine, maybe. I'm not clear on exactly when Kyler's birthday is; we celebrate it as the day Mom and Dad adopted him. Not even the day that became official in the courtroom. But the day Ky first came to stay at our house.

Anyway, she was thrilled that he could draw. Not because she wanted to pin a medal on his chest or something. Not like she wanted to say my son, Ky, is an artist, and my son, Jason, plays basketball, and my daughter Layla is a princess —Dad still treats Layla like a princess, and she eats it up. But I think Mom was excited for Ky, happy that he had something to be invested in and proud of. I overheard her talking to Dad about it one night when Ky and I were still really young. She was gushing—she doesn't do it that often, but she was so happy that night—about a picture Ky had done of a clown.

It was a really gross picture, actually, and though I wouldn't admit it, it scared the bejesus out of me. Mom and Dad talked about Ky's attention to detail, and all I could think of was how lifelike the damned thing was, and what if it came to life through the night? What nine or ten-year-old kid wants to admit to that kind of fear? I *accidentally* spilled cherry soda on the drawing, thinking they would throw it away. But they didn't. Mom got all pissy with me, and she batted the spilled soda off the paper with a dishtowel, and they saved the damned clown.

It hung on the fridge for weeks, and the red stain on the curled paper only made it scarier. Thankfully, Ky drew a horse in a barnyard or something, and Mom eventually replaced the clown on the fridge with the horse. Ky kept the clown, but he put it in his bedroom.

Dad wanted to sign him up for art classes and stuff, but Mom was against the idea from the beginning. Dad insisted that Ky needed to learn discipline with his talent, and Mom told him that was the most ridiculous thing she'd ever heard. They did put him in an art class at the community center. The teacher was a grandma type, and she drew stick figures and apples and rainbows, and Ky hated every second of it. In fact, he even had a few meltdowns, reminiscent of the days when we first got him.

Eventually, Dad gave in, and Ky got to quit the classes. He draws all the time now, but he doesn't just parade his stuff around like a kindergartner looking for star stickers. Most of the time, he tacks his latest piece up on his wall and starts something new. My bedroom is painted a pretty boring shade of blue. I don't remember what color Ky's walls are, really, because they're mostly plastered with his artwork.

"I gotta get Layla," I tell him now. He doesn't move, except to keep drawing. I stand at the side of his bed and watch his hand glide over the page. When the fluid movement changes and becomes choppy, I step closer and lean over him to see what he's drawing. I can't really tell at this point, but it looks like a forest. Kind of boring for him. "Wanna go?"

I don't expect an answer, and I don't get one. His eyes are glued to the paper, but his face is slack and smooth. I asked Mom once if he was an idiot, and even though that's not what I meant, she got really pissed off at me. She even smacked my butt hard enough to make my eyes sting. I hauled ass out of the kitchen because I was, like, eleven, and my mom had spanked me, but I heard my dad suggest that maybe I meant *idiot savant*. I looked it up; that is what I meant.

Ky's weird. He's really weird. But I don't know if he's autistic. Some of his behavior fits in a lot of spots on the spectrum that doctors and psychologists use to measure autism. But some of it doesn't. Sometimes, he's just slower than normal to pick something up. Sometimes he's the life of the party, and sometimes he can be in a one-on-one conversation with you and totally space out and stare right through you for hours.

He gets Cs in school. Sometimes he has to work his ass off for the average grades. Sometimes he just seems to know things. Mostly, he has trouble with reading, and that means slower learning in pretty much every other subject.

Mom apologized to me for spanking me that night. She told me Ky's biological parents had used drugs, and a lot of his issues were caused when his mom carried him. She also said that living with those people for the first five years of his life had been detrimental to his health and growth, and that's why family services had taken him from his parents.

Whenever I get mad at him now, I call him an idiot. Ky laughs, but Mom gets pissed, and she throws stuff around in the kitchen. Cracks open a bottle of red and gulps it down like she's dealing with a house full of toddlers instead of me and Ky, pretty much never in her hair, and Layla, who does no wrong.

I turn to leave his room—Mom must think I'm already gone, or she would be yelling at me to get moving—and notice the overflowing garbage can by his desk. Unusual. We don't often have paper homework; our school uses iPads and tablets, so almost every assignment we have to turn in is done online. And Ky has a steady hand when he draws. Rarely uses an eraser; in fact, the pencils he uses don't have erasers. And I've never seen him scribble anything out or start over.

Whatever he's been working on lately, he's doing a lot of starting over.

I take a peek at him to find that he hasn't moved, so I snatch the top paper, half wadded up, from the top of the can.

"Jason? Layla will be done in five minutes!"

"Coming, Mom!" I shout as I crumple up the paper into a tight wad and tuck it in my pocket. I glance at Ky one more time, because I want him to go with me. But he's out until he finishes whatever he's working on.

Mom did talk to our doctor about Ky's attention issues, about the fact that he can sit for hours when he's drawing. But every doctor that checks him out says he's okay. Maybe average intelligence with some learning disabilities, blah blah blah. Not sure if Mom wanted a doctor to say he was a genius, even if he's not on the autism spectrum, or if she wanted a churchy person to evaluate him and decide God was channeling him to make the world beautiful or maybe that he was slipping into a state of unconsciousness and doing astral projection or what.

The upshot is just that Ky's weird.

419

But Layla puts mustard on her pork chops, and I like museums.

Maybe we're all weird.

In the car, I shove the key in the ignition, but before I put the Accord in drive—it's ancient, but it runs, and I only had to pay half and Mom and Dad paid the other half with the understanding that I would chauffer Ky and Layla around when I got my license—I remember Ky's drawing I'd wadded up and stuck in my pocket.

Feeling kind of queasy now—I shouldn't have taken it, but then again, Ky took my phone earlier—I stiffen my leg and lift my butt off the seat of the car. I pull the paper from my pocket and smooth it out over my leg.

I can't make it out at first. It looks like just some lines, some arches. Definitely the beginning of something. I turn the paper a bit at a time until something clicks. It's a face. Ky's drawing a face. But there's not enough to go on to even take a crazy guess at who it might be. Honestly, I'm not sure if it's a man or woman, even.

With that same feeling of guilt, I crumble the paper up again and shove it back in my pocket. I won't tell anyone about it. Even if Ky was drawing naked chicks or hearts with someone's name in them, I wouldn't tell anyone. Just the way I know Ky would never tell anyone about something he might see on my phone.

We're brothers. We keep each other's secrets.

But I still feel weird about this one.

Layla is waiting for me when I pull into the school lot. She's talking to two of her friends, and I know they're trying to figure out a way to rope me into taking them home. One of them is all tomboy and giggly and goofy and what you think of when you think of grade school girls. The other one is cute—like pretty—and she knows it. She's the one who flirts with me, and that gets creepier than anything with Ky ever does.

"Can you give Megan and Grace a ride home?" Layla asks as she pulls the front door open. I can't. She knows I can't. I don't know why she asks every time I come to get her.

"I can't, Layla," I remind her. State law requires a driver to have a license for a year before he or she can have more than one minor in the car who is not a sibling. She drops her ball bag on the floorboard of the car and turns to look at her friends over her shoulder. I catch the eye rolling as she does.

"He can't. See you tomorrow, guys."

"Do they have a ride?" I ask as she drops in to sit down. She pulls the door closed, and I see that Megan and Grace are already giggling, heads tipped together, not too concerned about a ride home.

"Yeah." She shrugs.

I ease away from the curb and study Layla for a second. She's got thick, dark hair that she wears in a ponytail pretty much all the time. Freckles here and there, but nothing like Ky's. I have freckles, but mine are sort of spread out over my arms and legs. I might have six, tops. It's funny, though, because we all look similar, even Ky.

We moved here before I was a year old. I guess Mom and Dad met and got married somewhere in Missouri and then came here. They both have some family somewhere out west, but no close relatives and no one around here. A lot of people don't know that Ky's adopted; it's weird to hear their shock if the subject happens to come up.

It's funny to me how rude people can be. Sometimes, they back pedal hard and fast to get away from Ky's adoption. Sometimes, they say stupid stuff like how noble it was for Mom and Dad to adopt him. Dad gets mad about that, but Mom gets kind of quiet. Some people just come right out and ask why they needed to adopt a kid when they already had two of their own. Dad always says they knew someone who worked in family services, and they wanted to help Ky. There were rumors that Ky had a little sister that stayed with his biological parents, but I think that was just shit kids at school were saying to be mean when we were younger.

When people ask Mom that, she says yeah, of course they wanted to help Ky. But she gets all weepy, too, which makes Dad mad. Mom wanted more babies, and we're not supposed to know this, but I've heard her talking to her friend Carol about it. She had two miscarriages, and so she felt like it was meant to be that they take Ky and give him a good life.

"What's for supper?" Layla asks as I turn out of the school lot and head toward home.

"Something green and shitty, I'm sure," I answer. She'll tell Mom I said it, but I don't really care. Mom has been on this health kick for a long time now. At first, she was doing it for her and Dad. He was having severe chest pains last year, and once, it was so bad, she took him to the ER, and I kept waiting for a phone call saying he had a heart attack and he was dead. They said it was just stress, but Mom insisted that they change their lifestyle. Less red meat. Cut back on sodium and sugar. No more soda. Exercise. She goes to some kind of class every morning, pilates and spin. Dad goes to the gym a few nights a week, and he runs every morning.

Not long after that, Mom started reading health articles and stuff and decided to try changing Ky's diet to see if it would help any of his issues. To me, that ship sailed back when we got him. He is who he is now, ya know? And he's okay, so I hate that she's trying to change him. Or fix him. He's not broken, I want to tell her. He's just different.

A lot of my life has revolved around Ky. I wasn't allowed to have friends over often when we were kids, because having people around freaked him out. When he was supposed to be doing homework or studying, and he didn't get why *laugh* was spelled with a *gh* instead of an *f* or when he would get stuck doing a long division problem, and he would just freeze and refuse to do anything, Mom would get mad, and then Dad would get mad at Mom, and then the whole family would come undone, and the house was just miserable to live in.

I even missed some games when I was younger. Like on those nights when the homework meltdowns happened, and Mom and Dad were screaming at each other, they would forget that I had a basketball game. Or they would send me with Garrick's mom, and they would stay home with Ky. I liked Garrick's mom okay, but I wanted my mom there. My mom and dad.

That's when I hated him.

They were my parents first, and I hated that this weird, fucked up little kid came to live with us, and I was just supposed to like him and love him and be nice to him and call him brother. If Ky and I fought over toys, I was expected to give in and walk away. When dinner was served cold because Ky wouldn't budge from our room to come to the table, I was expected to eat without complaining. When there was never enough money for vacations, even weekend trips to amusement parks because we were paying specialists to observe and/or treat Ky, I was told to stop whining and grow up.

Dad and I used to shoot baskets after dinner. Even in the fall when it was dark early, he would turn on the floodlights on the garage, and we would have free throw contests. But when Ky decided he wanted to play, too, I had to stand aside and watch my dad show Ky how to dribble. He's not a good ball handler, but whenever we play—even now—I'm not allowed to steal the ball from him. I do, though, when it's just the two of us outside. Ky gets pissed for the way the whole world babies him.

So I don't.

We get along just fine.

There are times, though, when I wonder what life would have been like without him. It seems weird to say lonelier, because I would still have my parents and let's face it—more of their attention—and my little sister. But there's something really cool about me and Ky growing up together.

Sometimes, I look at him, and I look at my mom and wonder if I had to wish one of them away, which would it be. Because I used to miss having a mom, once Ky came, and she mothered all three of us. But now, it's almost like he and I are each other's shadows.

The house reeks when we get home. Layla grumbles as she steps inside and toes her spikes off. Right on cue, Mom turns and rips on her for wearing the cleats into the house; she knows better. Layla rolls her eyes at me. She pushes the screen door open and kicks her cleats outside and then gives Mom a hug.

I don't do that anymore.

I don't remember the last time I hugged my mom. Or the last time she hugged me.

I'm not saying she doesn't love us. I'm saying maybe her third child was more than she bargained for. Maybe there's a difference in the *idea* of helping a kid with special needs and *parenting* a child with special needs.

Although really, these days, there's not much more to parenting Ky than me and Layla. Like I said, the past several years have been easier and happier.

"Dad should be home in about twenty minutes," Mom announces, and then she asks Layla about practice. Layla hops up to sit on the counter—Ky and I used to do that, but we're too big for it now—and swings her legs as she talks about practicing bunting and turning double plays. I don't like baseball, but it is fun to watch Layla play softball.

"Ky, would you set the table, please?"

We take turns, and no one ever gripes, because that means someone does double duty, and one of us gets a night off. Mom has a veggie tray on the counter, and Layla swipes a carrot stick and starts crunching it. I look around, but Ky's not in the kitchen.

"Mom, Ky's not in here," I tell her, because I don't want her to get mad at him. "He was drawing something earlier."

She nods.

"Yeah, he showed it to me," she says and nods at the fridge. The last picture—a train bridge—has been replaced with a new one. A woman's face. It's a pencil sketch, so there's no color.

"Who's that?" Layla asks, but when she looks at me, I can only shrug.

"I dunno." Mom takes a casserole dish out of the oven and sets it on the stovetop next to the skillet of peppers and mushrooms. "Do you recognize her, Jason? Someone from school?"

First of all, the idea of Ky having a crush on someone almost paralyzes me. He talks *to* girls at school, and he talks to me *about girls*, but never anyone specific. Never like he wants to ask someone out. For his sake, I kind of hope he never does. Because I'm afraid even though the girls are nice to him, they would laugh at him if he tried to be more than friends with any of them.

"No." But I put my hands in my pockets and step closer to the fridge to study the picture. I don't recognize the woman; Ky has drawn her as an older woman. Not like grandma old, but not a high school kid, either. Her hair is pulled off her face, and he drew her in a bit of a profile, like she's just turning to look away, so you can see a ponytail. Her cheekbones are knifelike and as I study the picture, I decide that's what makes her look old.

"Ky?" Mom's voice is distant now. She's at the bottom of the steps, yelling for Ky to come down to set the table.

"He was freaking out about something this morning," Layla tells me. She hops off the counter and moseys to the stove to poke the serving fork into the casserole. I'm shocked when she shivers with disgust and then turns adoring eyes to my mom as she comes back to the kitchen.

"I know," I tell Layla. I look back at the picture on the fridge, and I wonder what he did with the picture he was working on when I was in his room. This is definitely not the same one.

The woman in Ky's picture is wearing a blouse, open at the neck. The picture is like a headshot, something you would see in a school yearbook. I look again, wondering if maybe it is someone from school. Maybe a teacher, since she looks older.

She's wearing a necklace, but again, it's a pencil sketch so I don't know if it's gold or silver or even one of those black cloth necklaces people wear now. There's a cross pendant, and it looks like something else there. I step closer and brush my fingertip over the cross. But what I'm seeing is a faded mark, something Ky erased.

"I'm gonna wash my hands for dinner," Layla announces.

"Please do." Mom nods. "Jas, would you fill the glasses, please?"

Since I finished the milk earlier, it's ice water for dinner. I step around her and glance at the clock on the microwave. Almost 6:00. Dad'll be home any minute, and the table's not set. I look up when I hear voices in the living room.

Mom ducks her head in there. "What're you watching, Ky?"

Layla answers her, but I can't hear what she says. Nothing from Ky.

"Honey, why are you glued to the TV?" she asks, and now

I move to stand behind her. Ky is on his knees in front of the big screen TV. It looks like he is praying, because he has to strain to see the TV hanging on the wall. The national news is on; Ky's not a big TV person. We have that in common; if we watch TV, it's *The Walking Dead* and maybe movies. He'd rather draw, and I'd rather play games.

Mom moves to stand closer to Ky, and Layla and I glance at each other. When he was thirteen, Ky got fixated on card tricks. Like, it made me and Layla nuts, because he was always trying to do these magic tricks, and he just wasn't good at it.

When I hear the word *body*, I look back at the TV. Harold Robards, the news guy is on remote, somewhere in the woods. I wasn't paying attention to the first part, so I don't know where this is, let alone if it's, like, a state park or if it's private property or what. The screen says *Body found last November,* and the trees look skeletal, and it looks cold, so I assume this is an old news clip they are replaying. Then the reporter is back in front of the camera, and the woods are in the background, and there's a guy there with deer-in-the-headlights eyes and a bright orange ball cap and on the bottom of the screen, it says *Travis Jochem, Deer Hunter.*

"Oh, wow." Mom sighs, and when I look at her, I see that she's biting her lip.

The camera moves again back to the woods, and then it pans out, and there's a dark-colored SUV parked at an angle, and there are some people milling about by the hatchback. Robards is talking now, as he walks backwards to those very people.

Mom covers her mouth with her fingertips.

Robards says, "Mrs. Bryant, what are you feeling right now?" And then a guy with the woman Robards addressed slings his arm around her shoulders, and the woman ducks her head away from the camera. But we see that she's crying. The whole world can see that she's crying.

Suddenly, the wooded scene and the people and the SUV are gone, and I look around to see who changed the channel. But Ky is still kneeling on the floor. His eyes are big and curious, his lips open just enough to breathe, and Mom is still standing there with her fingers pressed to her mouth, and Layla stares at the TV, looking just as confused as I feel right now.

The TV is now showing the news studio, and the news anchor is there now, and suddenly, there's a photo shown on the screen. It's the woman Ky drew, the one hanging on the fridge.

Before I can look too closely, before I can see if she's wearing a necklace, that picture is gone, and the camera is showing a brick ranch home, and the bottom of the screen says *Home of Jay and Ellie Bryant*.

"We've asked to speak to Mrs. Bryant," Robards is saying, but the camera zooms in on a face, and I'm disappointed to see it's not the same woman. Not the woman in the picture on the TV or the one on the fridge. "But Mrs. Bryant is not taking questions at this time. So we're speaking with Maeve Taylor, sister-in-law of Ellie Bryant. Mrs. Taylor, thank you for speaking with us."

The woman—this woman looks older even than the woman Ky drew—nods. She's tall and thin, and she has her arms crossed over her chest, her hands wrapped around them. Not like she's cold, but like she's holding herself together. Her eyes look a little glassy, almost like she's high, and her face is haggard and drawn in a frown so deep, you could get lost if you look too hard.

Like Mom is.

I glance at Ky to see he hasn't moved.

Who are these people? And why did my brother draw that picture?

"Mrs. Taylor, what was Ellie's reaction when you learned the body found was not that of her son, Luther Jordan?"

She swallows so hard, it looks painful, and turns those eyes on the reporter and arches her eyebrows in contempt.

"This has been an extremely difficult time for my family." Her voice is level and cool, though it's thin, and she's still frowning, and it still looks like she's doing everything she can to stand there in one piece, one body. "We've obviously had some dark times through the years. Each time a boy is found, we—Ellie—goes through that horrid, painful, hopeful rush of feelings—"

"I'm sorry, Mrs. Taylor, did you say hopeful?" The reporter—Robards—almost shrugs, but he tips his head to make it look like he's concerned for her.

"She wants closure," the woman says quietly. "Obviously, she would like to know that her son is safe out there, somewhere. Barring that, she would like to find Luther and bring him home. Give him a proper burial and memorial."

"Do you believe Luther Jordan is dead?"

"I don't know." The woman shakes her head. "I don't know. Maybe at *this point*, maybe on day *ten*, Ellie had to hope her son was gone, because the alternative could be so much worse."

"Are you saying Ellie Bryant wished her son—"

"Do you have children, Harold?" The woman interrupts him. Ky moves from his knees to a squat. I hear Mom sniffle, and when I look at her, tears streak her face. Layla is plastered against her side now; Mom's free arm is around her shoulders.

"No, ma'am," the reporter answers.

"Any parent out there gets what Ellie Bryant is feeling right now. Her son has been missing for fifteen years. She has lived fifteen years—five thousand four hundred and seventy five days—wondering if Luther is dead or alive. Scared to death of what he's suffering if he is alive. No parent should ever have to live with that feeling. And every time there's a body found, Ellie, my brother, my nephew, my sweet little niece…they all have to gear up for that possibility, Harold. That this body, this boy is Luther."

Harold looks a little green in the face now.

"And then, every time it's not Luther, they all deal with that rush of relief. Because even more than not wanting him to suffer, parents don't want their babies to be dead. Do you get that? And then, they all grieve, because it might not be Luther." The woman is crying now. Tears slide over her face, but her voice is hard now, like she's determined to say what is on her mind.

Slowly, Ky stands, and Mom reaches for his hand.

"It might not be Luther, but someone's baby is dead. Someone out there right now is grieving for that boy Travis Jochem found in the woods last November."

Harold nods and looks back at the camera. He looks stricken, like maybe the woman did get to him.

But before he can say anything to the anchor, she adds,

"And now, they try to go back to living their lives around a boy who's been missing five thousand four hundred and seventy five days."

The guy nods again and clears his throat. His voice is hushed when he identifies himself as Harold Robards and sends it back to the anchor in the studio.

Ky is pressed up against Mom's other side now.

My throat kind of aches, and Ky looks like he's five again, like that sullen, mean little boy who came to live with us. The boy I hated Mom and Dad for adopting. Layla's arm is around Mom's back, and her bony, little-kid fingers are wrapped around Ky's wrist, like she's afraid he might vanish.

And then Mom turns to me and reaches for me with the hand that had covered her mouth. Her fingers are wet with tears when she touches my arm, and then she pulls me to her to hug.

The back door opens, and Dad is talking, maybe on the phone.

But I hear Mom instead.

"One hundred and thirty one thousand and four hundred hours."

ABOUT THE AUTHOR

As an only child, Tracy Broemmer grew up with a wild imagination. An avid reader from a young age, she spent a lot of time with her nose buried in books and a lot of time making up her own stories. She penned her first book in grade school and hasn't stopped writing since.

Tracy is the author of the Lorelei Bluffs women's fiction series, the women's fiction series the Williams Legacy, and several stand-alone women's fiction novels. She has recently dabbled in contemporary romance as well.

For more information, visit her website at www.broemmerbooks.com

ALSO BY TRACY BROEMMER

Women's Fiction Novels

Fairytale (writing as Therese Kinkaide)
Just Like Them (writing as Therese Kinkaide)
Small Hours (writing as Therese Kinkaide)
Picket Fences
Two Story Home
Green-Eyed Girl
Say Everything
Come Home for Christmas
Sketching Litchfield Lake
Ever, Again
Safe as Houses

Every Little Thing, Lorelei Bluffs, Book 1
Two A.M., Lorelei Bluffs, Book 2
Blind, Lorelei Bluffs, Book 3
Leaving July, Lorelei Bluffs, Book 4
Hesitation Marks, Lorelei Bluffs, Book 5
Four Letter Words, Lorelei Bluffs, Book 6
See Kate, Lorelei Bluffs, Book 7
Loved You More, Lorelei Bluffs, Book 8
A Lorelei Ending, Lorelei Bluffs, Book 9
I Do, Lorelei Bluffs, Book 10

Truth Is, The Williams Legacy, Book 1

Other People's Ugly, The Williams Legacy, Book 2

Omissions, The Williams Legacy, Book 3

Contemporary Romance Novels:

Destiny's Calling: Your Future is Waiting

Wedding Day Shenanigans

Holiday Fling

The Kiss Off

Something Like Love

Love, Nashville, Mississippi Queen Trilogy, Book 1

Forever, Duncan, Mississippi Queen Trilogy, Book 2

Contemporary Romance Novellas:

Indian Summer, A Novella

Dear Jaclyn Perris, A Novella